CONFINED BY LUST

"Who put these chains on you?"

"You ask me that? You cast-off son of a spotted baboon! Who do you think? Your soldiers! Your orders!"

"No." He scowled. "Not by my command."

Roxanne's eyes narrowed.

They were beautiful eyes, he decided, golden-brown with flecks of black, nearly the same color as those of the cat, and they glittered as fiercely. Roxanne's green silk tunic clung to her like a second skin, and her glorious hair was a mantle of living fire. Confined as she was, arms high, full breasts thrust forward, nipples plainly showing, this savage little princess would wake a marble statue.

And he was not made of stone. Heat coursed through his loins as he wondered if her mouth would be as sweet as ripe dates. She was virgin, and she was his to do with as he pleased. . . .

The Conqueror

JUDITH E. FRENCH

LOVE SPELL NEW YORK CITY

For Bill, who went ahead to scout the trail.

LOVE SPELL®

December 2003

Published by

Dorchester Publishing Co., Inc.
200 Madison Avenue
New York, NY 10016

ISBN 0-505-52571-2

The name "Love Spell" and its logo are trademarks of Dorchester Publishing Co., Inc.

Printed in the United States of America.

Visit us on the web at www.dorchesterpub.com.

The Conqueror

Chapter One

The lamp flickered, casting grotesque, shifting patterns against the gray stone walls. Here in this cave, Roxanne supposed, there should be no difference between night and day, but she always knew. When the sun set, the weight of the mountain seemed to crush her, making it harder to breathe, chilling her to the bone.

She took a fresh sheet of Egyptian papyrus from a cedar-wood box. Her paper was precious, but there was no longer any need to conserve. Time was short. That which she had kept hidden in her heart these many years must now be written down or lost forever.

Once, the days had spread before her as many and vari-colored as the sands of the steppes, but no longer. Her ears ached for the sound of rain; her eyes wept for the green of lush valleys. She longed to feel the crisp wind of a mountain pass on her face and the rhythm of a galloping horse beneath her body. She was a child of light, born to sit an ancient throne. Was it possible that she had traveled so far to end her life in this dark cavern?

And yet behind her eyelids lay the white mantle of Sogdian

1

snows, silent and cold, flakes drifting one upon another in a rhapsody of swirling brilliance.

And here, here was the first pale flower daring to challenge the brown and sleeping plains. Another and another, spreading in a carpet of riotous color across the steppes: reds and yellows, blue and lavender, flanked by green of every hue, spreading on into tomorrow.

She bent to gather a handful of blooms. How their sweet scent filled the dark room, spilling sunlight into every corner, warming her soul. What bird was that she heard calling to his mate? Surely she had seen hundreds like him. Thousands. "Fly high," she whispered. "High enough to touch the clouds."

Her throat tightened. "Alexander . . . Did you do this to me . . . or I to you?"

For seven years this mountain dungeon had held her, but she had never doubted that death would bring her freedom. And she had long since ceased to fear the black horse and veiled rider.

But her waiting was over. At last night's changing of the guard, she had heard the muttered exchange between soldiers.

"A few more days and we'll be quit of this job," Silas had said.

"Good riddance, I say," Ciro had replied. "I didn't leave my father's goat herd to spend half my life shepherding a Persian whore."

Roxanne took a deep breath and continued writing.

Familiar faces rose in her mind's eye, clearer than her own right hand in the gathering shadows: her father Oxyartes, Soraya, and Kayan . . . her cousin . . . her dear one. Was he teaching another seven-year-old to ride wild Scythian ponies as he had once taught her?

"Grasp his mane, Roxanne!" Kayan's laughter echoed from the past, as the shaggy little horse reared on his hind legs and fell back on his haunches. The child she'd once been had grinned and brushed gravel from the seat of her green doeskin trousers.

"You're supposed to stay on his back!" Kayan taunted, but

2

there was no malice in his teasing. And she'd turned the joke on him the next day when she'd slipped a thorn branch under his saddle and sent him sprawling in the palace courtyard.

As the only living child of Prince Oxyartes and Queen Pari, she'd been the hope of her people. Together with the man she took to husband, she was meant to rule the twin kingdoms of Bactria and Sogdiana. She'd been no dainty Persian princess, hidden away in palace splendor. Descended from that race of fair-skinned warrior women the Greeks called Amazons, she'd been trained in the bow and short sword before she was old enough to read. By ten, she'd spent a month alone in the mountains guarding the horse herds, and at fourteen she had slain her first snow tiger with three shafts from a horn bow.

The twin mountain kingdoms, wealthy beyond belief and home to her family for more than a thousand years, had been her world. Her lineage was without blemish. Roxanne smiled at a half-forgotten memory. Had not Darius the Third, King of Kings, mighty bull of Persia, sent his ambassadors to offer for her hand?

She remembered how she had stood beside her father in the East Tower of the Blue Palace and watched the disappointed emissaries ride away. "What need has Roxanne of a Persian throne?" her father had asked. "Or the sheltered life of veil and purdah? But I can forbid you nothing, child of my heart. Say the word, and I'll send riders to fetch them back."

She'd answered with a barracks-yard oath, and her father had bellowed with laughter and enveloped her in a bear hug. How solid he'd seemed then, how proud she'd been of him—a prince with the pride and the power to refuse King Darius. He was a solid man of medium height, broad at the shoulder with arms like a blacksmith, a high forehead, and a proud nose. Oxyartes's shoulder-length hair had once been a bright auburn, but now was a darker russet with threads of gray. She'd inherited that red hair from her father, as she'd gotten her nutmeg-colored eyes and her dimple from her mother.

When she thought back, that shining moment—solid as the

3

rock beneath her feet—had marked the end of a life she had believed would last forever.

A week later, her father and her cousin Kayan had answered the call to arms, leading an army of fierce cavalrymen to aid the Persians against the Macedonian barbarians her people called Greeks. But the invaders had sliced through Darius's pretty soldiers like a sickle through ripe wheat. The Bactrians and the Sogdians had fought bravely, but the Greeks were too many, and they could not stand alone once the remaining Persian troops had fled.

Kayan had brought word of the burning of Persepolis, capital of the Persian Empire since time out of time. She had wept bitterly for the beauty of that city and for the books and the ancient art treasures of the palaces. But she had little time to waste in tears. A princess must think of her people first.

The women of her house had always been educated to rule. She had studied medicine, mathematics, and astronomy since she was old enough to toddle. She could read and write five languages and speak seven. And on that day, she'd set herself to study Greek.

Fortunately, Kayan had brought home two yellow-haired barbarians captured on the battlefield. One had lived only until his wounds healed sufficiently to lay hands upon her royal person. She'd pretended womanly weakness and then cut the Greek's stubbled throat with her dagger. Kayan had urged her to have the second soldier executed as well, but since the soldier had witnessed his companion's fate, she'd hoped that would be lesson enough. If she'd killed that one as well, how would she learn the primitive speech of her enemy?

Since she was a child, she'd ridden among rough soldiers and shared campfires, hunting expeditions, and long days in the saddle, but none had ever dared to forget her position as princess royal.

She had always believed that her husband would be her beloved Kayan. Astrologers had chosen him on the day she was born. Son of her father's cousin, he was both noble and wealthy in his own right. But wealth had never interested

Kayan. From boyhood on, he had been a warrior. He'd risen to the rank of commander, an honor for one so young.

Kayan was tall for a Sogdian and muscular, not handsome, but rugged with sharp, craggy features, nut-brown hair, and almond eyes so dark and liquid that anyone seeing him for the first time remembered little else. Kayan's crooked smile was made more so by the hairline scar at the corner of his mouth, a token of a Scythian skirmish.

Swept up in sweet memories that seemed more real than this dark cave, Roxanne raised her hand to brush back the wayward lock of hair that regularly tumbled over Kayan's high forehead. If she believed in witchcraft, she would be certain she had conjured him up, and he was standing in front of her. Bold, faithful Kayan. How she missed his dry humor and the mischievous gleam in his eyes.

Her father had loved Kayan as his own son, but he'd had his doubts about putting him on the throne. "No soldier is braver," he'd admitted when she pressed him as to why he had delayed her wedding. "Kayan is a general born, but a general is not a prince. Does Kayan have the wisdom to rule after me?"

"I do," she'd flung back with passion.

How young she'd been then . . . how innocent.

She remembered distinctly being at prayer, some months after that conversation, when the second message came from her father.

The sacred fire on the altar had flared as a messenger pressed a scrap of silk bearing her father's seal into her hand. This letter was worse than the first. Darius was no more. The fool Bessus had set himself up as High King of Persia. Even now, her father and his troops pressed hard for the mountains of Bactria. She must summon every available man and prepare the citadel for war.

Unbelievable that the barbarians should come so far! Bactria and Sogdiana were not Persia. Now the Greeks faced men. So had she believed . . . so had they all believed. She could not know that two years of bitter mountain fighting would pass before she saw her father again.

"This Alexander is not mortal," Oxyartes had declared when they were reunited after so long apart, and she was safe in his arms. "I fear the Wise God has turned his face from us to this golden hawk."

War with the Greeks went on. Brave Bactria fell. Sogdiana struggled for her life. Cities burned. Vultures preyed on the unburied dead. Enemy soldiers dragged free women of Sogdiana away as booty. More than a hundred thousand of her people died, and still the free people fought on. Each mile Alexander gained had to be won and then won again. And each step was mired in Greek blood.

Finally, the Bactrian and Sogdian survivors took refuge on Sogdiana Rock, a citadel rising above the valley floor like the hand of God. No army could scale its sheer rock walls or pass the narrow trail.

Oxyartes had stocked the fortress with provisions for two years. Here the nobles, soldiers, and their families took a final stand. With them they had brought the wealth of a thousand treasure houses: pearls and precious carpets, scrolls, art work, silks from the fabled land of Chin, furs, fiery jewels, pottery, golden chains, and ancient weapons encrusted with precious gems.

Roxanne, hiding her womanhood with the felt and fur clothing of a Sogdian warrior, stood beside Oxyartes to receive the Greek heralds.

"Tell your master, this Alexander of Macedonia," Oxyartes bellowed, "that we will never surrender. If he wants to take this rock, he must find flying soldiers!"

Kayan scowled at the departing delegation. "What now?"

"Now we wait," Oxyartes said. "There are easier lands to conquer. My spies tell me that his soldiers long to follow the caravan route to India. Let them. Here we are and here we stay." He laid a hand on Roxanne's shoulder. "Go to the women's quarters, Daughter."

"My place is here beside you. You'd not send a prince to cower among the crones and suckling babes."

Her father's powerful grip tightened as his temper flared. "A prince would know his duty to his liege, no matter what the command." He scowled. "Go! I will have no hysterical women throwing themselves from tower windows when you can calm them."

Flushed with shame, Roxanne bowed her head in wordless apology. If only she'd been born a prince, Alexander would never have come so far. "Let me be of some real use," she begged. "I know all the ways off this mountain. In Greek clothing, I could sneak into Alexander's camp and put an arrow—"

"No!" Kayan said. "You must—"

Her father silenced him with a stern look. "Slaying Alexander will not turn back this army, child," he said. "No man could be prouder of a son than I am of you. But you are a woman, not a man. You are made to bring life, not take it."

Swallowing the retort that sprang to her lips, Roxanne placed a fist over her heart in the soldier's gesture of obedience and hurried toward the gate that protected the women's section of the palace. Two guards stepped aside and called for the warden within to unbolt the door for the princess royal. As Roxanne stepped forward, she heard Kayan's call.

"Wait, Roxanne. I'd have a word with you. There may not be time later. I have the next watch."

She waited for him. Together they entered the secured gateway, walked through a courtyard, and ducked into a shadowy hallway. There, Roxanne turned and threw herself into his arms.

"Roxanne." He crushed her against him.

Rising on her toes, she brushed his cool lips with hers. "May the Wise God protect you, Kayan, and us all. As soon as Alexander tires of his sport, I'll ask Father to permit us to wed."

Kayan held her for a long minute, so close that she could feel the beat of his heart. "Words don't come easily to me— not as they do to you. But I swear no harm will come to you, except over my lifeless body. I'll send Wolf to be your shadow."

She pulled away. "As you wish. But I'd feel better knowing he was guarding your back." She had lent Wolf to guard

Kayan. Now, it seemed, her cousin would send the wild man to shadow her steps again.

Before she was born, Oxyartes had rescued the young son of a Bactrian bandit from the Scythians. The fierce raiders had already cut out the boy's tongue and were ready to geld him when her father's archers had made short work of them. Her father had carried the boy home, more dead than alive, and ordered him tended. When his wound had healed, Oxyartes bade the lad watch over his newborn daughter.

The butchery had cost the youth his speech. He had no skill at writing, but when they asked his name, the lad had sketched the crude outline of a wolf. So, Wolf he had become. Now, a man in his prime, his black beard and hair were as wild and thick as any wolf pelt, and he could kill as swiftly and silently as a steppe eagle. Until Roxanne had sent him to the war with Kayan, Wolf had never left her side, sleeping each night at the foot of her bed beside her hunting leopards.

"I will send Wolf," Kayan repeated firmly. "Once we're wed, we'll find him another lair to sleep in."

One final kiss, and then Roxanne went to soothe the women and children. "My father bids you all to pray for our deliverance."

"What if the cliff face does not hold them?" Mitra demanded in her grating voice. "What then?" She clutched her remaining son, a red-faced babe, to her ample breast. She had the right to fear. Her husband and thirteen-year-old son had fallen at the River Oxys.

"Then we must be prepared to die as Bactrians and Sogdians."

"No more talk of death," Soraya called. "It is time to feed the children." She laid a warm palm on Roxanne's cheek. "You too should eat. How long since you've tasted hot food?" Soraya clapped her hands and servants filed into the room with heavily laden trays.

"Perhaps a cup of wine," Roxanne agreed. She slipped the heavy fur hat off her head, pulled out the golden pins, and her hair tumbled unbound to her waist. "I ate earlier in the guardhouse."

"What did your father tell the messenger?" Soraya poured the strong Bactrian wine and mixed it with clear mountain water.

Roxanne smiled in spite of her worry. Nothing ruffled Soraya. The day she and Kayan had dragged a lion cub into a dinner for ambassadors from far-off Chin, Soraya had summoned the steward to remove it, declaring the cat "not of high enough birth to share supper with our honored nobles."

Soraya was Roxanne's mother's cousin, her late mother's dearest friend. When Queen Pari had died in childbirth, Soraya had raised her as her own daughter. Mother, friend, chief lady-in-waiting, all of these described Soraya.

Roxanne regarded her foster mother closely. Soraya was a handsome woman, her hair a soft brown, eyes gray-green, cheekbones high and pronounced. Oxyartes teased her about having a Scythian or Chinese look. She was tall, nearly Roxanne's height, and pleasantly rounded. Soraya had become a widow at seventeen, and Roxanne often wondered why, with all her male admirers, she hadn't remarried.

"Roxanne?" Soraya's brows arched. "What did your father say to the Greek invader's messengers?"

She repeated the tale, and the women laughed together at the thought of winged warriors. "Only in some children's bedtime story," Roxanne assured them. "We're safe enough on this rock."

"You should stay here," Soraya fussed. "A princess has no place on the ramparts."

"I am heir to the twin kingdoms. My place is with my father." Roxanne set the silver goblet on the low table. "The ivory box? You have it safe?"

Soraya paled. "You're certain there is enough?"

"Enough for those who wish to die honorably if worse comes to worst. The poison is lethal and quick. A bit on the tongue is enough." Roxanne bit her lower lip. Had they all gone mad that they could talk so calmly of suicide?

A final glance around the room told her that Soraya needed no assistance. Roxanne finished the last of her wine and returned to the walls with the soldiers.

* * *

Dawn broke late over the mountains. Rose-pink rays of light spilled through the thick clouds that enveloped the peaks rising over the citadel. Roxanne shivered, despite her wolfskin cloak. Deep snow remained on the mountain even through the height of summer, and the nights were frigid.

A sentry shouted an alarm. Armed men spilled from the barracks, some stringing bows, others tugging on boots and coats. "There!" one cried. Up above them, high over the citadel, enemy soldiers clustered on the rock face.

"Sorcery," her father swore. "It isn't possible."

Macedonian heralds under a white flag of truce were already riding up the narrow rock trail. The arrogant messenger thrust forth his missive.

Alexander's words were brief. "Come see my flying soldiers."

The heralds offered terms for surrender of the fortress.

"I must have a few minutes," Oxyartes said as he stepped back out of earshot of the Greeks.

"No, Father," Roxanne protested. "We must not surrender. Remember the slaughter at Maracanda? If we lay down our weapons, we will die like sheep." She eyed the bearded Greeks in their short tunics. "Let us fight. If we all die, we'll take a few of them with us to paradise."

Oxyartes shielded his eyes with a hand and surveyed the cliffs above the citadel. "The archers will rain destruction," he said wearily. "Attacks from above and below will divide our fire power." He shook his head.

For over three years he and his troops had battled Alexander of Macedonia. His old wounds ached when it rained; his bones acknowledged their years. Death . . . he had seen so much death. Slowly Oxyartes turned to look into the waiting faces of his officers. Their sisters, their mothers, their wives and children were within the tower.

"Alexander promises the lives of our women if we surrender," her father said. "Look above. There must be three hundred archers." His proud shoulders sagged. "It is over. Kayan!

10

Take my daughter to the women's quarters. See that she is dressed as befits her station."

"No!" Roxanne caught her father's arm. His face was tallow-white, suddenly old. "Don't ask this of me. I would stay with you. I would die at your side. If you love me, grant me this!"

"For that love, I cannot. Take her, Kayan, by force if you must. Take also a hundred of the palace guard to protect the women until we see if Alexander be true or false."

Kayan's obsidian eyes narrowed. "And if the Greeks betray us?"

"Then I trust you will find the strength to do what must be done."

Chapter Two

The women's tower echoed with soft weeping. The children were oddly silent. Even the babes had ceased their wailing and stared with frightened eyes. Servants had drawn and barred the shutters and lit the oil lamps as if it were evening. Stern Greek voices, the tramp of soldiers' feet, and the dull clank of armor seeped through the gray stone, an ever-present reminder of the foreign occupation of their citadel.

Fear hung in the air. Roxanne's mouth tasted of copper. She had waited to hear the clash of battle, but the only screams were those of slaughtered oxen.

"Did you see him?" Lilya whispered. "The Macedonian? Lord Alexander? Is he a misshapen dwarf as they say? My cousin's neighbor's wife knows the sister of a rug merchant in Balkh. She says that Alexander's only half human. He was fathered by their god, Zeus. Beneath his chest, this Alexander is as hairy as a lion. And his huge member is not like that of a mortal man. It is—"

"How can you believe such nonsense?" Roxanne could not keep the irritation from her tone. "He is a man like any other."

"No! It's true," Mitra argued. "The rug merchant's sister says that no woman comes out of his tent alive. He'll claim you as

12

spoils of war. Better you cast yourself from the top of the tower than be impaled by that enormous shaft!"

"Enough," Roxanne said.

Behind her, white-haired old Golnar began to whimper. "Mitra's right. The barbarians will have their filthy way with every one of us."

Roxanne scowled. "No more of that talk. You'll frighten the children." She suspected that Golnar might wish to be claimed as some lusty Greek's bedmate. She'd already buried four husbands, the last young enough to be her grandson. Ordinarily, Roxanne could deal with these foolish women, but not today when all her hopes had turned to ashes.

She had obeyed her father's last order, allowing the maids to dress her in a flowing gown and trousers of black Chin silk so sheer that you could almost read through the material. Her waist was cinched with cloth of gold, and the flat round hat that held her veil in place was heavily encrusted with gold and emeralds of deepest green. Her jewels were few: a slender gold torque around her throat and her ram's head ring. On her feet she wore pointed silken slippers, worked in a pattern of green leaves and milky pearls from India.

Her face was tinted in delicate hues, her eyes outlined with Egyptian kohl. She had washed her hair, brushed it until it gleamed in the lamplight, and let the heavy mass flow over her shoulders and down her back to her waist. When she glanced into the silver mirror, a princess looked back. Yet she felt no pleasure in her appearance. Better she had been born with the face of a sheep than to be degraded because of her beauty.

When she returned to join the other women, Kayan took one look at her, nodded his approval, and turned to admonish the nearest archer in gruff tones. Kayan had positioned guards at all the doors, with the greatest number grouped near the formal entryway where the Greeks would most likely appear.

It took all of Roxanne's willpower to keep from begging Kayan to hold her in his arms. But she couldn't.

Not only would it be inappropriate public behavior, but she was still irate with Kayan. Common sense told her that his

prince had ordered him to hold her here, that Kayan the soldier would want to be at Oxyartes's side to share whatever
fate the Macedonian decreed. But she resented being confined simply because she had been born female. Why
couldn't she and Kayan disobey her father? It would be more
honorable for her to die fighting beside the man she loved
than to allow the women to deck her in finery for her conquerors like some meek lamb led to slaughter.

A six-year-old, the shy daughter of a baron's second wife,
tugged at Roxanne's hand. "Please, lady. My mother wants to
know if you saw my father at the wall." Roxanne bent to answer the child when a great pounding echoed from the bronze
gates.

"Open in the name of Alexander! Surrender your weapons!"

Kayan's archers notched arrows on their bowstrings. Roxanne's bodyguard Wolf moved from the shadows, curved
Scythian scimitar clutched in lean fingers, to take a stand between her and the door.

"Hold your positions," Kayan ordered.

"Open or Oxyartes dies!"

Kayan glanced at Roxanne. His gaze locked with hers, and
she saw the indecision there. Oxyartes had not meant for
Kayan's archers to kill the Greeks, but rather the women. And
now that the moment had come, she wondered if he had the
resolve to carry out the terrible task.

"Put down your weapons," she said. "I command it." Wolf
tensed, and Roxanne laid a hand on his fur-clad arm. "Go,
hide yourself in the tunnels," she said. "Quickly!"

Wolf bared his teeth. His eyes glittered with rebellion, and
he uttered a low growl.

"Go, my friend," she said. If Wolf remained at her side, his
would be the first blood spilled on these tiles. "You may be
of more help to me later."

For an instant, puzzlement wrinkled Wolf's sharp features.
Then he sprinted away toward the ancient section of the palace where the damp passageways threaded into living rock.

Trying not to reveal her terror, Roxanne nodded to Kayan.
When he did not repeat her orders, she motioned to the sol-

diers. "I command you. Disarm yourselves. If you fight"—she glanced toward the frightened women—"they will all die with you."

"Do as she commands," Kayan said.

Roxanne nodded. "Any who wish to follow Wolf into the tunnels may do so without dishonor."

Not a man moved, not even young Saeed whose frightened eyes looked as large as dinner plates. One by one, the archers laid their horn bows on the floor. Roxanne went to the inner door and unbarred it.

Two score of Greeks filed in, all in heavy armor, all carrying short swords and javelins. For what seemed an eternity, women, children, and soldiers stared at each other. The only sound in the room was the sigh of a nursing babe.

A haughty officer, clearly someone in authority, stepped forward. Was this Alexander? Roxanne didn't think so. The Greek's hair was a sandy brown rather than yellow. He was taller than average with a haughty countenance.

"Which of you whores is the daughter of Oxyartes?" he demanded in awkward Persian.

Kayan threw himself toward Roxanne, and two Macedonians barred his way with sword tips at his throat. Mitra screamed. Roxanne lifted her chin imperiously and addressed the leader in Greek. "I am the Princess Roxanne. Who are you? It's plain to me that you've learned your manners in a gutter."

"Hold your tongue before you lose it, bitch!" a soldier threatened.

"How courageous you Greeks are before an unarmed woman," she said. "Give me a sword and you're welcome to try."

The commander's eyes narrowed. "I am Hephaestion. Follow me. And try none of your Persian tricks, or I'll have my men use Oxyartes for target practice."

"No!" Kayan twisted away from his captors, and a third man slammed the hilt of his sword into the back of Kayan's head. Her cousin staggered forward and crumpled to the floor. Roxanne glimpsed blood trickling from Kayan's hair before Hephaestion shoved her toward the door.

15

"Where is my father?"

"Silence!" Hephaestion said.

Roxanne glanced at Soraya. "Look after Kayan if you can," she called in Sogdian, "while I have words with this Macedonian sheepherder."

She followed Hephaestion out into the courtyard, ignoring the soldiers who fell in step behind her. Greeks were everywhere. They had thrown open the storehouses. Platoons of soldiers emptied them systematically. She saw no looting.

"If Oxyartes hopes to trade you for Alexander's favor, he'll be surprised," Hephaestion said. "Although you're not the squat, dark savage he bet me two gold darics you would be. He'll give you to me, if I ask. What say you, wench?" He took hold of her arm.

She jerked free. "Beg me from your master, you Macedonian pig, and I'll geld you the first time you sleep."

Hephaestion cursed, but Roxanne ignored him. She had caught sight of her father. Beside him stood a golden-haired man. She darted through the milling crowd and dropped to her knees in front of Oxyartes. "Are you well, sire?"

The stranger turned and smiled down at her, his face radiant in the single shaft of sunlight that broke through the heavy clouds. He took her hand in an iron grip, raising her to her feet. "The lady Roxanne, I believe."

To her surprise, the Greek's eyes were nearly level with hers. He was not three fingers' width taller than she. The gilded locks that curled around his face were damp and seemed as silken as any girl's. Roxanne inhaled sharply, stunned by the fair and unblemished face too godlike to be human. He possessed a high brow, square chin, sculptured nose, and large, intelligent eyes so startling a blue-gray that they resembled liquid opals. Averting her gaze, she stared at the dusty sandals on his shapely feet, taking in the sinewy calves and well-formed legs.

Though he was not tall, Alexander's physique was that of a virile warrior, tanned and muscular, crisscrossed with battle scars. His bare chest was hairless, shoulders broad, stomach flat, and waist thin. A lionskin wrap barely covered his loins,

and a cap of lion skin and teeth crowned his brow. He wore
nothing else except a heavy ring on his left hand.

"Don't be afraid," he said.

She met his gaze again and read amusement there. His familiar treatment rankled. "I am the Princess Roxanne. Why
should I fear a barbarian such as you?" Her father's eyes signaled caution, but she had exhausted her portion of patience.
"And you, my lord," she continued in Greek, "can be none
other than the Macedonian, King Alexander."

He laughed. "We're pleased that you speak our tongue so
eloquently, lady. I'm pleasantly surprised." Without releasing
her hand, he turned and led her across the court, through a
series of chambers and passageways to a splendid reception
room. Her father, Hephaestion, and a dozen officers hurried
to keep pace with them.

Alexander stopped before a marble bench and motioned
for her to sit. "Your people have delayed me sore," he said. "I
have not found such fighters in all of Persia. But . . ." He
switched from Greek to a courtly Bactrian. "Your beauty is
widely known. Roxanne, the little star, is said to be the fairest
in all the world."

"My father bade me beware of Greeks. Those who come
with swords in hand and honey on their lips must be doubly
dangerous." She flashed him a bitter smile. "Strange, sir, you
so quickly change your mind. Did you not bet Hephaestion
that I would resemble a she-ass?"

Alexander laughed again, then stood and folded sinewy
arms over his chest. "Wit and a quick tongue. I like you, Little
Star. Yes, I do. And I fancy your copper-gold hair . . . almost
flame-colored. It is quite unusual for a Persian."

"I am not Persian," she corrected him.

"Alexander," Hephaestion warned. "Don't—"

"Why not?" Alexander gestured grandly toward his companions. "Haven't you all been nagging me for months that
it's time I thought of giving the empire an heir?"

"With a proper Macedonian noblewoman," Hephaestion
said.

Alexander shook his head. "You have no imagination. Surely a princess royal should satisfy—"

"Burn in the deepest pits of the underworld!" Roxanne cried.

"Daughter!" Oxyartes admonished. "Don't be a fool."

"Yes, I think I will," Alexander said. "What say you, Prince Oxyartes? Will you give her in honorable marriage?"

"Of course," her father answered.

"I'd rather be thrown from the highest tower and eaten by vultures!" she cried.

"With spirit such as that," Alexander continued, "she'll bear me sons to—"

"You're mad!" Hephaestion said. "I'll be no part of this."

"Nor I," Roxanne agreed.

"You will do as I say," Oxyartes replied hotly. "Accept—"

"Accept what?" she cried. "That I'd give myself to this Macedonian sheepherder who burned our cities and laid waste our farms?"

The sting of Oxyartes's hand shocked her into silence. Never before had her father struck her. "You are heir to this kingdom," he said. "You have a duty to your people."

"Ask anything else of me, but I won't—"

Her father raised his hand to slap her again, but Alexander stepped between them. "Wait. Give her a little time to get used to the idea." The Greek drew Oxyartes away and spoke to him for several minutes. Roxanne fought to hold back tears of anger and frustration.

Then her father returned, took her arm, and led her to a small, windowless room off the reception area. "Compose yourself," he commanded. "Stop acting like a spoiled child."

"What have you done? Sold me to save your own life?"

His face whitened. "My heart aches that you would believe that." The pain in his eyes made her stomach clench.

Oxyartes drew himself erect, again the prince she had always known. "You make me say what no father should have to." His big hands tightened into fists. His body tensed, and a muscle along his square jawline twitched. "You are Alexander's property. He can use you as slave or concubine, sell you

18

in an open market, or pass you on to one of his soldiers . . . or to many."

"I will kill myself first."

"You reveal your ignorance. Do you think a man like this will give you the opportunity to take your own life if you're of value to him?" His deep voice cracked. "By this marriage you bring an end to the war. You join Sogdiana and Bactria to the Macedonian cause, not as a conquered nation, but as allies. If you become his wife, he will spare our people, men, women, and children."

"And if I refuse? What then, Father?" Tears spilled down her cheeks. She was suddenly so cold that her teeth began to chatter.

"If you will not have him, then he says he will put to death all men over the age of eight. The women and remaining children will be sold as slaves. Our horses and livestock will be slaughtered, our wells poisoned, and our fields strewn with salt. Alexander swears that if you refuse him, he will not leave one living thing so far as the naked eye can see from this rock."

"I am to be the sacrifice."

"For Bactria. For Sogdiana."

Gooseflesh rose on her arms. "And Kayan? He was to be my husband. What of our love?"

Her father's voice became a croak. "His name on your lips will be his death warrant. He is my trusted lieutenant, a no-bleman. Your love for him is that of a kinsman, no more."

She turned to the finely woven linen wall covering, pressing her face against the bright-colored embroidered flowers. Her nails dug into the minute stitching, rending it in silent rage. "God of my mother," she prayed. "Don't ask this of me. Give me an honorable death."

Oxyartes seized her shoulder and spun her around. "Death? Is that all you can think of? Coward! Where is the courage I saw in one who thought herself prince of Bactria and Sogdiana?" His words lashed with whiplike precision. "You could be queen of all Persia and Greece. Win Alexander's heart, and your children will inherit a throne."

19

"I don't care about Persia and Greece." She wept deep, dry sobs that ripped her inner soul.

"My armies have but a single champion, Daughter. History will record your tactics."

"And my tears? Who will remember my tears?"

In a private chamber, Hephaestion, Ptolemy, and Philip shared Alexander's meal. Skillfully Hephaestion, tallest of the three, sliced a crimson apple, still crisp after months of storage, and placed a section in his mouth. "You are mad," he said. "If you desire the saucy piece, bed her. She's comely enough. But marriage? When you choose a wife, it should be a Macedonian lady of high birth, not some mountain tribeswoman."

Alexander swirled the wine in his cup and looked thoughtful. "We can't invade India with Bactria and Sogdiana in revolt at our back. If I take Roxanne to wife, I'll make kinsmen of these people. Their swords will slash for me. That magnificent light cavalry will ride over my foes. I tell you, Hephaestion, I'll breed on her a son to rule the world."

"If she leaves you a root to breed with," Ptolemy said. "She threatened Hephaestion with the loss of his."

Hephaestion scowled. "This is a mistake. She's trouble. And if you go through with this, the men won't like it."

"I agree," Philip answered. "She has a face and figure to rival Aphrodite. But swiving a shapely redhead is one thing; marrying her is another."

"Stop thinking like a soldier, and think like a general." Alexander rearranged the golden plates and cups on the polished ebony table. "Here is Sogdiana Rock." He slid a bowl of dates into place. "The steppes are there. This way is India, and here, all of this is the mysterious land of Chin. Through these mountains move caravans of riches. We're at the crossroads. Silks, spices, gold, furs, slaves, gems. It all passes through here. These people are not savages, my friends."

His blue-gray eyes were shrewd as he drained the last drops of wine from his chalice. "Above all, these mountain people are warriors, the fiercest we'd had to face since we left Macedonia. They claim they're descended from the Amazons."

Hephaestion scoffed and muttered a good-natured oath. "Olympias claims you were fathered by a god. Are we to swallow this myth of Amazons as easily as your mother's tall tales?"

Alexander grinned. "I'll send her your best when I next write."

"Don't bother. Our queen has a long memory and sharp fangs."

"Don't try to change the subject. I mean to weld these Bactrians and Sogdians to our cause. Besides, if I were still at home, I'd have several sons by now. This is the time and the place . . . and above all, this is the woman. I will have her, and I will have her with honor."

"Do as you please," Ptolemy said, pouring himself more wine. "You will anyhow."

"The Companions complain you grow more Persian every day," Hephaestion persisted.

"And you? What do you think, old friend?"

Hephaestion's expression grew serious. "I have long ceased to judge you by the actions of mortals."

Minutes later, two burly guards ushered Oxyartes into the chamber. He saluted Alexander. "My daughter, the Princess Roxanne, is honored by your offer of marriage."

Alexander waved him to a seat. "Sit, my soon to be father-in-law. Tell me, how many soldiers do you have still fit for duty?"

"You'll want to talk to my second-in-command, my cousin's son, Kayan. He can tell you all you need to know."

"Send for him," Alexander ordered. "And make preparations for the wedding feast. Spare no expense. I would not have it said that the new High King of Persia slighted his bride."

Chapter Three

Senses reeling, Roxanne sipped the hot, spiced wine. Veiled dancers, their wrists and ankles gleaming with silver jewelry, whirled before the dais in a kaleidoscope of sound and color. Both Greek and Zoroastrian rites sealed the marriage. Alexander had cut the traditional loaf with his battle sword, and they had eaten of the bread. A priest had nicked Roxanne's wrist and her husband's with the tip of a golden dagger, so that their blood mingled.

Roxanne felt numb. She could not believe that her lips had uttered the sacred oath that sealed the marriage and bound her to this Macedonian barbarian so long as he drew breath.

The huge reception chamber was crowded with foreigners. Only here and there did she glimpse a familiar face. Despite Alexander's assurance that they would be under his protection, few of her countrymen had dared to bring wives and daughters to the wedding. Those who did come appeared frightened, barely able to taste of the wedding feast.

Kayan was not among the witnesses. With Alexander's permission, Oxyartes had sent Kayan, well guarded by Greeks, on a diplomatic mission to Balkh. Her father had known that Kayan could not have borne the marriage ceremony and thoughts of the night to follow. If she had gazed on Kayan's beloved features, perhaps her own courage would have failed her.

Roxanne glanced sideways under her lashes at Alexander. He had downed cup after cup of potent Bactrian wine, yet she heard no slurring in his voice, saw no indication that he was intoxicated. His raucous laughter matched that of his Personal Companions or *hetairoi*, the inner circle of noble courtiers who were his adjutants and closest friends. Of these, she recognized only Hephaestion.

Lean, sinewy fingers seized hers, startling her from her thoughts.

Pulling her toward him, Alexander turned her palm so that he could press his lips and sharp, white teeth against the underside of her wrist where blue veins were clearly visible beneath her fair skin. His moist tongue caressed the spot he had nipped, and a sensation of intense heat scorched her arm.

Butterfly wings fluttered in the pit of her stomach as his heavy-lidded gaze dropped to the tips of her slippers and then slowly seared a path up her silk-swathed legs and thighs to linger on her intimate folds before gliding higher to appraise the curves of her breasts.

Soon, his gray eyes promised. *Soon.*

She shivered, reminding herself that Alexander could see little of her shape beneath her ceremonial robes. Surely it was the closeness of the room, the unseasonable warmth, that caused moisture to dampen the undersides of her breasts and the apex of her thighs. The air seemed as thin as it had been the day, years ago, when she had scaled the heights of a cliff to snatch a Delijek falcon chick from its mother's nest.

She was no stranger to the act of mating. She was virgin, certainly, but a princess was no innocent shepherd girl. Within her library were Chin and Indian scrolls that told of the many ways a man and woman might give and receive carnal pleasure. Neerja, her father's favorite Indian concubine, had instructed her in the ancient arts of love.

Being pure did not make her a prude. Only a simpleton could live among soldiers and not hear the coarse jokes and see how men regarded sex. Many times, Roxanne had lain awake, dreaming of Kayan's kisses and contemplating the nights of passion they would share once they were married. But this mating with Alexander would be a mockery of love.

"Daughter?"

Roxanne realized that her father had been addressing her. She nodded, not really comprehending his words. She had not uttered a sound since her vows. As Alexander had removed her outer silk veil, she had drawn an invisible curtain around herself. Secure behind that invisible barrier, she could watch the world without being part of it.

She had chosen the white of mourning for her wedding garments. Her rings, bracelets, and even her coronet of pearls were as pale and glittering as glacier ice. Her people would know that she went to the Macedonian conqueror as an unwilling sacrifice, not as a traitor to the twin kingdoms.

Alexander's royal Companions were dancing now, stamping and clapping in a drunken frenzy more suited to a campfire than a palace wedding. Hephaestion shouted something, eliciting an explosion of approval from the clapping, stomping crowd.

"Alexander! Alexander!" they roared.

Laughing, he rose and joined the dance, whirling, kicking his legs high, and singing lustily. Roxanne concealed her shock behind an ivory façade. Had they wed her to a madman? What kind of king would dance in public like a common fancy boy?

Her composure shattered when the dance ended among cheers and huzzahs, and Alexander extended his hand to her "Come, wife! Dance with me!"

Murmurs of dismay rippled through the ranks of the Bactrian and Sogdian nobles. Oxyartes scowled and half rose to his feet. His hand moved to his waist, but halted when he touched the empty scabbard. Alexander had ordered her people disarmed.

She glanced back at Alexander to see a flicker of puzzlement cloud his blue-gray eyes. An oath rose on her lips, but she bit it back as her father's black stare shot a warning.

Shame Alexander, here in public, and our lives are forfeit! But nothing and no one could force her to perform before her own wedding guests. She buried her face in her hands and shook her head.

"Forgive her. She is shy," Oxyartes said.

Her husband roared with laughter. "My bride is shy!" he shouted. The Greeks joined in his glee as another group of professional dancers swept into the hall, accompanied by drums and pipes. Alexander returned to his throne on the dais. "Perhaps it is time you retired, little wife."

"As you wish." She knew she had to get out of this hall before she did something she would regret. Head high, ignoring the Greeks' catcalls and crude humor, she rose and left the celebration,

Four armed guards followed her. A steward attempted to guide her down the polished marble corridor to Alexander's chamber, but she brushed past him, striding swiftly to her own quarters and slamming the door in their faces.

Soraya met her with open arms, but Roxanne pulled away and ripped off her crown and the smothering headpiece and veils. "He wanted me to perform for his guests!" She threw the jeweled coronet. "He doesn't want a queen. He wants a dancing bear."

"I'm sure he meant no insult. Perhaps the Greeks' customs—"

"No!" Roxanne seized a flask of precious oil and heaved it at the door. The blue glass shattered. "Am I a whore? Does he expect the Princess of Sogdiana and Bactria to entertain at the bridal feast as well as in his bed?"

"Calm yourself," Soraya soothed. The serving women shrank away as a green vial of Egyptian perfume followed the oil. One maid let out a wail and fled the chamber as shards of glass rained around her head.

Still trembling with anger, Roxanne flung off the fur-trimmed robes and wrenched away her bracelets and rings. "Greeks do not exhibit their wives! They keep them as hidden from the world as any Persian noble." She kicked a low table out of her way, too inflamed with rage to feel the pain. "Since

25

I've wed a Macedonian pig, am I compelled to root in the mud like a sow? I'll kill the bastard before I let him into my bed!"

"Child, child." Soraya took Roxanne's arm and tugged her to an alcove at the farthest corner of the room where a full-grown hunting leopard lolled on a fur rug. "Mind your tongue. The Greeks are not deaf. I didn't raise you to be a fool." She handed Roxanne a goblet. "Drink."

"I won't go through with it! Let Alexander futter some camp follower. I'd sooner bed a Scythian!"

She drew in a ragged breath, suddenly realizing that her throat was parched. She took a deep swallow of the fiery liquid and found that it was not wine, but the potent elixir of the steppe tribes. "Oh!" she sputtered. "That burns all the way down."

"It will do you good," Soraya insisted. "The Scythians are weaned on it. One skinful, they say, makes a man fearless and gives him the strength to fight as twenty."

"If you say so." Grimacing, Roxanne forced down the remainder of the clear liquor. "Uhhh. It's bitter." She looked suspiciously at her foster mother. "Have you drugged me?"

Soraya averted her eyes. "I gave you nothing that will harm you."

"You did. How could you? I need my wits about me."

"It was just a sedative of poppy. To calm you."

"I don't want to be calm."

Agitated by her mistress's distress, the leopard rose, snarled, and strained at her chain. Roxanne dropped to her knees and cradled the big cat's head in her lap. "There, there, I've frightened you, haven't I, Akheera?" The cat mouthed her mistress's arm, gently nipping with needle-sharp fangs, and her growl became a rumbling purr.

"For shame, my lady," Soraya said. "She'll have you scratched and bleeding." Pushing open a hidden panel in the wall, she called. "Wolf! Take Akheera. She is not needed here, tonight of all nights."

Roxanne's mute bodyguard appeared in the hidden doorway with a chain looped over one arm and made a quick motion with his right hand. Akheera flattened her ears against her head.

"I should take her with me to the bridal chamber," Roxanne said. "That would give Alexander a night to remember."

Wolf's lip curled in a snarl as fierce as that of the big cat. One sun-scorched hand caressed the curved dagger at his waist. Wolf might not be able to speak with his tongue, but his expression-filled dark eyes conveyed his thoughts eloquently. Roxanne could see the question hovering there.

"No, Wolf. Make no attempt on Alexander's life." She snapped the chain on Akheera's heavy leather collar. "Go with Wolf." The leopard stretched languidly, and then allowed the Bactrian to lead her into the passageway in the walls.

"Hunting animals, both of them," Soraya said softly. "Sometimes I wonder which is more dangerous."

"Neither is dangerous, any more than a quivered arrow, dear friend. I am the bow that launches them. Without my command, they are safe enough."

Soraya brushed creamy cat hairs from Roxanne's silk trousers. "You must dress quickly. Your husband will—"

"Will want me naked."

"Perhaps a little more of the sedative . . ."

"No more of your help, Soraya. Luckily, it doesn't seem to have any effect on me. You were wrong to deceive me."

"You know that I have always loved you as my own child."

"I haven't been a child for years. And if I desire them, I have potions of my own." She shook her head. "No, I won't take my own life. Poison isn't my weapon." She paused and went on. "He expected me to be ugly, did you know that? I wish I were."

Soraya made a sign against evil. "Don't say such things. Your beauty may do what your father's soldiers could not. It may turn the fury of this demon elsewhere and spare our people." She took Roxanne in her arms. "It will not be so bad. A little discomfort, quickly over. And you may be thankful that he has made you his wife. There is no dishonor in losing your maidenhead to a husband."

"Then why do I feel such shame?"

"A few weeks he will tarry here, and then he'll move on. You may never see him again."

"A thousand years would be too soon."

Soraya signaled to the maids. They hurried to Roxanne, whisked off the trousers, and replaced them with a tunic and trousers of transparent, sea-green silk. One servant anointed her with perfume while another dusted her cheeks with powder and enhanced the red of her lips with deep carmine. Finally Soraya brushed out her hair except for a coronet of braids, pinning the matching green veil and thin diamond-studded circlet securely.

"There. You're lovely," Soraya pronounced. The waiting women murmured agreement. "And look." Soraya swung open a window and looked out. "Your people salute you."

The mountainside and valley below the citadel were ablaze with torches. The myriad lights mirrored the brilliant stars overhead. A lump rose in Roxanne's throat at the magnificent display, and she wondered if her father or Alexander had given the order. The torches signaled joy in the wedding and peace between the twin kingdoms and the Greeks. But between Alexander and Roxanne, she knew, there could never be peace.

Agreeing to this marriage didn't mean she had surrendered. It was a battle lost, not the war. No matter how long it took or what the cost, she would have her revenge. Alexander would never best her. By all that was sacred, she swore it.

A fist slammed against the outer door, tearing her from her musings. "We come for the bride!" a gruff voice shouted.

"Courage," Soraya said.

But Roxanne returned to the window, pushing back the heavy draperies embroidered with red dragons, and leaned on the wide stone sill. She felt strangely light-headed, and she breathed in the cold mountain air in an attempt to clear her thoughts.

"Open or we will break down the door!"

Roxanne heard the clank of armor, but the white tiger skin felt cool and soft beneath her bare feet, and she was reluctant to move. She stared out into the clear, still night, gazing beyond the campfires of the encircling army, beyond even the Hindu Kush. If she had the power to work magic, she would will herself away from this place, so far away that even a Macedonian sorcerer could not find her.

"Roxanne, please," Soraya whispered.

A weight struck the door, and the wood splintered. The women screamed as a dozen Greek soldiers crowded into the room. "Take her!"

"There is no need," Soraya protested, but a burly guardsman shoved past her and seized Roxanne's arm.

"No treachery, woman," Hephaestion called from the doorway. "Or I promise to see you and your kin flayed alive and burned, down to the last suckling."

Roxanne stood in a dreamlike state as the sergeant ran rough hands over her body. "No weapons on her, sir," he said.

The soldier clamped silver manacles on both her wrists, and Roxanne managed to get out a single word. "Why?"

"We had reports that you threatened the king's life," Hephaestion said. "Lucky for you that it was just a woman's hysterical blabber."

Nearly an hour later, Alexander gave his Companions the slip and made his way a bit unsteadily down the stone corridor to the king's chamber. His head was reeling, and he knew he had partaken of a great deal more wine than he should have, but he'd gone into battle many times in a worse state.

"By Zeus's foreskin, I'm not too drunk to ride a horse. Or to sample the delights of my new bride," he said.

Two guards snapped to attention. The High King slapped one on the shoulder, called them both by name, and exchanged a few ribald jokes. "No need of reinforcements tonight," he said. "Let no man pass until daybreak, if you value your sacks."

Alexander pushed open the door to his royal suite. For a few seconds, he stared into the room, letting his eyes adjust to the flickering torchlight, before stepping inside.

A ferocious roar brought him up short. Hair rose on the back of his neck as he wrested his sword from the scabbard.

"Roxanne!" he shouted. His gaze darted from the snarling leopard crouched in the center of the massive bed to the woman. She knelt on the bed, inches behind the big cat, both arms spread wide, wrists manacled to the carved posts with chains of gleaming silver.

The shock sobered him instantly. Swearing an oath, Alexander lunged forward, lifting his weapon to deliver a death-blow to the beast.

"No!" Roxanne screamed. "She's mine! Don't hurt her!" And then to the animal, she cried, "Down! Akheera! Down, girl!" The leopard bared ivory fangs and lashed her tail. Her snarl became a series of deep, rumbling coughs.

"What game is this?" he demanded.

"I am bound and helpless," Roxanne answered. "My servant loosed Akheera here to protect me . . . from assassins."

"To murder me, more likely," Alexander replied. He swore again. "Who put these chains on you?"

"You ask me that? You cast-off son of a spotted baboon! Who do you think? Your soldiers! Your orders!"

"No." He scowled. "Not by my command."

Roxanne's eyes narrowed.

They were beautiful eyes, he decided, golden-brown with flecks of black, nearly the same color as those of the cat, and they glittered as fiercely. Roxanne's green silk tunic clung to her like a second skin, and her glorious hair was a mantle of living fire. Confined as she was, arms high, full breasts thrust forward, nipples plainly showing, this savage little princess would wake a marble statue.

And he was not made of stone. Heat coursed through his loins as he wondered if her mouth would be as sweet as ripe dates. She was virgin, and she was his to do with as he pleased. He lowered his sword. "If I can't kill your pet, what shall we do with her?" he asked huskily.

"Call for one of my huntsmen."

"What then? Shall I loose you as well, kitten?"

"Unless you're afraid for your life."

"Should I be?"

She shrugged and moistened her lips. "Perhaps."

Alexander's rod stiffened, pulsing with blood. His breath came faster as he imagined what it would be like to feel her buck and plunge beneath him, to hear her cries of pleasure in his ears and feel the pain of her sharp nails dig into his back as he filled her with his seed.

"You're trembling," he said, as visions of her bared breasts filled his head. Sweet mother of Zeus! Her nether curls would be as soft as down, and her woman's juices . . . He groaned. "No need to fear my javelin's thrust, little wife. You're mine, and I care well for all that's mine."

"Send Akheera away, and I will show you how grateful I can be." Her throaty voice promised much.

"I will teach you such delights," he promised her, "that you will believe in paradise."

"Send away the leopard, and swear to me that she will be safe."

"Your wish, sweetheart, is my desire." Eager to begin the wooing, he returned to the door and shouted orders.

In minutes, two stout Bactrian kennel-men arrived. At Roxanne's command, the cat crouched as they fastened a bronze chain to her collar.

Alexander bolted the door behind servants and leopard. "Now, on to more pleasant pursuits," he said.

"Yes," she agreed sweetly.

Drawing his sword again, with two mighty strokes he severed the chains that held her captive. Roxanne slid down onto the couch in a heap, hair hanging forward to hide her face.

Alexander sheathed his sword, unbuckled his belt, and let the weapon fall to the floor. He reached for his bride, but she was too quick for him. She scrambled off the far side of the bed, dashed to the window, and flung open the shutters.

Her eyes were wide, and he could read the fear there. "Shhh, shhh," he murmured as he might to a skittish mare. "Come away from there. The night air is chill."

"Is it?" She braced one slim hand against the stone sill, and her muscles tensed.

"Roxanne! No." Suddenly he feared that she meant to jump. It was fifty feet to the stone courtyard below.

31

He crossed the room in the span of a heartbeat. His fingers locked on one shoulder and he pulled her into his arms. "Don't be afraid," he murmured. His mouth sought hers, and the ice shell broke.

"Afraid?" Roxanne's balled fist slammed into his right cheekbone as she exploded with fury.

Startled, he shoved her away from him and rubbed his throbbing face in disbelief. She regained her balance and faced him defiantly. "Afraid?" A dozen Bactrian curses rolled off her tongue.

He grabbed for her, and she spun away, leaving him with a handful of sea-green silk in his hand. "Come back," he ordered. "What are you—"

A golden platter flew past his ear. Raisins hit his face. He ducked, barely avoiding being struck by a silver pitcher. "You little hill savage!"

He charged, dodging left at the last moment. She ran into his arms, slammed a sharp knee into his groin, and then dropped to the floor, as slippery as an eel. He groaned and reached for her as she squirmed away.

He flung himself over her, pinning her face down on the bearskin rug. "I don't want to hurt you," he said. "But I—"

She twisted onto her back, panting from exertion, her fair skin sheened with moisture. "Am I to dance for your pleasure like a common whore? Do you expect me to service your infantrymen as well?"

"Enough talk," he said, forcing her head back, his mouth hot and hard against hers. Her lips parted, and he slid his tongue into the silken cavern. She arched her hips, grinding against his loins. Gasping, he pushed up to stare into her face. "You—" He broke off when he realized that what he read in those golden eyes was not lust, but danger.

Roxanne slipped a Sogdian dagger from beneath the bed hangings and pressed the razor point against the hollow of his throat. "If I am your wife, then I will be treated like a queen."

Chapter Four

"Drop the knife." Alexander's voice was deadly calm. "Drop it now, Roxanne, or die."

"You think I'm afraid of dying?" It was a lie, spoken more to convince herself than him. Terror numbed her limbs and filled her mouth with the taste of copper. Her heart thudded so wildly against her ribs that he must hear it pounding. "I'm no common herd girl to be used and discarded. I'd rather die than know the shame of—"

"Shame? How have I shamed you?" His powerfully muscled legs trapped hers in the thick fur of the bearskin. "You're the first woman I've taken to wife."

She could feel the swollen length of his erection pressing hard and hot against her thigh. Inside, she trembled like steppe grass before a storm, but her hand holding the dagger remained steady.

"Give me the knife." His tone softened as a crooked smile crossed his lips before spreading to his beautiful eyes. "Am I so ugly that you would choose death over life?"

His face was inches from her own ... so close that she could see the tiny scratch where he had cut himself while shaving. His voice was husky and beguiling.

One thrust, she thought. *One thrust and this Greek will burn no more cities . . . will put no more of my people to the sword.*

"Does your oath mean so little? The promise of a Sogdian princess?"

His question stunned her. It was true. If her word meant nothing—what was left to her? With a shudder, she let the dagger fall from her fingers. He seized the blade and hurled it across the room with such force that it bounced off the stone wall and clattered across the floor. She forced her eyes to meet his, certain that he would choke the life from her.

"Have I given you cause to think evil of me?" Gathering her roughly in his arms, Alexander stood and strode the few steps to the couch, carrying her as easily as though she were a child. "We are enemies no longer, Roxanne, but the next time you raise a weapon to my throat, be prepared to use it."

Alexander claimed her mouth before dropping her onto the bed. She watched numbly as he stripped away his single garment and flung his naked body over hers. She clamped her eyes shut, willing herself not to flinch, waiting to pay the price of a conquered woman. She expected pain . . . brutality. She steeled herself to bear what she must.

His assault on her body was much more devious.

His lips brushed hers, feather-light, almost like a lover's caress. His breath was warm on her face, as clean and tempting as spring mint. His scent enveloped her. He was undeniably a foreigner, but his virile body smelled both sweet and overpoweringly male.

She blinked back tears and turned her face away so that he could not see the fear in her eyes. "Do what you will," she whispered, "but do not expect ardor of me."

He might possess her body, but she would not allow herself to forget the spilled blood of her people . . . to become so enraptured by his touch that she could forget what he was—a barbaric invader.

Almost tenderly, he stroked a wisp of hair from her damp forehead. "Speak not of what happened in war," he said. "That is in the past. If you are a princess, you know well that a king must do things he does not find joy in. But when I saw you,

34

Roxanne, I didn't think of you as a Sogdian, but as a woman. A woman I wished to take as wife."

He kissed her left eyelid. "You tremble so, little one. I would not harm you. If I wanted to shame you, would I have asked your father for your hand?" He cradled her cheek in his callused hand and turned her head so that he could place a kiss on her right eyelid.

She lay as still as a marble statue, holding her breath, trying to ignore the rush of heat that skimmed her skin and made the room overly warm. He kissed her brows and cheekbone and sucked gently on her lower lip. She felt as though this Greek was overwhelming all her defenses at once, and she could not summon the strength to fight him off.

"My beautiful bride," he murmured; "you must be a goddess come to life. I have not seen a woman to match you in all of Persia." His fingertips traced the arch of her brow and trailed down her cheek to caress the hollow of her throat. "Is your heart made of ice, Little Star? Am I so unpleasing to you?"

Ribbons of bright sensation coiled and uncoiled within her as Alexander's lean, callused fingers brushed her skin, touching, exploring, claiming what was now his to do with as he pleased.

Her chest grew tight, her breathing strained, as her pulse quickened and tension knotted in the pit of her stomach. Her thoughts tumbled; impossible images formed in her mind. "You are a foreign dwarf!" she cried, as her eyes flew open. "A sorcerer!"

"How so?" He nuzzled her ear.

"To scale this citadel," she answered breathlessly. "No mortal could—"

Laughing, he kissed her mouth, hard and quick and teasing. "No witchcraft, but mountaineering," he said when he broke off the kiss before she could protest, leaving her shaken, both by the slyness of his attack and the intensity of her reaction. "The peaks of Macedonia are rugged." The clever fingers which had stroked her throat so skillfully dipped lower to skim the curve of her breast.

35

Her lips tingled; her heart skipped like a foal at first bridling. "Bastard!"

He laughed again. "So said my father often enough. My mother claimed Zeus as her lover. Apollo, as well. It's difficult to keep all her stories straight."

"You are no god!"

"That remains to be seen. You may think otherwise after this night." He nibbled her throat, sending ripples of gooseflesh over her bare shoulders. "Many women have said so—I am so well endowed."

"And men as well, I suppose."

He chuckled. "You have been listening to my enemies. Lies."

"I know about Greeks."

"Ask Hephaestion if you would know the truth about me. I have always favored women."

She turned her face away. "You think I will so easily forgive your insult at our wedding feast? How could you shame me before your men? Would you have asked a Greek wife to dance like a common entertainer?"

He cupped her breast in his hand, and she felt her nipple pucker and harden. "I did not ask you to dance to shame you," he murmured as he lowered his head to taste her breast. "It was only to show off your beauty. I never meant it as an insult."

She felt the tip of his tongue, moist and hot, flick teasingly over her tender skin. Her breath caught in her throat as he drew her nipple into his mouth and suckled, sending sweet, bright sensations rocketing through her body. "No need to woo what is already yours," she cried.

"I want you willing," he said. "I have never taken a woman by force." He lifted his head to stare into her eyes, and then returned his attention to her breasts, kissing, licking, and suckling on them until her anger and fear gave way to raw desire.

"I have heard otherwise." By the Sacred Fire, what was he doing now? A rush of blood heated her throat, and she moaned softly.

"Do you always believe everything you hear?"

36

All the while, his hands moved over her, touching her most intimate places, giving her physical joy in ways she had not dreamed were possible. "You are a soldier," she replied, trying to ignore the sweet sensations that threatened to undo her. "You are an invader."

"Am I?" His laughter stirred her blood, sending unfamiliar starbursts of pleasure skittering from the soles of her feet to the roots of her hair. He found her mouth, kissing her as she had never been kissed before. His tongue, hot and swollen, slid between her teeth, and she clung to him as the earth shifted beneath her. The fire in her blood became a torment, and she could not be still. He filled her mouth, breaching the barriers of her mind with his scent and taste and feel.

And to her shame, she found it impossible to resist touching him, exploring the broad, sinewy shoulders, the taut curves of his muscular arms, and the flat, hard lines of his belly with her own hands. She had never lain so close, had never been so intimate with a man. She felt the throbbing heat of his body against her, the sheen of his bare skin, and the rise and fall of his chest as she struggled to maintain her wits.

She met his gaze again when they paused for breath, and she read the amusement in his gleaming gray eyes. "You meant to insult me in front of your men," she accused. "Sogdian women, women of noble birth, do not dance in public, only for their . . ."

"For their husbands? I am your husband, your lord. Some day . . . some day you will dance for me." His powerful arms tightened around her. "You're right," he whispered hoarsely. "It is not for another man to see this body, only me. You are an enchantress, Little Star."

"Save your honeyed words for those who will believe them."

"You know I speak truth. You are no mortal. You are a mountain fairy who may turn to mist in my arms."

She felt her breasts grow heavy and full, her nipples harden against the pressure of his lightly stroking fingertips. Then she gasped as he lowered his head, drew a nipple between his lips, and sucked it gently. Ripples of desire spread though her body. "Don't," she pleaded. "Please . . . don't."

"No," she protested. "Surely . . ." She closed her eyes and fell back against the pillows.

She knew that such play was normal between a man and a woman. Her father's concubines had spoken of the use of tongues and teeth, but she had not guessed that it would feel like this.

"Sweet Roxanne," he murmured thickly. He nibbled at her shoulder and then slid down to kiss a path over her breasts to her navel. His fingers slid lower, caressing her nether curls and dipping to the damp heat between her thighs.

She could not remain still. She tossed and moaned as he sought entrance to her slit. *He is my husband,* she reminded herself. *Nothing that we do here can be . . .* "Ohhh."

Alexander slipped a finger into her moist folds. "Sweet, so sweet."

She cried out when his warm tongue replaced his finger. What sorcery was this? She had no defenses against her own desire.

He buried his face in her, probing, licking, sucking. She felt his teeth nipping, his hands beneath her buttocks, lifting her hips to delve still deeper. She arched against him, opening to his assault, tangling her fingers in his hair, urging him on with whimpers and quick, hard gasps.

Sweat broke out on her body. All reason fled as she gave herself over to lust, losing herself in wild, uncontained desire.

A powerful hand gripped hers, guided her fingers down to caress his rock-hard length. "What say you, little wife?" he murmured. "Shall I make you a woman?" His hands brushed against the curling hair of her mound, and she whimpered with desire. She felt the swelling of her flesh as his long fingers probed the core of her being. "Shall I love you, my Roxanne?"

She pulled him against her, reveling in his muscular body. "Yes," she urged, betrayed by her own need. "Yes."

Swiftly he plunged into the depths of her virgin body. He was too big . . . Surely, she couldn't . . . She felt the barrier tear, but her pain was short and sweet. Then she felt the sensation of fullness before he slowly withdrew and entered her again. She braced herself for discomfort, but this time there was none . . . only wonder that this should be possible.

She found herself rising to meet him as he buried himself in her body, clinging to him, crying out. Against her will, she was swept into the throes of passion, spiraling up and up until her reality exploded in a shower of falling stars, whirling on and on into forever.

Afterward, he held her in his arms and whispered words of love in his lilting Persian. She clenched her eyes, hiding the desperate confusion she knew must show there. What magic had he used that she could so forget Maracanda and the massacre at the River Oxys? She had yielded. Worse, she had been partner to his conquering of her flesh. This battle he had won and shortly would win again. The war, then, must be for her soul, which he would never possess. Could she not cast the dice for this? This man who had made her a woman held only a part of Roxanne in his arms. She sighed and cuddled closer. Flesh must yield to flesh.

Twice more he made love to her in the cool darkness, plunging them into a chasm of desire, teaching her things she had never dreamed of. And the third time, Roxanne was the teacher, using knowledge she had gained from the lore of darkest India. When they lay still and barely breathing, he kissed her love-bruised lips and whispered. "Swear to me," he commanded. "Swear that you will never take the coward's way out . . . that you will never commit suicide."

"I will not."

"You would not have done it. You love life too much, as I do." The gray eyes probed her soul. "Admit it, little Sogdian."

"Because I love life, I value it. I would have willingly thrust the dagger into your heart. Only for my people did I stay my hand, because I feared for their safety." She propped her chin on one hand. "I am no coward, Macedonian. I have been trained as a warrior."

"No warrior ever had such a body. You were created to inflame a man. You were created for me." His mouth closed over hers, and then he laughed and slapped her bottom. "I am hungry. I desire wine. The wine of Bactria is very good." He leaped from the bed and threw open the door. "Bring food," he commanded, "and cool wine."

Roxanne drew a fur over her naked body as the servants hurried to do Alexander's bidding. He carried a brimming goblet to the bed. "You drink first, my pet, so that I know I am not poisoned."

"Poison is a Greek trick," she flung back at him. Roxanne drained the goblet; it was unwatered and strong. "Where is the water?"

"I have ordered it served so." Together they devoured the meat and bread, and when it was gone, he reached for her again.

"Are you insatiable, Macedonian?"

"In everything."

Roxanne woke in the early morning as the first rays of sunlight were piercing the deep-set windows. Alexander, the conqueror, sprawled beside her, his tousled blond hair deceivingly boyish in the half darkness. His shoulders were impossibly wide, his arms muscular for one of less than average height, and his smooth, fair body was covered with scars of war. His eyes flickered, and he grinned lazily at her. "No daggers this morning, my lady?"

"None but your own, my lord." The words slipped guilelessly from her lips. Her father had taught her the Chinese game of generals and kings when she was five, and one did not telegraph future moves. Let this barbarian think he had clipped her wings. He would learn soon enough.

"Little Star . . . you are truly worthy of Alexander." He drew her to him, and the magic began again. There was no pain for Roxanne, only glory. Kayan's face passed before her eyes only once. She could not deny that her Macedonian husband was experienced in the art of love.

"Last night," he murmured drowsily, "you were untouched. I had thought otherwise. We heard tales . . ."

"No man has touched me," she said honestly. "I have been instructed, but . . . no man or woman has laid hands on me.

How then would our children be assured of being legitimate?" She flushed. "The Sogdian children, I mean. I am a princess. It is a matter of my honor."

He laughed. "I cannot admit to being untouched, little Sogdian. But never have I been with a woman such as you. I thought Persian women docile."

Roxanne sat upright, clutching a blanket over her. "I am no Persian. Again you shame me, Greek. My heritage goes back long before the Persians. My birthplace, Samarkand, is the Mother of Cities. From time out of time, Bactria and Sogdiana have been the center of the world. Our great master, Zoroaster, was born in Bactria. This is the crossroads of Syria, Chin— the land that some call China—and Persia, the hub of the world."

"So, you are not Persian. Well, I am not Greek. I have conquered Greece, but I am Macedonian. There is a difference, which you Persians do not seem to understand." He laughed. "Peace, little wife. You are truly Sogdian, and I will try not to refer to you as Persian. But you must remember your own lesson and not call me Greek."

At noon, Hephaestion banged at the door and was sent away by a good-natured Alexander. "Send us something to eat and another jug of wine." He strode about the room naked and fingered the rich wall hangings and the Persian carpets. "It is a beautiful chamber," he admitted as he opened a silver-bound chest. "What is this?"

"Be careful, my lord," Roxanne drew a blanket about her and crossed the room to his side. "The chest is mine. It contains medical instruments and rare drugs."

"Why are your things in my royal chamber?

"The rooms were mine first. Your people claimed it for your use because it was the finest in the citadel."

"You can have it back," Alexander said. "I have my own pavilion with my Companions. When I am here, we will be together." He picked through the vials and containers. "What is this?"

"Malachite for wound dressings and eye shadow. And that is myrrh. Give it to me. Are you a child that you must paw through other people's belongings?" She replaced the silver box and firmly shut the lid. "There is nothing in here for evil. I do not serve the lie."

"Ha, you are a Zoroastrian, a fire worshiper. I would have guessed you served some animal-headed god of darkness," he teased.

"You are thinking of Egypt. We do not worship fire. Fire is a symbol. We follow the teachings of the Zend-Avesta. There is Ormazd, the universal spirit of good, and Ahriman, the spirit of evil. They battle constantly, but we believe that Ormazd will prevail in the end." She took a comb from a table and began to run it through her hair. "Will you bathe, my lord? There are bathing pools beneath—"

"Of course I will bathe. But we will have water brought here. I am not ready to return to the world."

He stroked her breast, and she shivered with anticipation. "The baths are private," she said. "We could go there—"

"I will have a tub brought," he said. "I've no wish to share you with anyone."

"As you wish, my lord."

"Exactly." He smiled at her, and she wondered once again if the tale about his father being a god was so impossible.

"The day is already half gone," she said, covering her doubts with practicality. She retreated behind a draped screen and changed into a blue silk gown, stitched with threads of gold. "Surely a soldier does not spend his days lazing about a lady's bedchamber."

"What are you doing back there? Plotting, I'll wager. Come back to me." From a low stone shelf, Alexander pulled scrolls and spread them on a table. "What are these? Whom do they belong to?"

"What do they look like? They are books, and they belong to me. They are from the land of Chin. Be careful with them."

Servants entered the room with trays of food and drink, followed by slaves bearing a huge copper tub. Other serving men and women dumped hot water into the tub, and two scantily dressed maids came forward with oils and soap and thick towels. "Away!" Roxanne clapped her hands. "I will serve the king this morning."

He watched, amused, as she ordered them all from the room and tested the water. "If you are ready, my lord."

He stepped into the tub. "It's hot." He settled into the steaming bath and allowed her to soap his back and hair. "You do this as if you've had experience."

"I've seen men's bodies. Yours is not unique." She dumped a dipper of soapy water over his head.

He sputtered and reached for a towel. "Enough, woman! You mean to drown me!" He turned piercing blue-gray eyes on her. "What need does a woman have of books? Who reads them to you?"

"My education matches yours, Macedonian," she replied. "I read Persian, Chin, Greek, Sanskrit, and other languages that you would not be familiar with."

He laughed heartily as he climbed from the tub and wrapped his hard body in a towel. She could not help noticing his many battle scars. "An educated bride? I am astonished, and more so if you speak truth. Have you heard of Aristotle, little Sogdian?" He shook his wet blond curls and ran his fingers through them.

"You are as vain as a woman," she accused.

"Do not change the subject. Admit it. You cannot be as learned as you pretend. Someone has taught you to recite these pretty speeches like a trained parrot."

"Aristotle," she scoffed. "Your teacher was a pale imitation of his master Plato. Soo Lung, my tutor, is schooled in the ancient wisdom of the East."

Alexander advanced on her menacingly, then grinned and swung her up in his arms. "I agree with you. I ventured to tell Aristotle that once myself." He kissed her soundly. "And I was whipped for impertinence—as I deserved." He kissed her again and pushed her back on the bed. "Aristotle believes that the Greek city-state is the ultimate form of government," he murmured between caresses. "I will prove him wrong."

Roxanne's gown parted, and he slipped a warm hand inside, clasping her breast, stroking the swelling nipple until it

43

hardened for his seeking mouth. "I will conquer India and then Chin. Can't you see? One empire . . . one political unit! A blending of the best of all cultures." He tightened an iron fist. "And I will hold it all. It has been foretold, Little Star. I will bring Greek law and order to the world."

"And freedom?" she dared.

"Freedom was born in the campfires of the Greeks." He covered her with his hard body.

She laughed softly. "My lord, you would put Apollo to shame." She pulled him down against her, arching to meet him, filling her nostrils with the sweet, virile male scent of his body.

"This I will give you, my little hill savage. Greece has no woman to match you. You are an Amazon."

Chapter Five

For five days, Alexander did not leave the bridal chamber. On the morning of the sixth day, when Roxanne awoke, she found that she was alone. Her husband had returned to his Companions.

Weeks passed. Alexander's army rested at Sogdiana Rock, grazing their weary mounts in the lush valleys and allowing the horses to put on weight and muscle. The Macedonian officers formed Bactrians and Sogdians into companies of light cavalry under Greek commanders. Roxanne's father, Oxyartes, Alexander kept close, cautious yet of his loyalty, but recognizing the military genius that had held his army at bay for so long. Alexander ordered every able-bodied man enlisted in the forces; none would be left behind to cause foment when he crossed the Hindu Kush into India.

During this period, Roxanne saw little of her husband. Alexander informed her that Macedonian noblewomen lived sheltered lives, having their own duties and keeping to the women's quarters. The nights he did come to her, he proved an ardent and attentive lover. It was plain to Roxanne and her supporters that the Greeks expected Alexander to tire of his foreign bride, but he did not. He even spoke publicly of taking her with him when his army marched.

"Leave her," Hephaestion advised. "We need no noble-woman's household with her whining maids, seamstresses, and hairdressers holding us back."

"There are women with the army." Alexander stood beside a rough wooden table in Ptolemy's tent, scanning a supply list. Around him, gathered for the morning staff meeting, were a half-dozen Macedonian Companions, including Ptolemy, Philip the royal physician, and Alexander's rough-spoken kins-man, Leonnatus.

"Whores travel with the troops." Perdiccas spat on the floor. "You can have your pick of them. No need to drag along your native wife." The jagged scar along his cheekbone, souvenir of a Bactrian arrow, reddened.

Ptolemy glared at Perdiccas. "She might be more dangerous left behind. Here, she's a queen in her own right."

"What could she do?" Perdiccas said. "Raise an army of women?" Leonnatus's harsh laugh echoed from the back of the tent.

"I don't trust these Sogdians," Philip said.

"Nor I." Alexander handed the scroll he'd been reading to an aide. "But the time will come when you'll be glad to have them with us. They're tough, absolutely without fear, and un-matched as light cavalry." He took a cup of unwatered wine and led the way across the encampment toward the horse lines. To the left, two hundred recruits, newly arrived from Macedonia, were learning the basics of phalanx maneuvers.

"By Ares's rod, they look young. Were we ever that green, Hephaestion?"

"Raw as fresh-shorn lambs, but they'll toughen."

"Some will."

"They're Macedonians, aren't they?"

A huge black warhorse raised his head and whinnied. "Bu-cephalus!" Alexander called. He beckoned to a groom, sig-naling him to bring the animal. Leaving his Companions, Alexander went out to greet his old friend, scratching the horse's forehead and offering a sweetened cake. Even with the gray of age, Bucephalus—Ox Head—remained a magnificent animal, and Alexander loved him as he loved few men.

He took hold of the horse's rope halter and called over his shoulder, "Hephaestion! Walk with me. Ptolemy can make the final assignments."

Perdiccas scowled. "He prefers that damned beast's company over ours."

"Who wouldn't?" Leonnatus said. "Bucephalus's arsehole is prettier than your face."

Hephaestion made a final suggestion to Ptolemy and joined Alexander. Together they walked through the camp toward the stables.

"A few more weeks and we'll set out," Alexander said.

Hephaestion glanced at a square of rolled sheepskin. "The scouts' reports of the passes through the Hindu Kush aren't favorable. We're bound to suffer heavy losses." They were alone now, too far from anyone to be overheard. "You're not serious about bringing this barbarian woman with us? She'll be trouble."

"You too?" Alexander vaulted onto Bucephalus's back. "He needs exercise. Let's ride together and clear our heads of wood smoke and petty obstacles. Maybe we'll sight ibex or antelope and bring one back for dinner."

Hephaestion was his closest friend and had been since they were boys together. He valued Hephaestion's opinions and depended on them. It was his plan to name his friend as *Chiliarch*, second-in-command of the army, what the Persians would call *Vizier*, but he would not be constrained by Hephaestion, any more than he would by any other man. "Sometimes," Alexander continued, "I think war is ten percent fighting and ninety percent scribe's work. Do you deny me a little pleasure in my bed?"

"A woman is a woman. And this one is trouble. I say leave her here."

In the stables, Hephaestion commanded a horse and Alexander threw a bridle and leopard-skin saddle cloth on the black stallion. Together they rode away, following a narrow valley through a rocky pass and out onto an open plain. The grass was knee deep and the air sweet with the scent of wild-flowers. Far above them, a Balaban falcon screeched and circled the flatland, seeking prey.

Alexander reined in as he sighted movement on a rise half a mile away. "Look there." He pointed. "They're not Greeks." In unspoken agreement, both put heels into their mounts' sides.

As they drew nearer, Alexander could make out the leather garb of native tribesmen. One looked like a Bactrian, his companion veiled and garbed in the custom of the wild Scythians. The strangers waited until they were almost within shouting range, then wheeled their horses and galloped away.

"Should we send out a patrol to run them down?" Hephaestion suggested. "It may be a trick to lure us into ambush."

Alexander grinned. "We came out for some fun. I've no intention of riding into a trap. If we wait to fetch soldiers, they'll be long gone." With a shout, he took up the chase. Hephaestion swore and followed, lashing his mount down the grassy slope at a full run.

At first, Bucephalus's long, powerful strides ate up the distance between Alexander and his quarry. As he neared the two riders, Alexander could see that the Bactrian's raw-boned bay was nearly a hand taller than the Scythian's gray. The youth lay low on the mare's neck, guiding it only by knee pressure, his hands free to use the short horn bow slung across his back. He glanced over his shoulder, and the gray's pace slowed to a rolling canter.

Alexander urged the black on. They were running on open ground with no hiding place for a larger party. Two savages presented no problem for seasoned Macedonian warriors, even if they were armed.

The man on the bay reined his animal in a wide circle, leading them back almost to the spot where Alexander had first sighted them. Then the two split up, the Bactrian heading due west, the Scythian east toward the mountains. "The archer's mine!" Alexander shouted. He wheeled Ox Head to follow the gray.

48

The Scythian led him on a zigzag course toward hilly country until Alexander cursed the pride which had made him take up the challenge on old Bucephalus. Still, the black warhorse had endurance, and the strain of the chase was beginning to show on the gray.

Yard by yard, they gained ground, and Alexander watched for any sign that the Scythian would reach for his bow. At close range, the weapon was deadly, able to drive arrows with enough force to pierce hardened leather armor. Alexander carried only his hunting spear and his short sword, but that weapon had severed the Gordium knot, and he had no doubt it would do for a bandit.

Alexander's doubts increased as the ground became more rugged. He was no fool to be led into a blind canyon where the Scythian might turn and wait for him in hiding. The gray's course was erratic, first lagging and then spurting ahead with renewed vigor. Alexander had long lost sight of Hephaestion, but he could take care of himself.

Suddenly the gray skidded to a halt, so abruptly that its hindlegs tore clods from the earth. The rider vaulted upright on its back, and they circled Bucephalus with the horseman first standing, then leaning from the animal's back to touch the ground on either side of the flying withers. Puzzled, Alexander drew his mount to a stop and watched this strange pantomime.

The little horse wheeled in a tight circle, reared on its hind legs, and screamed a challenging whinny. The Scythian's soft leather boots touched the ground, and he gave an arrogant salute, tossing back the deerskin headgear which had concealed his face.

"You!" Alexander went taut with anger, driving his knees into Bucephalus's sides and charging the horseman. Roxanne laughed merrily, seized a handful of mane, and leaped onto her mare's back.

"What think you of my lady's mount, Macedonian?" She pressured the gray's neck, and the animal shot off like an arrow from a horn bow in the direction of Sogdian Rock.

Cursing, Alexander slid from Ox Head's back and began to

lead the sweat-streaked old warhorse. His wife's jest would be an expensive one, he vowed. The day was fast fading. He took his bearings from the tall peaks, but knew it would be dark long before he reached the citadel.

Where had his wife learned to ride so? He felt his ire rise. How dare a woman, his woman, make such a fool of him? He doubted any man in his cavalry could equal her skill. The little gray mare was too precious to be ridden. "I'll breed her to Ox Head and get a line of colts from her to carry kings." He continued to stride beside the stallion long after the black was rested enough to remount.

Then, abruptly the big horse stopped short, threw up his head, and whinnied. To the east, Alexander made out a pale horse and rider running full out. Behind them came a group in hot pursuit.

Roxanne clung to the plunging mare's neck and searched the horizon for Alexander. The Scythian raiding party had taken her by surprise, springing from a ravine directly in her path. Now the race was in earnest.

The five warriors behind her had crossed the Oxys in search of scalps and booty, and she was as ripe game as any Greek. Worse, their horses were fresh, and her riding skill novice to their own. Their war cries rang in her ears, and childhood tales of Scythian brutality numbed her mind as she urged the gray on, faster, ever faster.

A woman taken by the Scythians was better dead. Used as common whore and slave, she'd not last six months in their filthy camp. They'd captured her cousin Laleh five years ago, and none had laid eyes on her again.

Roxanne risked a glance behind her. One man was gaining ground. She could make out the black paint that streaked his features. Why had she sent Wolf off on a child's jest? He was a match for any two Scythians blindfolded! If she did not return, Oxyartes would have Wolf's head on a pole.

Alexander watched as two riders veered off to encircle the gray. There was no mistaking Roxanne on her little mare. Her game had turned ugly. He drew his sword and urged Bucephalus toward her.

The Scythian was close enough behind her that Roxanne could see his black eyes above his deerskin mask as he whipped his stallion after her. His companions had taken up his battle cry, howling like a pack of steppe wolves nearing a kill. She whipped an arrow from her quiver, twisted, and let it fly. Her first two shots missed, but the third shaft pierced the Scythian's neck, and his scream turned to pain as he slowed his mount to rip the arrow from his bleeding flesh.

Alexander met the faster of the two outriders head on, dodging arrows to slash with his sword. Bucephalus reared and brought his front hooves down with hammer blows against horse and man. Alexander's blade bit through the Scythian's soft bronze one, cleaving the tribesman nearly in two. The other outrider reined to join the remaining three. Alexander dashed the blood from his face and pointed to a rise of ground.

Roxanne drove the mare toward it with her last remaining strength. The gray was tiring fast, the little horse's neck soaked with sweat, her gallant head drooping. She gulped air in great strangled gasps. A misplaced hoof on this rugged ground, and they both could break a neck before the Scythians even reached them. An arrow grazed Roxanne's leg and she dove off the horse, rolling onto her feet, and sprinting the last few yards toward the rise. The gray mare galloped on. One Scythian followed the animal for a short distance, but then gave up the chase. Unburdened by her rider, the gray was as fleet as a mountain deer.

"Friends of yours?" Alexander shouted. Roxanne scrambled behind a boulder and notched a feathered shaft. The Scythians retreated out of arrow shot. Roxanne leaned against the stone, breathing hard. "We could use your army now, Macedonian. Keep your wits about you, or we'll be their evening meal. These steppe devils are eaters of human flesh."

"Surely they could find better to do with your flesh," he replied.

She cursed and counted her arrows. This husband of hers seemed strangely exhilarated in the molten rays of the setting sun. His eyes glowed with an inner fire. "My mare will return to the citadel, and Father will send out search parties."

"You forget Oxyartes commands nothing," Alexander answered gruffly. "How do I know this is not a trap of your setting?"

"Scythians? One does not bargain with Scythians! Sooner ally yourself with a pack of demons. My Bactrian guard, the one your friend followed, his name is Wolf. When he was a boy, Scythians cut out his tongue and ate it. Wolf has no speech, but you have only to look into his eyes to know Scythians."

"Darius had a Scythian unit of mounted archers at Gaugamela." Alexander flexed the muscles of his sword arm. "They fought well, until they turned on the Persian supply camp and looted it."

"Didn't I just tell you? Never trust a Scythian. Trust a Greek before a Scythian."

"Hephaestion will bring my soldiers. We have only to hold out until they arrive. Give me your bow. You shoot well for a woman, but—"

"I shoot well." She gripped her bow stubbornly. "It was made especially for me. The pull would be too light for you." She scanned the open plain in front of them. The Scythians had halted their ponies and sat, still as statues, staring back. "They will wait for the cover of darkness. Then they will attack. Even you cannot wield bow and sword at the same time."

"You should have held on to the mare. Rested, she could have carried you to safety." Alexander glared. "How is it the Persians teach their women the art of war? And how did you learn to ride like that?"

"How many times must I tell you that I am not Persian?" Dusk was falling over the valley; the wind had dropped so that even their hushed voices seemed too loud. "Mountain women have always fought beside their men. My grandmother, queen of Bactria, once led an all-women troop of archers and javelin throwers. She died before I was born. My cousin Kayan taught me to ride."

"Then he shall teach others. My young recruits could benefit from such expertise." He caught her shoulder and turned her to face him. "I forbid you to ride in such a reckless manner again. If you quicken with my seed, you might miscarry the child."

"I am not with child. If you wished a porridge-faced ewe for a wife, you should have wed one. My blood was noble when your ancestors were herding sheep. No man will tell me how and when I shall ride."

He raised his hand as if to slap her, and a Scythian arrow plowed a furrow along his cheekbone. Alexander whirled to meet the onslaught. The four horsemen plunged toward them from the gathering darkness. Roxanne's arrow caught one man full in the chest before the remaining three were upon them.

The Macedonian's sword carved a ring of havoc around them, decapitating one warrior and sending a second galloping away with blood pouring from his upper leg. Alexander scarcely noticed the arrow in his own leg, just below the knee. Roxanne dropped to her knees on the grass and snapped the shaft.

"Leave it!" he shouted.

He was bleeding from the cut on his cheek and a sword scratch on one arm. His yellow curls were soaked with the Scythians' blood. The headless body of the tribesman lay only feet from where they stood. "I said leave the arrow alone, woman!" Alexander snapped. "Do you ever do as you are told?"

"Hold still. The point is poisoned. I must cut it free and cleanse the wound. Have you water?"

"No." Swearing, he braced the leg against a rock as she sliced at the wide bronze arrowhead with her dagger. She squeezed the wound, then sucked at it and spat out blood and poison.

"Am I not bleeding enough?" Alexander said. "Leave it! That's good enough." He ripped a bit of cloth from his garment to bind up the wound. "Let's look at you." He yanked her to her feet. "Not a scratch. You've the luck of Artemis."

"You must not take a Scythian poison lightly. Horse urine might do to wash out the—"

"You'll put no horse piss on my wound."

They waited, straining their ears to hear anything but the wind through the grass. Minutes became an hour and then two.

"Maybe they've gone," Alexander whispered.

"No. They're thinking this over and—"

There was a whoop, and then the thud of hoofbeats growing fainter. "They've had enough," Roxanne said. "You handle that sword like a warrior, Macedonian."

A ram's horn echoed across the valley. "That's Hephaestion. He'll hunt that Scythian war party down and peel the hide from their backs."

"Not likely. Your Greeks will never find a trace of them. They come and go like the wolves they are. There is your trophy." She pointed to where she thought the raider's decapitated head lay in the tall grass.

"No." He laughed. "Here is my trophy." He caught her by the waist and crushed her against him. "I have not forgotten this afternoon's chase. You will pay dearly, wife." He kissed her hungrily. "I have many soldiers and only one wife. You must learn your place, my little hill savage."

She struck at him with both fists, and he threw her to the ground, pinning her beneath him, his hands like iron bands on her wrist. "Let me go!" she said, struggling wildly.

He kissed her again, muting her cries of anger. She met his kiss with her own, a long, deep caress that set his blood to boiling. He let go of her wrists and cradled her against him, while she clutched at his chest and neck and stroked his face. "Woman, you madden me." He groaned as she moved beneath him, blocking out the pain of his wounds, filling him with a surge of power, of immortality.

Slowly he began to strip away her boy's deerskin garments, kissing her naked throat and nipping at her shoulder. He slipped her shirt off and pressed his face against her naked breasts, kissing each in turn, licking the nipples until they grew taut.

She slid her trousers down and kicked off her high skin boots. The brilliant moon, moving free of the clouds, revealed her pale body in all its beauty. "The Scythians would not have taken you," he said. "I would have slain you myself before they laid hands on you."

"We had them outnumbered," she answered. Her fingers brushed his injured leg and he winced. She bent to kiss the wound, running her mouth the length of his leg to tease his engorged shaft. Lightly she kissed the swollen length until, unable to contain his lust another heartbeat, he threw her to the earth and drove into her willing body. Wildly he pounded deep and hard, seeking the release of her hot flesh. She met him with equal fervor, bucking against him, reveling in the feel of his ardent assault. She stiffened and cried out on his third thrust, and then he felt her climax again when he reached his own.

She closed her eyes and curled against him. Silently he held her for a long time, as the bite of the evening air cooled their fevered flesh. Then Bucephalus nickered a warning. Listening intently, Alexander heard the sound of approaching horses. "Cover yourself. Someone is coming."

"I have ears, Macedonian." She reached for her skin trousers. "A score of riders, at least. Heavy horses. Your Greeks."

"She rides, she fights, and she has ears. A paragon. I don't suppose you play at dice?"

"Better than you, my lord."

"We'll see." He whistled for Bucephalus, swung up on the stallion, and pulled her up before him. "Try to hold your tongue in front of my men. This will be difficult enough to explain. Making a proper Macedonian wife of you may be harder than scaling Sogdian Rock."

Chapter Six

As the army waited for Alexander's command to begin the new invasion, unrest spread through the ranks. Alexander's leg wound healed slowly; some said too slowly. Among the Companions there was open talk of poison. And those who dared to mention witchcraft did not hesitate to name Princess Roxanne as the culprit.

The unseasonably mild weather turned angry as storms swept down out of the mountains to pile drifts of snow across the valleys and steppes. The high passes could only be crossed in early summer, so Alexander's army waited, training new troops and holding what maneuvers they could in the bitter weather.

In Balkh, Alexander drafted thirty thousand Bactrian and Sogdian youths to be trained in Macedonian battle tactics and taught the Greek language. If he took the sons of the conquered nation to India as part of his army, Alexander reasoned that their families would be more inclined to remain peaceful at home. These young men would owe their loyalty to him; he would make Macedonians of them.

Bactrian and Sogdian veterans he incorporated into regular units, although this action was not without strife. Old hatreds were slow in dying, and blood often stained the dirty snow as Macedonian and mountain warriors struggled to adjust to strange faces, speech, and customs. Sogdian noblemen resisted the melding of troops, and tempers flared under Greek discipline.

"It will never work," Roxanne declared as she removed the bandages from Alexander's leg in the privacy of her bedchamber. "Your men hate mine. They will never treat them as equals." She washed the suppurating wound with woolen pads soaked in vinegar and dressed the injury with a paste of alum, malachite, and honey. "You must stay off this leg if you want it to heal."

"The leg is fine. Your fussing has kept it draining." Alexander downed a goblet of wine. "Keep to women's matters and let me command my army."

"Form separate light cavalry units of Bactrians and Sogdians," she persisted. "Even my father liked to keep them apart. Bactrians are stubborn. They must be led, not driven!" She signaled to a slave girl who brought wool and linen for bandages. "The wine would be better on your leg than down your throat, my lord," she added tartly.

"You would have me allow your Bactrians to form their own companies? And have them turn on me in battle? I think not." He lifted his goblet, and the girl refilled it. "My mother gave up counting my drinks when I was seven. I drink what I please, and I do not take military advice from women." He caught a lock of her unbound hair and rubbed it between his fingers as she bandaged his leg. "Well for you that your caustic tongue is wrapped in such a lovely body." Leaning forward, he raised her chin and claimed a lingering kiss.

She yanked tightly on the knot she was tying in the bandage, and felt him flinch. "Remember that I was royalty when you were a naked lad herding sheep. I am not one of your Greek whores."

His brooding eyes narrowed. "Someday you will go too far." Abruptly he stood and yanked on a pair of woolen trousers, cut and stitched in the Persian style. "Do not forget who is master here."

She withdrew, putting distance between them. Her lips stung from the ferocity of his kiss, and it took all her will not to back down. Many spoke of Alexander as a god. She knew that he was all too human . . . yet there were times when he seemed to possess qualities that went beyond those of mortal men. He frightened her . . . and yet he held for her a terrible fascination.

"There is something more," she said, unwilling to keep silent when her people were at risk. "You do not endear yourself to the families of these boys you force into your army. Some are very young to go to war. Many will die in the passes of the Hindu Kush."

"Many of my own soldiers will die. Those youths who live will toughen. You do not train soldiers like milkmaids. Some of my Macedonians were no older when they followed me from home to Babylon." He threw open a window, letting in a cold wind. "Damn this accursed weather! We should be on the march."

Hephaestion appeared in the open doorway. "Philip said you were here. How is the leg?" He reached for Alexander's cup and drained it. "Bring another goblet," he ordered a serving girl. Roxanne noticed the gleam in Hephaestion's eye as the shapely slave hurried to do his bidding.

"Leave us, Farah," Roxanne commanded, taking the wine ewer. Hephaestion's reputation had spread throughout the citadel. He would have to seek his bed partners elsewhere than among her women.

"Shut the window. It's bad enough outside." Hephaestion warmed his hands over the charcoal heater. "Two mares foaled this morning. How the colts will live in this weather, I don't know."

"Did you have them brought inside?" Roxanne asked.

Hephaestion ignored her. Drawing up a stool, he continued his conversation with Alexander.

Cheeks stinging, she turned to her husband. "With your permission, my lord, I have duties."

He dismissed her with a nod and turned again to his friend. "Scouts brought new maps of the area near the Jhelum River.

I want you to study these and compare them to what we already had."

Roxanne slipped unnoticed from the room. For the most part, Alexander seemed to regard the enmity between her and Hephaestion with tolerant amusement. There was nothing that the tall Macedonian might not say or do in Alexander's presence, and she hated Hephaestion with unconcealed venom.

Since she had married, she had kept her wardrobe of boys' garments in a chest in her room. She changed quickly into leathers and tossed a wolfskin cloak around her shoulders. Wolf shadowed her footsteps as she hurried down the passageways.

She would see to the colts herself, since the Greeks had so little concern. Horses were valuable. Her father often brought mares and their colts into the barracks during bad weather. One could not fight the forces of nature, he had told her many times, one must learn to live with them.

On the kitchen staircase, she came upon the slave girl Farah chatting with a young Greek guard. The girl ducked back into an alcove. "Come here, wench," Roxanne commanded.

As if reading her mind, Wolf made a few quick motions in the air with his hands, and his lips formed the word *Lilya.* Roxanne nodded.

"You're right," she said. "Lilya did ask for a new maid."

The widow Lilya would be returning to the city of Maracanda and her estates as soon as her things were packed. Her only son was six, young to be drafted into Alexander's company of boys, but tall for his age and sturdy. Other boys not much older had been chosen. She had warned Lilya to take her child away.

She decided to send this serving girl to Maracanda with Lilya before she could come to trouble here. In Maracanda, Farah would be Lilya's worry. Roxanne did not demand chastity of her maids, but this girl was too foolish to look after her own interests.

"Go at once to the Lady Lilya in the North Tower," she ordered the slave. "Tell her that you are a lady's maid, and that I make a gift of you to her. She is as silly as you, but she will treat you kindly and find you a worthy husband among her staff. If you are shrewd, you will gain your freedom in the bargain."

In the stables, Roxanne paused to offer an apple to her gray mare, Nata. Her saddle no longer hung by the stall door, and Roxanne could do no more than curry the mare or take pleasure in the feel of the animal's velvety nose against her skin.

Alexander had forbidden her to ride Nata. "The mare is too precious to risk losing her bloodline in a careless fall. Her hooves have wings. I will breed her to Ox Head. Choose another horse."

"Nata is mine!" she had protested. "You cannot take her from me!" Kayan had given her the mare as a gift on her fourteenth birthday, a horse worthy of a princess, one trained as one horse in a thousand.

Alexander's reply had been curt. "You forget who is conqueror here." And then, after a long silence between them, he had added. "The mare is royalty. She will not carry a rider again."

Once he'd made a decision, Alexander would not be swayed. Anger and reason had both failed. Sorrowfully she had picked a long-legged chestnut with one white hind foot. Her new mount, Roi, was full brother to her swift gray mare, and Kayan had trained him as well. The gelding was powerful, and she loved him for his courageous heart. But he was not Nata, and she could not forgive her husband.

"Alexander reminds us that we are slaves in our own kingdom," Roxanne said to Wolf. She glanced around the stables and then called for a groom. "Boy! This mare needs fresh water. If she sickens, your master will have you crucified." Properly chastised, the young Greek hastened to fetch a full bucket from the well in the courtyard.

Roxanne noticed a bearded Sogdian enter the barn leading a familiar horse. The warrior's furs were iced and heavy with snow, his features red with cold. He slung a leather case over his shoulder and strode toward her.

Her heart leaped with joy. "Kayan?" She started to run to

him; then caution prevailed, and she motioned him to an empty stall. Wolf took up a position of sentry, and Kayan pulled her into his arms. "Are you well, my heart?" she whispered.

"Hush," he answered. "I am well, but you . . ." He inspected her closely. "Does he mistreat you? If I thought for an instant—"

"No." She shook her head.

"Not a murderer? Tyrant?"

"Do you think I have forgotten the deaths of so many of our people? But I don't want to talk about him. Tell me of my father—of Balkh." She gasped as he caught her again in a fierce bear hug.

A warning whistle tore them apart, and Kayan dropped to one knee and handed a leather satchel to Roxanne. "These are for your lord, Princess. The High King will want to see them immediately."

Ptolemy and a man Roxanne recognized as Cleitus paused at the stall gate. Ptolemy's questioning gaze brought a quick response from Roxanne. "My cousin has returned from Balkh with important reports."

"Your cousin, eh?" Cleitus said. "Does Alexander allow you to meet in secret with Sogdians in a stable? Where are your guards?"

"My guard is here," Roxanne said. "I need none but Wolf. Must the wife of your master be guarded from his own army? Ptolemy, perhaps you would deliver the messages to Alexander. My cousin is cold and weary."

"Gladly." The hawk-nosed Macedonian paused and seemed to choose his words carefully. "I am not your enemy, lady. Nor yours." He nodded to Kayan. "But the king has been my friend for many years. Do not give him cause to distrust you. If he suspected that you—"

"I do not need to be told my duty as a wife, Ptolemy," she replied coolly, "but I believe you mean well."

"I warn you, he can be utterly without mercy. Do not mistake his temper. He is not like other men. He allows no mistakes . . . in himself or in others." Ptolemy saluted her and turned to his comrade. "We'll take this up to Alexander. I'm anxious to see these reports myself."

Neither she nor Kayan spoke until they were alone, and then he broke the stillness between them. "You were right, little cousin. I am like to drop on my feet. I outrode the Greek guards. They are used to warmer weather. Perhaps you and I will talk again later." His eyes said what his lips could not.

"Yes," she agreed. "Ptolemy is right. We must give Alexander no cause to distrust us."

She and Wolf walked alone to the west stables. Here the roof had been raised to give shelter to Alexander's three war elephants, captured at the battle of Gaugamela. Persian mahouts slept beside the huge beasts, keeping charcoal braziers burning to warm the stables. Once, as a child, Roxanne had ridden on the back of an elephant. She did not think highly of them. They could not be controlled as readily as a horse, and they were prone to panic in the heat of battle.

The female elephant trumpeted a greeting, and Roxanne produced another wizened apple. The cow took it daintily in her gray trunk and tucked it into her mouth, munching greedily. Roxanne exchanged a few words with the mahouts, and then followed their directions to the newborn foals and their dams.

"Do not stare at me so," Roxanne murmured to the swarthy Bactrian who shadowed her. "I am no fool. I would not deceive my husband, not in *that* way. But I have loved Kayan since I was a child."

The grim mute pursed his lips and whistled an eerie refrain that caused the hairs on the back of Roxanne's neck to stiffen. For the pace of a heartbeat, the swirling chasm of the Bactrian's desolate soul was revealed in his sloe-black eyes. Then the ebony lamps shuttered, and human desire vanished, leaving Wolf with eyes as expressionless as a hawk's. Roxanne shivered, and turned her attention to the mundane world of the horses.

Wolf unlatched the low stall door for her. Both mares stood content, knee deep in sweet hay, the tiny foals curled beneath them. One little one was a roan, the other black as night. Both were horse colts. She wondered if Alexander's Ox Head was the sire.

"They are fine, licked dry and fluffy. Both seem healthy." She nodded her approval to the groom. "Cover them with blankets tonight, and check on them in the deep hours of the night. Be sure the dams have plenty of water and enough grain."

Roxanne commanded horses to be saddled, and she and Wolf rode out across the snowy valley, the leopard Akheera loping beside them. The cutting wind blew raw, and Roxanne drew her fur hood down around her face as the animals plunged through the knee-deep drifts. She had chosen a sturdy warhorse that would not tire in the snow. The peace of the valley was what she needed. Here there was no sound but the heavy breathing of the horses and the crackle of the crusty snow beneath them. The sky was clear; no hint of a cloud marred the tranquil blue expanse.

What would she do? Seeing Kayan had brought back all her confusion, her doubts. He was the man she loved, yet she belonged to the barbarian. Could she bend her will to Alexander's, or would her spirit perish in defense of freedom?

Two hours later, they returned to camp. Roxanne's limbs were numb with cold, but her mind was clear. Dogs ran out to bark at the leopard, and Roxanne ordered Wolf to return Akheera to her kennel. "No harm will come to me here," she assured the Bactrian. "The hour grows late, and I must change for the evening meal."

Reluctantly Wolf fastened the chain on the big cat and led her snarling away. Chin high, Roxanne rode through the Greek encampment. Heads swiveled as she passed. Most had seen the commander's foreign bride at a distance, but she supposed she must appear outlandish to them in men's garb. Greek and Macedonian women, she had been told, were kept close to their homes, hidden from the world. She ignored the coarse remarks, keeping up the pretense that she did not understand their foreign tongue.

The camp, laid out in a mathematically exact grid, teemed with motion. Merchants hawked their wares among quarreling laundry women, beggars, whores, and camp followers. Veterans swaggered before green recruits. Men repaired armor and polished weapons; children squealed, racing through the drifts of dirty snow. Open pit fires burned, and each tent had its own campfire. Horses, oxen, camels, and mules stamped and snorted, adding to the smell and organized pandemonium.

An old woman selling hot spiced meat pies blocked Roxanne's path, and she tossed a coin in payment. The Macedonian delicacy was steaming, and it burned Roxanne's hands through her thick mittens as she devoured the pastry. The ride had made her ravenous, and she thought ahead expectantly to this evening's feast. Alexander would be dining with Hephaestion, Perdiccas, and Ptolemy. He had asked that she share the meal with them, an unusual honor.

She hoped Hephaestion would be on his good behavior. She wondered at his dislike of her, a hatred he had made no attempt to hide from the first day he had laid eyes on her. Hephaestion was so damn egotistical, a trait he shared with Alexander, but he lacked her husband's charm.

She thought of Alexander's closest friends. Next to Hephaestion were Ptolemy and Perdiccas, and the crude Leonnatus, all Companions and friends of his youth. Ptolemy was the only one she liked, perhaps even trusted, if one could be said to trust a Greek. His dark face was thin and serious, his light eyes gentle. Yes, she did trust Ptolemy. Perdiccas was an unknown, and Cleitus too coarse to earn her respect.

Tonight's dinner would be intimate with challenging conversation. If she and Alexander did not argue, he would return to her bed for the night, a not unpleasant realization.

A painted eunuch minced through the mud, lifting each fur-trimmed boot precisely, like a dancer. Roxanne turned her horse aside in mixed pity and distaste. Castrated as children, the eunuchs were neither male nor female, and usually possessed the worst attributes of both sexes. The Persians kept eunuchs to serve their women and families, a practice borrowed from the Orient, since eunuchs were supposedly free from the lusts of the flesh. But those Roxanne had known had adopted darker practices, and she could not bear to have them serve her.

Among the Greek conquerors, the eunuchs had gained much favor. The Hellenes were ever known as boy lovers. Some even hinted that Alexander and Hephaestion were lovers. Roxanne knew better. The ties that bound the two were stronger than flesh; it was a linking of souls. Hephaestion had his pleasures, male and female, but Alexander was not one of them. She wondered whom this pretty eunuch belonged to. He must have a strong protector, or he would not have survived here long.

To the left, Roxanne noticed a large scarlet tent with yellow streamers. Precious Persian carpets lay in the doorway, and two Thracian guards stood attendance. Curiosity got the best of her, and she watched as the eunuch entered the tent. This was not the officers' section of the camp. She wondered who could be the owner of this elaborate pavilion.

Laughter erupted within, and a beautiful Greek woman, clad in a cloak of leopard skin, emerged. Roxanne reined in her warhorse and stared. The woman was small and dainty with a lush, curving figure and black curls piled high over an olive, heart-shaped face. Her fingers bore precious rings, and her wrists heavy bracelets of beaten gold. She turned eyes heavily lined in kohl in Roxanne's direction and laughed again in bell-like tones, making some comment to her unseen companions. Two Macedonian officers ducked through the low tent entrance, and one caught the woman up, kissing her possessively.

There was no mistaking those shoulders, that golden cap of leonine curls. Roxanne's heart stopped, and she jerked the horse's head around, lashing at him with her whip. Alexander. Alexander in the arms of that woman.

She sawed the gelding to a halt, forcing him down as he reared, throwing foam from his open mouth. "You, boy!" she called to a half grown lad. "Do you know the scarlet tent yonder?"

The boy frowned as though he resented the commanding

tone of this strangely dressed horseman. "I should think so. That is the tent of the concubine Europa."

A Greek whore. Had her husband hidden his concubine all this time? Roxanne had heard no rumor, no whisper. Yet she could not deny what she had seen with her own eyes. She jabbed her heels into the bay's sides, sending the youth scrambling for his life.

Roxanne felt the heat of blood tinting her throat and cheeks. Had Alexander come to her bed fresh from that of his harlot? Did he spend the nights he was absent from the royal bedchamber in Europa's tent? Did he whisper to Europa the same love words he had given her? How could she have been such a fool, so blinded by the physical pleasure he gave her? He was a Greek and never to be trusted.

The taller officer with Alexander and Europa had been Hephaestion. Did they all share the jest? Were they laughing at her together? Hephaestion knew about the concubine, had known from her wedding day. So had they all . . . all but his wife.

So intent was she that she almost missed the cry of pain. Seething with anger, Roxanne reined the big horse around. Beyond the line of tents, beside a central fire, a circle of soldiers ringed a stake. Bound to it was a boy, whip-thin and sunken-faced. She lashed her horse through the group of men. "What are you doing to him?" she demanded in Macedonian.

"It's Alexander's woman!" one shouted.

A bearded sergeant snarled. "This is none of your business. This thief has been caught and sentenced. Cut and be damned!"

A razor-edged blade gleamed in the sunlight, and the boy screamed. Roxanne spurred her horse over the sergeant, slashing her riding crop across the swordsman's cheek. He dropped his weapon and backed away, wiping at his blood-streaked face.

She leaped from the saddle, her own curving saber in her hand, and placed her back against the hysterical boy. "Keep your distance," she warned, wielding the deadly Scythian blade in a warrior's grip. "Touch him at your peril!"

The sergeant rose from the mud, clutching a bleeding arm and curdling the air with his curses. Drawing his sword, he advanced on her. "By the gods, I'll split you—"

Roxanne's weapon flashed an arc of silver. She twisted her body, making herself as small a target as possible, and met the man's blow with her own. The shock nearly knocked her off balance.

"Are you mad?" a soldier warned the sergeant. "Titos! Don't, man! It's the High King's foreign wife!"

Titos's sword descended again, low, aimed to cut her legs from under her. But he sliced only air. She leaped aside, drawing blood with her own saber, making a long, shallow cut along his right arm.

She tried to concentrate on the man's eyes. Her instructors had taught her that a careless swordsman gives away his moves. The powerful Macedonian short sword drove straight for her midsection. She spun away, circling her opponent, the point of her saber stinging over and over like a swarm of angry wasps. Roaring, the sergeant charged, deadly in his fury. She hit the ground and rolled, coming to rest abruptly at the feet of a warhorse.

"Enough!" A commanding voice cut through the clamor of the crowd. Alexander dismounted and pulled her roughly to her feet.

Trembling, she sheathed her blood-tipped saber. "They were going to cut this boy's hand off. I stopped them."

"Silence." Her husband's withering gaze turned on the sergeant. "You raised a weapon against my wife?"

The Greek threw himself prostrate in the mud. "Lord . . . I . . ."

Alexander waved, and two men dragged the sergeant to his knees and bound his arms behind his back. "Garrote him." Alexander swung back onto his horse and thrust out a hand to Roxanne. "Bring the boy and witnesses to the audience chamber."

Awesome in his fury, he yanked her up behind him. They rode in silence through the camp until they reached the palace. "Dress yourself as befits your station and be in the audience chamber in half an hour," he said. "What were you doing in that camp?"

She slid down. "What were *you* doing there?"

He frowned, taken aback. "Me? Ah, you saw Europa. Are you jealous, little Sogdian?" His stare was unnerving.

"I saw you. You cannot deny that you were with her."

"Why should I deny it? Did you suppose I was celibate before I met you? It is not the place of a wife to question her husband." He shrugged. "Hephaestion and I share many things."

Stunned by the magnitude of his statement, she struggled to keep from saying words that could not be taken back. "It was not necessary to have that soldier executed."

"I have known him all my life. He served my father."

"Then why order him garroted? It is senseless!"

"You belong to me. To touch you is to defy my authority. I would do the same to anyone who touched Bucephalus. No matter the reason, my rules are not to be broken."

"Damn your rules! I could not stand by and let those soldiers mutilate a child!" She trembled with rage, more irate with Alexander than with the soldier who had tried to kill her. Her husband considered her property, a thing he owned like his horse!

Alexander forced back the urge to sweep Roxanne into his arms and ravish her intoxicating body. His anger at her bold interference in military justice was tempered by curiosity. What kind of woman could hold her own against a seasoned warrior? He wondered for an instant what the outcome of the match would have been if he had not intervened. The possibility that Roxanne could have been killed shook him to the core.

"I'll hear the boy's case," he conceded. "But if he's guilty, it will not be a hand, but his head that rolls. Take care for your own."

Still infuriated, Roxanne dressed herself in the royal purple of a Sogdian prince. If this Macedonian would put her on trial, she would not hide behind a woman's skirts. She thought of the boy. Where had she seen him before? She called a servant to make inquiries. She would not yield the child's life easily. In any case, to lose a hand would be as bad as death. Had these Hellenes no more heart than Persians?

As she entered the audience hall, she saw that her lord had been joined by Hephaestion and Ptolemy. They were seated on the dais, leaving one place for her. Wolf signaled the steward, who announced Roxanne with all her titles. She took her seat beside Alexander. He clapped, and the boy was brought before them.

In Sogdiana, trials were open to all free men, both noble and commoners. Standing by the wall were a group of Roxanne's countrymen and among them Kayan. She felt his eyes on her, but did not dare to acknowledge him. She did not think Alexander would order her executed without good cause, but she was certain that he would have Kayan put to death for the slightest infraction. The soldier's garroting had driven Alexander's lesson home vividly.

A corporal stepped forward nervously and said that the boy had been hanging around the tent for weeks. Soldiers had fed him occasionally, and twice he had been hired for rough chores. But this afternoon, the youth had been caught stealing a sword. The law stated that a thief must have the offending hand cut off. Sergeant Titos had been carrying out the sentence when Princess Roxanne had ridden up. At first, no one had known who she was. She had attacked Titos.

Alexander turned to Roxanne. "So you interfered with the punishment of a thief."

Hephaestion frowned.

"My lord," she answered, "the boy has not yet been permitted to speak in his own behalf. By Sogdian law, it is his right."

Alexander nodded, and a guard thrust the accused forward onto his knees. His bruised face was streaked with mud, and he'd obviously been crying. Alexander shifted in his seat. "What do you have to say in your defense?" he demanded.

The boy stared at the floor, and his words tumbled out in broken bursts. "It's true." His lower lip quivered. "What they said. I . . . I did try to steal . . ." Emotion overcame him, and he sobbed, unable to continue.

Alexander stood up and strode to the kneeling boy. He seized the ragged tunic and dragged him to Roxanne. "Here, my lady. He is one of yours. Show us Sogdian justice for an admitted thief."

Ptolemy coughed. He himself had been put on the spot by Alexander. It was never a pleasant experience, and he felt pity for Roxanne.

"As you wish, my lord." Roxanne's speech was clear and precise. "I have learned something of the case. The boy's name is Jason."

Alexander raised one fair eyebrow quizzically.

"Jason is the illegitimate son of a Thracian mercenary and a laundress of unknown lineage. Both of his parents are dead, and he has supported a younger sister for the past three years by herding a flock of goats."

"And where are these goats?" Alexander had the uncomfortable feeling that he already knew the answer.

"They have vanished, my lord, perhaps into the cooking pots of your army. The boy, then, had no means of feeding himself or the sister, and so he has sought work in your camps."

"And begged."

"No, sir," the boy protested. "I am no beggar."

Roxanne rose from her seat and approached the accused. "Why did you attempt to steal the sword? Was it your intention to sell it?"

Jason's eyes widened. "No, lady. Who would believe I owned a sword? No one would buy it from me."

"If it was no use to you, why did you steal it?" Alexander asked.

The boy flinched. He bit his lower lip and covered his shaggy head with chilblained hands.

Roxanne faced her husband. "You must speak, child, or all is lost." She stepped down from the dais and touched the lad's bony shoulder. "You have acted the part of a man. Now you

70

must be brave a little longer. Why did you take the sword?"

The boy swallowed. "I wanted . . . wanted to be a soldier. I thought if I learned to use the sword, I could join your army. I would have given it back, once I could wield it."

Roxanne nodded. "So what we have here is not a thief, but an overeager recruit."

A twitter of laughter rippled from the corners of the room. Alexander scowled, and the audience fell silent. "Is that the truth, boy? Or a fine lie you concocted to save your skinny neck?"

Roxanne dropped to her knees beside the child. "Mercy, lord. Do not put such a brave child to death for wanting to be a soldier."

His fingers clasped hers and he lifted her up. "Do not bow to me, Princess. Not here. Although in our chambers, I might reconsider."

More laughter erupted from the assembled nobles.

Roxanne stiffened. She raised her head high and met Alexander's unsettling gaze. All is lost, she thought. He will kill the boy as he killed Titos, to hurt me.

"My judgment is that you must judge him," Alexander said. "Your decision will stand. What justice in Sogdiana for a convicted thief?"

For an instant, Roxanne's knees felt unsteady. "Stealing is a great sin, and to steal from the army of the king is a terrible wrong, one that must be punished. I sentence this boy to serve as one of your royal pages. Under your watchful eye, he will learn duty and obedience. In time, when he has learned to be useful, he may enter the army, but you will be a better judge of that than a mere woman. I will find a foster family for his sister, and I trust that you—in your generosity—will provide for her care and will offer a suitable dowry for her when she comes of marriageable age."

"And if he repeats the crime?" Alexander asked.

"If Jason ever steals again, so much as a crust of bread, he is to be torn apart by four horses. So be it; so speaks the ancient law of Sogdiana." She motioned to the boy. "Justice must

71

ever be tempered with mercy. Serve your master well so that you may bring honor to your name and his." She saluted Alexander in the Sogdian manner and swept from the room with Wolf in attendance.

Chapter Seven

Roxanne thought of the Greek whore as she dressed for Alexander's evening banquet. She was not certain that her husband would still welcome her, but since he hadn't told her not to come, she allowed her servants to dress her and to arrange her hair elaborately. Carefully Soraya shook out the priceless lavender silk that had been Roxanne's grandmother's wedding gown.

The garment was of the sheerest weave, embroidered with a map of the heavens over Bactria at midsummer in deeper purple and set with diamonds for each star. On her head, Soraya placed a veiled, silk cap sprinkled with diamonds and sapphires. The embroidered tunic fell in points over full silk trousers, gathered at the ankles and slit from thigh to calf. Roxanne's grandmother had been the warrior queen of Bactria, and the monarch's tiny curving dagger, with its hilt of gold filigree and rubies, graced one leg. The dagger alone was worth the price of a nobleman's ransom.

"I would hesitate to wear my heirlooms before these greedy Greek savages," Soraya advised. "Careful!" she warned the maid who knelt by Roxanne's feet, lacing the purple silk slippers.

A girl came forward with a tray of precious scents, and Roxanne chose a blend of the essence of mountain violets. She had told Soraya about the boy Jason and the trial. All would be palace gossip before the evening was past.

"Stay as far from these invaders and their affairs as possible." Soraya tugged a copper curl into place and placed the cap in position. "There. Do not tilt it backwards like a dinner plate." She dismissed the women. "I saw Kayan," she confided when they were alone. "It would be better for you both if he had remained in Balkh."

Roxanne fastened on a favorite bracelet, lapis lazuli crudely set into old gold, a piece so ancient none could say what people had fashioned it. "My lord is too honorable to deprive his wife of her personal jewelry."

"He is a thief at heart. They are all thieves."

"The time may come when these gems will be needed to provide an army for the twin kingdoms," Roxanne said. "Let Alexander believe me a foolish woman until then." She hugged the older woman. "Did Lilya depart this afternoon?"

"With that worthless Farah. Good riddance, I say. Lilya was blessed with wealth rather than wisdom. She will only come to grief here, and Farah is trouble. That wench will be big with child before she takes marriage vows, never doubt it."

A knock at the door revealed a nervous steward. "Please, Your Highness . . ." Macedonian soldiers stood at the man's back.

"The princess is ready." Soraya smoothed the back of the tunic a final time. "Caution," she whispered.

Tonight Alexander and his friends dined in the small banquet hall. The high arching chamber glittered with the light of hundreds of oil lamps. The walls of dark paneled wood were hung with tapestries and paintings on silk; the floor was marble strewn with priceless Persian carpets. Beneath the tiles, pipes carried hot water which heated the stone, making the room comfortable in the deepest cold of winter. The low tables were polished wood, inlaid with semiprecious stones in patterns of leaves and grass. Rugs and heaps of pillows and bolsters were arranged beside the tables for reclining.

The men rose to their feet as Roxanne entered the room, and she saw immediately that most were garbed in the costume of some Greek god or ancient hero. Astonished, Roxanne glanced around. There was Ptolemy dressed as Hermes and Perdiccas disguised as Poseidon, lord of the sea, complete with trident. But where was Alexander?

"Welcome, my lady." Her husband turned from a group of Companions and smiled. She stared at him, momentarily speechless. Tonight he was no longer Alexander, but Herakles. He'd dyed his yellow curls a midnight black and was barefooted, wearing nothing but a lionskin that left one massive shoulder bare and exposed his tanned, muscular legs. A wide armlet of gold enhanced his magnificent biceps. "Well, do you approve?" he demanded.

"Yes, my lord," she murmured, making obeisance. The dark hair was startling, making him look more dangerous—almost a stranger. She couldn't tear her gaze away from him.

Grinning, he offered his hand and led her to a place at the head table. Attempting to regain her composure, she nodded graciously to his guests. One place was still empty; Hephaestion had not yet arrived. "I trust I have not kept you waiting," she said.

Alexander smiled at her, a formal smile that did not reach his blue-gray eyes. "Such beauty is worth waiting for."

Roxanne was not deceived. Anger still lurked in the recesses of his eyes. But she was not so easily cowed by a bully. She settled gracefully on the cushions beside Alexander and murmured greetings to those of his friends she knew.

In a curtained corner, musicians began to play; Persian by the sound of their instruments and probably all blind. The Greeks and Persians had much in common, Roxanne thought. Civilization must be measured in thousands of years, not in centuries. No Sogdian would blind his child to advance a career in music as the Greeks and Persians did. Children were precious to her people, worth more than gold, and harming one was considered the most heinous of crimes.

"Roxanne."

She realized that her husband was speaking to her, and she

gave him her full attention as he lifted his goblet in a toast. "To Sogdian justice," Alexander declared.

He was already a little drunk. Too bad the Greeks did not realize the potency of Bactrian wine. It should be liberally diluted with water, allowing one to enjoy the rich flavor without losing control of the senses.

"Thank you, my lord." She left her own wine untouched, sipping instead from a golden cup of pure mountain spring water.

Slaves began to carry in trays of roasted ibex, goat, and lamb, cunningly contrived pastries of meat and vegetables, figs, plump dates, olives, and all manner of dried fruits. Rounds of cheese, flat bread, and honey cakes baked with berries were arrayed before them. Young girls carried silver basins heaped with bright-colored fruit ices to cleanse the palate, while directly behind them came bearers shouldering great platters of golden-brown game birds, stuffed with onion and apples, and nestled in nests of highly spiced saffron rice.

Young Macedonian pages stood behind Alexander and his favorite Companions, alert to keep every goblet brimming with wine. Roxanne did not recognize the lad who served her husband. He was a sullen-featured child, perhaps some noble's son, newly arrived from Greece. The boy seemed awkward and nervous. Alexander should see that his youthful attendants were better trained before allowing them to serve at state banquets. She resolved to speak to him about the matter at a more opportune time.

Alexander ate heartily as usual. His manners were without fault, despite his huge appetite for both food and drink. Roxanne barely tasted her own meal: fresh-picked greens, a sliver of roasted antelope, and orange sherbet. The men around her laughed and talked, seemingly unaware of the tension she felt in the air. Her skin seemed too tight for her body, and gooseflesh prickled the nape of her neck. She glanced sideways under her lashes at the king, still fascinated by his change in appearance.

He caught her look and smiled charmingly. "You are not hungry this evening? The meal is excellent." Deliberately he peeled an apple and offered her a section. She accepted it casually, returning his smile with a guarded one of her own.

There was rustling and footsteps from the archway as Hephaestion entered the room with a woman. He wore an old-fashioned plumed helmet and carried the distinctive shield of Achilles. As the two stepped into the torchlight, Roxanne stifled a cry of indignation. It was Europa, the Greek harlot, on his arm.

"Hephaestion!" Alexander called. "Or should I say Achilles? You're late." He rose. "Europa, you honor our presence with your beauty."

Hephaestion replied with a crude jest which brought laughter from the Macedonians. The king grinned and glanced at Roxanne. "I don't believe you've been formally introduced. This is Lady Europa, the toast of Athens."

Roxanne seethed. The black-haired bastard had been planning this—sitting there smugly stuffing himself like a tame ox. Europa's painted mouth turned up mockingly as she curtsied. Hephaestion led Europa to the empty table without a glance in Roxanne's direction, but knowing looks passed between the other guests.

Roxanne stood. "With your permission, my lord. As the professional entertainers have arrived, I shall retire for the evening."

The Greek whore's cheeks flamed scarlet.

"You will not insult my guests, wife," Alexander said. His hand tightened around hers. "Where are your manners?"

"In Sogdiana, such women are not brought to respectable tables."

"I am lord here," he thundered. "I will bring a camel to your table, if I wish."

Roxanne nodded obediently. "It appears that you have already done so." She sat and lifted her chalice. "A toast to your guests and the honor they deserve." She downed her water defiantly, and Ptolemy's laughter warmed her trembling soul.

"Europa has been called worse than a camel!" Ptolemy shouted. "As I recall, Alexander, you have called her worse." He drained his own cup as others joined in his ribald laughter.

"I am not offended, Lord Alexander," Europa purred. "Your new bride is scarcely more than a child, unsophisticated and ignorant of civilized society."

Roxanne averted her eyes, shielding the murderous intent that must show there. She would provide no evening of amusement for her husband's friends. The whore had been brought here to shame her, as punishment for the incident in the camp this afternoon. Alexander had mastered his temper tonight, bending it to his will. Did he think less of his wife? Let the whore think her helpless; Europa would learn.

More toasts were offered. Servants brought fresh courses, and conversation turned to war, Alexander's favorite subject. An argument ensued, concerning the value of war elephants in battle, ending only when a troupe of dancers from the mists of Chin gave a performance which included tumbling and feats of magic to delight the eye and amaze the mind. Alexander was enthralled, commanding that the most thrilling tricks be repeated and then explained in detail. Finally, he rewarded the dancers with a purse of silver darics and dismissed them before calling for a lyre.

"Europa is an accomplished singer," he declared, proceeding to play a Macedonian love song. The Greek woman joined in, and Roxanne yawned daintily. Alexander played with great skill, but she could not account Europa's singing anything but second-rate and artificial.

When the song was finished, Alexander laid the stringed instrument down and motioned to his wife. "I have never heard you sing. It would be unfair to ask you to compete with Europa's trained voice. But you must do something. Will you not favor my guests with a dance of your country?" He patted Europa's backside familiarly and sent her back to Hephaestion's table with a gentle shove.

Roxanne studied the Greek woman from under her lashes. Europa was dressed in vivid shades of pink with strands of pearls woven in her dark tresses. Her face was painted unnaturally, giving her a masklike quality. Roxanne wondered about the harlot's age; Europa must be in her late twenties, already past the first bloom of beauty. The woman, obviously pleased with herself, leaned against Hephaestion and shared wine from his cup, looking slyly over the rim at Roxanne.

"Well, lady wife?" The drink had taken its toll. Only one intimate with the Macedonian conqueror would know how much of the fiery liquid he had consumed. He never staggered or slurred his speech. If anything, he became more precise, more cunning, and, she guessed—more deadly. For an instant, caution restrained her, and then her own fierce pride swept it away.

"As my lord commands," she murmured. She rose, whispered to a servant, and then crossed to the curtain to speak to the musicians.

Alexander laughed. "It seems my bride will honor our gathering with a rare performance."

Servants extinguished most of the lamps in the banquet hall and carried in a bronze kettle containing a glowing fire as the music changed to sensuous harmony. A primordial air filled the shadowy chamber, high pipes plunging beneath the deep call of the drums and rising again to lure the mind to ancient echoes.

Roxanne knelt in the center of the room, her motionless form enveloped in a veil of sheer amethyst gossamer, her gleaming auburn hair a waterfall of copper-gold, hiding her ethereal face. The cadence flooded the hall, seducing listeners with memories of lost loves and fiery passions, striking responsive chords in both Greek and Asian hearts.

Then Roxanne's finger cymbals came slowly alive, faintly at first and then more boldly, anticipating and blending with the sensual rhythm. For a space of time, only her hands moved, and then she rose from the floor as gracefully as water flowing over rock, her face and form swathed in veils.

Draperies of silk flowed around her, caressing her body, accentuating her womanly curves . . . revealing nothing of her face but dark, haunting eyes that seemed to see into each man's soul. She swayed before them, a bewitching illusion more legendary than real, hovering between heaven and earth.

Extending her arms, Roxanne moved fingers and limbs to

the throb of the drums. A reed instrument added a hypnotic refrain. She dropped a veil to the floor and began to roll her hips as the dance evolved from mystical enchantment to carnal intensity.

Alexander's mouth went dry as desire made him hard. A lock of dark hair fell over his face as he leaned forward, gripping the edge of the table.

Roxanne dashed a handful of blue powder into the fire, and the flames flared. The tempo of drums and pipes quickened. Illuminated by the flickering light, her hips moved faster and faster; her bare feet, reddened with henna, flashed beneath the hem of her sheer silk trousers, which revealed more than they concealed.

Alexander's brow beaded with sweat.

Another veil fell away. Roxanne's tunic swirled as she danced, allowing glimpses of silken-bound breasts and naked midriff as she leaned backward until her hair brushed the floor and the veil covering her face dropped away. Alexander stared at her undulating body with naked desire. Unconsciously he rose and stepped down from the dais, his gaze riveted on her.

Wilder and wilder the music rose, faster and faster, ascending to a crescendo of primeval lust before ceasing abruptly as Roxanne came to rest at Alexander's feet, her skin sheened with moisture, her kohl-rimmed eyes hot with challenge.

For a long moment there was silence, and then Perdiccas and Ptolemy rose to their feet with shouts and thunderous applause. Hephaestion joined them. "Well done," he exclaimed, and the other guests followed suit.

Alexander caught Roxanne's hand and raised her to her feet. Drawing her into his arms, he kissed her lips. The men laughed good-humoredly. Only the Greek woman remained sullen. "I bid you all a good night," Alexander said as he threw Roxanne over his shoulder and strode out of the hall.

"I should claim you here, before them all for that demonstration," he said. He crushed her against him, his mouth caressing her neck and breasts as he carried her through the passageways to her chamber.

"You bade me dance, my lord," she replied. "Yet now you are angry."

"Not angry . . . damn you, Roxanne! You drive me mad." He kissed her hungrily. "You'll regret this night's game, woman," he promised. His hands searched out the secret places of her body.

The astonished guards at her chamber threw open the door for them, then quickly closed it. Alexander lowered Roxanne to the tiger-skin rug, baring her high, rounded breasts and burying his face in them. "Your Bactrian failed in his duty to protect you this afternoon," he accused. "You could have been killed."

She wiggled free of his embrace and sat up. "It was my fault. I sent him to return Akheera to the kennel. I didn't expect danger in your camp."

His face darkened. "I will not have you in danger. You will have other guards. I will find you one myself. What is the name of that cousin of yours, the one who taught you to ride?"

Roxanne pushed the damp hair back from her face and got to her feet. "You know his name. It is Kayan. He is too valuable a soldier to waste in guard duty."

Alexander ripped off his tunic and reached for her, splendid in his nakedness. The muscles rippled across his broad chest and down his flat stomach. His chest was crisscrossed with scars, but nearly hairless. Below, blond curls nestled about the base of his erect manhood.

"I would not trust you to the care of one of my Macedonian Comrades. You would be too crafty for him, witch." His fingertips stroked her breast, and she tried to push his hand away.

"Nothing I do pleases you. Why don't you set me aside? Divorce me. You could easily find a hundred women more pliant to your will." She stood her ground, unmoved by his fondling.

"You are jealous." He twined an auburn curl around his index finger. "Her body does not match yours, Little Star."

"I am more than a body! I have a mind to match your own!"

81

Her eyes flashed liquid flame. "You thought to shame me with your whore! Instead you shamed yourself."

His temper flared, and he seized her wrist, pulling her against him roughly. "No woman tells Alexander what he may and may not do! I'll have a hundred whores if I so desire." He kissed her cruelly, and her teeth closed on his lower lip, drawing blood.

"Have your hundred harlots! Have a thousand! Sleep with sheep, for all I care! But you'll not bed me!" She faced him defiantly, fists clenched, eyes nearly level with his own.

He wrestled her to the bed and ripped away the lavender tunic and trousers, leaving her alabaster body revealed in all its beauty. Her breasts were heaving, her nipples hard and pink. One sinewy hand stroked her throat. "To deny me is high treason."

She struggled wildly, and he pinned her legs with his own. Blood trickled from his lip where she had bitten him. He pinned both her wrists with his free hand above her head. "Submit!" he commanded. "I will have you, with or without your consent."

She read the madness in his eyes, but she was past caring. "I will not wait in line for the leavings of an Athenian harlot!" Ceasing her struggle, she lay still. "Take what you desire, Macedonian, but you will find no joy in it."

Cursing, he forced her thighs apart with his knee and pressed her body to the bed, his tongue invading her mouth. Roxanne lay as one asleep, refusing to surrender to the passion he stirred within her.

Infuriated, he rolled off her and got to his feet. "Have it your way. I will find another woman's thighs more inviting." He stalked from the room, leaving her shaken but dry-eyed.

Roxanne lay on her back and stared at the ceiling. If she had driven him to the arms of Europa, so be it. Some insults were too great to bear, and she would have her honor. Slowly she rose and dressed in a sleeping gown. The star map tunic of diamonds was beyond repair. No matter. The diamonds would go into her secret cache. She was more disturbed about Alexander's command that Kayan be her bodyguard. How could she bear it if her love were near her day after day, so close but forever separate?

Perhaps Alexander would forget. He was, after all, very drunk. And he might change his mind. . . .

For a week, she did not see him. She had duties enough to keep her busy. Her father returned to the palace, and together they sat in judgment on the many civil cases and criminal prosecutions that had piled up in the period of political turmoil during and after the war. There were widows and orphans to provide for, marriages to arrange. Alexander's troops were under strict military discipline, but it was not prudent for an attractive female to be without husband or guardian with so many soldiers present.

Alexander's method of governing a conquered province was unique. Subject to his will, native laws were still enforced and taxes collected. Roxanne could give judgment, assured that her decision would rest in the majority of cases. It was dry work and tiring; she wearied of the quarreling litigants, but she had duties which must be attended to. In normal times, most of the legal matters would be handled by magi, but these were not normal times. Many of the judges were dead, the others scattered to the far ends of the twin kingdoms.

On the eighth day, Roxanne was called from the chamber of judgment by her husband's command. She hurried to the crowded audience hall. Today the room was packed with Persians, Medes, and ambassadors from neighboring lands, including one from India.

The steward saw her as she entered the Arch of Hope. "The High King will see you at once, Princess," he said respectfully. The man was a stranger. It troubled her that there were so many in her own court that she no longer knew.

Alexander rose to meet her, offering a ringed hand, and leading her regally to the smaller throne beside his own. His eyes were icily polite as they inspected her from the toes of her velvet boots to the silk pillbox cap on her head. "You are lovely today," he whispered for her ears alone. "I trust you have slept well this past week."

"As well as you, my lord." What new mischief was he planning? she wondered. Today Alexander had donned the trappings of a Persian High King, and no ancient hero-prince ever wore them so magnificently. His hair was still dark. His face and form were those of a god. When he entered a room, all eyes were drawn to him. Alexander radiated a virile essence, a spark of life so bright as to dim all those around him.

Her husband claimed the god Zeus as his father, but logic told her that the tale was impossible. Alexander bled blood as any other man. He slept—although very little, so far as she could see—and he ate and drank as common men did.

He was all too human. No immortal could be so vexing, so stubborn. But even she was not immune to his charm. She couldn't prevent her heartbeat from quickening at his nearness, and she couldn't keep from admiring the grace of his movements. He reminded her of Akheera. Yes, if Alexander were a beast instead of a man, he would be a mountain leopard.

"We have decided . . ." He paused and stared at her.

What was he saying? She shook off her reverie and met his gaze. When had her husband begun to refer to himself in the royal *we* of the Persian kings? she mused. Was that why he had dyed his hair? To look more Persian?

". . . that the threat to the Princess Roxanne, heiress to the throne of the twin kingdoms, demands . . ."

What was he up to? Roxanne forced her features to conceal her thoughts as her father had taught her.

". . . The Sogdian nobleman, Kayan, has been chosen for this honor and will be awarded suitable rank in my army. Kayan, stand forth and be recognized."

Her cousin came forward, his face dark with subdued anger.

Do not imagine I had any part in this, she cried silently. She could not trust herself to look into Kayan's eyes.

Stiffly he approached the throne.

"On your knees, Sogdian," Leonnatus growled.

Kayan had come to the throne room straight from the barracks. His clothing, although clearly that of an officer, was meant more for the battlefield or the hunt than a king's court. He had not shaved in days, and his eyes were hollow with exhaustion. Roxanne's heart went out to him. She knew her cousin's pride. If Alexander did not show him respect, Zoroaster alone knew what Kayan might do. She heard the slight intake of her husband's breath as his muscles tensed.

Kayan stopped, touched two fingers of his right hand to his lips, and gave Alexander a slight bow, that of high-born man to his superior. Then he straightened and stood, waiting.

Angry muttering rumbled. Hephaestion swore, and Philip took several steps forward, hand on his sword hilt.

"Welcome, Kayan," Alexander said smoothly. "We have heard much of your bravery and wish to reward you. We entrust you with care of the Princess Roxanne. We give you command of her personal guard. Keep her safe, at peril of your life." Her husband glanced at her. "Does this suit you, lady?"

She bowed her head. "As you wish, my lord." This was not the time or place to contest his will again. What reason could she give? *Husband, do not give me my cousin as bodyguard because I desire him above all things?* She forced a smile. "You are too kind."

"So be it," Alexander pronounced. "Wait, Kayan. Have you wife and children?" His voice was as smooth as raw Chin silk.

"No," Kayan answered. "I have never married."

Roxanne wondered at the control Kayan demonstrated, he who was never known for a mild or compromising temper. How proud she was of him today; how handsome he looked with his olive complexion and raven eyes above a thin mustache. He was a tall man, topping Alexander's height by a full hand, hard and muscular, in the full strength of his manhood.

"We must observe the proprieties. The princess, my lady wife, may not be guarded by an unwed gentleman. Choose a wife—today. As soon as the ceremony is complete, you will take up your duties at court."

"My cousin is not a slave to be ordered . . ." Roxanne began, before taking a gentler tactic. "Surely he must have time. A

85

marriage among our people is a serious matter. Kayan is his father's only legitimate son. He cannot marry carelessly."

"Is there a prior contract with any woman? Are you betrothed?" Alexander demanded of Kayan sharply.

"No, lord."

"Then, if you favor no lady, we will choose one for you." He glanced at her. "Does any noble lady come to mind? Perhaps the Lady Europa would—"

"No. She must be Sogdian," Roxanne said. "May I have leave to discuss this with my cousin? My father or his might—"

"Our time is precious," Alexander replied. "What say you, Kayan? Shall the Princess Roxanne choose a wife for you? Or shall I?" He smiled, a smile that did not reach his gray eyes. "Since you are cousin to my wife, this makes us kin, does it not? Speak, Cousin."

How much does he know? Roxanne felt icy dread run down her spine. *There has been nothing since our marriage that he could find fault with—except that day in the stables. But no one saw us . . . no one heard. Alexander may suspect, but he has no proof.*

She forced herself to nod agreeably and smile at her husband. "There is a lady, pious and gentle, a noblewoman, newly widowed. She is the Lady Lilya of Maracanda. She is in need of a protector for herself and her son." Lilya at least was rich. What matter that she possessed the common sense of a roasted onion?

"Do you object, Cousin, to this Lady Lilya?" Alexander demanded. Kayan shook his head. "So be it. Send me word when you have wedded and bedded the woman, and we will provide a suitable wedding gift. You have our leave to depart, Captain."

"As the High King decrees." Kayan saluted and backed away from the throne.

Roxanne sat silently while dozens of ambassadors presented their credentials and gifts to Alexander. He was well pleased with himself, and the glances he gave her were not unfriendly. She was too shaken to respond. It was Kayan's right to marry; there could be nothing between them so long as Alexander lived or did not divorce her. But for Alexander to force a wife on Kayan without giving him a choice—it was insupportable.

Her reverie was shattered by a commotion in the hall outside the audience chamber. One ambassador did not come willingly. "It is the Scythian," Alexander informed her. "We captured a band of horse thieves two days ago. This one fancies himself a prince."

Burly guards dragged the struggling tribesman into the room, arms and legs chained. They flung him face down before the throne. "Welcome to our court, Scythian," Alexander said.

Snarling, the man raised a swarthy, blood-streaked face. His greasy black hair hung in a half-dozen braids over his shoulders. The slanting eyes above the ritually scarred face were like twin coals, and Roxanne felt the hatred emanating from them. Her nostrils caught the unwashed scent of horse piss, and vomit; the leather clothing he wore was filthy and stained with gore.

"He does not understand Greek," she said. "Shall I translate for you?" When Alexander nodded, she repeated what the man had said.

Obscene curses spat from the tribesman's thin lips.

"We understand that well enough." Alexander laughed, and his Companions joined in. The Sogdians and Bactrians in the room remained silent. "Is he indeed a prince?"

"The Scythians have many self-styled chieftains," Roxanne explained, "and every chief has many sons." She called a Bactrian officer to the dais and conferred quietly with him. "My lord," she said after a few moments. "This Scythian is known to us. He is Prince Khem, the oldest son of a powerful chief."

"Tell him that we seek treaties of peace with his nation."

Roxanne translated, and the Scythian spat at Alexander's feet. "We make no treaties! We are people of the sword!"

"Take him to the dungeons," Alexander commanded. "We will talk again when his manners have improved." To Roxanne, he murmured. "You are fortunate you do not join him, little Sogdian. Your own manners need improvement."

"You, great king, are my example," she replied sweetly. "I strive to follow your lead in all things."

Alexander stood. "This audience is at end. Come, wife." He grinned disarmingly and reached for her hand. "There is a newborn colt I would have you see. He has the very markings of old Ox Head, his sire."

Chapter Eight

"Your clothing is not suitable for the stables, wife," Alexander observed when he met Roxanne coming down the stairs one morning nearly two weeks after Jason's trial. "Dress in your riding leathers and meet me at the north barn."

"I had planned to meet with a delegation of merchants from Samarkand," she replied. She noticed that he had dyed his hair black again, but she refused to comment on it. Her husband would have to play his childish games without her as partner.

"They can wait." He grinned. "I was supposed to prepare a report for my mother's chief councillor. But it's too fair a day to remain inside. I want to hunt ibex." He looked down at his own gold-embroidered tunic with a wry grin. "I'll change, too, lest I be taken for a court dandy by my soldiers."

She nodded. "As you wish."

"If you prefer, you can stay in the palace and haggle over the price of grain with your fat merchants."

She smiled. "No, I agree. Give me but a quarter of an hour, and I'll join you."

By mid-afternoon they were ten miles from Sogdiana Rock and the army camp. They had sighted two Greek patrols, but no big game. The weather had turned mild in the last weeks. The wind off the steppes smelled of springtime, and flocks of migratory birds filled the great bowl of blue sky. Roxanne reveled in the motion of the black gelding under her. Too long had she been trapped indoors.

"You are unlike any woman I have ever known," Alexander said. "I'm not certain if you should take that as a compliment." The accompanying soldiers rode far enough behind to give them privacy. "Sometimes I think you have the mind of a man."

Roxanne decided that she far preferred this Alexander. Here, without his lion head-cap and regal trappings, away from his Companions, he seemed younger, less driven. Alexander's mind never ceased working. He was curious about everything, from the teachings of Zoroaster, to the verses of Bactrian saga-songs, to the art of telling perfect gems from flawed—sometimes all in the space of an hour. He loved poetry, plays, music, and all manner of games and toys. And when he set himself to charm her, as he did today, he was hard to resist.

"Race you to that hillock," he shouted, and they were off with their escort scrambling to keep up. She was a length behind when they reached the rise. Grinning, he slowed his stallion to a trot and guided the dapple-gray so close to hers that his bare calf brushed her knee. "You're either fearless or crazy. The best woman rider I've ever seen."

She smiled, certain that had their animals been evenly matched—and had she judged it to be in her best interest—she could have left her husband eating dust. "I'll beat you next time."

"You wish." His mood grew serious. "We depart for India soon."

"So you say, but the days go by, and your army waits."

"I have good reason. The signs have not been favorable."

"Sacrifice a bull to your god of war and reward your priests. The signs will be whatever you wish them to be."

He scowled, but she read no real disapproval in his liquid gaze. "You make light of my decisions."

"No, of your superstitions."

"You ill-wish me?"

She shrugged. "Why shouldn't I want an occupying army to fold its tents and march? Your troops eat like locusts."

"Those are not the words of a dutiful wife."

"True. And you will sleep better if you take Europa with you instead of me." Alexander's laughter was genuine. "I'm serious," Roxanne continued. "Take your painted plaything and leave me to govern Bactria and Sogdiana."

"For once, you and Hephaestion agree. He and Perdiccas spoke to me of that just last night."

Her eyes widened in surprise. "Hephaestion suggested that I remain here and rule in your place?"

"Not precisely." Alexander's lips twitched as he tried to control his amusement. "It would please all my Companions greatly if I set you aside and chose a Persian princess as wife." He pulled a goatskin canteen from a strap at his waist and offered her a drink. "The snow pack is melting in the Hindu Kush. As soon as the passes clear, my army will move. It may be years before I come to Sogdiana again. I will take you with me. I have no doubt you will survive the journey."

"And the trouble I will cause you?"

"Even gods have their afflictions. I don't suppose you speak the tongue of India?"

"India has many tongues. I have some knowledge of Sanskrit."

"Taught to you, no doubt, by some great holy man."

"No. Neerja, my father's favorite concubine."

"The same Neerja who taught you that trick with the balls and the feather?"

"And the honey. She is a woman of great talent."

"Perhaps I should make her acquaintance."

Roxanne brushed away an annoying gnat. "Not possible. My father is too fond of her to allow her to associate with strange men." No need to tell him that Neerja was much older than her father, or that the concubine had gained so much weight that she no longer walked but was carried from place to place by her adoring servants.

"Neerja must be—" Alexander reined in abruptly. "Wait, there on the left . . ." He slid from his dapple-gray's back and pulled a dagger. "This plant—do you know it?" He fingered a pale purple blossom.

"Yes." She halted her horse. "The root is used in the healing of burns. It grows in quantities beyond number on the steppes. In the summer, it makes a carpet so beautiful the gods might have woven it."

"I must have it for my collection. I've sent wagonloads of plant and wildlife specimens back to Macedonia. There I have the greatest museum the world has ever known. Each piece is carefully documented," he explained. "The idea was Aristotle's, but even he didn't realize how—"

"The flower will wither," she said.

"I'll have it dried and pressed. You must write down all you know about it, so it can be classified. I wouldn't expect a woman to understand. But you did not tell me the name of the plant. What is it—" His blue-gray eyes sparked a warning. "There!" He dropped the flower and vaulted onto his stallion's back. "Look!"

Roxanne gathered the reins as she saw the flash of movement in the tall grass. Almost as one, she and Alexander turned their horses and sped toward the two score of their accompanying soldiers. Behind them, a hundred savage horsemen galloped across the valley, undulating war cries issuing from their throats.

"Scythians!" Roxanne shouted.

"Ride for Sogdiana Rock!" Alexander ordered, waving his men into combat position. "We will hold them here."

The Macedonians donned battle helmets and yanked round shields from their saddles. Forming themselves into a flying wedge, they charged the lighter horses of the enemy attackers.

Roxanne gauged the distance to safety—ten, maybe twelve miles. If she had been astride Kayan's gray stallion or her own swift mare, she might have chanced it. But the Greek gelding she rode this day was bred for muscle, not short bursts of speed. She would be ridden down by the swifter steppe ponies. She dug her heels into the black's side and raced after Alexander and his Macedonians. If a Scythian arrow found her, she vowed, it would not be in her back.

Her horn bow was in her hand as Alexander's well-trained troops sliced through the Scythian line. Her feathered shafts joined a rain of arrows; men and horses screamed. The smell of blood maddened her gelding, and the black lashed out with his hooves at a fallen Scythian, crushing the man's skull. She fired another arrow, shooting a graybeard through the throat. Just ahead of her, a Greek's horse plunged into a hole, sending mount and rider sprawling. Roxanne yanked the reins, and her gelding leaped the sprawling mass of man and horse and continued the wild charge.

A Scythian cut his pony close to Roxanne. Steel gleamed in the bright sunlight as the warrior's curved saber sliced the air. She gripped the black's mane, and guided her heavier mount in a direct collision course with her attacker. The two animals struck with bone-shattering force, and she was nearly wrenched from the high-pommeled saddle. Two arrows slid from her quiver, but she kept hold of her bow. The rough-coated Scythian pony went down, screaming from the pain of a snapped foreleg, sending the rider tumbling into the destructive path of his own howling comrades.

Alexander wheeled his cavalry and formed for a second charge, parting just enough to allow Roxanne and the black warhorse through the lines. The Greek soldier who'd fallen had somehow remounted and was closing fast on his comrades.

"Damn you, Roxanne!" Alexander yelled. "I told you to run!"

She spat dust and threw him an obscene gesture.

Three dozen Macedonians were still mounted; the field was strewn with dozens of fallen Scythians, some dead, others mortally wounded. The killing force of these battle-hardened Greek veterans was terrifying in its perfection, Roxanne thought. No wonder Alexander's army had cut such a swath across Persia. The prince within her thrilled at his military genius.

"Stay close to me!" Alexander shouted. His eyes blazed beneath the red-plumed helmet, their normal blue-gray color so dark as to be almost black.

The bastard was having fun! "I'll try," she flung back. "You'll need someone to guard your back!"

Again the two lines charged. At the last moment, the Macedonians swung left and drove through the right end of the Scythian horde, then turned again with almost mechanical precision, striking the Scythians from the rear, inflicting terrible carnage. Alexander seemed invincible as he destroyed one opponent after another without slowing his horse's stride. Stunned by the Macedonian tactics, the larger Scythian force scattered to regroup. And in the ensuing confusion, Alexander signaled his force to attack.

Roxanne drove her steed hard on Alexander's flank. Her husband's muscular body was streaked with blood, his sword crimson to the hilt. The war cry on his lips rang as fierce as any Scythian's. Finding her quiver empty, Roxanne fired her last arrow and defended herself with her scimitar, slashing her way past one fiercely tattooed tribesman and then a second.

The din of battle deafened her; time seemed to stop so that men and horses moved in slow-motion. Then a Scythian rose from the grass and drove a spear into the throat of Alexander's horse. The dapple-gray's forelegs folded under him, and he crashed to the earth. Her black was following too close. She vaulted out of the saddle at the instant her horse slammed into the dying gray stallion. She hit the ground hard and rolled, her scimitar gripped tightly in her fist.

Alexander lay pale and still, his dark hair scarlet with gore. Shaken, sucking in great gasps of air, she scrambled to his motionless body and stood over it. A screaming warrior galloped toward her. She dodged the charge and sliced a wicked gash across the Scythian's thigh.

The battle had dissolved into small knots of fighting around her. She had no time to wonder about the remaining Greeks. She swung her sword again and again, until her arm numbed, and she could hardly stand from weariness.

A cry behind her broke the icy trance of battle frenzy. She whirled to face a red-haired Scythian wielding a two-headed axe. Abruptly her world tilted and dissolved in blackness. She felt the grass open beneath her feet and tumbled down into oblivion.

The gray void jarred, and Roxanne became aware of a steady grinding pain in her head. Her mouth was dry; her body ached in a dozen places. Cautiously she opened her eyes just wide enough to make out the shapes of a horse's head and ears. The movement, she realized, was the rolling gallop of a horse. What held her upright? She shifted her body and was rewarded by a harsh male voice and a tightening of the iron grip around her waist.

"Good. You are not dead. I was afraid I had wasted my time and energy in dragging you along." The tongue was Scythian, the stench of horse and rider as sour as uncured cowhide.

She let herself go limp, pretending unconsciousness.

She tried to remember... If only her head would stop throbbing. Alexander? Did he live? Or did his beautiful head swing from the saddle leather of some Scythian raider? Bile rose in her throat, and she choked it down. There were steppe horsemen in front and behind; she could not guess how many, and all were riding hard.

It was full night. Not even a star shone in the cloudy black sky. The grassy steppe rolled before them endlessly, and the war party rode on, guided by some primitive sense of direction.

How much time had passed since the battle? She had no way of knowing if it had been minutes, hours, or days. Without moon or stars, she could not tell. It could be anywhere between dusk and dawning. Had any of Alexander's troops escaped? Were there other prisoners? Again, she had no clue.

Terror reared its head, stalking her with ghostly horror. Fear seeped through her veins, chilling her soul. Scythians. All the childhood dread of nightmares and nameless monsters attacked her intellect, and she bit her lip until she tasted the salt of her own blood to keep from weeping. She scrambled for some shred of hope.

Alexander could not be dead. He claimed to be immortal,

the son of Zeus. He must be alive. And if he lived, he would come to claim her. He considered her his property; she was his. Alexander would come for her though all the demons of Hades barred his path.

Strength poured through her body. A Sogdian prince and warrior would not fear these steppe wolves. Was she any less? She had only to stay alive long enough for Alexander to rescue her. If only the pounding in her head would allow her to reason. She must have a plan . . . she must outwit her captors.

Unconsciousness flowed over her again.

The fall jarred Roxanne awake. Coarse laughter and jeers greeted her as she opened her eyes to the glare of dawn over the steppes. A Scythian with tangled orange-red hair stood over her. She blinked, remembering something . . . A confused image slid into place. This was the man with the double axe.

She fixed her gaze on his rough, knee-high, horse-skin boots, struggling to focus, willing herself to stop seeing two of him. She drew in a deep breath and studied the baggy trousers and greasy hide shirt. The Scythian was short and stocky with bowed legs and long, muscular arms. Slanting black eyes and front teeth filed to wolfish points were nearly obscured by a tangled beard and a sweeping mustache of startling orange. Clan tattoos covered the low forehead and sharply-chiseled cheekbones.

Her inspection was cut short as the object of her attention aimed a vicious kick at her. She rolled aside and staggered to her feet. "I am no dog to be kicked!" He backhanded her, sending her sprawling into the grass, and laughed again.

"Get of a poxed camel!" she cried. "May demons twist your bowels!" She found her feet again and backed out of range of his blows. "Your brain is as thick as a horse's ass. Do you not recognize me? I am Roxanne, princess royal of Bactria and Sogdiana!"

His pig eyes clouded with puzzlement, and his face flushed beneath the caked dirt and sweat and blood. "What magic is this?" he asked, "that I understand the tongue of this foreign bitch?"

His companions roared with laughter, slapping each other, hopping up and down, and calling advice.

"Ox dung! Turd of a dog!" Roxanne replied. "I speak Scythian, bonehead! Not only that, I hear your thoughts before you utter them! I am not only a princess. I am magi! A sorceress!" She fixed him with a fierce glare and gestured with both hands in what she hoped passed for mystical signs.

"We have a cure for sorcerers." The red-haired Scythian snaked his saber from its sheath. "I'll have your head on a pole!"

Terrified, she kept up her bravado. "Touch me, and I shall curse you. For time out of time, you will wander among the leprous undead, pursued by demons of fire and the ghosts of unclean creatures."

Her tormentor hesitated. His tattooed lips thinned and grew taut. She noticed with disgust that human finger-bones, some with rotting bits of flesh still clinging to them, were knotted into his hair and beard.

"Kill her!" another warrior said. "Kill the witch!"

"Yes, kill me—if you can," Roxanne taunted. "My powers will be greater on the other side. Shall I cause your spear to wither, your seed to dry up, and your sacks to rot? Anger me not, Scythian! For the plague will fall not on you alone, but on all your tribe, so that your women will wail and curse your name. Their wombs will lie barren, their cradles empty."

"You lie," Redbeard reasoned. "You are a mere woman."

He lowered his sword, and hope quickened in her breast. This man was clearly a warrior, not a thinker. "Take me to your chief. Your shaman," she urged. "Let them decide if my words are empty."

The Scythian took a step backward and made the sign of the horns to ward off evil. "I like not your talk of demons and curses," he admitted. His friends had fallen silent, and more than one edged away.

"I wear a woman's body," she said. "I am human. But I am a powerful sorceress. I can cast spells that would trouble your sleep and twist your bowels." She straightened and brushed the dirt from her clothes. "Take me to your chieftain. He will understand my powers and what use can best be made of them." She folded her arms and tried to hide the dizziness that threatened to land her facedown on the ground again.

The sun was climbing higher. The great globe of fire on the eastern horizon lit the endless sky, tinting it with streaks of purple and orange. The sunrise gave her a sense of direction. There were few landmarks on the steppes, but now she knew which way was home. And she didn't have to escape. Her Macedonian conqueror would come for her with a mighty army at his back. He would find her. She must survive until he did . . . survive by any means.

A one-eyed warrior rode his pony through the group. A terrible disfigurement distorted half of his face, leaving the crown of his head bald and ridged with scars. "You are a fool, Chaba!" the man rasped. "She is no magician. Her legs will part as soft as any slut's." Saliva oozed from twisted lips, trickling down into his greasy beard as he slid from his mount and came toward her.

"Touch me," she warned, "and your root will shrivel like wet rawhide. I'll make a eunuch of you."

"Watch out, Skunxa!" a bald veteran jeered. "Your young wife Tagi won't care for that!"

"Go ahead. Call her bluff!" another urged. "We'll keep Tagi satisfied."

Roxanne stared into Skunxa's single bloodshot eye. "You are powerless," she said in slow, measured tones. "Your hand is numb. The numbness spreads through your fingers. Your hand cannot hold the weight of the saber. Every muscle . . . every vein, is limp and useless." Her voice droned as she stepped closer, never breaking eye contact with the man.

Skunxa's saber trembled and dropped from his fingers. With a curse, he twisted away, clutching his sword-hand.

"She is a witch!" a man in a peaked leather hat shouted.

Milling warriors edged away. "Sew her into a fresh horse skin and drag her!" one yelled. Others muttered agreement.

"Do you think to deceive the gods of darkness so easily?

Woe to the fool who touches the handmaiden of the mighty!"
Roxanne advanced on her captor, the red-bearded man
whose name appeared to be Chaba. "Take me to your camp.
Your war chief will know of what use I can be to your tribe. I
am a blade to be directed against your enemies! The gods
have decreed it!"

She forced herself to appear calm. "I will prove my good-
will." She pointed at the one-eyed man. "Your hand is whole
again. But—you may not lie with a woman for three journeys
of the moon. If you have not angered me in that time, your
vigor will return." Her fist clenched in the air, and she hurled
an imaginary essence in Skunxa's direction.

"Very well, handmaiden," Chaba said, eyeing Skunxa's at-
tempts to flex his fingers. "I will take you to our camp. But if
you lie, your death will be long and exceedingly unpleasant."

"So be it," she declared. She shouldered past him to his
horse and removed a water bag from his saddle. She drank,
almost gagging on the curdled mare's milk and blood. "I must
have my own mount," she added. "Yours will tire carrying
two."

"You cannot escape," Chaba warned. "Not even a witch can
ride faster than our arrows."

"Why would I wish to escape?" she answered. "I do not
question the will of the gods."

Alexander opened his eyes to see Hephaestion's grim face,
pushed aside restraining hands, and sat up on the edge of the
bed. Blood-soaked pads and bandages littered the floor.

"It's about time," Hephaestion said. "You had us worried."

Cautiously Alexander flexed his shoulders, ignoring the
pain of three different wounds. "How many of our men escaped?"

"Twenty-six. Eleven wounded. Three lightly. Two will not
live to see another dawning." Hephaestion shrugged. "We
drove off the raiders, but you'd lost so much blood that we
thought it wise to return to the citadel. We didn't do badly,
considering their numbers."

"Roxanne?" Alexander glanced around the chamber. "Why isn't she here?"

"Lie back. You'll start the bleeding again, and Philip will have a fit." Ptolemy motioned to a servant. "Wine for the king."

"She was behind me. She fought at my side." A spasm passed over his features. "Is she alive?"

His friend nodded.

Alexander let out the breath he had been unconsciously holding and reached for the wine. "Have the bodies of our men been recovered?"

"Yes. We'd not leave them for scavengers."

The blue-gray eyes narrowed. "Was she hurt?"

"Your lady was not among the dead. I'll have the city searched."

Alexander swore an oath foul enough to shrivel marble. He threw the wine goblet against the nearest wall and rose unsteadily to his feet. "If she's not among the dead, then she's captured. She would be here if . . . if . . ." He swayed and clutched at Hephaestion's shoulder to keep from falling. "What did you give me? The wine . . ." His last words were lost as his knees folded. Hephaestion caught him and lowered him gently to the bed.

Ptolemy's gaze accused Hephaestion. "He'll have your eyes for drugging him."

"I doubt it. He needs rest. Tomorrow will be soon enough to go in search of his bride."

"Tomorrow may be too late," Ptolemy answered. "Her head may join those of our lost comrades. He'll not forgive you if—"

"I am Chiliarch of this army and second in command. If the king's not fit to ride tomorrow, I'll lead a company against the Scythians myself. That Bactrian . . . Wolf? They claim he can track a shadow over rock. I can use him. But tonight, Alexander will sleep."

Time and distance have little meaning on the steppes. Dull with fatigue and weak with hunger, Roxanne clung to the saddle and rode on between the horsemen for days or weeks. She couldn't be certain. Three warriors had succumbed to their wounds, and their corpses were tied across saddles beside rotting Greek heads. Roxanne almost envied the dead. They felt nothing and feared less.

Her tricks had worked, at least for a little while. But what if the chief was not as easily gulled? The Scythian shaman would demand proof of her powers, and Roxanne feared she had exhausted her store of illusions.

The Scythians worshiped gods of death and destruction. She had heard tales of human sacrifice and cannibalism, tales that . . . She chewed at her lower lip. She would think no more of such stories. She must hold the beasts at bay until Alexander came for her. And if he didn't . . . If he abandoned her to these wolves, she'd haunt his dreams into the next world as she had threatened the Scythians.

In mid-afternoon the war party crossed a small river, pausing to water the tired animals. Roxanne slid from the saddle and let the cold water flow over her aching body, carefully washing her cuts and bruises. Her hair was matted with dried blood. She held her breath and ducked under the flow. Gingerly she used fingertips to examine the gash across the top of her head. The wound was painful, but not serious. But her strength was failing her. She could barely summon the energy to remount.

No man spoke to her, whether from fear or hatred mattered little. At least she didn't have to keep up a performance. Instead she concentrated on summoning all she knew of the Scythians, both good and bad. Some said they had once been a mountain people, but she doubted it. These tribesmen moved when and where they wished. War, horses, and their own twisted code of courage were all that mattered. They treated their women worse than the beasts of burden that pulled their wagons.

Scythians were extraordinary horsemen; she would give them that. On foot, they were awkward, bowlegged, and almost comical. But mounted, they were magnificent. A Scythian was not a rider; he was part of the animal itself. As a mounted warrior, the Scythian was fearless. Only his lack of discipline and an unwillingness to band together under one leader detracted from his ability.

Roxanne didn't believe she'd ever heard of a Scythian woman riding unless she was carried off by another band as a prize of war. The females walked in the mud and dust and horse dung.

It was said that Scythians were skilled in the crafting of beautiful objects of gold. It was certainly true they prized gold; the precious metal was easy to carry and could be traded anywhere. A half-Scythian smith kept a forge at the citadel, but she did not know if he was an exception or if his ability had come from his mother's race.

The Scythian encampment came into view more than an hour's ride away. Oxen pulled wagons that served as the only shelters of the tribe. The beasts moved slowly, and boys drove the vast herds of horses and cattle behind the wheeled dwellings. At first sighting of the wagons, the war party cheered and set off for them at a gallop.

Roxanne estimated the number of wagons and the size of the herds. The tribe was large with several hundred warriors. This would be a powerful chief, then, one who commanded many fighting men.

"Guardian of Light, be with me," she prayed. "Lend me strength and courage to face what must be faced."

Chapter Nine

Roxanne lay bound hand and foot beneath a wind-stunted tree, a hundred yards or more from the nearest Scythian wagon. The high-wheeled shelters had been drawn into a closely interlocked square, with prized livestock safe within. The larger herds of ponies, cattle, and goats—the true wealth of the Scythians—were guarded by half-grown boys. The sun was setting and the air already turned cooler. She knew that she would suffer from cold once night had fallen, but she would not think of that now. Instead she remembered her first meeting with the leader of this tribe, soon after they had reached the camp.

"Prove you are who you say you are," the wrinkled old chief had demanded when she was dragged before him.

"Prove that I am not."

The village shaman, Gog, was a mountain of a man with small, piercing eyes nearly hidden in rolls of fat. His voice, high and shrill for a male of such size, had risen to a squeak as he'd thrown ashes over her. "Bind her tightly and leave her on the steppe tonight! What the wolves leave, we will deal with tomorrow. If she is indeed the handmaiden of powerful spirits, they will protect her." He had laughed, well pleased with his wisdom, and Chief Karachi had agreed. Let the gods punish the wolves if they so desired.

Steppe wolves. Roxanne shuddered. She'd hunted the carnivores, but always on horseback with hounds and armed companions. These wolves were massive—some standing as tall at the shoulder as a yearling colt—with fearsome teeth that were powerful enough to snap a horse's leg bone. In a pack, the wolves feared nothing, least of all man. When she was a child, she had heard the beasts howling in the darkness around a campfire as she burrowed close to her father.

The great wolves—gray, white, black, or brown—shadowed the Scythian herds, and they would hunt when darkness fell. Tonight she would have no horn bow, no spear, not even a knife to defend herself. She would be the prey, as helpless as a newborn foal.

Roxanne twisted and tugged at the rawhide thongs. They had been applied wet, and as they dried the bonds shrank and cut deep into her flesh. She cursed every Scythian back to the dung heap from which their ancestors had climbed. Would there be nothing but scattered fragments of her bones when Alexander got here?

Once, when she was barely ten, Roxanne had been thrown from her pony onto an icy ledge. She had slid over the precipice and managed to grab a gnarled tree root, leaving her feet dangling over hundreds of feet of emptiness. She'd been stunned and hurt, too frightened to cry. She hung there for what seemed hours until she heard Kayan calling her name. She'd shouted, and Kayan had knotted a rope around his waist, made it fast to a rock, and climbed down the mountain to retrieve her.

"You did well, both of you," Oxyartes had said when she was safely in his arms. "Men who tell you that courage is having no fear are either fools or liars. Bravery is thinking clearly in the midst of fear and doing what must be done."

Kayan would not come tonight to help her, nor would Alexander. It was too soon. She must rely on her own wits and prayers. The light was fast fading, and an unnatural silence hung over the steppe. Even the birds were still. Roxanne could hear the thumping of her own heart. Fires flickered from the circle of the camp, and from somewhere on the endless rolling steppes came the hunting cry of a wolf.

Alexander and his Macedonians rode their first mounts to ground, changing to fresh remounts, and leaving drovers to drive the exhausted animals back across the river to the citadel. Each soldier followed Alexander in full battle array with two relief horses roped behind him. The ranks of veterans were swelled by Bactrian and Sogdian troops.

At Alexander's side rode Hephaestion and Ptolemy. Alexander's fury at being drugged had receded to a simmer. He would not forget the incident, but his full attention was on finding the Scythians and recovering his wife, dead or alive.

The mute Bactrian was as good as his word. He showed Alexander where the war party had crossed the small river and where they had paused to rest. A smaller boot print in the dried mud of the riverbank brought Wolf to his knees, and he motioned to Alexander.

"Are you certain?" the king asked. Wolf's answer was a grin.

The Macedonians filled their canteens and allowed their mounts to snatch a few mouthfuls of grass and drink their fill. Men would eat in the saddle. There would be no rest until they found the Scythians.

"If she is alive here, she'll be alive when we find them," Alexander declared. "They may think to trade her for our Scythian captive." Prince Khem was dead, but the Scythians couldn't know that. The fool had swallowed his earring in his cell and choked to death.

Hephaestion shrugged. "It would be a sensible course of action. But we are dealing with savages, not civilized men."

A night wind rolled across the grass; the only sounds were the anxious lowing of cattle and the occasional nicker of a horse. Roxanne's hands had lost all feeling, and her legs ached with shooting cramps. "Damn you, Alexander," she muttered. "Where are you?"

Overhead, masses of black clouds raced, and in the distance she heard the rumble of thunder. The horse herds stirred restlessly. It was too early in the season for grass fires, but storms on the steppes were terrible, and both beasts and men feared them. Far off to the east, a finger of fire splintered the sky as the wind increased in intensity.

The rain came first, light spatters, and then heavier, the drops cold and stinging, soaking Roxanne to the skin. Her teeth chattered as thunder boomed and lightning struck just beyond the horse herd, sending animals stampeding toward the camp.

In the third flash of brilliant light, Roxanne saw the flood of panic-stricken horses divide and stream in two separate herds as they neared the square of wagons. Men leaped onto their ponies and galloped after the horses. The earth shook with the vibrations of hooves. The air burned with the stench of sulfur.

The teeth of the storm ripped at the encampment for perhaps half an hour before moving westward. The thunder grew less deafening, and the lightning strikes hit farther away. The rain slowed to a steady drizzle and gradually stopped. Shivering almost uncontrollably, Roxanne raised her face from the grass to watch a pale crescent moon peek through the clouds to bathe the steppe in wisps of silver, incandescent light.

Drawn by the scent of blood, the wolf pack fell upon the horses that had been injured in the stampede, razor-sharp teeth slicing hide and bone. A stranded foal, separated from its dam, was run down. Roxanne shuddered as she heard the animal's death screams. The wolves floated like gray ghosts across the grass, growling and snapping.

Driven by fear, Roxanne wrenched at the leather thongs on her wrists until one section loosened enough to free one hand. Quickly, she slipped the ties off the other. Pain shot up her arms and down into her numbed fingers as she clumsily untied her ankles. She welcomed the pain as blood flowed into her hands and she regained the use of them. But now that she was free—how could she save herself? The tree behind her was too low to provide sanctuary; the soft grass yielded no weapon, not even a rock.

She forced herself to her feet. She'd not lie there and wait to be devoured. Then she spied a length of wood, a branch, half hidden in the grass. It wasn't much of a weapon, but it was better than nothing.

A snarl behind her in the darkness snapped her head around. Ruby eyes glowed from a shapeless form. Roxanne's nose wrinkled as she caught the foul stench of carrion mingled with a musky odor that could only be that of a wolf. The animal growled, deep in his throat, and inched forward. "Get away from me!" she yelled, jabbing at the wolf with her stick. "Back!"

The beast crouched and sprang. The weight knocked her backwards, slashing teeth striving for her throat. She screamed, and the weight suddenly rolled off her.

"Do you live, witch?" Chaba asked as he materialized from the darkness.

"Barely." Roxanne drew a ragged breath and shuddered as she looked at the gray wolf with the arrow protruding from its side. "How did—"

"Quiet. It would be worth my head if I am found interfering in the shaman's affairs." He yanked her to her feet. "Did you call up the storm?"

"No."

"Good. You are not lying. Storms are just storms."

"But I did summon you to slay the wolf." One forearm burned like fire, and she felt something warm and sticky running down onto her hand. She was scratched and shaken, but she didn't think she'd received a serious injury.

Chaba grunted. "Maybe. Maybe not. You make me think. If you have this power, can you make me the next chief?"

"Maybe. Maybe not."

He covered her shaking shoulders with a foul-smelling robe. "Fortunate for you the wolf was gray. If it were black, I think maybe I might not see him clearly and shoot you instead." He chuckled. "You do not think that is funny, witch?"

"Hardly. But I'm freezing. If I don't get warm, I'll be dead by morning."

"Is not safe to make a fire." He shoved a piece of cooked meat into her hand.

"Thank you." Gratefully she took a bite and sank to the ground, clutching the wrap around her. "You know that Lord Alexander has Prince Khem as his prisoner."

"We know. We were ordered to find Khem." He dropped to his haunches beside her. "Khem is my half-brother, favorite of our father."

"Why didn't you try to trade me for him?"

"Better he dies. Dead he cannot warm his wife's bed or become chief after our father is gone."

"Logic." She took a drink from the skin of mare's milk Chaba offered and willed her stomach to hold the vile liquid down.

"Skunxa could not please his woman this night. I listened outside his wagon." Roxanne could hear the respect in Chaba's voice as he said: "Your man must be strong to overcome your magic."

"My husband, Lord Alexander, is the son of a god."

"Why didn't you use your powers on the wolf?"

"The wolf was a test. I did not need to kill the wolf. You did."

"You could take away my manhood if you wished?"

"In this life and the next."

He grunted again.

"Or I could make you a mighty bull. A legend among tribes."

Three pairs of red eyes gleamed in the darkness. Chaba let fly two arrows. A yip told them that he had found a target. "I should be the next chief. But I do not say words my father wishes to hear. I am not his favorite."

Roxanne felt sick, and she was nearly overcome with weariness. Her eyelids felt weighted with rocks. "And the shaman?"

"He is my enemy."

"You need a more powerful shaman?"

He grunted, stood, and rubbed his hands together. "Fire would keep the wolves away, but fire would tell the others that someone had helped you." He grasped her chin and lifted her head. "My eyes say that you are a woman. How can a woman be shaman?"

"Demons come in many shapes. I would sleep now. You keep watch. I need my strength if I am to make you chief." She uttered a small sigh. "Only my outer skin looks like a female. Inside, I am a terrible spirit. Remember the one-eyed man."

Chaba notched another arrow. "I will keep watch."

Sometime before dawn, Roxanne was shaken awake. "I return to camp now," Chaba whispered. "I will do what I can to help you, but you must not forget your promise to me, witch woman." He took the robe. "You must tell no one I was here."

She looked for the body of the wolf. It was gone, and she surmised that Chaba must have dragged it away. "I will not forget," she assured him. She watched as Chaba moved through the tall grass toward the wagons, and wondered how far she could trust him.

Chief Karachi, Gog, and a group of warriors came for her when the sun was high. She stood and faced them, arms folded across her chest. "Well, are you satisfied?" she asked. "The wolves did not eat me."

The owl-eyed shaman wound his ringed fingers in her hair and shoved her to her knees. "Trickery!" he snarled. "I have dealt with tricksters before. Who loosed your ropes, woman?"

"The spirit of the storm."

"So?" He twisted her head back, exposing her neck to the blade of a spiral dagger and pressed upon the skin until a thin, scarlet line appeared. "Shall I feed the steppes with her blood?"

Roxanne could not stop tears from welling in her eyes. "Kill me and you will never see Prince Khem again."

The chief knocked the shaman's dagger away with a casual swipe of his hand. "What do you know of my son, woman?"

Roxanne got to her feet. She did not see Chaba in the group. "Prince Khem lies in prison. The High King, Alexander, who is my husband, will trade him for my safe return."

"What proof do I have that Khem is alive?" The chief was past middle age, his face wrinkled from the harsh climate of the steppes. Stringy, graying front braids hung nearly to his waist, but the fingers that grasped Roxanne's shoulder were powerful.

Karachi was still counted among the warriors; when he was not, another would rule in his place. A chief of the Scythians held his command through birth, cunning, and physical prowess. The steppe tribes felt no mercy for a man whose wits or strength had begun to wane.

Roxanne shrank from the sourness of the chief's breath. Did these steppe wolves never bathe? "Your son was alive when last I saw him. He spat at Lord Alexander's feet."

The old chief roared with laughter, and the others joined in. "That is Khem," he admitted. "My men tell many strange tales of you. Can it be that you are not a woman at all?" He seized the leather ties at the front of her shirt and tore them away, exposing the curve of her pale breasts to the eyes of the onlookers. "It is a woman's body," he said.

Roxanne drew the sections of her tunic together. "If I am harmed, you will have nothing of your son but his head. My husband will not pay for soiled goods."

The chief's eyes narrowed, and he drew back and spoke quietly to the shaman. Then Gog squealed orders in his high voice. "Take her to my wagon. Bind her tightly so there will be no tricks. I will seek answers from the gods on how best to recover Prince Khem. You need have no fear of this witch woman. Her spells are child's play compared to my own." His heavy-lidded eyes were as lifeless as wet stones. "If she is her lord's favorite, I think he will be glad to get her back, no matter her condition."

Rough hands seized her. It was useless to struggle as she was dragged back to the camp and thrown into a wagon. She wasn't offered food or water, and she lay in a heap of flea-ridden animal skins in the semidarkness.

After a few hours, someone hitched oxen to the wheeled shelter. Around her she heard the voices of women and children, but no one came inside or took heed of her in any way. Then the wagon began to move.

Hours passed, the monotony of motion broken only by the annoyance of biting insects and vermin. Roxanne's wrists were numb from the leather ropes that bound them, her injured arm throbbed, and the rocking of the wagon made her so nauseous that she wondered if she might be pregnant.

Alexander desired a son. She had done nothing to prevent a child, but she was not sure that she wanted to give him one. If she bore his child, the Macedonian might never let her go. Even if she were not a prisoner of the Scythians, her future was uncertain. She didn't know how she would feel about Alexander's baby. She didn't know how she felt about him. Perhaps it was best to leave some things to heaven.

In late afternoon, a deep voice filtered through the hide walls of the wagon. "Witch woman. Listen. It is Chaba. Do not believe my father. No matter what he promises, you will never return to your man alive. The shaman desires you for his bed."

"Help me to escape."

"I can't. I don't trust you, but if I can save your life, I will. Do not expect me to risk my own again."

"Chaba—wait." He was gone. She struggled with her ropes, but the knots were strong.

At dusk the wagons stopped, and shortly Roxanne smelled the smoke of cooking fires. After what seemed an eternity, a round-faced woman brought a bowl of stew. "I have a knife," the Scythian warned. "If you give me the evil eye, I will cut your throat."

"Thank you for the food." Roxanne took the wooden bowl between her bound hands and sipped at the greasy contents. "Water?"

"I will give you water." The woman tossed a beakerful into Roxanne's face. Laughing, she backed out of the wagon.

Roxanne's wrists were raw and bleeding from the tight leather thongs, but the water soaking into the leather made the ties stretch a little. She worked at the knots frantically, but was unable to get free. She felt ill. Her injured arm throbbed painfully, her head ached, and she thought she was feverish.

From outside she could hear mingled male and female voices, a baby cry, and the laughter of children. Roxanne squirmed and crawled forward until she could peer beneath the entrance flap. Just outside her wagon stood two warriors, their backs turned to her. One was the bald man who'd been a member of the war party that captured her. Beyond them, several other men sat around a fire, passing a skin container and drinking from it. Gog, the shaman, was among them.

Firelight shone on the back flap of the wagon. Wary of being seen, Roxanne crept to the front and pressed the side walls to feel for any weakness in the seams that held the covering together, but they were tight. Tired and discouraged, she lay down on the skins and closed her eyes.

She came instantly awake when a rough hand touched her breast. She tried to twist away as a hard mouth ground against hers. A thick tongue probed between her teeth. She bit down hard, and a closed fist rocked her head. "Be still," a shrill voice rasped. Groping hands tore at the fastenings of her trousers.

"No! No!" A man's weight pressed her into the stinking furs. She screamed and clawed at her assailant's face. "No!" she protested.

He rolled on top of her, pinning her, his erect penis hot and pulsing against her thigh. Roxanne slammed her palm up, striking her attacker in the Adam's apple. He let out a groan and began to cough. Freeing a knee, she drove it into the fat man's groin. He clutched his testicles and moaned as she struggled to wiggle out from under his sweating bulk.

Abruptly the unmistakable wail of a Greek battle horn pierced the air. Once. Twice. The wagon vibrated with the sound of charging horses and Macedonian war cries.

Roxanne screamed Alexander's name.

Instantly the shaman clamped a hand over her mouth and seized her by the throat. "Quiet!"

She caught his middle finger between her teeth and bit down just as a flaming arrow sliced through the hide canopy of the wagon. Gog yanked his hand free. She tried to scream again, but she could utter no more than a yelp before he wrapped both hands around her throat. Roxanne's struggles grew weaker as he squeezed tighter, and waves of blackness threatened to drown her. Desperately she jabbed at the shaman's eyes with her fingernails.

Outside the wagon, Alexander's forces hit the sleeping

Scythians with the fury of a whirlwind. They drove through the encampment with naked swords and a hail of deadly arrows.

In the darkness, havoc reigned; fear-crazed animals rushed within the circle, overturning shelters. Smoke and fire made it difficult to tell friend from foe as hand-to-hand combat raged. Sword clashed against sword. Bodies were trampled underfoot as the herds stampeded through the wagons. Macedonians hacked and stabbed, killing anything that moved.

Another shaft struck the wagon. The arrowhead pierced Gog's massive thigh. He howled with pain, released Roxanne, and tried to burrow under her as a sword slit the wagon cover asunder. Roxanne's eyes widened as she saw a familiar warrior astride a black warhorse illuminated by the flames.

"Alexander!" she gasped, throwing up an arm to shield her eyes from the light. "Alexander!"

The shaman gave up his efforts to hide and scrambled for the back of the wagon. Alexander wheeled Bucephalus, leaped a fallen Scythian, and caught the shaman as the fat man's feet touched the earth. A single sweep of Alexander's sword sliced Gog's head from his shoulders and sent it spinning into the darkness.

Roxanne scrambled to the opening, threw up her arms, and Alexander pulled her up in front of his saddle. Hephaestion and two Companions moved to the king's side, and he held Roxanne against him as he urged the big warhorse away from the battle onto the steppes.

Trembling, she clung to him, holding on to him with all her remaining strength, afraid that if she let go he might vanish in the mist of a dream.

"I have you," he crooned to her. "It's all right. I have you." Still he had to pry her fingers loose before he could lower her into Wolf's arms. "Keep her safe," Alexander commanded. A dozen soldiers formed a ring around them. "Guard her with your lives," Alexander said. "I have Scythians to kill."

Someone threw a robe over her, and Wolf raised a water skin to her lips. Flames from the burning camp lit the area nearly as bright as day. Wolf's face was full of concern, and

113

his gentle fingers sought out the swollen bite on her arm. He snatched something from a bag at his waist, chewed the mixture, and pressed it against the wound.

"How badly are you hurt, lady?" Ptolemy asked.

"I don't know." Her voice came out in a harsh whisper. "A wolf bit me." Her bodyguard's gaze met hers.

They carry poison, his expression said.

"I know," she murmured. Her throat hurt, and it seemed that she couldn't draw in enough air. "Alexander? Where is—"

"Well," Ptolemy answered. "Rest now, lady."

Daylight showed smoking wagons and stacked corpses. Macedonians cooked an ox over an open fire and were eating. A group of women and children huddled together under guard. Everywhere was death and the smell of dying. Roxanne took a little more water, but had no taste for food.

Alexander dismounted and came to her side. "You are indeed trouble, little Sogdian." His hand brushed her cheek tenderly.

"Your losses?" Her voice was coming back, but her throat still ached where Gog had tried to strangle her.

"Not many. We had the element of surprise." He gestured toward the prisoners. Roxanne saw Chaba among the wounded Scythians. "That man," she said, pointing. "The one with the orange hair. He saved my life. Not once, but twice."

"I am tempted to put them all to the sword."

"He is the son of the old chief. Brother to Prince Khem. His name is Chaba."

"Prisoners will hinder our journey back to the citadel."

"I owe him a debt," she said.

He examined her arm and frowned. Ptolemy and his Companions withdrew to give them privacy.

"You are silent," she said. "Ask what you most wish to know."

"Did they violate you? No, by the Gods—it does not matter. You are what matters." He drove one clenched fist into another. "They will die to the last suckling."

"No, my lord," she reasoned. "Leave them. It will be years

114

before they dare to raid us again." She caught his hand and lifted it to her cheek. "A Scythian is a wild beast. They act by instinct. Men must live by honor. Mine is not stained. Nor yours. No man has used me in that way." She shuddered. "Had you been but a few minutes later . . ."

He tilted her chin up. "It does not matter. I would be no king if I put you aside for that which was not your fault."

"Why is your skull so thick? No man has had me. I have never lied to you, and I will not lie now. Although if I believed you would divorce me for it, I might be tempted."

His strong arms enfolded her, and he lifted her. "I'm sure you will weave a fantastic tale of your adventures, and I will be at a loss to deny the truth of it."

"I told them that I was a sorceress."

"And so you are." He carried her to the place where his physicians were caring for the wounded Macedonians. "Do what you can for her," he instructed. "Let your fingers be skillful, for if she dies . . . you die also."

The Macedonian force turned toward the mountains in midmorning, after scattering the horse herd and confiscating the Scythians' weapons. They left women wailing beside their unburied dead, which included both their shaman and chief. Chaba marshaled the remaining men, all of whom were wounded, some gravely.

Roxanne was not strong enough to sit a horse. The physicians had given her opium to dull the pain, and she lay only half conscious in Alexander's arms. Her cheeks burned with fever.

"Take me home," she murmured between cracked lips. "If I am to die, let it be in my mountain homeland."

"I am taking you there, woman," Alexander replied sternly. "But I forbid you to die." His eyes were fierce. "Do you hear me, Roxanne? I forbid it."

Chapter Ten

All during the journey back to Sogdiana Rock, Roxanne's cheeks were flushed scarlet with fever. Once they reached the citadel, physicians and magi traversed the halls of the palace with potions to aid in the princess's recovery. As the weather warmed to full spring, and the hills turned from brown to green, the Companions were anxious to cross the treacherous passes into India. But Alexander refused to give the order to march.

"Roxanne goes with us," he repeated, dashing his wine goblet off the table. "When she is able to travel, we will leave. Not before."

Ptolemy and Perdiccas exchanged glances. "There is bickering among the men," Hephaestion continued. "Many are for turning home to Macedonia while they are still hale enough to enjoy their wealth."

"Your lady could be brought along when she is better," Ptolemy suggested. "It may be weeks or—"

"She will not die!" Alexander shouted. "Think you these Sogdians would yield her later, when I am hundreds of miles away? No! There will be delays and excuses, though nothing that could be termed treason. If I leave her, they will make of her a queen, and we will have to invade Bactria and Sogdiana all over again!"

"If you cannot trust her . . ." Hephaestion paced the tent. "By the gods, Alexander! I have never seen you so distracted over a woman! What spell has she cast over you? You would delay for no man on earth. But for this . . . this barbarian Amazon . . ."

"Careful, my friend." Alexander's eyes narrowed dangerously. "You go too far." He got to his feet. "If you cannot control the troops under your command, then perhaps I should choose my officers among the Asians. I am High King here, not you." He swept more wine goblets off the table. "I find the conversation here repetitive. I'll look for more stimulating company." He strode from the tent, his features an ivory mask, and crossed the area to Europa's scarlet pavilion.

"He's mad for Roxanne," Ptolemy said. "Until she dies or recovers, we'll get nowhere with him." He motioned the aide to clear away the spilled wine and bring more refreshment. "You know how he is when he gets something in his head."

Perdiccas cursed loudly, his face red with anger. "It's these damned Persians; they've convinced him he's more than a king."

"More than a man," Hephaestion muttered. "Maybe he is, but no god has ever led an army, and our men won't be led by one. He must come to his senses. If it would help, I'd cut her throat myself."

"As our king said, this conversation is repetitive." Ptolemy forced a wry chuckle. "And dawn seems to come earlier these days. I'm for my own cot and a night's sleep. You might as well join me, Hephaestion. Europa will have no warm arms for you tonight."

"Later, perhaps. Perdiccas and I will kill this wineskin."

Ptolemy went to his own quarters, more disturbed by Alexander's behavior than he would admit. His faith in his commander had never faltered, but he knew Alexander was on dangerous ground.

The army was changing; nearly half was Asian. An officer needed to speak three or four languages just to give orders to

117

his troops. The Asians would give loyalty only as long as Alexander held the reins of power. The real strength was in the Macedonian troops, and they were unsettled and complaining. It was time to march. Simple men understood fighting. Alexander must move on to India or turn back.

Oxyartes left his daughter's chambers with the fatigue of sleepless nights evident in the dark hollows under his eyes. He nodded to Kayan outside the bedchamber door. "She's sleeping."

"The fever?"

"The same. It is a potent poison." Oxyartes was a man who had faced death fearlessly many times. He had watched as his wife labored to give birth to three stillborn sons, and later as she died. Roxanne was his only living child and heir, and fear of losing her brought him near the edge of dementia. "These physicians are all fools. One day it is honey, the next a paste of myrrh. On the battlefield, I would have cauterized the wound immediately."

"If I had been with her instead of in Maracanda . . ." Kayan drove his fist against the gray stone wall. "I am useless to her, Lord Oxyartes . . . useless as a man and useless as her guardian."

"Hold your tongue," the older man cautioned. "The fault is not yours. It lies with Alexander if it lies anywhere. You were ordered to Maracanda to wed Lady Lilya. It is better for you and for my daughter that you have a wife. Her husband is no fool. Did you bring your wife back with you?"

"Yes, lord. She is in her quarters in the women's tower. Lilya was not pleased. I think she is fonder of a certain fat merchant in Maracanda than of me." He stiffened to attention as Alexander appeared at the top of the curving staircase. "Your Highness."

Alexander spoke briefly to his father-in-law and to Kayan before entering Roxanne's chamber. The room was tightly shuttered and thick with incense. Candles burned by the curtained bed. Waving away the Persian physician, Alexander sat on the edge of the bed. "Out of the room," he commanded the attendants. "Wait—open the windows. How is the princess to breathe?" He laid his palm on Roxanne's forehead, and her eyelids flickered.

"You did not need to come again tonight. What time is it?"

"Three hours past dusk." He took a fresh cloth from a bowl of water and seeping herbs, squeezed the rag, and placed it on her forehead. "My army is restless. You're holding up all my plans."

"If you would have me well, send away these cursed physicians. The squint-eyed one would have me drink curdled tiger's milk." She fell back against the pillow, and the pupils of her dark eyes were wide and glassy. "I have been dreaming strange dreams."

"It is the poison," he soothed. "Had I known how badly you were hurt, I would have buried those Scythians alive instead of showing mercy. You are a bad influence. You make me soft so that my enemies will take advantage of me."

"Greeks are born soft."

A snarl from beyond the inner door drew his attention. "What is that?"

"Only Akheera, my leopard. The physicians are afraid of her. Wolf keeps her in the anteroom with him." Her eyelids drifted shut. "I am serious about the doctors. Send them away."

"They are here to help you." He lifted a goblet and sniffed the amber liquid. "Are you supposed to drink this?" He raised it to her lips, lifting her head so that she could sip from the cup.

"No." She clenched her teeth. "I vomit after I drink their potions. I don't trust your physicians. I have many enemies."

"Why must you be so stubborn? I order you to drink."

"No. I will not." She pushed the cup away.

"Do you suppose I would poison you?" He tasted the drink, then spat it out and cursed. "It tastes like camel urine!"

"I wouldn't know. I've never drunk camel pee. You, of course, are much more experienced, being Hellene and civilized."

"Half dead and still your tongue cuts like a briar." He kissed her forehead. "You have lost too much weight. I prefer you soft and round." The green silk gown barely covered her breasts. Gently he cupped one and bent to kiss a rose-tinted nipple. "I have missed you, wife."

"How so, when you spend your nights in Europa's arms?"

He stiffened. "I weary of that tune. She means nothing to me."

"I did not mean to anger you. You must listen to me. I fear . . . my dreams tell me that you are in great danger."

"Danger from what?"

"I don't know, but . . ." She drew in a ragged breath and focused on his face. "The dream is always the same. There is darkness . . . then a swirling mist. I am afraid." Her fingers tightened on his. "Please. Remain in the palace tonight. Do not go back to the camp."

"What danger could find me in my tent in the midst of my army? Not a man but would give his life for me." He offered her the potion again. "Take a little. Even a god cannot hold fighting men waiting indefinitely. You must get better."

There was a tap at the door. Two Greek physicians bowed and entered the room. "Your Majesty. We did not think to see you here tonight. The princess seems much stronger. Do you not agree?"

Alexander glared at them. "No, I do not agree. How can you call yourselves men of medicine when you cannot cure a wolf bite?" He scowled at them. "Asklepios, you I know. Who is this rogue with you?" He indicated the older man.

"Galen, High King," the stranger answered. "Come from Athens to join your forces only last fall. My credentials, Highness, are the finest. I assure you. I trained under—"

"I don't give a fig for your credentials. I care only that you have not cured my wife. Unless you wish to have your skin peeled and stretched over my horse for a blanket, you'll heal her."

Galen flushed and drew himself to his full height. "We are only men, Your Majesty, not gods. Some things are not in our power."

Asklepios took Roxanne's wrist. "Her life force is bolder this evening, High King." She tried to pull her arm free.

"Who prescribed this medicine?" Alexander lifted the goblet.

"I did." Galen's long-nosed face was solemn. "An elixir of white hellebore to strengthen the blood and destroy the infection."

Alexander scowled. "The princess detests it. Find another remedy." The doctor cleared his throat and averted his eyes. "The drink is bitter. Taste it yourself," Alexander ordered.

Galen's hand trembled as he took the cup and downed the contents in one gulp.

"It is a familiar recipe, Your Highness," Asklepios soothed. "Your teacher Aristotle himself recommends it."

"If I do not see results in two days, you will both be replaced." He bent over Roxanne. "I will come again tomorrow, and I'll bring my own doctor, Philip. Sleep well."

She seized his hand. "No. You must not leave the palace. Just then, I saw something form in my mind. A tent flap. Danger awaits you in your tent!" She tried to sit up, and her breathing became irregular.

"There, there," Galen murmured. "You must rest, Princess." His eyes met Alexander's. "You see her condition."

"By the Wise God!" Roxanne cried. "Stay, Macedonian. Death stalks you this night!" At her outcry, the inner chamber door flew open, and Wolf leaped to her bedside, dagger in hand.

Alexander stopped him with a glance. "She is in no danger, Wolf. She is befuddled by her fever."

Galen backed away. "We cannot tend the princess with this savage present."

"Enough! All of you!" Alexander declared. "Roxanne, will you have Wolf to guard you?" She nodded. "So be it. But he must remain out of the way. And the leopard must be chained. My Companions are right. Sogdiana is an outpost of barbarism. Until tomorrow, Little Star."

Galen took a bottle from an inner pocket and refilled the cup, wiping the edges with a clean cloth. "Drink this, Highness."

When he lifted the cup to her lips, she bit his index finger. He jumped back, spilling the amber liquid over the coverlet. Wolf's dagger flashed a warning. "Kayan!" she called. "Kayan!"

The door banged open. Kayan filled the doorway, sword in hand.

"Captain," she said weakly. "These men have displeased me. Imprison them." Kayan's shout brought four burly Sogdian guardsmen.

"You can't do this!" Asklepios protested. "The king—" A soldier seized him by each arm.

Galen wailed and dodged for the doorway. Kayan blocked his way. "Take him," he ordered. "Not that way." He swept aside a hanging rug and pressed a loose block of stone. With a creak and a groan, a narrow stone door opened, revealing steep steps leading down into the darkness. "Take them to the deepest depths of the citadel," he ordered. "They are not to be harmed . . . yet."

When the guards and physicians were gone, he turned to Roxanne. "What game are you playing, little cousin? I think you are not so weak as you pretend. And what is so revolting about your husband's Greek doctors that you would have me risk my head to satisfy your whim?"

"It's true that the fever doesn't muddle my mind as much as they think. But I need your help. They're poisoning me."

A muscle twitched in the lean hawk face. "At his orders?"

She shook her head. "I don't think so. It's not his way. But he is too trusting of his own."

"Has he had his own physician, Philip the Macedonian, examine you?"

"No, I refused. Philip hates me. I told Alexander I would not let him touch me." She tore aside the bandage. "See for yourself, Kayan. The wound heals. But I am possessed by an all-invading weakness. I should be gaining strength, not losing it."

"And if you are wrong? The king will not be pleased."

"You and Wolf and my father are the only ones I can trust. Have the physicians questioned." She lay back and closed her eyes. "One more thing. I feel Alexander is in great danger.

Send word to Ptolemy that I must see him at once. If I have one friend among my husband's men, it is Ptolemy."

"If he will not come?"

"He must."

"I'll be just outside the door. Take nothing to eat or drink save from Wolf's hand."

"Thank you, Kayan."

Emotion flickered in his dark eyes. Then he was gone, closing the door behind him.

"Carry me to the window," Roxanne said to Wolf. "I need fresh air."

Tenderly he gathered her up, coverlet and all, and took her to the window. Setting her down gently, he pushed the heavy shutters open.

"Smell it, Wolf," she said. It was too dark to see the mountains, but she could imagine them crowned in caps of snow and shades of green spreading down toward the deep valleys. "It is full spring," she whispered. "And I lie here like a sickly calf."

He frowned and made the signal for food.

"A little goat's milk laced with wine," she said. "I will not die this way. I won't. No, leave me."

She pressed her face against the stone sill and half dozed until Wolf returned with the warm milk. "Any sign of Ptolemy?" she asked. He shook his head. "I am so helpless. Alexander distrusts me." She clenched her fists and whispered the worst barracks-yard oath she knew. Wolf draped a tiger skin around her shoulders against the cool night air. "Wolf, I will be no woman in my next incarnation. I swear!"

He went to the antechamber and slipped off the leopard's chain. Akheera stalked into the room, growling deep in her throat.

"Akheera, here," Roxanne called. The big cat sniffed her curiously, padding in circles, then sank down with her head in her mistress's lap. Roxanne scratched the wide, flat head and the base of the leopard's dark ears. Akheera's growls softened to a low, rumbling purr. "If my husband were a leopard, he would be easier to deal with," Roxanne observed.

Wolf dropped to the floor and sat cross-legged between Roxanne and the door, a naked blade across his lap.

"I doubt that they will come with swords to take off my head," she said. "Why would they bother when they are doing such an efficient job with poison?"

An hour passed before a knock on the wall brought the Bactrian to his feet as the secret passageway opened. Kayan stepped into the room and brushed cobwebs from his tunic. "You were right." He stepped aside to let the guards enter with a prisoner between them. They threw the weeping physician to the floor. "Speak up! Tell her what you told us!" Kayan ordered. Whimpering, the man drew himself into a ball.

Roxanne bit her lower lip. They had tortured him. Her stomach lurched. The man's fingers were crushed and bleeding. "If he will not repeat his words," she began, "return him to—"

"No! No," he protested. "Mercy, lady, I beg you. Mercy!" He crawled toward her. "I was only following orders."

Loud voices sounded outside in the hall, followed by scuffling. "Open the door," Roxanne ordered.

Ptolemy and Hephaestion burst into the room followed by two heavily armed Macedonians. "What mischief is this?" Hephaestion demanded. "Where is Alexander?" He drew his sword, and Wolf stepped between him and Roxanne.

"Hold. There is no danger to Alexander here," Roxanne cried. "I sent for you, Ptolemy. There is much for you to hear from this physician. He has been poisoning me."

"The plot is greater than that," Kayan said. He nudged Galen with his foot. "Speak, carrion."

"They . . . they seek to murder the High King."

"Who does?" Hephaestion seized Galen by the throat and pulled him upright. "Who would kill Alexander?"

"Black Cleitus—the general. Cleitus said Alexander was bewitched, possessed by the Sogdian whore. He promised to restore the Macedonians to power."

Hephaestion threw Galen to the stone floor. "Crucify him!" he ordered. "And have Cleitus placed under arrest at my command!"

"Wait," Ptolemy cautioned. "Sound the general alarm," he

told an aide. "And do not let this man die yet. We will need his testimony if the plot involves Macedonians. We must find Alexander and warn him." He glanced at Roxanne. "I went to his quarters. He wasn't there."

"Europa?"

"No," Hephaestion said. "I just left the lady's pavilion. No one has seen Alexander since he came to the palace. Four pages were in his tent, but they were not his usual aides. The boy who was to have stood duty tonight is nowhere to be found."

"What is the page's name?" Roxanne asked.

"Jason." He nodded. "Yes, the same lad you rescued in the camp. This is how he repays Alexander's mercy."

"This treachery was not made by my countrymen," Kayan said. "This doctor sought to murder the Princess Roxanne and the king. The poison they gave her was a slow one, administered a little at a time. Asklepios seems innocent of any involvement."

Hephaestion nodded. "Perhaps I owe you an apology, Princess Roxanne. Now, where by all that's holy is Alexander?"

The thud of tramping feet echoed in the palace corridors. Trumpets blared as troops mustered to battle formation. Torches blazed. Hephaestion and Alexander's inner circle of Companions brought the army to highest alert while Roxanne waited and prayed.

Sometime in the early hours before daybreak, a Sogdian soldier brought word to Roxanne that searchers had discovered Jason's body in a ditch. The youth's wrists and ankles had been bound, and he'd been strangled. But of Alexander there remained no trace. The High King of the Greek lands and Persia seemed to have vanished from the face of the earth.

As the first streaks of dawn broke over the peaks, a rider on a black warhorse neared the outer guard station. A small party of soldiers, including several high-ranking officers, and a general and two grizzled veterans rode out to meet him.

"Alexander!" the senior man called. "Where the Hades have

you been? Hephaestion has called a general alarm."

"Black Cleitus." Alexander grinned at his old companion. "Don't get your bowels in such a twist. Bucephalus and I thought we'd get a few kinks out. I can't ride out for a few hours without my army going to pieces? What's happened? Another insurrection in Persia?"

"Not so far as I know," Cleitus answered gruffly. "Hephaestion gave the order sometime after midnight." He glanced around uneasily. "Trouble with some of the barbarian tribes, most likely." He reined his mount close to the king's horse.

Alexander caught the glint of sunlight on a spear point. "Cleitus?" Alexander threw himself sideways off the saddle cloth as the general's spear pierced the air where his chest had been only an instant before. Alexander found his footing on the damp grass and drew his sword.

"Death to traitors!" Cleitus roared. He slashed at Alexander with his own sword. The rider behind the general, a man Alexander recognized as a Macedonian noble named Nestor, spurred his roan toward them.

Bucephalus reared, driving Cleitus's mount backwards. Bronzed blades clashed. Nestor let fly an arrow. It missed Alexander and glanced off the big black's rump, sending the animal into a killing rage. The bowman reached for a second arrow, then slumped sideways when a Corinthian sergeant behind him pierced the rebel with a spear.

Cleitus charged. Alexander's hand closed on Cleitus's spear shaft. He wrenched the spear out of the ground and hurled it into the general's chest. With a groan, Cleitus fell forward to the ground.

The group scattered. Three riders rode their horses away from the camp. Two of the younger officers drew their weapons and took positions to defend the king. The sergeant rode down the slowest of the three remaining assassins and dispatched him with a mighty blow.

Alexander grabbed a handful of Cleitus's hair and lifted his head. Blood ran from the general's mouth. "Why?" Alexander demanded. "You risked your life to save mine in battle. Why would you betray me?"

Black Cleitus's eyes glazed with death.

* * *

"More than twenty of my Macedonians," Alexander said that night as he paced Roxanne's bedchamber. "Black Cleitus, Galen the physician, Thanos, Eugen, six of my pages. They were my friends. Why? And why Cleitus? He was among the closest—"

"Simple enough," Ptolemy said, turning from the open window. "They wanted power. To get that, you have to be dead."

"And us as well," Hephaestion said. "No doubt the three of us would have shared a single grave."

"Now they will share one."

"Will you put them all to death, my lord?" Roxanne asked quietly. "Even the boys?"

"All must die," Hephaestion growled. "As a lesson to traitors. But Alexander is merciful. Their executions will be quick."

"Not quick enough. Many will refuse to believe Cleitus was a traitor," Ptolemy said. "Already there is grumbling among the troops. They say he slighted the Princess Roxanne and you killed him for it."

"They call her a witch," Hephaestion added.

Alexander scoffed. "Witch she may be, but if she is . . . I control her. She does not control me."

"I am no sorcerer," Roxanne said. She sat propped up in her bed, modestly covered from the eyes of her husband's Companions.

"Why did you ride off alone into the mountains?" Hephaestion asked. "It was madness."

"Old Ox Head was bored. We needed time to stretch our legs . . . time to think. We've waited too long. The troops are growing stale."

"There is a cure for that," Ptolemy said.

Alexander nodded. "Ready the men. We march for India."

Within a week, Roxanne was well enough to rise from her bed and join Alexander on one of the stone balconies overlooking the valley. He greeted her with a kiss and slipped an arm around her shoulders. "Your color is better today."

"I feel stronger." She noticed that he'd cut his hair short, clipping away most of the dark locks, letting the golden roots shine through. "No longer the hero Herakles?" she teased.

"No." He ran a hand over his close-cropped head. "Bucephalus acted as though he didn't recognize me."

She smiled. "Good. I prefer you as a yellow-haired barbarian."

"So you approve of something I do?"

She nodded. "A few things."

His mood grew serious. "I was wrong."

She gazed out at the herds of horses milling on the plain below. Outriders divided the groups into nursing mares and foals and young mounts for breaking. The trained warhorses were tethered on the far side of the camp. These animals would remain in the lush valleys of Sogdiana while Alexander's army marched east. The priceless mares and their foals would grow fat on the new grass. Nothing would be demanded of them until the colts reached three years of age, the time for schooling.

"I said I was wrong." Alexander's boyish charm manifested itself. "Am I forgiven?" She shrugged. He kissed her. "You are a bitter enemy, little Sogdian. I have given apology to few men in my lifetime. You should be honored."

She laid her head against his bare shoulder. "You don't trust me. You never will. Let me go, Alexander. Divorce me. We will bring each other no happiness."

"I never let go of what is mine." He imprisoned her in his arms. "The men are right. You have bewitched me. I love you as I have loved no other."

"But you don't trust me."

"I don't trust my mother. I did wonder enough about your dream to stay away from my tent the night of the attempted coup."

"You trust Hephaestion."

"We are brothers of the soul."

"Leave me in my mountains, Macedonian."

"Never."

She stared away at the far mountain peaks and blinked

128

back tears. "If you take me from this country, I will never see it again."

"I will take you and bring you back. I give you my word. Our son will ride these high meadows. On my honor." His mouth silenced her protests with a kiss; his hands moved over her body. "Grow strong," he said. "I would have an heir of you by this time next year. His kingdom shall be the greatest any man has ever ruled. It will stretch to the ends of the earth." The gray eyes held hers. "Give me a son, Roxanne."

"Karma rules us all, my lord. What will be, will be."

He stroked her glossy auburn braid. "You must have more faith in me. I told you that you would not die, didn't I?"

"I will die when the number of my years has spilled, and so will you, my lord." She stepped away and turned to gaze at the flawless features of his noble profile. The sunlight haloed his head, and she laughed. "Perhaps you won't die. You still claim to be Zeus's son, don't you?"

"So my mother told me often enough." He grinned. "Either Zeus's or Apollo's. It was dark, and she couldn't quite tell who her lover was. Either way, I'm half a god."

"Then you deserve to live as long as these mountains, Alexander. Yet I am but mortal flesh, only a woman, as you yourself have so often pointed out to me. There is no place in your legend for me."

"Then I will carve one." He gathered her in his arms and lifted her, and she marveled at his strength. "If ever I am mortal, it is when I look into your eyes, Roxanne. When I think I understand the workings of your mind, I find that in reality I hold nothing but a handful of mountain mist. Come lie with me, Little Star."

"It seems I have no choice."

He carried her inside and down the curving stone steps to his own chambers, which he rarely used, preferring his tent amidst his army. He'd returned her apartments to her and taken others, more Spartan and suited to his nature.

Here, only a wide couch with silken sheets and piles of scattered scrolls and maps gave evidence that a king slept in this room. His armor lay where he had discarded it; his round embossed shield stood against a wall. The plain battle helmet with its red crest lay on the foot of the bed. Roxanne took it between her hands as he placed her on the bed.

Her fingertips traced the dents on the helmet. "You have used this hard," she observed. "Who gave you this dent?" She rubbed a deep depression thoughtfully.

"A souvenir of Tyre." He took the helmet from her and tossed it aside.

"And am I a souvenir of Sogdiana?"

He bent and kissed her shoulder. "You tremble like a leaf before a storm." His kisses trailed a fiery path up her throat and into her hair as he cradled her with chest, and loins, and powerful legs. "You need not fear me," he whispered, pressing her back against the bolsters. "I want only to feel your presence next to me. I can wait to possess you until you are strong again. Sleep here in my arms, where none can harm you." Strong fingers stroked her neck and shoulders, easing the tension from her muscles until she drifted off.

At dusk, servants came with trays of food and drink. Alexander bade them leave the provisions and go away. With his own hands, he served her, choosing choice bits of fruit and mountain greens and tender meat. "This wine is watered, a special favor to you," he assured her, sipping from her cup. "And you must taste the bread. It is a Macedonian recipe and still hot from the oven."

"You will stuff me like a roasting pigeon," she protested.

"Only so you will be too dull to beat me at my new game. Pachisi. Have you played before? Answer 'a little' and I shall suffocate you with the bedcovers, wench!" He fished the gameboard from under his bed. "Well? I've never known you to be speechless before, Sogdian. Do you know the game?"

"It is Indian, is it not, my lord?" she asked innocently. "Do you play the game of your enemies?"

"Always." He pinned her back against the pillows and kissed her soundly, then nuzzled his face against her breasts. "I will not stand for you to be an invalid long," he warned. "Another week perhaps. My loins burn with the thought of your warm, slick folds." He let go of her and spread out the

130

game. "I go first." He shed his tunic and sat cross-legged on the bed, wearing only a self-satisfied expression. "I will not tolerate cheating."

She was not deceived by his disarming smile. "I do not cheat, my lord."

"I won't tolerate dishonesty. I must have no shadow on my son's birth." His low voice was deadly. "The captain of your guard—"

"Is my kinsman, whom you in your wisdom appointed to the post." She did not flinch from his gaze, instead meeting his steady look with courage. "I play to win," she said, "but I never cheat."

"So be it. And if you lose . . ." He chuckled. "If you lose, what forfeit will you pay?"

"You shall have your heart's desire . . . at high noon on an elephant's back." She reached for the playing cubes.

"And if I lose?"

She forced herself to smile at him. "If you lose, Europa shall lead the elephant."

Chapter Eleven

The army of Alexander the Great assembled to march on India, more than 130,000 strong; including the elite Companions, Macedonian heavy and light cavalry, Asian cavalry, foot archers, infantry, the Bactrian camel corps, slingers, and native irregulars. Drums rolled. Divisions formed into ranks; elephants trumpeted, and green-broke horses bolted from formation to the cursing of veteran soldiers. Herds of horses and cattle, provision wagons, and pack animals bearing the mechanisms for onagers and machines of war were followed by merchants, wives, mistresses, laundrywomen, camp whores, and children.

The Princess Roxanne came to the marble steps of the palace accompanied by her personal bodyguard Wolf, Kayan and his company of guards, Roxanne's serving women, and Soraya. Day by day, Roxanne recovered from the effects of the poison. Alexander had promised that she could ride beside him as soon as she could sit a saddle. His sense of adventure had infected her with a desire to see what lay beyond the Hindu Kush, and her sadness at leaving Sogdiana was tempered with an inner exhilaration.

Today she would not ride horseback, and she had dressed

accordingly in a formal cloth-of-gold tunic and trousers with a Persian feathered cap and a mist of a veil. On her feet she wore soft boots of hand-tooled leather worked with silken thread in ancient designs but made to give stout service. The women she had chosen to take with her were young and daring, skilled in horsemanship and the use of weapons. Who knew if any of them would ever see their homeland again? But with the army of Alexander lay dreams of romance and adventure.

Alexander waited at the foot of the grand staircase on Bucephalus, as restless as any raw recruit. "Come, wife," he called, pulling her up before him on the big stallion. "Your transportation is at the bottom of the mountain. The sun is already two hours high. We must ride."

Together they maneuvered the steep pathway cut out of living rock that led to the valley floor more than a mile below. "We will not cover much distance today," he said. "It takes time to establish routine on a march." His eyes sparkled with excitement. "Gold becomes you. I'll deck you in the treasures of India. When our son is born, I'll reward you with his weight in precious gems."

"You are generous, lord, with the wealth of kings you have yet to conquer. I'll hold you to it. I am partial to emeralds."

"Emeralds it shall be. And now, see what I have here. You shall ride in style, little savage."

A great cow elephant stood patiently swaying from side to side, her wizened mahout leaning against her trunk. The elephant's yellowed tusks were capped with points of silver, inlaid with a pattern of golden leaves and flowers. Her back was draped in scarlet and gold blankets. Strapped to her wide back was a howdah with wooden turrets and a silken canopy. A magnificent harness of red leather with sparkling jewels covered the elephant's head and shoulders.

Roxanne laughed merrily. "This is my punishment for all my evil deeds. I detest elephants. And this riding box looks fit for . . . for a Persian eunuch."

"Nevertheless, wife, she is yours," Alexander assured her.

"Her name is Tuma, and she is fifteen years old. This is your mahout, Niki."

The little man kneeled, and Alexander waved him magnanimously to his feet. The mahout tapped the cow's trunk with an iron goad, and the massive beast groaned and sank to her knees in the dust.

A servant produced a set of wooden stairs, and Alexander helped Roxanne from the saddle, and then led her to the steps. "Your elephant awaits, Princess," he pronounced solemnly.

Spasms of laughter seized her. "I can't," she protested. "My warriors will die of embarrassment."

"Will you defy a royal command?" Alexander struggled to maintain his own composure, but she knew he wanted to laugh as well. "It is a conveyance worthy of the first wife of the High King."

With a helpless shrug, she climbed the steps to the howdah. The interior was cushioned with silk and cotton bolsters and was much larger than she had imagined from the ground. She settled herself royally, and the elephant lurched to her feet. "I'll never forgive you for this," Roxanne promised as her husband saluted her. Chuckling, he mounted Bucephalus and rode to join his Companions at the head of the procession.

Wagons drawn by sleek mules carried Roxanne's personal possessions. Her ladies would travel in the wagons when the weather was too bad to ride horseback. Wolf fell in behind the elephant on a shaggy steppe pony with a big head and one white stocking. Kayan and her honor guard rode just ahead. As she'd mounted the steps to the fanciful howdah, Roxanne had caught her cousin's amused expression. Let them all enjoy the joke, she vowed. She would give her husband proper repayment when the time was right.

The elephant's stride was regular, and once Roxanne got used to it, not unpleasant. The view from the swaying howdah was magnificent. Sogdiana in spring was at its most glorious. Best of all, the army of occupation was marching out of the country, leaving Oxyartes once more in control. He would join the force in a few weeks when a new governor was fully established. Alexander had no fear of Oxyartes's betrayal while he held Roxanne and the pride of the Sogdian and Bactrian noblemen.

In truth, Roxanne's countrymen were mostly resigned to Alexander as overlord. He had not proved to be a harsh master, retaining most of the Sogdian laws and tax structures. He put no restrictions on the extensive trade that was the life blood of the twin kingdoms. A new government would be made up of Macedonians and Sogdians. Alexander had promised that Oxyartes would return as prince after the Indian campaign.

The sparks of independence were not extinguished, only banked until the balance of power shifted. Bactria and Sogdiana had a history of freedom that stretched into the mists of time. For now, they would deal with the Greeks and with Alexander peaceably. Tomorrow might be another day.

The beauty of Roxanne's towering perch was that she could see all without being seen herself. Although she longed for the feel of a spirited steed beneath her, she was content to bide her time until her full strength returned. It would be a long campaign, and she had been out of training since her capture by the Scythians. As a woman, she was lighter and had weaker muscles than a man of the same size. She must combat her weaknesses by agility and wit, and by keeping her body in top condition.

She sighed and watched a golden eagle soar from the peak of the citadel toward the valley floor. King of the air, the eagle was a symbol of her country. On horseback, Roxanne felt akin to that eagle, fast, and free, and untouchable. Wolf had assured her that her own string of riding horses was with the main herd. Soon she would experience the feeling of freedom again. The rocking of the howdah lulled her, and she dozed.

Roxanne's lashes fluttered as the curtain parted and she started, suddenly wide awake as Alexander vaulted into the howdah beside her. "I've come to claim my forfeit, wench," he said, offering her a golden goblet. "Here, take this before I spill it. The wine is excellent."

"Alexander?"

"Who else would you expect? I'll demand the head of any other man who touches so much as the curtain of this howdah." He grinned. "It is high noon, and you did lose the wager."

"What are you talking about?" She rubbed her eyes, and for a moment wished he were a god. Dealing with Apollo himself could not be nearly as difficult.

He settled into the cushions across from her. "Most of the wine spilled, but the thought was there," he said, taking a wineskin from around his neck and filling the cup to the brim. "Drink, sweet wife . . . to us and to the son I hope to get of you."

"Now?" She looked at him uneasily. "You're joking." He wrapped a lock of her hair around his finger. "You're not joking."

"Can you think of a more propitious time?" His fingers strayed from her throat to the top button of her tunic. She tried to twist away, and he pulled her on top of him. His lips, firm and warm, brushed hers. "Roxanne," he whispered. "I have waited long enough." The empty goblet rolled forgotten on the carpeted floor.

"You're mad. Here? With all your army looking on? And mine?" She tried to wiggle away, but he held her firmly. His lips were sweet and tender against her own. His eyes glittered with inner fire.

"Roxanne. My own . . ." He buried his face in her neck and kissed her over and over again. Somehow his seeking fingers found the second button and released it.

"My lord," she protested weakly. "No."

"They can see nothing. Let them think what they will. I might be beating you. You are unruly enough to be beaten soundly." He chuckled and nibbled amorously at her lower lip. "What is the worst they can say? The High King is ensorcelled by his wife? It's true." He kissed her again and murmured, "Is it a sin among your people for a man to desire his wife?"

Alexander's presence was intoxicating, and the more she

struggled, the closer their limbs became entwined. "I am wed to a madman," she sputtered.

But she knew that if there was madness, she shared it. What was this charisma that her Macedonian conqueror held for her? Why did his nearness cause her to abandon reason? More than a physical lure, more than intellectual, Alexander drew her spirit to his as surely as a desert oasis entices life.

Her pulse quickened as he undid her tunic's third golden button and pressed hungry lips against the throbbing pulse in the hollow of her throat. She wanted to protest, but her words died unspoken. It would have been easier to stop breathing than to deny him what he sought.

She lifted his dimpled chin and brushed her lips to his, letting the wonder of the kiss enfold her in a cloak of enchantment. Alexander's strong hands skimmed over her body, caressing, stroking, cradling her, until heated passion ignited the fire within her.

Their kisses deepened as tongues met, and probed, and tasted, pulling them far from the world around them to a place where nothing mattered but the heat of his flesh against hers.

Alexander whispered her name, and the sound of his voice thrilled her to the depths of her soul. *Hold back*, an inner voice cried. *Hold back*! But there was no denying the virile magnetism of this man as he tongued and kissed every inch of her, all the while murmuring her name. Swept up in the storm tide of his seduction, Roxanne surrendered once again, returning his lovemaking with equal fervor.

Uttering deep whimpers of desire, she caressed the iron-hard muscles of Alexander's powerful shoulders and the bulging thews of his upper arms. His were hard male hands that could draw a bow or wield a sword for hours without end; she nibbled and licked and sucked them, taming their strength to her will. Her joyous exploration with fingertips and lips and tongue continued across the broad, smooth chest to tease first one male nipple and then the other to taut rigidity before moving lower to caress his iron-muscled stomach.

"What do you want?" he whispered hoarsely. "Tell me."

"You."

"Say it," he insisted.

"Only you." Sinewy thighs and powerful legs submitted to her touch, and she brushed her fingers lightly over the thin garment that covered his burgeoning sex.

"Kiss me," he commanded.

Slowly she obeyed, cupping the weight of his sacs in the palms of her hands and blowing soft breaths along his swollen length. He groaned, pushing her head lower. "What do you want?" she asked him.

"Kiss me," he said breathlessly. "Take it . . . take all of it."

"I cannot. I'm only mortal."

He drew in a shuddering breath, and his muscles tensed as she first kissed and then flicked the tip of her tongue over the surface of his hot, engorged flesh. His taste was so clean and sweet that the act which began as teasing increased the intensity of her own need. The deep aching in her loins flared to incandescent heat, and she felt herself grow slick with anticipation.

"Torturer," he rasped. His fingers twisted in her hair. "Yes, yes."

Wantonly she drew him between her lips, giving all that he asked for and more, enflaming his animal passions, luring him to the brink of the precipice again and again. Each time, in the last instant before Alexander lost control, she withdrew, leaving him moaning and shuddering with desire.

"Enough!" he cried suddenly, claiming her mouth with his and ripping away her fragile cloth-of-gold tunic and trousers. She felt no shame, only equal hunger as she tore at his own garment.

Her breathing deepened and came in quick gasps as he pushed her back against the cushions and fed hungrily at each breast until her nipples throbbed and flames licked her secret places.

His hard, sensual lips trailed a path of fiery kisses down her belly to her inner thighs, and she moaned as his fingers traced small, slow circles in her russet curls, before probing the damp folds below. She groaned as he sought the source of her pleasure, and massaged the sweet nub before sliding one finger deep and then two.

"I can wait no longer," he said, rolling onto his back and pulling her on top of him. She clung to him, her wildly erotic kisses adding to his raging lust as he drove into her.

Wordlessly she met his thrusting length with the fervor of her white-hot desire. The sway of the great beast beneath them was lost in the frenzy of wild lovemaking that culminated in wave after wave of joyous abandon.

"You have never said you love me," he whispered to her, in the sweet aftermath of their mutual rapture when they both lay breathless and exhausted, skin slick with moisture and bodies sated with desire. "Can you deny it?"

She murmured sleepily and burrowed into his chest. "Is it not enough that you have claimed your winnings? Must you shame your enemy?" She teased his nipple with an exploring tongue. "A captive must say whatever her lord desires." She felt the power build in him again. "Ask and I will give it, mighty king," she tempted.

"Yield up your treasure," he replied. "Whether you are willing or nay, I will not be turned aside."

She laughed and drew him down to her. "Gently, my conqueror," Roxanne whispered hoarsely. "For I know this day's work will produce the heir you desire."

Much later, as she descended the steps at evening camp, dressed in a new tunic and trousers, Roxanne felt a thousand eyes on her. Alexander had been back at the head of the column for hours, and yet the whispers had passed through the vast army. "She is once more in favor."

Kayan's gaze was accusing. Roxanne met his scrutiny with a haughty stare. What right had he to judge her? Surely he had tasted of his new wife's favors.

In the privacy of her pavilion, Roxanne bathed and washed her hair, anointing her body with precious oils and perfumes. She ate only a bit of bread and cheese and then retired to her curtained bed. The first day of a march is always tiring, and Soraya and the women were soon asleep. The single torch burned, and Roxanne lay awake staring into darkness.

Alexander's words echoed and reechoed in the recesses of her mind. Did she love him? Were love and hate two sides of the same knife blade? She knew that she would not hesitate to risk her life in his defense, yet she was also willing to risk her life to be free of him. And now there was something more. Her instincts told her that she carried the heir of Sogdiana and Bactria under her heart. She did not deceive herself that Kayan and his company of guards could protect her against her Macedonian enemies. If Alexander died, neither she nor her unborn babe would survive more than a few hours.

So protecting her husband might only be self-preservation on her part, not love for the man who had conquered her country and put so many of her people to the sword. But even if Alexander lived and claimed her child as his own, the danger would not be over. He would want to make a Greek of his heir. She might be allowed no influence over the child's upbringing. How then could she both preserve her babe's life and teach him to love and cherish the twin kingdoms?

She was certain that she was carrying Alexander's son, and that she had quickened with his seed before she had been captured. Yet it might be better to keep those thoughts to herself, because she feared her husband had not believed her when she'd told him she'd not been raped by the Scythians. Alexander's stubbornness was legendary. Once he seized on an idea, he could not be shaken from it. And if he had any question that this wasn't his child, it would bode ill for her.

Footsteps outside her tent made Roxanne reach for her dagger. And then reason reassured her. Kayan's men ringed the tent; her Bactrian guard lay sleeping at the flap. Only one person would dare to approach.

"Roxanne?"

"My lord, I am awake." She drew aside the curtain, and he came to her, shedding his armor as he crossed the tent.

"Good, for I don't have to wake you." He pulled her into his arms. His hair and body were damp and clean, his tunic fresh. "Another fourteen days and we reach the foothills of the mountains."

She tasted the strong wine on his lips. "You have created a scandal," she warned. "Europa will be jealous."

"It is my generals who are jealous. They are still drinking and rehashing old battles. You have pulled me from good company, Little Star. Now you must make it worth my while."

As days spilled into weeks, the army's march fell into a routine. Scouts reported the passes of the Hindu Kush clear, a far cry from the first crossing Alexander had made two years earlier when so many lives were lost amid the bitter cold and snow. Before they reached the high lands, Roxanne was on horseback. Followed by Wolf and Kayan, she joined Alexander and his Companions at the front of the procession. The cool mountain air was invigorating, and Roxanne felt the strength pour back into her tanned and glowing body.

It was a rare night when the king did not retire to the princess's pavilion, a fact that drew bitter warning from Hephaestion and his friends. "You give too much power to the Sogdians. If you will not have a royal Persian woman to wife, send back to Macedonia for one."

"I have a wife. One that suits me well enough," Alexander replied good-naturedly. "Two would be four times the trouble."

The climb through the high passes progressed slowly, and Alexander's army was strung out for miles. The horses were surefooted, but the camels and elephants had to be driven along the narrow inclines. Several supply wagons were lost when rocky ledges gave way, tumbling screaming men and horses into the chasm below. Here, the mountain tribesmen proved their worth. Sogdians and Bactrians had been bred in the thin air, and mountain travel came naturally to them. Even the mighty Hindu Kush, the "Hindu Killer," held no terror for them.

"Set my cousin Kayan to lead a regiment," Roxanne urged Alexander. "He's too valuable to waste guarding a woman's pavilion. Hector, a Macedonian, commands your Bactrian light cavalry, but the 'Flying Devils' hate him and Hector doesn't appreciate them. They are a rough lot with much to gain and nothing to lose. Kayan would make a crack company of them." She rode close to her husband astride his latest gift, a gray gelding that much resembled her beloved mare.

"And Hector? Is he to be shamed by losing his command because his men don't respect him?" Alexander's voice was stern, but the gray eyes studied her tenderly. This morning, she had told him that she was with child, and he'd offered her whatever her heart desired as reward.

"Send me home," she'd begged. "Free my kingdom."

"Choose something else. Something within reason. A palace? Your weight in Persian gems?"

She thought about what advantage she could gain by his favor, and decided that Kayan's safety was more important than anything else she could beg of Alexander. "You could find another command for Hector," she suggested. "Promote him. There is one among my guard who could fill Kayan's position. Bondoor. You know him—the man with the burn scar over half his face."

"His face does not frighten you?"

She chuckled. "No. He is a good man, skilled with arms, and smart."

"Another relative of yours, no doubt?" When she shook her head, he continued his line of attack. "And you do not feel the need for your cousin's protection?"

"You are protection enough, my lord."

Alexander reined in Bucephalus and patted the animal's powerful neck. "I have watched Hector, and I agree with you. He does not know how to lead the Flying Devils. I would have replaced him anyway. But what proof do I have that Kayan is as good a soldier as you say he is?"

"He was my father's second in command. They held your army back for two years, didn't they?" She smiled at him. "Kayan will not fail you. He has the courage of a lion."

"Then we would be foolish to keep this *lion* caged in women's quarters, wouldn't we? I will give him a chance," Alexander agreed. "My scouts tell me there are unfriendly tribes ahead in the mountains. It will be good practice for the Flying Devils. The tribes are small and scattered, but we can-

142

not allow the army to be harassed. It will be a different story when we reach the Punjab. The Indian kings will confront us with war elephants. Do you know what a line of charging elephants can do to a wall of infantry?"

"I don't like elephants, and I don't trust them. Not only are they a danger to us, but to the Indian forces who use them. Spear an elephant's tender trunk, and the beast will go mad. He is as apt to trample his own troops as the enemy. The bulls are uncontrollable during musth. Give me a horse any time, my lord. Horses are not as impressive, but they are predictable."

"I would not expect a woman to understand."

"The words are not mine, but Oxyartes's. My father has fought Indians before. Send for him. He has knowledge that would be of great use to you. He speaks the language of the Punjab like a native."

"Oxyartes will join us soon. Naturally, I will consult with all my generals before battle. But I do not need a woman to teach me the art of war—not even one as beautiful as you."

"As you say," she replied. "But if you bring them to a ditch, they cannot jump."

"What nonsense is this?" He stiffened with impatience. "Who cannot jump?"

"The elephants. Their legs are not made for jumping. And some do say they are terrified of mice."

"Enough," he snapped.

"Maybe I should have my ladies catch mice and turn the battle for your Greeks."

"Your tiring women are not afraid of mice?"

"Mice?" Her eyes widened in astonishment. "Are Macedonian women?"

"Usually."

She shrugged. "A pity. No wonder your warriors are so attracted to Sogdian women. It must be difficult to train the sons to courage when the mothers are such cowards."

"Go back to your bodyguards. I have plans to make with Hephaestion. I'm dividing the army and sending him on to the River Indus with my engineers. We can clear the foothills of hostile tribes while he prepares a crossing for us. Herakles himself crossed the Indus in full flood."

"Is this Herakles one of your many gods? I'd heard that he was a giant."

"A half-god, but no giant."

"No taller than you, my lord?" He threw her a black look and turned his horse back toward Hephaestion. "Will you join me in my tent for dinner?" she called after him.

He did not answer. Likely her sarcasm would drive him back to his Greek whore. Roxanne sighed. Why couldn't she learn to guard her tongue? She must remember that her husband was not like other men, and toying with him was a dangerous game with higher stakes than she might wish to pay.

She wondered about Alexander's wisdom in splitting his army. She supposed he must have his reasons. So far, they had encountered no danger. They had not even sighted any native peoples.

Kayan and Bondoor galloped to meet her. The lieutenant's scarred face was ugly, but he was kind and intelligent, a man she could rely on. She had noticed interest shown toward him by one of her ladies, a young woman named Parvona. Roxanne would question Kayan about Bondoor's family. His promotion would make him a catch, and if he served her faithfully, he would make his fortune.

Kayan reined in and saluted. "Princess." His words were icily polite, and they stung so that tears formed behind her eyelids.

"Cousin, we have much to discuss." She motioned for Bondoor to fall in behind them. "Alexander has promised me that you are to have command of his Flying Devils." The gleam in Kayan's eyes told her that she had made the right decision. "You're a cavalryman born," she said. "You must show these Greeks how it's done."

His eyes narrowed. "I'm sworn to protect you. Your father took my oath to—"

"You will better protect me if you rise in Alexander's army. Many will wish me dead . . . especially now that I carry his child."

Kayan's dark eyes absorbed the blow. "I am a soldier," he said. "It doesn't matter about that. The child will be part of you as well."

"And heir to my throne." Her lower lip quivered. "I had thought . . . wished . . ." She swallowed. "It should have been different."

"My son, not his," Kayan said.

He was so close, yet she dared not touch him.

One of Alexander's pages rode toward them. "I thought to raise Bondoor to your place as captain of my guard," she said quickly.

Kayan nodded. "As you wish, Princess."

"Highness." The boy halted his pony beside them. "The High King would see the captain at once."

"Bondoor!" Kayan shouted. "See to the princess." He saluted her, and for a second their eyes met. "If there is anything that I can do for you, my lady," he promised, "you have only to command."

Head high, back straight, she turned her mount and rode back through the column to her women. And not until night fell and she lay alone in her bed did she let the salt tears flow and her heart yearn for what could never be.

Chapter Twelve

Now that Hephaestion and the main body of Alexander's army had taken a southern route to construct a crossing of the Indus, Alexander engaged in constant warfare with the hostile hill tribes. The rugged terrain was strewn with forts, and the Greeks could not permit the natives to cut the main supply route back to Persia. Alexander knew he must subdue and scatter the tribesmen. For an organized army, it was the worst sort of fighting: running battles, ambushes, night attacks, and constant harassment.

When Oxyartes rejoined Alexander's force, he was not pleased with Roxanne's suggestion to promote Kayan from captain of her guard to commander of the Flying Devils. "Why?" Oxyartes demanded of his daughter. "I trusted Kayan to watch over you."

"I was at greater risk with him nearby. Alexander is suspicious. If he takes the notion that the child I carry is not his . . . I need not tell you that my husband can be utterly ruthless. Do you want to see Kayan's head roll?" She frowned. "Stop glaring at me. I've done nothing to compromise your honor or mine."

Oxyartes hugged her. "I never thought you would."

146

"Being Alexander's wife is like riding a heavily laden camel over thin ice. The ride is bumpy, and you never know when you're going to be plunged into frigid water." She led the way into her pavilion. "I'm sorry. Being with child makes me far too emotional."

Oxyartes smiled. "Your mother was the same."

"I never thought I'd miss Hephaestion, but I do. Alexander drinks more now, and he takes too many chances. He thinks nothing of engaging in hand-to-hand combat with enemy patrols. He's been wounded twice in the last month."

"When I arrived, Lord Alexander met me personally. He gave no indication that things are going badly between you."

"They aren't. Hephaestion took Europa with him. But Alexander listens less to me and more to the Persians. He will not be content with India. Mark my words, Father. He is possessed."

"Mind your tongue. It's not wise to speak such thoughts."

"Whom then may I open my heart to, if not you?"

"It's true that Alexander becomes more Asian day by day," her father said. "But is that bad? He sees each man's talents rather than his nationality. It's not easy being a king."

He settled onto a cushioned bench. "I am delighted at how well you look. There is a glow about you." He patted her arm. "A woman takes strange fancies when she carries a child."

"He is convinced that this child is a son," she confided.

"Then he may be surprised at how much joy a daughter brings." Oxyartes accepted a goblet of wine and chuckled. "I've never quite decided if you were a blessing from the Wise God or a curse."

Alexander ducked under the tent flap. "I'll wager Roxanne is filling your head with tales of my ill treatment," he said, moving to her side and draping an arm around her possessively.

"I say no more than I do to your face," she said. "You are too careless with your life. I don't want our child born an orphan."

"Would you have me ask more of my soldiers than I give myself? I didn't come here for lectures. I need this bandage changed." He held out his left forearm, which had been wounded several days before.

Roxanne went to fetch her medicine chest. "You should be as scarred as an old warhorse."

"My wounds are within." Alexander clutched his chest dramatically. "My heart has been pierced by my lady's scorn."

Oxyartes laughed.

"It's good to have you back." Alexander's mood shifted. "Do you know King Ambhi? Will he resist my army or yield?"

The men fell into a tactical discussion as she tended Alexander's arm. He'd been grazed by a jagged rock thrown from a sling, and the flesh was gouged and badly bruised. Careful washing had kept it free from infection, and now the swelling was beginning to subside.

For weeks, Alexander's army had laid siege to the town of Massaga, stoutly defended by high walls and a large army of professional soldiers. The city walls were rock and wood, and the recent rains made it impossible to breach the walls with flame. Battering rams were useless because of the chasm surrounding the fort. The main bridge had already fallen.

From the shelter of those walls, defenders inside could deliver a rain of arrows and missiles. As usual, Alexander was in the vanguard of the attack, and his helmet hadn't protected his arm. When Roxanne had first seen the injury, she'd feared that the bone was broken. A fractured arm in this heat could easily prove fatal.

Massaga was ruled by a self-styled prince, more bandit than monarch, who was wealthy enough to maintain a private army. The hill town was well supplied with food and water, making a long siege costly to the Greek forces. Yet Alexander was determined to breach the wall.

He'd repeatedly commented on how impressed he was with the captured Indian prisoners. They were a tall, lean people, dark of skin and eyes, who followed the custom of dyeing their beards in fanciful colors. "They are utterly fearless," he'd explained to Roxanne. "Warlike by nature. Such warriors cannot be left to savage our army's rear."

"I hope the treasure you take from Massaga is worth the

cost. We seem no closer to victory now than when we took up the siege."

"What we do here is marked well by Massaga's neighbors. I will take the city, and soon," he promised. "Besides, it's good practice for the men until we get to the real fighting." He'd paused and tilted his head in the way he did so often when he was thinking. "You will remain within the confines of the camp until I give you leave to ride out. Bands of lawless mercenaries roam these canyons."

His stubborn expression warned her not to argue.

"I mean what I say."

She nodded, far from convinced.

After he and her father left her tent, she had her ladies set up targets to practice their archery. Bondoor, her new captain of the guards, was only too eager to assist in any way he could. "Any news of Lord Kayan?" she asked.

"The Flying Devils surprised a bandit camp not five miles from here and put them all to the sword. Commander Kayan suffered only four casualties. Rumor is that the High King is pleased."

"I thought he would be. My cousin is an able leader. Bactrians are brave men who cannot be driven, but can be led by the right man."

Parvona sent an arrow into the center of the target, and Bondoor grinned admiringly. "The lady has skill. But if she would hold her bow a little differently . . ."

Roxanne nodded, and the captain put his arms around the woman and positioned her hands correctly on the horn bow. "You will have more striking power. Thus."

Parvona's next arrow buried itself to the feathers in the straw target. "Good!" Bondoor said.

Roxanne's arrows were made especially for her, and she had practiced with the bow daily from childhood. She had no intention of stopping now, even though her pregnancy was beginning to show; the exercise kept her from boredom. She, Parvona, and two other women shot for nearly an hour before a loud commotion drew their attention.

"Princess! Princess!" A Spartan page boy urged a dun geld-

149

ing toward the royal pavilion at a fast trot. "We have bridged the chasm! The High King leads the charge against the fort!"

"Give me your horse," Roxanne commanded. Ignoring Bondoor's protest, she vaulted onto the boy's mount and tore off, leaving Wolf and her guard to follow as best they could. She galloped through the camp toward the city walls. By the holy beard of Zoroaster! Did Alexander believe this was some child's game, and that he was truly immortal?

Smoke hung over the walls of the hill fort, and hundreds of warriors lined the parapets, screaming and brandishing weapons. From inside the town came a terrible din of horns and clashing cymbals. Archers rained a steady flight of deadly projectiles, and machines hurled rocks and burning logs. At the site of the ruined causeway, a huge tree had been shoved across the yawning crevice, and Alexander's men swarmed over this new "bridge," widening it with planks and rope.

On the far side, a unit of daring Thracians had built a bonfire against the huge wooden gate. A human chain of soldiers passed straw and buckets of oil to aid the inferno. Infantrymen interlocked their oval shields to protect the attack party from the defenders above. On the Macedonian side of the chasm, catapults hurled boulders into the fort. Foot archers on the walls returned fire.

Roxanne strained her eyes to make out the figures on the bridge. "Leonnatus!" she called to a Macedonian Companion she recognized. "Is he over there?" The dun horse danced nervously and reared, frightened by the noise and smoke. Easily she held her seat on the animal's back and forced it back to earth. Wolf, Bondoor, and four of his guardsmen galloped up behind her.

"Princess." Leonnatus left his unit and reined his horse toward her. "This is no place for you." He reached for her mount's bridle, and then pulled back his hand when Wolf threw him a warning look. "Yes, he's there. See!" The Companion pointed. "There under the wall."

Roxanne swore. Indian swordsmen had lowered rope ladders from the parapets and climbed down hand-over-hand with weapons clenched in their teeth to engage the Macedonians. The iron-bound gate smoldered; black smoke enveloped the struggling soldiers. The clash of weapons and the moans of dying men echoed across the bridge. Screaming reinforcements poured across the walkway.

To the right, Roxanne saw a troop of Sogdian horse archers charge across open ground, shooting arrows as they rode. A draped figure appeared at the fort's main tower. The Sogdian cavalrymen leaned to one side of their mounts, presenting little more than a leg as target to the archers on the wall. Like a flock of birds, the Sogdians wheeled as a single unit and passed the area again. One horse went down, fatally wounded, and the following two leaped over him. A comrade offered a hand to the rider, sweeping the fallen horseman up behind him and carrying him to safety.

One of the Sogdian arrows struck the bright-robed figure in the tower, and the man tumbled in a slow arc to the foot of the walls and lay motionless on the rocks. Within seconds, a great cheer arose from the attacking force.

Minutes later, a signal flag waved, and firing from the wall ceased. Someone shouted for an interpreter. Two men crossed the bridge and came back toward the Macedonian troops. To her relief, Roxanne recognized Alexander. He favored one leg as he climbed a rise to confer with his generals. Quickly a ripple passed through the watching troops.

Roxanne sighted her father and rode to join him. "Do they wish to surrender?" she called. He turned from a wounded Sogdian and scowled at her.

"Why are the Indians surrendering?" She counted the casualties among the horse archers. A few were boys still in their teens. Several she had known all her life. "Such a waste," she said. "To die for this."

"Women have not the heart for war," Oxyartes said.

"They are hardly old enough to be called men."

"They fight as warriors, don't they? Our Spitimes's arrow killed their prince. Didn't you see him fall?"

He ordered the wounded taken to the field hospital, and then turned back to his daughter. "It was luck, pure and simple. Most of the city's defenders were mercenaries. They offer

151

to surrender the fort if Alexander will spare their lives and accept them into his army." His frown became an accusing look. "The High King will not be happy to see you here at the front. I suggest you return to your quarters."

"Little I do pleases Alexander. There is nothing to see from my pavilion. I will go mad not knowing what is happening."

"Bondoor! Wolf! Escort the princess back to her tent." Her father's eyes were hard. "Your husband will not wish to have his wife make a fool of him in front of his army. Go while you retain your dignity, lest I be forced to take other measures."

She nodded. "But send me word whether Alexander is hurt."

Troops occupied the town and disarmed the citizens. At Alexander's orders, there were few deaths and no rapes. He ordered house-to-house searches to seize valuables and adult men. Females and boys under the age of nine were unharmed. The Companions placed noncombatant males under heavy guard. The High King offered the Indian mercenaries the opportunity to join his army, and more than five thousand accepted.

It was long past midnight when Alexander finally appeared at Roxanne's tent, still wearing his torn and bloody battle tunic. He was nearly rigid with exhaustion when he sank on the edge of her bed.

"My lord!" she exclaimed. Taking one look at his condition, she ordered her servants to bring hot water, medical supplies, and bandages. She poured him wine and then bathed his filthy body with her own hands.

"We crossed the chasm. Another hour and we would have burned through the gate," he bragged. One of his shoulders was blistered, and the back of his leg bore a sword gash. His right eye was purple-black, and the knuckles on his sword hand were split open to the bone.

"Have you eaten?"

"Not hungry." He downed the wine. "The mercenaries offered up the city in exchange for their own lives. It's a major weakness with soldiers-for-hire. They have no loyalty." He chuckled. "I was offered the daughter of the prince. Nine years old at the most. Too young and skinny for my taste." He ran a hand down Roxanne's leg. "I prefer my women full-bodied and grown."

She smiled at him. "What happened to the child, lord?"

"I left her safely in the care of her mother, with a warning as to my retribution should the girl be wed before she turns thirteen. I respect the customs of other peoples, but bedding children turns my stomach!"

"This is what happens when women are treated as chattel. It was never so among the Sogdians or Bactrians."

"I heard that you were there, at the end, when the prince died." He raised his eyes to her. "You are forbidden to put yourself and my son in danger. If it happens again, I'll hang Bondoor and his company as a lesson in obedience."

"It wasn't their fault. The responsibility was mine."

"And my command is that you are to be kept safe!"

Her cheeks grew warm as her anger rose. "Explain to me the wisdom of men, husband. Women are considered too weak for war, too delicate to be trained to defend their own soft bodies. Yet when war comes, women are raped and slaughtered like flightless birds. What reason is there in this? To arm and train the women of a city is to double its strength. Who would be more loyal? Nothing is so fierce as a lioness or a she-bear defending her cubs!"

"There is much in what you say, little Amazon. In ancient days of Greece the legends tell of such fighting women. I like the idea well enough . . . so long as you do not turn your sword on me."

"Your own sword is sufficient for us both," she replied. Laughing, he kissed her.

She spread a soothing ointment on the burn and stripped away his dirty clothing and offered him fresh garb. "Later," he said, stretching out naked on the coverlet and holding up his cup to be refilled. "You saw me at the wall. I was magnificent. Admit it." She pulled off his sandals and washed the cut on his leg. "What did you think? Admit it. I am invincible."

"You are a warrior without fear." She packed away the precious medications, mentally reminding herself what must be

153

replenished. "I was . . ." She stopped, realizing that Alexander had fallen asleep. Carefully she took the goblet from his hand, lay down beside him, and pulled a silken cover over them both.

Sometime before dawn, the Indian mercenaries attempted to overcome their Macedonian guards, and a battle ensued. A rider came to inform the High King, and Alexander leaped naked from the bed, sword in hand to join the fighting. By the time the sun rose, all five thousand Indians lay dead on the hill. Rather than bury so many of the treacherous enemy, Alexander ordered that the camp be struck and his army march east toward the Indus.

Roxanne lost count of the skirmishes, the tribes, the forts they captured. As they left the high mountain passes, the land became more fertile and the towns larger. Envoys of petty kings sent offers of peace treaties and pack trains of gifts to placate the foreign invader. To his delight, Alexander added twenty-five war elephants to his elephant corps. The rocky trail had become a wide highway, leading toward the vast plain below. Still, it was a shock to Roxanne to reach the crest of a final hill and view the panorama of the Indus stretching from horizon to horizon.

The river was unlike any Roxanne had ever imagined. Even the great salt sea must be awed by such a river. Surely her husband did not mean to cross that flow with his army. And yet, she knew he did and somehow would. She put her heels to her swift pony and galloped along the road to catch up with the head of the procession, her guard trailing behind her. "It's magnificent!" she cried when she caught sight of Alexander.

He pulled up and waited for her. He was wearing his favorite lionskin cap this morning, and his spotless tunic was embroidered with gold. She never saw him among his Companions that she wasn't taken by how young and vigorous he looked. He was a man who only seemed small among others until you looked into his eyes and saw a hero-king gazing

NAME: _____

ADDRESS: _____

_____

_____

TELEPHONE: _____

E-MAIL: _____

_____ I want to pay by credit card.

__ Visa   __ MasterCard   __ Discover

Account Number: _____

Expiration date: _____

SIGNATURE: _____

Send this form, along with $2.00 shipping and handling for your FREE books, to:

Love Spell Romance Book Club
20 Academy Street
Norwalk, CT 06850-4032

Or fax (must include credit card information!) to: 610.995.9274.
You can also sign up on the Web at www.dorchesterpub.com.

Offer open to residents of the U.S. and Canada only. Canadian residents, please call 1.800.481.9191 for pricing information.

back. Under that intense stare, the observer took a second look and realized that Alexander was a giant among men.

"After we cross this"—Alexander motioned toward the mighty river in front of them—"we'll begin to see some excitement."

"How far until we meet up with Hephaestion and his engineers?" she asked. "I'd like to see the bridge that could cross that river."

"A few days," Alexander replied. "I had a message from him this morning. The city of Taxila lies on the far side, and Hephaestion is not certain of our reception there. King Ambhi would be a formidable adversary if he should decide to oppose us." He grinned. "Wait until Hephaestion sees my new elephants. He's been bored out of his skull these past weeks. Only the results of bridge building are interesting, unless you're an engineer by trade."

"I'm certain Europa has done her best to keep his nights interesting."

Alexander laughed. "You are thickening at the waist, wife. I'm glad your mind is still lean and sharp. In time, you and Europa may come to enjoy each other's company. She's a remarkable woman, educated as you are."

"I sincerely doubt it, my lord." Roxanne fished in her saddlebag for a piece of fruit. "Taste this—it's delicious. I'm sure you were in too much of a hurry to eat this morning."

"It's my strict upbringing. My tutor, Leonidas, believed a starving boy learned faster." He bit into the juicy fruit. "Thank you. I believe motherhood has improved your disposition."

"I will never understand the Greeks. They school colts with sugar and soft hands, and princelings with cruelty. Your boyhood must have been difficult."

"Earlier this morning, Ptolemy and I were discussing a name for my son," he said, swiftly changing the subject. "I lean toward Herakles, but Ptolemy thinks Philip would be a better choice. What do you think?" He waved to a page, and the lad produced a small, peacock-blue, velvet pouch. Alexander tossed it to her. "A gift in return for your own. I always pay my debts."

She loosed the drawstring and poured out a pair of gold filigree and pearl earrings, and a large pearl attached to a pin. "But what is this?" She held up the single pearl.

"It goes in the nose." Mischief twinkled in Alexander's eyes. "A gold ring with a chain would be better, but I couldn't find one."

"The earrings I shall wear with pleasure, but you may give the nose plug to Europa. It would suit her nature better than mine."

"You see, Bucephalus, I told you she was jealous." Alexander grinned and leaned forward to scratch his horse between the ears. The stallion's black hide was scattered with gray hair. Roxanne knew the old horse was long past his prime, but he still pranced and tossed his noble head, dwarfing his handsome master. "You have not given an opinion, Roxanne. What name is best for the future High King of Macedonia, Greece, Asia, India, and Arabia?"

"Arabia? I had not heard that." She smiled. "But, my lord, your choice of names seems limited. I would not have a daughter named either Herakles or Philip."

Alexander's countenance darkened under the lionskin helmet. "It is not a joking matter. You carry a son. I must have a male heir, and soon. Let there be no more jests about girls until you have given me a quiver full of sons."

On the third day, as they neared Hephaestion's camp, cheering troops rode out to greet the king, calling his name over and over. "Alexander! Alexander!"

It seemed to Roxanne that he gloried in the adulation. He had ordered Roxanne to dress in her finest robes and ride beside him. "Let them see you and our son," he said. Still, he couldn't resist galloping ahead to meet Hephaestion. They embraced, too glad to see each other for words.

Roxanne rode up to them, and Hephaestion saluted. "Princess, you look well."

She murmured polite phrases. Like Alexander, Hephaestion was changeless. Blunt-spoken and shrewd, he made no pretense of being her friend. He tolerated her for Alexander's sake. She wondered if he would support the child she carried. Which would be stronger, his love for his friend or his hatred of her? If Alexander died without an heir, Hephaestion would inherit the crown. He had never given any indication of a desire to rule . . . yet. Hephaestion was an enigma.

"Wait until you see my bridge," he boasted. "The river was too wide and the bottom too treacherous to sink pilings, so we built a floating bridge. It rests on a chain of boats!"

Nothing would do but that Alexander must go and see this marvel immediately. Roxanne was overwhelmed by the ingeniousness of the plan. The men had linked wooden boats together and constructed a road of wood, dried grass, and dirt over them. The pathway was wide enough for seven men to walk abreast and stretched to the far side of the Indus.

"Even your elephants can cross without getting their feet wet," Hephaestion assured Alexander. "The wealth of India lies on the other side. We have only to grasp it."

Chapter Thirteen

Roxanne was certain that Alexander's crossing of the Indus was a tale men and women would relate to their grandchildren. Slowly, methodically, the great army crossed the rocking bridge. Heavy cavalry, archers, wagons, strings of horses, and women and children on foot were interspersed with the great elephants, which balked and had to be coaxed and prodded along.

The second day, the army's passage was complicated by rain and wind. Alexander had commanded that Roxanne wait until his army had secured the far side of the river and set up camp before she traversed the floating road. Most of her ladies had already gone ahead to make preparations for her welfare, while she remained in the care of Bondoor and her personal guard.

Roxanne missed Wolf's company. With Alexander's permission, Oxyartes had sent her personal bodyguard with an urgent message to the Bactrian governor. A simmering rebellion there would soon damp down once the patriots received news that Roxanne was well and with child. Her babe would be born heir to the throne of Bactria and Sogdiana.

Meanwhile, under Bondoor's vigilance, she enjoyed the

freedom to ride among the common soldiers and their women. Soldiers' wives, too shy to approach royalty, would exchange gossip with a plainly garbed Sogdian noblewoman. With her hair modestly braided and hidden by a scarf, Roxanne could admire fat-cheeked babes and ask advice about her coming infant from experienced mothers.

The child in her womb had begun to stir, and she felt herself consumed by the miracle of life. Alexander was right—being pregnant made her softer, more fragile emotionally. She felt a fierce protectiveness for her babe and wished with all her heart she were safe in her mountain kingdom instead of here in this foreign land with its unfamiliar customs.

"Lady! Lady!"

Roxanne turned to see a small boy with tangled blond hair dashing toward her. Heedless of the weather, five-year-old Jem, son of a laundrywoman and only the Wise God knew who else, wore nothing but a filthy loincloth and overlarge sandals tied together with bits of twine.

"What have you got for me?" He held out a grimy paw.

"Where have you been?" she demanded. "What makes you think you deserve anything but a switching? You haven't been at lessons for weeks."

Dark eyes, nearly hidden by the mop of shaggy hair, narrowed, and he studied the big toe on his left foot. "Don't need no damned reading," he mumbled in coarse Greek. "Gonna be a soldier."

"Even soldiers need to know how to read. And to mind their tongues around the king's lady." She dug a sugared plum from her saddle pack. "You show up tomorrow morning—or else!"

Grinning, Jem snatched the sweet and darted away, dodging the wheels of a cart and snatching a melon from a basket as he ran. "Stop, thief!" the Persian drover shouted.

Roxanne couldn't hide her amusement. Jem would sell the melon to the first soldier with a coin in his pouch. Neither he nor his sluttish mother had any desire to better themselves. Jem rarely appeared at the school she'd established for the children of the camp followers, and the clothing she purchased for him was always gone the next day.

Roxanne shook her head. As her father had often said, "The boy is born to hang as a bandit." Perhaps Oxyartes was right, but she was fond of the little rascal, all the same.

A line of elephants, including Tuma, Roxanne's personal beast, lumbered past. The cow's small eyes glared, and she huffed and swung her great trunk from side to side in annoyance as she neared the bridge. When she balked, Tuma's Indian handler first cursed and prodded, and then pleaded with the stubborn animal. Finally, after great confusion and a heated exchange of temper between soldiers and mahouts, a nudge from the elephant directly behind Tuma broke the impasse. She trudged onto the bridge and the column of men and elephants moved forward.

Roxanne was glad to be crossing on foot and not riding in the swaying howdah. She was certain that the double motion of the bridge and the elephant would have been more than her stomach could take.

Abruptly, just ahead of Roxanne, an axle snapped, and a cart dumped passengers and supplies in front of a line of bullocks. Horses shied sideways, drovers shouted, and women cursed. One of the last elephants to file onto the bridge raised her trunk and trumpeted, sending a green-broke gelding galloping through the chaos.

Roxanne held tight to her pony's reins and spoke soothingly to him. Her pavilion would be erected on the far side by the time she got there, and she was looking forward to dry clothes and a hot meal.

Soldiers heaved the cart aside and started the procession again. After what seemed an eternity, Roxanne's turn came. She dismounted, wrapped a scarf around her pony's head so that he couldn't see the water, and led him onto the river roadway.

The bridge showed evidence of the multitude that had already crossed. Engineers had directed workmen to drop bundles of reeds to fill in gaps and tie additional lines to hold the boats securely together. The matted path was uneven and muddy, the footing not unlike that of soggy marshland. Although the roadway was obviously strong enough to hold the weight of elephants, Roxanne was certain she'd feel easier once she set foot on solid land again.

She glanced over the side at the churning brown tide. Bits of flotsam, including a dead cow, banged against the row of boats upstream. Clouds closed in, and the rain began in sheets, cutting vision to a minimum. Roxanne's pony plodded on, ears pressed against his head, ignoring the downpour.

Light cavalry rode back and forth on the artificial roadway, keeping order. Kayan was assigned to just such duty, and midway on the bridge, Roxanne had the opportunity to speak with him. When her cousin dismounted to walk beside her, Roxanne glanced back meaningfully at Bondoor. He nodded, slowing his step and that of her guardsmen so that she and Kayan could exchange words in relative privacy.

"You've done well with the Flying Devils," she said. "I told Alexander you would."

"Does Bondoor suit you?" Kayan was lean and tanned from long days in the saddle. His hawk face was inscrutable, revealing none of the good humor she knew he possessed.

"Yes," she replied. "I like him. He wishes to wed one of my ladies. Parvona."

"Give her a rich dowry. Bondoor's family lost their wealth in the war."

Roxanne nodded. "I will." She hesitated, and then said, "I miss you."

"It's better that we are apart."

His manner was so reserved that she winced. "Don't make this harder. You know how I feel about you . . . how I've always felt."

"Do I?" Kayan looked into her face, his almond-shaped eyes full of anguish. "Do you know? You are wed to another man. You carry his child and go to his bed . . . not unwillingly. From this, I am to understand the great passion you feel for me?"

"You know why I married Alexander." Shakily she smiled, wishing to give any who saw them the idea that she was idly trading family gossip with her kinsman. "But I made a vow of faithfulness at my wedding. I am a princess of Sogdiana. I

JUDITH E. FRENCH

cannot make a cuckold of my husband. Not for *his* honor, but for yours and mine."

"This small man—this yellow-haired barbarian—slayer of our people, burner of our cities, holds what should be mine!"

"Keep your voice down."

"Can you deny you care for him?"

She summoned courage. "I've never lied to you."

"By Ormazd, this playacting we do is the greatest lie."

Roxanne glanced away, ignoring the needles of soaking rain. "Let me finish. I would be lying if I told you that I perform a wife's duty against my will. Is that love? I don't know. But this much I am sure of: What I feel for Alexander is different from what I feel for you. It takes away nothing from my love for you." She began to shiver, despite the heat.

"You don't have to stay with him. We could turn back across this cursed river, flee to the mountains. They'd not miss us for hours."

"Just ride away? You think it so easy?"

"Bondoor and your guards are loyal to you. Once we reached the hills, Alexander's men would never find us."

"And where would we go? Home to Sogdiana?"

"Anywhere," he said. "With you beside me, I'd be happy herding sheep or—"

"Trade honor to live a life hiding like criminals? Don't you know Alexander would level the Hindu Kush to get me back?"

"We could bribe someone to say you drowned in the Indus."

"Both of us? Not unless he places the coins on my dead eyelids with his own hands would he believe." She shook her head. "You don't know him, Kayan. I carry his heir. He'll never let me go."

"I'd accept your child as my own."

"If I agreed—if we did escape, we'd only come to hate each other. You're no sheepherder. You were born to be a soldier and I a queen."

Kayan shook his head. "I can't accept that."

"You must. It is our fate to make this sacrifice."

It took all of his strength not to pull her into his arms. How

162

could he give her up after all their plans and hopes? Somehow deep in his gut, he'd always felt that there was something about Roxanne that set her apart from other women.

He swallowed and gazed at her. Wet from the wind-driven rain, her hair hanging in strings and without weapon or crown, his little cousin was indeed a queen, and the soldier in him saluted her.

She'd been a daredevil from the day she could walk. Once, when they were hunting wolves, she'd crawled into a bear's den to steal a cub. He'd had to risk his own neck fending off three hundred pounds of raging sow while Roxanne scrambled up a tree. It had taken her father and a score of soldiers to rescue her, and they'd both been whipped soundly. Undaunted, she'd taken her punishment without a whimper and made plans for months to go back and find—

Her voice cut through his memories. "You'll see Sogdiana again, Kayan. You and Lilya will grow fat with dozens of grandchildren—"

"Like as not, you and I will sicken and die of pestilence here in India."

"I'm serious." She reached out to take his arm, and then pulled her hand back self-consciously. "I'm not the only one who is married."

"Lilya?" He scoffed. "I sent her back to Maracanda."

"That was not wise."

"I was ordered to *wed* the lady, not to live with her."

"She may be a simple woman, but Lilya is without malice. And she's wealthy."

He glared at her. "Think you I care for her gold? Lilya is better suited to quiet gardens and lazy afternoons than traveling with an army. In Maracanda, she has the protection of my name and the freedom to do as she chooses."

"I should have picked a clever wife for you."

"I want but one. You."

"Hush. Such talk could see us both crucified."

"You fear Alexander so, and yet you love him?"

She shook her head. "Love is not as simple as the poets make it in their rhymes. And I'm not afraid of what he might

163

do to me, only to those I love . . . you, my father . . . my country."

"Say the word and I'll kill him for you."

She shook her head. "The only thing worse than a live conqueror is a dead one. Alexander is both our tormentor and our salvation. Leave him to the justice of the Wise God."

"You would protect him. Admit it."

"No more, I beg you. I'm torn apart. You are the only constant in my life. If you turn against me, I'm lost."

"Never," he vowed. "I am yours, little cousin, until death."

"You must not speak so. You'll put your neck—"

"Captain!" An aide rode toward them, shielding his eyes from the blowing rain.

"Captain! We need you!" the soldier shouted. "On the approach to the bridge. Xoni is threatening to carve a drover from chin to heel."

"I'm coming." Kayan swung up onto his horse and turned to Roxanne before riding off to settle the dispute. "The Wise God be with you, Princess."

"And you," she answered. "Always."

Strange thoughts tumbled through her mind as she watched Kayan thread his way back through the plodding procession. Would she regret not running away with him? Would Alexander care if she vanished? Her wet clothes weighed her down, and she was suddenly weary. If she did disappear, she mused, how long would her husband wait before taking another wife? Would it be the Persian princess, Barsine, the daughter of Darius, or some Greek noblewoman? And if the child she carried under her heart was a daughter instead of a son, would Alexander take a second wife to increase his chances of producing an heir?

The questions troubled her as she reached the far bank of the Indus, pulled off the pony's blindfold, and led him through the ankle-deep mud and slime toward her pavilion.

Alexander joined her within the hour. She'd barely had time to bathe and change into dry clothing when he appeared in the entranceway to her inner chamber.

"You look terrible," she said, offering him a length of cloth to dry his face. "Will you eat—"

"No." He shook his head impatiently. "I wanted to see if you'd arrived safely. I'm leaving a company of my finest infantry to support your personal guard. My scouts have brought word of a large force of Indian cavalry, including units of war elephants, drawn up on a rise less than two miles away."

She took cold meat from a tray and pressed it into his hand. "You can eat this as you ride. Even Herakles took sustenance."

"Leave off, woman," he said gruffly. "I've called the general alarm. The men are forming into their divisions. Would you have me stuffing my mouth with cheese like a goatherd while I lead the charge?"

She handed him a cup of watered wine. "Better that than have some Indian swordsman cleave you in two because you're too weak to defend yourself."

He fixed her with a steely gaze as he gulped the wine. "You should live to see that day."

"Eat and I will cease to nag you." She threw a dry cloak around his shoulders. "It is kind of you to think of my welfare when—"

"Remember what happened when the High King of Persia left his royal camp unprotected?" Alexander clenched his right fist. "Nothing stood between my troops and his greatest treasures. I could have captured Darius's household and wealth single-handed." He glanced down at the meat in his left hand, took a bite, and tucked the remainder into a pouch on his belt. "You're turning into a shrew, Roxanne. If I wasn't in a hurry, I'd—"

Hephaestion burst into the chamber. "It's King Ambhi of Taxila."

"You're certain?" Alexander asked.

Roxanne drew on a robe.

"Positive." Hephaestion took Alexander's goblet from his hand and drained it. "Two scouts saw his standard." He glanced toward the platters of food. "Bring me some of that," he said to Roxanne. "I haven't eaten since daybreak."

She rolled bread, meat, and dates in a cloth and handed it

to him. Without comment, he added a joint of lamb to the bundle.

"Get Perdiccas and a company of Companions," Alexander ordered. "We'll ride out and see what kind of reception this Ambhi means to offer us."

"No envoys?" Roxanne asked.

"Tend to your sewing," Hephaestion said. "He has no time to placate you now."

She stiffened. "Will you tell your king what he may and may not say to his wife in her chamber?"

"Stop it," Alexander admonished. "The two of you are worse than fighting cocks." He took hold of Roxanne's shoulders and kissed her soundly. "Too late for envoys, my dove."

"Be careful," she warned.

Hephaestion shrugged. "Don't count on it. If he is, it will be the first time."

Roxanne's eyes narrowed as she heard their footfalls fade away. If they believed she would remain in this tent like an obedient slave while Alexander faced Ambhi's army, they were greatly mistaken. Minutes later, she sneaked from her tent in the guise of a fat washer-woman and pondered how she would steal a horse.

Rumors spread like wildfire through the army and filtered through to the camp. "The Taxila king's forces have murdered Alexander's envoys!" . . . "Two hundred thousand Indians are about to attack!" . . . "King Ambhi's charge is led by three thousand war elephants!"

Rumors or no rumors, the years of strict military discipline in Alexander's army prevailed. Regiments fell into rank; phalanx commanders readied their units. No one supposed that Alexander would do anything but fight, and where he led, the army would follow.

Companions dressed in their finest uniforms. Hephaestion laughed when the grooms led Bucephalus forth. The stallion wore steel armor, overlaid with thin sheets of pure gold, to match the gold of Alexander's red-crested battle helmet. "You may not prove you're immortal," Hephaestion said wryly, "but at least King Ambhi will know you're rich."

The clouds parted and a pale sun peeked out, bathing the plain in soft light. Green fields stretched on either side of the road as far as the eye could see. The city of Taxila lay only a short distance away, a metropolis of trade and learning. Alexander had hoped he would not have to do battle with King Ambhi. If he could take the city peacefully, it would be a tremendous psychological advantage, sending a potent message to both his own followers and to the hostile country ahead.

Alexander, Hephaestion, and the Companions urged their warhorses into a slow canter, weapons ready but not yet drawn. The line of war elephants in front of them seemed without number. Alexander tried to estimate the opponent's cavalry units and foot archers.

"Artemis protect us!" Hephaestion grinned. "We're in for it this time."

They reined in their mounts, and Alexander motioned a herald to ride forward to meet the Indian messengers. There was a brief exchange before one of the Indians turned back to King Ambhi's forces. Tension mounted. Bucephalus arched his neck and pranced restlessly. Alexander sat motionless.

Suddenly, in a single motion, the line of war elephants dropped to their knees. The Macedonian herald galloped back to the king. "Lord Alexander!" the messenger shouted. "King Ambhi welcomes you to his city! They've not come to fight but to honor you!" He saluted. "That's Ambhi himself on that big tusker in the center."

The Companions moved forward slowly, and the Indian king advanced with a small group of cavalry. The bejeweled elephant lumbered toward them, and they could make out the waving figure of a delicate youth in splendid attire. "Greetings, Great King Alexander," the young monarch called out in badly accented Greek. "Welcome to Taxila."

Alexander grinned and nodded regally in response. Taxila had fallen into his fist like a ripe nut.

*   *   *

An hour later, Alexander stood in the center of his wife's tent, eyes blazing. "Where is she?" he demanded. "The king of Taxila dines with me within the hour, and you dare to tell me that the Princess Roxanne is missing? Find here! Find her at once," he roared. "Or heads shall roll!"

The High King's meeting with the Indian king was both as brief as diplomatically proper and amiable, considering Alexander's anger over his wife's absence. Ambhi placed Taxila entirely at his disposal. King Ambhi would continue to rule the province with Alexander as overlord. Money and Indian troops would be forthcoming. It was a total victory for Alexander, and equally rewarding for the boy king, Ambhi. Alexander's army would take possession of Taxila the following day, there to rest and make ready for the invasion of India proper.

Ptolemy was waiting a few paces from the pavilion. "She's safe," he said quietly to Alexander. "They found her near camp with her cousin. She was mounted on a good horse and disguised as a boy."

Chapter Fourteen

"I told you to remain in your pavilion. Where have you been?" White-lipped with rage, Alexander dragged Roxanne into his tent, amid the gaping astonishment of his troops. "Speak, or I shall have that treacherous cousin of yours skinned alive!" He pushed her roughly onto a camp stool and glared at her.

"Don't threaten me, you Macedonian barbarian!" she flung back at him. "I'm not afraid of you!" In truth, she was, but she'd suffer torture by fire and sword rather than admit it.

"You should be frightened. Any other husband would beat you—"

"Strike if you dare, but beware my sting." Swiftly she drew a curved Indian short-sword from the jeweled sheath on her thigh. "You boast of your honor, but you don't know the meaning of the word."

"Hold your tongue, woman," he said. "Do you want the whole camp to hear you? It's bad enough they saw me hunting for you."

"You didn't care if they saw you drag me in here as though I'd committed a crime."

"You were discovered in men's clothing. In Kayan's company. Were you running away with him?"

"Would we be riding toward camp if I was trying to escape?"

"I told you to stay in your tent."

"I heard rumors that you'd been attacked by three thousand war elephants. That you'd all been slaughtered. If it was true, how safe would I have been in camp? Do you think a company of your foot soldiers could have held off an elephant charge?"

"How did you get past my infantrymen without being seen?"

"That's not important." No need to tell him that she'd bribed a laundry woman, hidden her face and hair with veils to make her escape, or that she'd stolen a horse from under a sentry's nose and men's clothing from a wash line. And no need to tell him how her fear for him had made it impossible to stay hidden away . . . waiting to hear.

"If I can't trust my infantry to guard one woman . . . I'll have the skin off their backs!"

"It wasn't their fault. If anyone is to be whipped for disobeying your commands, let it be me."

"Have I struck you? Have I put a single bruise on your soft skin?"

"You've done worse. You've insulted my honor."

"Your honor? What of my honor when I catch you with that damned Kayan?"

"My cousin was with the cavalry. He found me halfway back to camp and insisted that he escort me to my pavilion to ensure my safety. I didn't lay eyes on him until after your confrontation with King Ambhi."

"What am I to think? I ride straight to your pavilion to tell you about Ambhi's surrender, and your women tell me that you're sleeping. When I go to wake you, I find nothing but pillows heaped under a spread. What childish game is this?"

"An act you drive me to by treating me more like a possession than a wife."

Alexander swore foully. "A wife. You've never acted like a wife. And give me that sword. I warned you about ever drawing a blade against me again."

"Through your Greek heart!" Murder lurked in his eyes. Such rage was caused by something far more than this night's escapade, she sensed. She leaped off the stool and put her back against a center tent post. "You'll not bully me. By Ormazd's blood, I swear it."

He advanced on her. "I've never hit a woman, but I swear—"

"If you strike, strike hard. For if you do not kill me, I shall kill you," she vowed, lapsing into her native tongue. "You are the father of this babe and the only man to know me. Believe what you will! A Greek would not know the truth if he uttered it."

Alexander made a lunge for her weapon, and her sword sliced the air. He twisted sideways, and the blade cut through his tunic and laid a thin scarlet thread across his chest. He swore and jumped out of reach of her blade.

"You call me a hill savage, Macedonian! Come closer, and I'll prove whether or not you're immortal."

"You're overwrought, Roxanne."

'You swore that you loved me," she reasoned softly. "You cannot love me and trust me so little. I hold my honor dearer than my life."

The deadly fires in his eyes receded to a smoldering glow. "Swear by your one god that you have not betrayed me with any man."

"By all the Defenders of the Light, I do swear."

For long seconds he hesitated before nodding. "Then I have wronged you." He exhaled slowly. "Put down your weapon. You're safe from me." He lowered his arms to his sides and moved into her killing rage. "Strike if you will, Roxanne. I will not defend my life from my own wife."

She hesitated, muscles tensed, watching Alexander's eyes as her Chin sword master, Shu-sai-chong, had taught her. *Watch the eyes of your opponent. Mind reacts before muscle.* Gooseflesh prickled on the nape of her neck as she wondered if she could trust him or if this was a ruse to get past her guard.

"You were telling the truth," Alexander said. "Before . . . when you said no Scythian took what was mine."

The air between them lost some of its tension, like a taut bowstring relaxed. "So this is the source of your rage? It isn't my sneaking out to see what was happening tonight that troubles you so much. It is what might have happened to me when I was captive of the Scythians. Admit it."

"I admit nothing."

"If I'd been raped, I would have told you. Among my people, there is no shame for a brutalized woman. Is a river polluted because a trespasser drinks of the water? If a crime is committed, who is at fault—the evildoer or the victim?"

"Don't try to tell me that you don't love Kayan."

"He is my kinsman. Is it so wrong to have feelings for those of your own blood? I love my father. Do you find fault in that?"

Alexander grimaced. "It's an admirable trait, but not one I can share. Philip of Macedon, my own father, commanded respect and fear, but never love."

She swallowed, attempting to ease the constriction in her throat. Suddenly the tent felt overly warm. "Kayan is innocent of any wrongdoing—as I am. I couldn't stand being locked up like a prisoner so I went to see what was happening. I was afraid for your—"

"Alexander!" Hephaestion burst into the tent. "The Asian troops are massing in rebellion. Oxyartes leads—"

"They think I'm in danger." Roxanne sheathed her sword. "Let me show my face and—"

"By the gods! I'll finish this traitorous bitch!" Hephaestion grabbed Alexander's short hunting spear and drew back his arm to run her through.

"No!" Alexander leaped between her and his friend. "This is between me and my wife. Harm her at peril of your life."

"And let this Sogdian sorceress cuckold you and bring down your army?"

"Out of my tent," Alexander said in a voice so low it was a grating whisper. "For the love I bear you, I will forget you ever uttered those words. Roxanne carries my son in her belly. None other's. What passes between us here is a love game. No place for you. Now leave, before I lose my temper."

Swearing, Hephaestion backed through the tent opening, Alexander's lance still gripped in his hand.

Trembling, Roxanne sank to her knees on the thick rug in

front of her husband. "Why didn't you let him kill me?" she asked. "You would have been well rid of such a traitorous bitch." She closed her eyes, as dizziness threatened to overcome her. "I am weary, my lord. Do what you will."

He raised her to her feet and enfolded her in the safety of his arms. "What am I to do with you?"

Her tremors became shudders as she began to sob. "Hush, hush," he crooned. "You are exhausted. You will do harm to yourself and our child."

"Why can't there be peace between us?"

"I don't know. Maybe the lessons I learned at my mother's feet made me wary of believing in a woman's honor." When she didn't answer, he said, "I have been accused of murdering my father, but I'm innocent of that crime. I've often wondered if she did it."

"I'm not Olympias."

"No, you're not." He carried her to the couch, laid her back against the pillows, and lifted a cup of wine to her lips. "Rest now."

"I can't," she said after taking a single sip of the strong drink. "I must show my father and his troops that I am unhurt."

"I've been half out of my mind with worry. What was I supposed to think?" He shook his head. "Do you seek out trouble, woman, or does it seek you?" He traced her right eyebrow lightly with the tip of his index finger. "Would you have killed me?"

She sighed. "I don't know. Perhaps."

"Hephaestion swears you will poison me or cut my throat while we sleep."

"Don't suppose I haven't thought of it."

Alexander laughed. "Come, we will both go out and do our duty. You must show your admirers that I haven't murdered you, and I must try to convince Hephaestion that he isn't High King.

"And as soon as your father and his savages are satisfied that you are unharmed, you are to return to your pavilion and go to bed. I'll join you tonight."

She touched his forearm. "Why do you believe me now

when you didn't earlier? About the Scythians?"

He tilted his head slightly to one side and regarded her with a half smile. "Because you didn't beg for forgiveness. You got angry. If you'd been lying, you would have tried to save yourself."

"And would you have shown me mercy?"

"Do you think me a monster? I would have no Scythian's brat inherit my throne. But I wouldn't have blamed you."

"But if I gave birth to a child of rape? What would you have done to that innocent babe?"

"Some questions are better not asked," he replied. "And not answered."

Once Roxanne had assured her father that all was forgiven between her and Alexander and that Kayan would not suffer for her mischief, she obeyed her husband and went to her tent. She lay down and fell into a deep sleep that lasted through the afternoon and night. When she opened her eyes in the morning, Alexander was stretched out beside her, his eyes full of concern. "Are you rested? Would you like something to eat?"

"Yes, and yes, my lord."

"Say nothing to remind me of yesterday," he said firmly. "Today I will spend the entire day with you. I will show you my new city, Taxila. You will meet the king and tour the market. The native craftsmen do magnificent metalwork in this region."

"Did you keep your word about Kayan?"

"His skin is whole and on his back. I've promoted him and sent him to action in the passes. The bandits near Massaga have come out of hiding, and the Flying Devils are well suited to deal with them."

"Thank you. You will not regret it."

"I hope not."

She stretched and threw aside the coverlet. He kissed her bare shoulder and stroked her rounded belly. "You are more beautiful now than the first day I set eyes on you," he said.

Her braids had come undone and her hair lay in tangled

waves over her breasts and shoulders. "And I suppose I will be just as lovely when I'm swollen with child like a full wineskin." Alexander kissed her stomach. "You are the most outrageous man I have ever known," she protested as he kissed his way down her hip and bare thigh.

"Lie still and be ravished. I am the conqueror today, and you are a helpless maiden at my mercy."

She chuckled. "I was promised cities and palaces and shopping stalls, and instead I am to be assaulted by a yellow-haired Greek?" He nibbled at her knee and then retraced his path with greater fervor, brushing warm lips across her belly to linger at her breasts, teasing first one and then the other with his lips and tongue.

She groaned with pleasure. "Am I to be tortured as well?"

"I can see that you are a wench who must be bribed," he said, leaning on one elbow. "I happen to have a few trinkets that I'm willing to trade for your favors."

From under the pillow, he produced a delicate gold chain set with rubies and two heavy gold bracelets of Egyptian styling, exquisitely wrought in the shape of curling asps with emerald eyes. "These go on so and so." He slipped the priceless jewelry on her wrists and linked them with the golden chain.

"Not snakes," she teased. "First elephants and now snakes. I am terrified of snakes."

"Now you are truly my captive and must submit to my Macedonian perversions." He kissed her mouth. "Don't struggle so, you'll break them. I could hire a hundred Indian bowmen for a year on what the chain alone cost." The golden links snapped, and a ruby the size of Roxanne's thumbnail rolled across the carpet. She locked her arms around his neck.

"You are mad, Alexander of Macedon; outrageously insane." Her body arched against his, and she returned his kiss. They did not call for food until the sun was midway overhead.

The afternoon they spent in Taxila as Alexander had promised. Roxanne loved the ancient market with its rutted winding streets and stalls of silks and spices, jewelry, and wares of every kind. Snake charmers sat cross-legged, playing strange melodies, while cobras swayed hypnotically before the onlookers. Magicians demonstrated feats of magic, and peddlers hawked trays of pastries and fanciful sweets of spun sugar. Roxanne munched a cone of sugared flower petals and coaxed a pair of emerald earrings from her husband.

"You are too expensive," Alexander grumbled good-naturedly. "I should have left you in Sogdiana."

"I warned you," she reminded him, tossing a candied date to a monkey on a leash. "Oh, look, isn't he precious?" The monkey doffed his feathered hat and danced a jig. "He looks like Perdiccas when he's had too much wine."

"No monkeys! Don't even ask."

In the palace, Roxanne was introduced to the young king, and then went into the inner court to meet his many wives and consorts. She sat on cushions beside a blue-tiled fish pond and played with the lovely dark-eyed children, listening to soft sitar music and chatting with the women. They looked to her like so many exotic birds in their bright gowns and sparkling jewels. Still, Roxanne was glad when Alexander summoned her away. Despite the quiet luxury, she felt stifled there, hemmed in. It was not the life for her. In such a golden cage, her soul would wither.

In Taxila were many holy men, self-named philosophers who spent their lives in prayer, contemplating the mysteries of the universe. One of these scholars, Calanus, accepted Alexander's offer to travel with his army. As always, Alexander was fascinated with new religions and was glad to add another philosopher to his retinue.

All too soon, the army's pleasant stay at Taxila came to an end. Messengers brought word that the armies of King Porus were forming beyond the Jhelum River to repulse the invaders. Alexander, supported by the new troops from Taxila and her subject cities, readied his men to march. "King Porus will never surrender," King Ambhi warned. "He is an old enemy of my late father and a veteran of many battles. He won his throne by force."

"I wager he's not faced an army such as mine," Alexander

said. King Ambhi was riding with Alexander's troops in his first action, nervous but eager to take part in battle.

"The Jhelum is swollen by spring rains. It is a mighty river."

"We'll cross it."

Spurred on by Alexander's promise of vast wealth, the army moved swiftly over the flatlands toward the Jhelum. Steady reports kept them informed on the strength of King Porus's army. "A riverbank is not a good battle site for us," Roxanne worried. "Could we not march around and come at him from another side?"

"Too costly in time. His elephants will be our biggest concern. His cavalry wears only cloth armor. They're no match for mine. We have elephants, but crossing the rivers will be difficult, and my Macedonians are still not comfortable around them. The elephants terrify most of the horses." Alexander paced the tent. "You will keep out of the way this time, wife, if I have to have you bound hand and foot and sealed in a trunk. The only reason I won't leave you here in the women's court in Taxila is that you'll be safer with the army, where I can keep an eye on you. Who knows what mischief you'd be up to if I abandoned you to your own devices?"

She had chosen garments of pale green today, an embroidered silk tunic and trousers the color of new leaves, a perfect foil for her hair. "I told you what to do with the elephants."

He scoffed. "Mice."

"You know I was not serious. Instruct your men to fire at the elephants' trunks. The beasts become uncontrollable if they are in pain."

"Uncontrollable is the key word, little Sogdian. My soldiers do not fancy being trampled into jelly. They would prefer to avoid rampaging war elephants. Porus also has companies of chariots. On the flat plain, they could be used to advantage."

"But not against you," Roxanne replied. "My father told me what your Macedonians did to Darius's scythed chariots at Gaugamela." Alexander grinned boyishly, and, encouraged, she continued. "You outmaneuvered them."

"We did," he said. "They were useless."

"So we are agreed, you need not worry about Porus's chariots." She massaged the tight muscles at the back of his neck. "What says your new holy man, Calanus?"

"He predicts that it will rain harder."

Roxanne laughed and called her ladies to bring food for the High King. If she didn't see to it that he ate, he would go without. Her husband was a man who thrived on hardships. Thirst, hunger, and fatigue did not seem to affect him as they did other men.

"My soldiers fight as well in wet as in dry weather," Alexander boasted. "Snow or desert heat—they are magnificent."

"How could they do less, my lord, with you to lead them?"

Roxanne did not care for the rains of India. Regardless of what Alexander said, mud slowed the army's progress, and the downpours made it impossible to find dry firewood for the cooking fires. The horses' hooves softened and had to be inspected daily for rot. Only the elephants seemed to like the rain, and then only when it wasn't blowing into their faces. Reluctantly, Roxanne was again riding in the howdah on the lumbering Tuma. If she was uncomfortable, at least she and Soraya were dry.

When the army reached the Jhelum, Hephaestion ordered the camp to be set up well away from the swiftly running river. Drovers brought supplies from surrounding areas, and soldiers were put to work erecting stockades for the animals. Roxanne could see King Porus's troops amassing on the far side. Companies of elephants and mounted archers patrolled the river banks. Earlier, Alexander had spread the word among his men that they would be camping here until fall. His excuse was that the change of season would shrink the river and make crossing easier.

From the first day of their arrival, Alexander ordered heavy cavalry and Sogdian archers to ride back and forth on this side of the river, to venture into the stream yelling battle cries, and to do all they could to create confusion and concern among the Indian defenders. The Companions sent archers in boats floating down the river, always keeping just out of arrow shot of the enemy. Their mission was to fire missiles at King

Porus's war elephants. Even the elephants of Alexander's legions were not spared by their handlers, who rode them over and over again in formation to the river, as though attack were imminent.

Alexander commanded that this psychological assault continue through the nights. Regiments marched to the cadence of drums and trumpets. Officers ordered soldiers to build bonfires, and horsemen to carry torches as they galloped up and down the riverbank.

The steady harassment went on for several weeks while Alexander and his trusted inner circle of Companions planned their battle strategy. Roxanne's nerves were raw. It was near impossible to sleep in the constant state of readiness for war. And through it all, the rains fell without respite.

King Ambhi came often with Alexander to Roxanne's pavilion, where they shared her evening meal. Conversation remained general. Alexander confided his plans for confronting King Porus to no one but Hephaestion, Perdiccas, and Ptolemy. Roxanne could see that young Ambhi was somewhat miffed at being shut out of Alexander's confidence, but of that the Indian monarch dared not complain.

"King Porus's position is invincible," Ambhi observed for the third or fourth time that evening. "Even if we wait until the dry season, you cannot move cavalry across the river in the face of war elephants. Each elephant carries six or more master archers. The Jhelum will run red with our blood. Do you think to cross on the bodies of our own men?"

"It is true," Roxanne said quietly. "Indian archers are a force to be reckoned with. Your own foot archers, King Ambhi, are magnificent." The Indian bows were much larger than Sogdian or even Scythian weapons. Indian bows were as tall as a man, the arrows more than four feet in length and shot from a sitting position. Even Greek armor could not protect a soldier from such deadly missiles.

Ambhi's mouth opened and closed, fishlike, and his pale, pimpled complexion flushed. He had not lost his astonishment at having her present at meals, and whenever she ventured an opinion, he looked as surprised as if Alexander's

Bucephalus had suddenly begun to spout Sanskrit. The king made a point never to address her directly, speaking instead to Alexander or one of the Companions.

"Our position is hopeless," Ambhi said, casting his small, nearsighted eyes toward the roof of the tent. "Quite hopeless."

Roxanne waved away the Greek servants and poured wine for Alexander and Ambhi. Alexander smiled and sipped in silence while the Indian continued to talk of the excellence of King Porus's cavalry.

"You have not seen my husband's army in battle," Roxanne said politely. "They are the best the world has ever seen."

Alexander nodded. "If you prefer to return to the safety of your own city walls, King Ambhi, I—"

"No, Your Majesty." Ambhi's sallow skin took on an even more yellow hue. "I am no coward. It is the waiting . . . and . . . and the rain."

Alexander's smile became a disarming grin. "Calanus tells me that India will teach me patience." Roxanne doubted it, but felt this was not the time to express her opinion on her husband's faults.

After they finished the meal, Alexander and Ambhi played Pachisi until nearly midnight. Then the younger man bade them good night and left the pavilion.

"About time," Alexander said. "I have a meeting with Hephaestion and Ptolemy. They will be here within the hour."

"Here, milord? Not in your own tent?"

"This is better. Tomorrow we attack. I'm leaving Craterus in charge here. You know him. He's one of my most able generals. I'm taking Hephaestion, Ptolemy, and Perdiccas with our squadrons of Companions upriver about sixteen miles to an easier crossing. We ford the Jhelum tomorrow night and take Porus by surprise." He chuckled. "Perdiccas has such a mouth on him, we don't dare let him in on the strike until we're in the saddle."

"You won't tell Perdiccas what you're up to, yet you tell me?"

His smile widened. "Our fates are joined. You might lead a

rebellion of Bactrians and Sogdians against me, but you'd never betray me to the Indians."

She nodded. "It's true. Our fates are entwined. And the fate of the child I bear. You will lead the attack?" She put her arms around him and laid her head on his chest. "I would feel better if I could ride beside you as I did when we faced the Scythian charge."

"What? Do my ears deceive me? Love words from my Little Star?"

She sighed. "Whatever you say you will do, you will do, for this is the hour of your glory. But I have a woman's fears." She pulled him toward the curtained bed. "Lie with me, Alexander. Give me something sweet to think of tomorrow while I wait."

"Would that you could always ask a boon so easily given." He kissed her hungrily. "One thing I will tell you, Roxanne. Were you a man, I could choose no one better to ride beside me. Not even Hephaestion."

He drew her to the bed, not bothering to pull the curtains, and they coupled fiercely, united in desire and passion.

For long moments after, Roxanne lay in his arms, and then Alexander rose and drew on his tunic. "Stay there. Sleep if you can. We will need but a single lamp." He kissed her mouth tenderly. "Tomorrow will be long and the night longer, but I warn you, do not cross the river until I send for you. Do you understand? I will have no disobedience in this."

"Yes, my lord. I will await your command." She drew a sheet over her naked body. "But you must promise to tell me of the battle so that I can boast of you to our son."

At dawn, the first morning of sunshine in weeks, Alexander said his good-byes to his wife and mounted leisurely; giving no indication that today's routine would be any different from the day before. He rode back toward the horse pens and met with Hephaestion.

Together they led squadrons of Companions back along the road to Taxila for several miles. Then they turned upriver and rode hard for the spot where the Jhelum narrowed. Long before dusk, they were well hidden in the thick forest that lined the river. Alexander knew that there were enemy scouts on the far banks, but by the time Porus received word that they were crossing, it would be too late.

Through the early hours of the evening they waited, standing beside their mounts, talking in whispers. Alexander stroked old Ox Head's neck and scratched the tender places on his belly. The black charger sniffed and rubbed his lips against his master's cheek. Alexander slipped him a sugared date, and the horse nibbled it daintily.

"It's time you retired Bucephalus," Perdiccas advised.

"It would break his heart if I left him behind when I rode into battle."

Ptolemy laughed softly. "For an old man, Ox Head's still got what counts. Half the foals born this spring were black as Hades."

"No wonder. Alexander reserves every choice mare for that stallion," Hephaestion said. "Bucephalus is in more danger of collapsing in the breeding pen than in battle."

They laughed and joked, swapping boyhood stories and tales until the weather turned and thunder rumbled in the distance. "We're in for a bad one," Hephaestion warned.

"We've crossed rivers in storms before." Alexander moved among his officers, giving last-minute instructions. Fording a flooding river in darkness was never easy, but he soothed them by saying, "Surprise gives us the edge we need."

Lightning struck a tree less than a mile away, and Hephaestion laughed above the pounding rain. "Alexander's relatives are lighting the way for us." Hephaestion swung up onto his tall bay and moved into position at the head of his regiment. Ptolemy and Perdiccas did the same, and Alexander led them through the trees toward the river crossing.

The fast-rushing water quickly rose to Bucephalus's withers, but the sand beneath his hooves was solid, and he plunged forward faithfully. The scent of battle was in the black's nostrils, and the years seemed to fall away from the old horse. Alexander spoke to him reassuringly.

The far bank was a line of faint trees illuminated by flashes of lightning. Rain fell in deafening torrents, muffling the sound of his army. Alexander drew his sword as Bucephalus neared the river's edge and climbed the muddy bank. The trees swayed before the fury of the storm, but no enemy troops barred their way. Alexander grinned. Porus's scouts were lax on such a night, and it would cost him a kingdom.

Chapter Fifteen

As night approached, Roxanne went to her father's tent and told him of Alexander's plan, as she had been instructed. Oxyartes was to take designated regiments of Sogdian and Bactrian light cavalry downriver a few miles and cross there once the fighting began. Craterus would wait with infantry and elephant corps on this side, ready to ford the river if Alexander sent word. Her husband had planned that most of the fighting would be done by his heavy cavalry, with special detachments of foot companions, using the dreaded phalanx to combat Porus's elephants. The foot soldiers would cross the Jhelum by boat downriver, form ranks, and march into battle once Alexander was firmly established on the other side.

"A large part of my lord's army will never see action unless the battle crosses the river," Roxanne said.

"He is wise. This will be no fight for men afoot," Oxyartes agreed. "My own informants tell me that King Porus's numbers are greater than ours. But troops are always exaggerated in war. You know what I think of depending on the elephant corps for a main line of striking power."

"Horses are always more reliable in battle," she said.

Oxyartes dressed quickly. "Kayan is back; his regiment will

ride with mine. I'll take the responsibility with Alexander. Better to have them on the far side of the Jhelum in the thick of things. There will be too many old enemies here." He looked at his daughter meaningfully. "What are his orders to you?"

"To remain in camp until he sends for me." Roxanne stepped behind a screen and donned her battle attire. "I can't obey."

"No, but after what happened when we faced King Ambhi, Alexander may not forgive your disobeying him again."

"I have the safety of my child to think of."

"I agree. To leave you here would be too dangerous. You have many enemies among the Persian faction, not to mention the Greek. The Council urged Alexander to take Barsine as wife only a week ago. Your pregnancy makes you even more of a threat to their ambitions."

Roxanne laced her high leather boots. "Greek deception is child's play compared to that of the Persian court."

"Take care. If you are lost, Bactria and Sogdiana are lost."

"No, not so long as you're alive." She grinned at him mischievously. "You can always take a young wife and sire a household of strong sons to inherit the throne."

"If it were that easy, I would have done it long ago." He shook his head. "Just because I've wanted no wife since your mother died doesn't mean that I've been celibate all these years. But no woman has quickened with my seed. There will be no sons of my line. Our hopes rest with you, Daughter. They always have."

Alexander's Companions crossed the Jhelum safely and rode hard toward the enemy position. When he discovered the trick, King Porus sent a force of heavy cavalry and chariots under the command of his son to engage and destroy the invading army. The two opposing groups met in the fury of the raging thunderstorm, fighting under terrible conditions.

In the blinding rain, the battle was quickly reduced to hand-to-hand combat with sword and spear. Regiments broke into swirling pockets of screaming horses, overturned chariots, and fleeing wounded soldiers. The heavy rain turned the plain to mud, chariot wheels bogged down, and the drivers and archers were slaughtered by the hundreds.

Alexander and a group of his best warriors drove through the strongest Indian cavalry charge, the heavier horses and armor of the Macedonians taking a terrible toll on their enemies. Verbal commands were useless before the earth-shattering bolts of lightning and rolling thunder. A direct strike on the chariot line blasted dozens and turned the battle into a rout. King Porus's son fell with mortal wounds and was lost in the terror of the night.

In the midst of the confusion, Bucephalus stumbled and went down on one knee, nearly throwing Alexander to the ground. The big horse recovered and charged again, trampling an archer underfoot. In the darkness and falling rain, it was impossible to register the magnitude of the destruction. The fighting stopped when the Macedonians realized they were alone on the field except for the dead and dying.

Alexander slid from Bucephalus's back. There was a bad gash along the black's hindquarters and at least two arrow wounds in his neck and side. The old horse was breathing heavily. Alexander laid his face against the warm neck and wept as the animal sank to the ground.

"Alexander!" Hephaestion rode up, leading a riderless charger. "Take this one. Philonicus won't need him any longer."

Alexander got to his feet and gave his Ox Head a last pat. Ordering an honor guard to stand watch over the dying horse, he leaped up on the new mount. "How bad are our losses?"

"Light. It was a slaughter. Porus is a fool."

"He's no fool. The gods turned against him. Come, we must hit him before he has time to reorganize."

As quickly as it had struck, the thunderstorm passed on, leaving only a softly falling rain and patches of fog. Alexander's Companions galloped along the road toward the main enemy encampment. The sun would soon be up, and they must take position before the balance of power shifted.

Oxyartes's forces met resistance on the far bank of the Jhelum, but the Sogdians poured ashore, battling fiercely. The thin ranks of the defenders broke, and Roxanne was able to cross without coming under direct fire. Bondoor and a half dozen of her guard were augmented by fifty of her father's best soldiers. "You are to stay clear of any action," Oxyartes ordered. She was wearing the garb of a Bactrian archer, and no one would notice the slim youth, so carefully protected by her outriders.

King Porus drew his defense lines on high ground, sacrificing valuable men to hold the river against the main body of Alexander's army. Porus's elephant corps took the center, with cavalry and foot soldiers ranked behind the elephants and heavy cavalry on both flanks.

The elephants looked invincible with padded armor, spiked harnesses, and master archers protected by howdahs on their backs. Trained to kill, the great beasts struck down the enemy with smashing feet and metal-tipped tusks. Even the sound of their trumpeting was unnerving to the opposing force. Porus himself was mounted on a great tusker in the center of the line.

Roxanne rode a chestnut gelding that her father assured her was unafraid of elephants. She was well armed, her bow and arrows slung over one shoulder and a lance tied across her saddle. Two swords, one straight and one curved, hung in scabbards at her waist. Still, she had no desire for an active part in the battle. She would defend herself if she must, but she was there mainly as an observer.

Alexander's troops lined up facing those of King Porus. Roxanne's heart chilled as she saw how few they were compared to the Indians. Even with the solid regiments of Shield Bearers on foot, armed with broadsword, heavy armor, and axe, she was afraid. No one could miss Alexander. He rode back and forth in plain view on a big gray charger. *Where is Bucephalus?* she wondered. Something had happened to him. She prayed it was not a bad omen.

Oxyartes's forces were well to the right, behind the squadrons of Perdiccas. The Shield Bearers were in the center with Alexander and several regiments of Companions in front of them, and Hephaestion and Ptolemy and their followers on the left.

With a mighty cacophony, the Indian line surged forward. Alexander's regiments wheeled left in mechanical precision, joined with those of Hephaestion and Ptolemy, and struck the Indian line on the far left flank. Perdiccas, Oxyartes, and their men galloped around the end of the Indian line to hit from the rear. Heavy armored infantry raised shields and met the elephant corps head on, slashing at the tuskers' trunks and legs with axes and swords.

The Indian cavalry on the right flank charged straight ahead, while the Sogdians raced to get beyond their line of attack. Roxanne's chestnut was swift of foot, and she had no trouble keeping up with the leaders. As they swung left, a regiment of Indians detached themselves from the main force and attempted to engage them. They were met with a rain of arrows from the Bactrian archers. Roxanne's warriors moved between her and the Indians, shielding her from the charge.

The battle stretched over three miles. It was hard for Roxanne to tell whether Alexander had succeeded in breaking through to hit Porus from the side and rear. Perdiccas's squadrons wheeled into position and attacked the main Indian force from the rear.

Roxanne drew her mount up on a rise. Kayan's Flying Devils were below and to her right, fighting fiercely. Perdiccas's heavy Macedonian cavalry was driving Indian foot soldiers forward into the elephant corps. Oxyartes took his Sogdians parallel to the Indian battle line, the light horses and riders striking hard and fast, circling and dividing the enemy. Bondoor held his post by Roxanne, despite his overwhelming desire to take part in the battle.

"Ride to Perdiccas," Roxanne demanded. "See if there is word of the king. I must know if Alexander is safe."

"I will send a man, Princess," Bondoor offered. "But your father will have me castrated if I leave your side for an instant."

The plain below dissolved into a mass of surging animals and men, making it impossible to tell friend from enemy. The rider galloped off, and Roxanne strained to see her father's elite guard of mounted archers.

Fog closed in around the rise, and Roxanne's vision was cut further by the rain. The sound of battle surrounded her: the clash of swords and spears, the cries of men and beasts. Suddenly a company of Indian cavalry appeared in the mist. Bondoor shouted an alarm and Roxanne's guard formed rank to face them. The fierce Indian horsemen with their heavy two-handed swords galloped toward the Sogdians. Roxanne split her soldiers, and they rose in opposite directions along the crest of the hill, firing arrows as they went.

With Bondoor and a man on either side, Roxanne retreated, leaving the hill to the heavy cavalry. Three Indians were dead and several wounded without a single casualty among the Sogdians. It was not easy to regroup her men on the plain below. "Ride toward Oxyartes," Roxanne ordered as the little band galloped toward the intense fighting.

Alexander's soldiers had split into three sections, trapping the Indians and hitting them from all sides. The elephant corps, Porus's greatest asset, took a terrible toll on the Shield Bearers, but the cost was dear to the Indian forces. Wounded elephants ran amuck, trampling Indians as well as Macedonians.

Perdiccas's regiments pushed the Indian foot soldiers in among the carnage, rendering them almost useless. Alexander, Ptolemy, and Hephaestion drove the Macedonian heavy cavalry through the ranks of Indian cavalry like a scythe through ripe wheat.

It was the elephants who turned the tide of battle. Maddened by blood and pain, exhausted and confused, they broke ranks and fled in all directions, leaving trails of carnage in their wake. When the cry went up that the elephant corps was disbanding, Indian cavalry units dissolved, and each petty chieftain sought to escape with his retainers.

Swept along by the pockets of fighting, Roxanne drew her sword and fought off fleeing Indian warriors. A spear nicked her horse's neck, and he reared and broke into a run. She lost track of Bondoor in the confusion. Suddenly her path was blocked by an injured elephant. She sawed at the reins. The chestnut fell back on his haunches, and the elephant struck at them with his truck. The blow caught Roxanne and knocked her senseless. She slipped from her mount, rolling beneath the feet of the massive tusker. Her horse struggled up and galloped away, reins trailing.

Cut off from his men and severely wounded, King Porus made a stand alone. His elephant had taken more than a dozen arrows; his mahout was near death. Alexander saw him and galloped up. Porus raised a javelin to throw, and Alexander wheeled out of range. "Ambhi!" he cried. The boy brought his horse to Alexander's side. "Speak to him. Tell him to surrender. He is too brave a man to die."

Cautiously King Ambhi rode forward and signaled to Porus for a truce. King Porus lowered the javelin, and they talked heatedly for a few minutes. Then Porus's elephant dropped to his knees.

Alexander and Ptolemy rode forward to accept the king's surrender. There was no hint of fear in the fierce dark face of Porus. He walked toward the Macedonians straight and proud, despite the arrow protruding from his chest, a man nearly seven feet tall.

"There is a king!" Alexander exclaimed and had Ambhi translate. "Assure him that he shall be treated as one." He commanded Ptolemy to see that King Porus's wounds were tended and that he was offered every courtesy.

Medical teams crossed the Jhelum to bind up the wounds of those able to survive, and to give the death thrust to those who could not. Soldiers rounded up prisoners and secured captured elephants. The sun broke through the clouds and shone on the blood-soaked plain. Already, vultures circled overhead.

A page lashed his foam-specked horse to where Alexander and Hephaestion had set up a command post. "Lord Alexander!" He dropped facedown on the grass. "Your Majesty, I come with an urgent message from General Craterus."

Hephaestion looked up. "What is it?"

"The Princess Roxanne! She's . . . she's dead."

Alexander stiffened, and his blue-gray eyes turned opal hard. "How?"

"I know not, Your Majesty. Only that she has been killed!"

"Dead . . . you are certain she is dead?"

Hephaestion laid a hand on Alexander's shoulder. "I'll go and learn the truth of the matter."

"I'll go myself."

Alexander crossed the Jhelum to the camp by boat. General Craterus waited on the far side. "I'm sorry, Alexander," he offered.

Craterus had never cared for the Sogdian woman, but she was the wife of his king. He was a soldier who held his tongue in matters that did not concern him. Although he'd not taken part in the battle against King Porus, he'd followed orders. Still, the High King did not look kindly on bearers of bad news. He pulled at his graying beard nervously.

Aides held horses for the king and General Craterus. They rode back to the encampment in silence. A large group of men milled before Roxanne's pavilion; they drew back respectfully as Alexander approached. "She's inside," Craterus said gruffly. Alexander waved him away and entered the tent alone.

The body lay on the curtained bed. Alexander approached and drew back the draperies. The Sogdian tunic was soaked with blood, a white hand mutilated by a sword stroke. He steeled himself to lift the silk that covered her face.

"Roxanne!" Soraya, her head wrapped in bloody bandages, ran to the side of the bed. She seized the cold, lifeless hand and raised it to her lips. "They would not let me see her. They told me Roxanne, her guards, and two of her women were slain in the attack. I have tended her since she was a child, and they would not let me come near her."

Alexander raised the woman to her feet and led her from the bed. "What happened?" he asked gently. In the lantern light, he could see that her temple and half her face were bloody and swollen.

"They came in the night when we were sleeping. There were horses and the sound of fighting. Her guards fell, pierced

191

with arrows. I never saw the raiders. They say it was King Porus's men . . . Indian soldiers, but I don't believe it. I know I heard men shouting in Greek. One of them clearly spoke her name. 'Make certain the Princess Roxanne is dead,' he said. I was in the other tent. A man hit me, and then I knew no more until . . . Oh, Lord Alexander." She wept. "She was as dear as any daughter to me, and they will not let me look on her. They say her face is shattered, but I don't care. I must see her."

"Sometimes it is better not to look."

"I love her," Soraya said simply. "I must."

"So must we both." Alexander turned back and lifted the silk, exposing the ravished face. "By the gods!" he swore. The woman was not Roxanne. The size and shape were close, the features crushed beyond recognition, but the woman's bloodied tresses were light brown, not auburn. "It is not Roxanne! Who is it?"

Soraya reached for the other hand. A silver ring gleamed on the girl's thumb. "Parvona, Lord Alexander. It is the princess's lady-in-waiting, Parvona. Where, then, is my Roxanne?"

"I don't know, but I'll find out!" Alexander strode from the tent. "Craterus! Who was captain of the camp guard?"

"Bondoor, but we haven't found him. We lost eleven men and several women besides those belonging to the Princess Roxanne." Craterus frowned. The security of the encampment was not his responsibility. He had been ordered to hold the Jhelum. Let the High King's fury fall on other heads.

"Were any of these raiders killed? Any captured?" Alexander's voice was low and controlled.

"No, lord. By the time I had word of the attack and sent a company to deal with it, they were gone." Craterus was beginning to sweat. If Alexander blamed him, it could mean his career.

"The dead woman is not the princess. I want an explanation of what happened here, and I want my wife found. I place you personally responsible for the investigation, General!" Alexander swung up on his horse. "Find her! Alive!"

*　　*　　*

Something brushed Roxanne's face and a foul stench filled her nostrils. She opened her eyes and stared into the hideous beak and glassy eyes of a giant vulture. She screamed and struck out at it, and the creature hopped away. All around her lay piles of dead. The smell of the battlefield was sickening.

She tried to sit up, and pain knifed through her body. She looked down at her tunic and trousers; they were soaked in blood. "Ormazd, help me," she whispered. The sun was setting and dusk settled over the plain. Everywhere birds of prey fluttered, tearing at the dead and near dead. Roxanne drew her saber and bit her lip against the cramps that gripped her. She was nauseous, and it was hard to think clearly.

Shadowy forms moved in the dusk, not soldiers . . . human scavengers, come to ravage the valuables and weapons of the fallen. A dead Indian soldier lay with his head across her feet. Clutched in his hand was a waterskin. Roxanne pried it from his stiff fingers. The liquid was warm and acrid, but she swallowed it gratefully.

The yipping of dogs echoed over the wasteland. It was said that spirits moved over a battlefield, dividing the dead between paradise and hell. Spirit or human, they would have a hard time taking her. She propped herself up and clenched her saber tighter, hoping she would not vomit.

A horseman moved through the carnage; it was too dark to see his face or uniform. She lay still, pretending death.

"Roxanne!"

"Kayan? Kayan?" she cried. "Here!" He lifted her in his arms, and she felt him wince. "You've been hurt," she murmured. "Your shoulder."

"I've been searching for you everywhere. I found your horse. Are you wounded?" He felt the wet stickiness of her clothing. "Can you sit a horse?"

"Yes. No . . . I . . ." Pain took away her breath. "You can't . . ." The cramping returned. She gave a low groan, and her head fell back as she went limp in his arms. He carried her for nearly a mile until he came to a team of Macedonians recovering their fallen comrades.

193

"It is the Princess Roxanne," Kayan called in rough Greek. "She has been wounded."

A rider went for Alexander. Someone took Roxanne from Kayan and helped him onto a horse. Quickly the two were taken to the nearest medical tent, where two physicians took command of Roxanne's case. An attendant examined Kayan's javelin wound and began to wash out the injury with unwatered wine.

"This is the princess," one of the doctors said. "I recognize her. I'd heard she was dead."

"She may be yet. Look at this."

The ceiling was blue. Light filtered through elaborate grating and cast geometric patterns on the floor. The tinkling of bells reverberated through the airy chamber. Something wet and clean touched her forehead, and Roxanne's eyes flickered. Soraya's face wavered before her and then vanished. It was all a dream . . . a dream of a dream and far away. Nothing mattered.

"Roxanne, open your eyes." She obeyed. Alexander stood over her. "Roxanne? Can you hear me?" She nodded, but her lips felt too dry to speak. He sat on the sleeping platform beside her and put a cup of water to her lips. "Do you know me?"

"Yes . . . lord," she murmured. "Where am . . . where am I?"

"In the palace of King Porus. We won the battle. It is mine now."

Roxanne's hand went to her flat stomach. She ached with a terrible emptiness. "My baby?"

"Lost." Alexander held her tenderly against him while she wept. At last, when there were no more tears, he laid her back against the bolsters. "Hush now, woman. Dry your tears. We will make another son."

"It's my fault. I disobeyed you," she agonized. "I crossed the river and killed my child."

Alexander shook his head. "No, the fault isn't yours. Perhaps it is the karma you speak of. Had you stayed in camp as I ordered, you would be dead. There was an attempt on your life, disguised as a raid by Indians. Your woman Parvona was killed."

"Parvona? Bondoor's Parvona?" She shook with dry sobs. Parvona was too young and full of life to die senselessly.

"She was in your pavilion sleeping. In the darkness, the assassins took her for you. I was told you were dead."

Alexander lifted her hand to his lips and kissed it. "Your guards and some of your waiting women were murdered. The attack may have been by Greeks. I crucified four men, but I still do not know who gave the order." He stood up. "Rest now and recover. You are sick more often than any woman I have ever known. You have lain here long enough."

"How long?"

"Five days, six if you count the first day in camp." He paused. "I lost Bucephalus too. I'm founding a city in his honor and another for our child on his resting spot. I'll name it for him, if you want to choose a name. Shall it be Philip, or would you prefer some heathen name?"

"Build your city, my lord. But do not name it for the dead. Our lost babe will live again in another body. Name your city instead for your great victory . . . Nicaea."

"As you wish, lady. I will come again tomorrow." She stared after him as he left the room. In his heart, she feared, Alexander blamed her for the loss of their child. Would he ever forgive her? Or would this be the sword that cut their union?

Exhausted, heartsick, she fell back against the pillows. "All victory must be paid for," she whispered. . . . And they had paid the price with heart's blood!

Chapter Sixteen

Amid the decadent luxury of the Indian palace, Roxanne mourned the loss of her child. Her body healed quickly, but emotionally she was far from recovered. Alexander was busy with the details of establishing an occupation government under General Craterus. He had promised King Porus that he could retain his throne, but Alexander would put no real power into the Indian's hands until he was sure of his loyalty. Alexander met daily with Porus and with the members of his council, leaving little time for Roxanne.

King Porus's wives, concubines, and female relatives were of a different breed from those of the young King Ambhi. The royal women regarded Roxanne as strange and exotic, and since she was established in Porus's most elaborate suite, as a threat to their own positions. Roxanne found no companionship in the palace; only icy courtesy.

Once again, Alexander had forbidden Roxanne to leave the confines of her spacious quarters. The rooms were large and stretched one into another around a great open-roof garden. But still, she could not shake the feeling of being imprisoned. Ptolemy had been given the responsibility for her security, until Kayan recovered enough to recruit new Sogdian guards from among her father's men.

The garden was a delight with its pools and fountains and flowering trees. Strange multicolored birds sang in the foliage, and a pair of peacocks strutted about the pool. The grass between the paving stones was thick and smooth as velvet, and the fountain gurgled and sighed so contentedly that an hour might easily stretch into an afternoon. Music filled the garden too, drifting from somewhere beyond the wall, sensual and languid.

Roxanne spent the mornings absorbed in books and in the refinement of her language skills. The holy man, Calanus, visited her quarters, and they spent hours in deep discussion.

"Your soul is intertwined with that of Alexander," he said. Calanus had not seemed to notice that Roxanne was a woman, an oversight which greatly pleased her. He answered her questions and argued points of philosophy as sincerely as he did with the High King. "Souls are neither male nor female," he observed. "Therefore it is of little importance in the cosmic scale."

"I must live in this female body. It is of greatest consequence to me," she argued.

Calanus was naked but for a scrap of cloth twisted about his middle, and his hair hung freely about his shoulders. He was scrupulously immaculate, another trait which endeared him to Roxanne. He spread his long fingers and smiled. "Let go of the past. Only this moment is relevant. Your tears accomplish nothing."

Ptolemy came occasionally to share her mid-morning meal. "Alexander means to drive still deeper into India," he said one day when he arrived unannounced. "The men are unhappy. The land ahead is deep forest with many strange creatures. We hear tales of tigers the size of horses and crocodiles that climb trees. Porus says the kings of the interior are powerful beyond belief, with armies of elephants and soldiers sworn to fight to the death."

"And what does my lord say?"

"He won't rest until all the world is in his hands." Ptolemy finished his slice of melon. "The streets are laid out for the cities of Bucephalus and Nicaea. Alexander is nothing if not ambitious." He laughed. "At least these are not named *Alexandria*. Do you know how many Alexandrias we've established in the last six years?"

"I can guess." Roxanne smiled to cover her distress. She'd not seen her husband in three days, and her messages to him had gone unanswered. She looked long and hard at the polished gentleman before her.

The Indian sun had darkened Ptolemy's skin and lightened his sandy-brown hair. His face was lined far beyond his years, but wisdom and ambition lay behind that cheerful countenance. Ptolemy was a more complex man than many supposed. Was he her enemy? Someone had gone to great lengths to see her dead on the banks of the Jhelum. It could well be Ptolemy.

"Am I under arrest?" she asked frankly.

"No! What gave you that idea?"

"I am confined here." She waved a servant to clear away the remains of the meal. "A Macedonian guard stands before the door. No one may be admitted except by the king's orders."

"For your protection."

"If Alexander wishes to be rid of me, there are simpler ways than to drive me mad. I am no tame songbird, content to sing my days away behind ivory bars." She brushed back a lock of auburn hair angrily. "I have been patient, Ptolemy, but I grow weary of waiting."

"Is there anything you desire?" Ptolemy was not immune to Roxanne's enchantment. Were she not Alexander's property and had a more amiable temper, he would find her damned attractive in spite of her willful nature.

"I desire freedom!" Roxanne rose from the silken cushion and paced the edge of the pool. "I could translate for Alexander, draw maps, train boys in horsemanship or archery. You tell me he is weighed down by the rigors of administration. Whatever he bids me, I would do willingly. But I cannot sit here idle! One entire afternoon was spent by Porus's wives on the choice of a new color for the king's beard. And when they had come to this momentous decision, it was meaningless because they would not dare to suggest to him he dye it that shade!"

Roxanne's hennaed eyes grew large and pleading. She was dressed in the costume of Porus's women, the linen garment so thin and clinging that it brought heat to Ptolemy's loins. The wrap was the softest blue, the blue of Mediterranean skies. Her midriff and feet were bare, her nails painted after the Indian fashion. She wore no jewelry except earrings of beaten gold and a large sapphire pendant.

Ptolemy shifted his knees to ease the pressure of his arousal. "I can promise nothing. He has his reasons. And I've never known a man more difficult to sway." He stood. "Alexander's mood will change. Until then, we wait."

"For once, I agree with your Macedonians. This land is too soft and cloying. I would gladly turn back to Persia, or even to Arabia." She knelt by the pool and dipped a hand in the clear water. A silver fish slid away to hide among the water lilies. "Do you know what happened to the widows of those Indians that were slain beside the Jhelum?"

Ptolemy shrugged.

"They were burned alive, sacrificing themselves on the funeral pyres of their husbands. Calanus told me. It is called *suttee*. What kind of place has our lord taken us to, Ptolemy?" The water ran through Roxanne's fingers, and she stared at her empty palm. "Our victories will be like that, Ptolemy. We will shed our blood here, and in a little while, not even the wind will remember that we passed this way."

Two more days passed without Alexander coming to her chambers. Roxanne's servants whispered behind her back. "The lady is no longer in favor."

Her outward agitation vanished, and she spent the afternoon composing poetry and soaking in her bath. Soraya was not deceived. "What mischief are you planning? Lord Alexander is a dangerous man. Take care you do not push him too far," she warned, brushing out the princess's long auburn curls.

Roxanne draped an ankle-length, leaf-green silk robe about herself and regarded her foster mother from under thick lashes. "Must I always be plotting some evil deed? You sound like the Greeks. 'The Sogdian witch is turning the king into an Asian!' 'Roxanne has put him under a spell.'" She sank onto a low couch and signaled for an Indian servant to begin applying her makeup. "The green eye shadow today, Valli."

"Don't take that stance with me, Roxanne!" Soraya snapped. "I have seen your antics since you were a child. Your father and Kayan dine with us this evening. Save your mischief for another day."

"Mischief?" Roxanne stretched and took a piece of fruit from a Chinese lacquerware tray. "I am my husband's most loyal subject."

Valli skillfully applied kohl to the princess's eyes, then curled and darkened the lashes. A second maid came forward with a silver bowl containing red powder to color the soles of Roxanne's feet and her palms. With a feather brush, she tinted her nipples and the inner parts of her thighs. Two more women hurried in with an array of silk garments in every color of the rainbow. "Which will you choose, Highness? Perhaps the yellow?"

"Green."

The maids whispered among themselves and produced four shades of green saris, ranging from turquoise to a deep emerald.

"It doesn't matter," Roxanne said peevishly. "Soraya?"

The older woman quickly selected a sari and jewels to match. She directed the maids to dress Roxanne and arrange her hair before dismissing the lot of them. Finally, when the garden was blessedly empty of chattering women, Soraya hugged her. "You are lovely, Roxanne. More beautiful every day."

"For how long?" Roxanne regarded her features in a bronze Egyptian mirror. "My beauty is a weapon, but one that will last only a little time." She waved a hand. "I like all this decadence. The female in me revels in the luxury, the jewels, the scented baths. But the prince inside warns me of coming to like it too well. If I ever waver from my karma, Sogdiana and Bactria are lost."

"A willow bends before the storm."

"But even a sapling will snap if bent too far. Damn his black Greek soul. I will not submit to Alexander or any other man." She turned away. "Leave me, please."

"Roxanne—"

"I would be alone." She strode to the far end of the court-yard, where strange trees hung with sweet-smelling fruit and exotic birds screeched and fluttered. "I will not bend," she murmured. "Never."

A few minutes before the appointed hour for the evening meal, Valli scurried in to tell Roxanne that the High King himself awaited her in the adjoining garden. "Tell him I will come at once," she said, and then resettled herself on the couch and picked up the scroll she had been reading. It was an ancient Egyptian text on the benefits of nitron and alum in wound care. The minutes ticked by.

"Why have you kept me waiting?" Alexander demanded. He filled the archway with his presence. "How dare you?"

She rolled the kidskin scroll carefully. "You have kept me waiting. For how long? Days? Weeks?" She smiled sweetly. "You are punishing me for the loss of your son." She rose and faced him at almost eye level. "Deny it, if you can."

He took several strides into the room and stopped, his gaze as scorching as the midday Indian sun. "You seem to think I have nothing more to do than to dally in a lady's court," he said in the soft tone that so often preceded an angry explosion. "Battles are but a fraction of war. My days are too short for all that must be done."

"It is not the days we are concerned with, is it? What of the nights?"

Alexander scowled at her. "Is it any wonder I absent myself from your apartments when I am greeted in such a manner?"

She rose and came to him. "I am happy to see you. It is just that being imprisoned does not improve my disposition."

"You call this a prison?" He glanced about the lavish chamber.

"Give me leave to travel about the city. Let Hephaestion and Ptolemy trail after me if you so desire. But I cannot be confined here. Give me something worthwhile to occupy my time," she pleaded, laying her head on his chest.

He traced her bottom lip with a rough fingertip, and she felt a shiver of anticipation slide down her spine. "The guard is for your protection. You have been ill. I am not convinced that all those responsible for the plot to murder you have been taken. Even you must realize that Ptolemy has more important things to do than play bodyguard to a woman." He gripped her face tighter and kissed her fiercely.

She broke away from him and signaled a servant to pour wine for the king. He downed the goblet and tossed aside the empty container. "I came to see if you would be well enough to travel soon. We ride east in four days. I have received tribute from two kings to the south, but Porus's uncle sends only threats. We will persuade him to see things differently."

Alexander's eyes were shadowed and red-rimmed. She knew the signs. He had been drinking too hard and sleeping little.

"You look lovely this evening." His tone deepened. "I do not blame you for the baby . . . at least not consciously."

"Then why are you suddenly so cold?"

"Cold! Woman, I have been the epitome of restraint! I am your husband and your king! You willfully disobey my orders before my subjects until it becomes a joke among my best friends. Yes, I am angry with you. But the anger does not concern the loss of our child. It is your attitude!" He glared at the servant.

"Leave us, Valli," Roxanne said. The girl fled, her bare feet soundless on the marble floor.

Alexander poured another tumbler of wine and drank it slowly.

Roxanne fought to control her own ire. "If I'd had my head crushed in, instead of Parvona, would that please you? Would you name a city after me?"

"You know I do not wish you dead. But that does not change the fact you disobeyed me in the midst of battle. By my own laws I should have you beheaded!" He turned away, his back stiff and unyielding.

"Then do so! Don't disappoint your friends!"

Alexander turned back and laughed. "You continue to astonish me, Roxanne." He seized her and kissed her long and hungrily. "It is not to prove anything to Hephaestion that I stay away, Roxanne. It is to prove something to myself. Even you cannot control me. I have broken my own decree and pardoned you for the love I bear you." He shoved her away. "Perhaps we will ride together tomorrow. I bid you a good evening."

Roxanne stared after him, speechless, as he strode from the room.

Not long after Alexander departed, her father and cousin came to share her evening meal. Neither man was in a good mood. Oxyartes still waited for Wolf's return and news from home. Kayan was deeply concerned with the losses his regiment had suffered in the battle and with finding good replacements.

The servants were clearing away the second course when Ptolemy came to share wine—and to spy, she suspected, on her father and cousin. "You have heard that we march in a few days?" Ptolemy asked.

"Yes, my lord told me. Thank you for taking my message. For once, I will be glad to move on, although I do not look forward to jungle travel. Calanus tells me there are snakes more than twenty feet long that can wind about a horse and crush him to death."

"And other beasts like elephants with a single massive horn in the center of their heads," Kayan said. "Let them come. My Flying Devils will hunt them like any other animal."

"You are not dining with Alexander tonight?" Roxanne asked Ptolemy, offering him a sweet.

"I was not invited. He didn't leave here happy, and my association with you doesn't help my position."

"So we are all in disfavor." She laughed. "What did you tell me, General Ptolemy? 'His mood will pass.' " She motioned to a servant, and a dozen dancing girls entered to provide entertainment.

Roxanne waited until her guests were gone and the lamps extinguished in the reception rooms. She bid Soraya a good night and retired to her sleeping area. The girl, Valli, was on duty by her door, and Roxanne summoned her.

"Do you know the palace well, Valli?" When the maid nodded, Roxanne produced a wax tablet and a writing tool. "Draw it for me. I would know where Lord Alexander's courts lie and where he sleeps." The girl's eyes widened. "Here!" Roxanne shoved the tablet into her hands. "Draw."

Trembling, she obeyed.

"And do the servants use these hallways and stairs?" Roxanne demanded. The girl nodded her head and quickly sketched in smaller passageways and hidden doors.

"Please, Princess. I do not wish to die. I have a husband and child."

"You will not die. Here." Roxanne slipped a heavy gold ring off her finger. "This should please your husband."

"They will think I stole it." She wavered. Roxanne pulled off her dangling earrings and added them to the tally.

"Take off your clothes and give them to me. Dress in something plain of mine." Speechless, the girl did as she was told. "You will flirt with the guard at the servant's entrance, offer him wine, and distract him. When I have passed, you may hide your loot and return here. I'll be back before dawn, so you needn't worry." Valli looked uncertain. "Are you slave or free?" Roxanne asked.

"Free, lady."

"Good. With the jewelry I have given you, you will no longer need to be a servant. Your husband can buy a shop and sell pots."

"But he is a baker," the girl protested.

"Little fool! Then you can open your own bakery! I will guarantee your safety," Roxanne soothed. "If anything happens to me, go to the Lady Soraya and tell her what happened. She will protect you."

Roxanne donned the woman's sari and twisted her hair up into a similar hairstyle. "In the darkness, I will pass for a servant." She gathered up an armload of clothing. "A washwoman." She bowed to Valli, and the girl let out a whimper of distress but followed obediently through the courts.

When they reached the servants' entrance, Roxanne tucked dates into her cheeks, threw a scarf over her head and shoulders, and bent over. She began to walk with the shuffling gait of an old woman. The guard was bored and more than willing to chat with an attractive woman who offered fresh bread and wine. He hardly noticed the old woman who passed with a basket of laundry.

Roxanne ducked into a niche and pulled the wax tablet from under the clothes. The palace was a warren of twisting passageways, courts, staircases, and tunnels. She hoped Valli's map was accurate. Alexander would have a surprise tonight. If he would not come to her, she would go to him.

The corridors were dark and shadowy despite the flickering oil lamps that lined the whitewashed brick walls. Macedonian patrols marched by, but Roxanne merely shrank against the wall and averted her face. Most of the palace slept as she found her way through the labyrinth to Alexander's court.

Roxanne heard familiar voices and ducked into a storage room as Hephaestion and Perdiccas swaggered by. There had been much drinking at her lord's table, if they were any indication. Perdiccas was singing a Macedonian ditty about a shepherdess, and Hephaestion joined in lustily on the chorus. She wondered who was holding whom up. She almost stepped out into the hall when Alexander came through the door.

"Hephaestion! Perdiccas! Wait!" he called, hurrying after his friends.

"We left you a gift," Hephaestion shouted back.

When the guards followed Alexander, Roxanne slipped into the king's chambers. A reception room led to an enclosed garden with many doors opening off it. The girl had marked the far left entrance as leading to the king's sleeping area.

Roxanne crossed the garden and went through the shadowy arch.

The outer room was obviously her husband's; his armor lay on a low table; his bow and arrows hung against a wall. A small altar with burning incense had been set up in honor of Zeus. The sleeping platform in the inner room was large and draped. Roxanne pulled aside the purple silk curtains and gasped. The bed was occupied!

"Come to bed, Your Majesty," the woman murmured sleepily.

Roxanne's eyes widened in surprise as she recognized the sprawling figure. "Europa!"

Chapter Seventeen

"Who are you? What are you doing here? It's you!" Europa sat up, clutching the silk spread around her naked breasts.

"You Athenian bitch!" Roxanne seized a handful of black curls. "How dare you creep into my husband's bed like some cursed vermin?" Roxanne dragged her from the platform screaming and punched her full in her shapely nose.

Europa wailed and began to kick and scratch, succeeding only in tearing out handfuls of her own hair. One hand struck Roxanne in the face, and in a fury she hurled Europa to the floor. "I'll give you reason to weep!" she promised, easing the dagger from her waistband.

Europa sobbed and crawled backwards across the rug. "No . . . no . . ." she cried hysterically. Wails caught in her throat as Roxanne bent over her, knife in hand.

More than an hour passed before Alexander returned to his bed. She heard him as he crossed the garden, singing the same tune she had heard earlier in the hall. "Wake up, my pretty!" he said. "The night air is chill and you are warm." Alexander threw back the draperies and fumbled with his tunic. "I am hot for you," he boasted, drawing aside the silken cover.

Roxanne lay naked on the sheets, her hair spread on the pillows. "Come," she whispered enticingly. "I will warm you."

"Roxanne?" His senses reeled. She sat up, placing her hands behind her head and looked at him innocently.

"Yes, my lord, it is I. Where else would your wife be?"

"Vixen," he said hoarsely. One hand stroked an ivory breast with its red-tipped nipple. "Enchantress." Her arms drew him down to her, caressing his burgeoning erection, stroking the tense muscles of his shoulders and arms.

"Whatever you desire, Alexander," she said, running a pink tongue lightly over his full lower lip. "Whatever you desire, I shall give you." He kissed her mouth and pressed her body against the silken sheets.

"How?" he murmured between kisses. Her skin was velvet fire, her flesh intoxicating. Driven by lust, he drove into her body. She met his thrusts with her own passion, digging her nails into his back and crying out as they rose to a crescendo of ecstasy.

Through the night, he made slow, passionate love to her and whispered thoughts he would never utter in the day. At last, satiated, Alexander slept, and Roxanne lay awake, exhausted but triumphant.

Dawn was breaking over the garden when Alexander stirred. His gaze rested on her serene face, not knowing she had risen and bathed in the pool in the early morning darkness and brushed out her hair until it gleamed. "Are you real?" he teased. "Or some goddess come to steal away my soul?"

"I am real enough, lord." For the first time he noticed a bruise on her right cheek.

"What happened? I couldn't have—"

"No, my lord." She laughed. "I could not accuse you of being a gentle lover, but you didn't hurt me."

He touched the bruise lightly, and then suddenly remembered. "Where is she? What have you done with Europa?" Alexander propped himself up on one arm and looked stern. "Well, Sogdian? Where is my countrywoman?"

Roxanne rose from the bed and led him to another room. A pile of cloth on the floor moaned and moved. Roxanne pulled back the linen, revealing Europa, bound and gagged. Alexander bent to unfasten the ties, and the woman began to cry and babble hysterically.

"Alexander!" Hephaestion's voice came from the bedchamber.

Roxanne drew on a robe of the king's. "In here, General!" she called. Hephaestion hurried into the room.

"What's going—" He stared at Europa.

One eye was black and nearly shut, her nose was swollen and bloody, her naked body bruised. But worst of all was her hair. She wailed and tried to cover her head with her hands. It had been cut within inches of her scalp so that chunks and jagged points of hair protruded in all directions. "By all the gods!" Hephaestion swore. He looked from Europa to Roxanne and back to Alexander and began to snicker. "Two at once? I thought you were drunker than that last night."

Alexander shrugged and joined the laughter as his friend wrapped the sobbing woman in a scarlet coverlet and carried her from the room. "I shall return this wild one to her quarters."

"It was no match, my friend," Alexander chuckled. "A doe against a she-wolf."

When they were alone, Roxanne sank to one knee and bowed her head. "I have been willful, lord, and my tongue is sharp. The High King may have whatever woman he wishes in his bed."

"Is this an apology?" He pulled her up. "Are you sorry you shamed and abused Europa?"

"No." She flashed a smile. "For it made me very angry to see that slut in your bed. But I will try to be a more obedient wife, I swear."

"Will try. Try is the relevant word here." He pulled her against him and kissed her love-swollen lips. "We have unfinished business, little Sogdian."

"What is that?" she murmured.

"The making of another son." Alexander swept her up and carried her to his bed. "And this time we will make no mistakes."

*   *   *

The army's path through the thick forest was perilous. The rains continued to fall, ruining supplies, rotting uniforms, and making cooking and sleeping difficult. Horses sickened in the damp and were attacked by tigers and wild dogs; poisonous snakes killed men and animals alike. Strung out for miles along the jungle road, the army was easy prey to sneak attacks by hostile tribesmen.

Roxanne, again in Alexander's favor, rode by his side. She had chosen a gray mare from the main horse herd and had named her Nicaea. She drew the horse close to her husband's and offered Alexander a small lump of ointment. "Rub this on your horse's head, my lord. It will keep insects from troubling him."

He smelled it, making a sour face. "Yuhhh! No wonder it drives flies away. Maybe I should use it myself." He reached up and anointed the animal's ears and neck. "Cursed creatures! Spawned by the lord of the underworld." Alexander slapped a mosquito. "Where did you come by this miracle salve?"

"One of King Ambhi's men told me. He says these insects carry sickness." Roxanne's mare wore an elaborate Indian harness with dangling fringe to discourage flies. "The ointment is made from the sap of a tree."

"There are more kinds of trees and plants here than I ever dreamed of." Alexander waved at the dense foliage around them. Monkeys chattered in the trees and peered through the branches at them as they rode by. "It would take a hundred years to catalog and record them all."

"The flowers are very beautiful," Roxanne said. "But it is not a place for horsemen or mountain folk. My Bactrians are nervous as cats."

"Don't mention cats," Ptolemy said, joining them. "We lost a woman and two more horses to that lame tiger last night. It seems to be stalking us. All we see are tracks and what he leaves behind. He came within a yard of one sentry, and the man never saw a hair of him."

"I've hunted snow tigers," Roxanne admitted. "But judging

by the tracks, these jungle cats are bigger. He must be old or crippled to have become a man killer." She ducked her head to avoid a trailing vine. "Hunting tigers in the hills is different from this."

"It's been a while since I've hunted anything challenging. If the scouts can't find him, I'll track him down and kill him myself," Alexander declared. "A tiger is a tiger. His skin would make a fine present for Aristotle, wouldn't it?"

Roxanne dropped back to ride beside her father as Alexander and Ptolemy talked. The tiger would have to be hunted down and destroyed, and if Alexander meant to hunt him, she wanted to go along. She had an uneasy feeling about this dark forest. The men were grumbling to turn back, complaining openly, and the tiger only added to their discontent.

Alexander's tunic was water-soaked, clinging to his body like a second skin in the heat. The rain turned his hair into a mat of curls. Roxanne noticed an insect bite on his cheek. The mosquitos seemed to single him out for attack, but he usually paid no more attention to insects than to rain. She thought longingly of Porus's palace. It had been so long since she'd been dry. The sensible thing in this climate would be to go without clothes altogether. If it weren't for the insects, she supposed Alexander would go naked.

"Well, Daughter, have you nothing better to do than stare at your husband's leg?" Oxyartes asked.

Roxanne chuckled. "He does have a comely calf."

Oxyartes's rugged face split into a grin. "I hadn't noticed."

She smiled at her father, thinking what a handsome man he was for two score and ten. He was still a warrior to be reckoned with, she thought with pride.

"We have reinforcements coming, an army from Greece with thousands of pack animals bearing medicine and weapons and new uniforms. Word of them just arrived by special messenger." He motioned toward the king. "Alexander will be glad to hear it, even if they'll be weeks getting here. The army needs fresh blood. I don't trust these Indians he's recruiting."

"And the Persians don't trust us," Roxanne answered. "It's a fine mixture my lord has assembled. The Greeks hate us all.

Did the messenger come by camel?" Oxyartes nodded.

Alexander had been quick to adopt the Persian High King's mail service. A series of riders mounted on Bactrian racing camels could carry a message across his empire in unbelievable time. Armed with only a light bow and the royal seal, the messengers were safe from all but the most desperate of bandits. Interference with the mail was a crime punishable by an excruciating death for the offender and all his family. Few dared to ignore the consequences.

The two-humped Bactrian camel was shorter than its Arabian cousin and of better disposition. Prized for their intelligence, endurance, and strength, and bred for speed, the animals could travel vast distances without food or water. Bactrian kings had used them in warfare for centuries. No racehorse could keep up with them on rough ground. The gods, it was said, had taken beauty from the hairy beasts and given them both wings and stamina in return.

"Any news from Sogdiana?" Roxanne asked. "Has Wolf returned?"

"Not yet. It seems his journey was for nothing. You must become pregnant again, Daughter, and soon," Oxyartes warned. "With every step, Alexander goes farther from the mountains of Bactria. You know the Bactrians; they are used to a tight rein. You must provide an heir for the twin thrones."

"I'm trying, Father, I'm trying."

A cry up ahead brought the column to a halt. An Indian came running toward Alexander, shouting and waving his arms, trying to make himself understood. Roxanne recognized him as one of a group cutting the road ahead of the army. She dug her heels into the gray and cantered up to Alexander.

"Calm yourself," she ordered in Sanskrit. "Now repeat slowly what you said." The man did, and she turned to her husband. "He says that they have found the mother of all snakes, my lord. And he begs that someone come and slay it."

Hephaestion frowned. "Beware of a trap, Alexander. The jungle is dark as the underworld ahead. Let me send—"

Alexander laughed. "You're becoming an old woman. Let's go and see this *mother of snakes*. Roxanne?" he dared.

She flinched inwardly. "Yes, my lord. By all means, let us not miss this wonderful opportunity." They galloped forward, together with Hephaestion and Oxyartes.

The snake lay half in the path, grossly swollen by the meal it had recently eaten. It raised its flattened head and stared at them regally, sending shivers up Roxanne's spine. Her mare snorted nervously and danced sideways, trembling.

"By the gods," Alexander swore. "It's thirty feet or more." He slid from his horse, sword in hand.

"Careful," Roxanne cried. The snake's head was the size of a yearling calf's, and its scaly, patterned body appeared to be made of stone. She bit her lip and forced back the terror that the huge serpent inspired.

More swiftly than they could have imagined, the snake slithered toward Alexander, and he swung the razor-sharp sword in a mighty arc to strike just below the neck. The muscles in her husband's shoulders rippled beneath the damp tunic as the sword bit deep in the snake's flesh. Instantly the giant coils wrapped themselves about him, and Hephaestion leaped to his aid.

Alexander's sword struck again, grating on bone, and he was caught in a tangled mass of writhing serpent. Oxyartes and Hephaestion struggled to free him as he hacked at the creature's neck, severing the head. Seconds later, they pulled him free and jumped back from the thrashing body.

Roxanne dismounted and ran to the king, her knees weak. He looked at her pale face and laughed. "Herakles slayed the nine-headed Hydra. This snake had only one head, and I'm glad. If it had had two, you'd have had to get the other one." He hugged her and groaned. "The thing nearly broke my ribs. Shall I have a quiver made for you from the skin? It's magnificent."

Roxanne shuddered. "No, thank you, my lord. I prefer emeralds to serpents. The honor is yours."

"Skin it," Alexander ordered, mounting his horse again. "And save the flesh. We'll have it cooked and see what it tastes like." He wiped his sword on a handful of leaves. "It would have gladly made me its dinner."

Hephaestion slit open the abdomen, and a full-grown boar rolled out. "You eat the snake. I'll have roast pig." He kicked the snake's head into the bushes. "I hope it doesn't have a big brother out there somewhere. That's as large a worm as I care to deal with!"

"You?" Alexander protested. "I killed the damn thing. You were just a bystander."

"If you want your men to think you killed it, naturally I'll relate that version," Hephaestion agreed. "You do have to keep up your image." Alexander called him an unspeakable name, and they both laughed.

Roxanne exchanged glances with her father. She would never understand these two. By the Wise God! She would never hear the end of this snake! She would probably have nightmares about it for a month. She cursed softly, and Oxyartes, seeing her lips move, laughed.

"I warned you, Roxanne. He's not like other men."

"But your warning makes him no easier to live with. If this is the father . . . what am I to expect of the son?"

The heat of the wet forest seemed to increase Alexander's thirst, and he drank late into the nights with friends, coming often to Roxanne's bed only a few hours before dawn. He was drinking far too much unwatered wine, and his temper shortened with every cup. He had become increasingly arrogant with men he had known since he was a boy.

And always the Persians stood behind him, whispering, "You are a god!" . . . "The High King answers to no human!" . . . "Your Majesty's authority comes from heaven!"

Sporadic fighting interspersed with long, weary days of cutting through the rain-soaked jungle eroded morale, and the army's grumbling grew day by day. Naked tribesmen hurled themselves from trees into the line of march, dealing death without warning, especially among the noncombatants. The women were afraid, and they spread their fears in the dark hours of the night with the same repeated message: "This land is cursed. Let us turn back."

Roxanne woke in a cold sweat, trembling from the terror

of her dreams. Instantly, Alexander's strong arm went around her. "Shhh, Little Star. You are safe," he murmured, his words slurred with drink. He cradled her head on his muscular chest. "Is it the snake?"

"No . . . nothing," she lied, clinging to him. Her nightmares were not so solid. In her sleep she was haunted by a nameless stalking dread. She seemed to be running in a shadowy mist, pursued by . . . by what . . . she could put no name to it. The jungle was cursed, and if her lord did not lead them out of it soon, they would all perish.

The rain stopped the following day, and spirits lifted. Fresh supplies reached the army from Porus's city, and Alexander declared a day of rest. They camped beside a nameless river and the remains of an ancient city, so old no one remembered its name or who had lived there. Alexander prowled its fallen walls, marveling at the stone faces of forgotten gods, despite warnings from the Indians that such places were favorite haunts of the dreaded king cobra.

"Someone built this city," Alexander said to Roxanne. "The ruins stretch far into the jungle. Men and women lived here, loved, fought battles, and died. Now they are only dust, and we cannot even honor their accomplishments." His fathomless eyes regarded her thoughtfully. "It shall not be so for me. Men shall say, 'The great Alexander passed this way. The great King Alexander built this city.' " He perched on a crumbling stone block. "Who knows what treasures lie beneath?"

"Have you not treasures enough, my lord?" She took his offered hand, and he pulled her up beside him. His free arm circled her waist and slid under her short linen tunic to stroke her abdomen.

"Never enough. And the one I desire most, you must give me. Is there a son nestled there yet, Roxanne? If there is not, the fault cannot be mine."

She laughed. "No, Alexander, the fault can never be yours." He tipped her chin up and kissed her full on the mouth.

"They are pestering me again to wed the daughter of King Darius. Would it pain you greatly? It is the Persian custom to have several wives." A trace of a smile played over his firm lips.

"Have you seen this paragon?"

"I believe the lady is somewhat taller than I, if that is what you mean, Princess." He began to brush away at a worn inscription cut into the rock. "What does this say?"

Roxanne stared at the writing. " 'Those who dare the gates of heaven may live to regret it,' " she read.

"What?" Alexander looked at her suspiciously. "You lie." He grabbed her wrists in mock struggle and pinned her back against the stone, looming over her threateningly. "A translator who gives false information to the High King shall be . . ."

"Shall be what?" she teased, her eyes sparkling with mischief. He released one wrist and cupped a full breast.

"The truth, wench!" he demanded. "Or it shall go hard with you."

"It always does." Laughing, she twisted away. "My education does not extend to obscure Indian inscriptions. It isn't Sanskrit."

"If I were forced to marry Barsine, it would be a political move. Then the Persian factions would be forced to support me." He traced the carvings with a finger. "You know that if I wed other brides, you will always be first and most important."

Roxanne stiffened, her playful mood lost in the reality of his words. "Most important?" She fisted her hands on her hips. "Do as you will, Alexander. But if you wed the Persian, there will be a price. I will never forgive you! Nay . . . even more . . . I will have revenge."

"You dare to threaten me?" Anger showed in the intensity of his voice. He came toward her menacingly.

"Save your black scowls for those you can frighten." She vaulted to the ground and walked away.

"Come back here!"

Untying her horse, Roxanne took hold of the mane, pulled herself up on the animal's back, and rode off toward the campsite. The bastard! Better if she did not become pregnant again. More fool she for not taking Kayan's offer. Alexander was like a little boy who constantly desired new toys. She was no plaything to be tossed aside when it suited him. If he took Barsine to wife, let them both beware.

Kayan shadowed her as she rode back through the camp. The men were taking advantage of the holiday in the manner of soldiers everywhere: drinking, feasting, and dancing. Games of chance were rampant, and the camp followers did a good business. A merchant had organized a wrestling match, and soldiers were lining up to square off with a mangy brown bear.

How different these soldiers looked from those that had taken the citadel at Sogdiana Rock. Were it not for their extreme fairness and speech, one would not even realize they were Greek. Their uniforms were an assortment of Persian, Asian, and Indian. Most were bearded and surprisingly young. Scattered through the crowd were Medes and Persians, barbarian horsemen, Bactrians, and dark-skinned Indians. No wonder the Greeks felt so far from home.

She paused to speak with Ptolemy as he waited his turn in a contest of arm wrestling among a few of the officers of the Companions. He had stripped to only a loincloth and was flexing his muscles. It was obvious he had been drinking since early morning. "You will be lucky to see your opponent, let alone best him," Roxanne teased. "Philip outweighs you by two stones."

Ptolemy laughed and drained another cup of wine. "You're in the presence of a master. My mother could beat Philip."

The burly Macedonian made an obscene gesture. "You're next, Ptolemy!" The onlookers roared.

Ptolemy bowed theatrically to Roxanne, staggered, and caught her arm for support. "A kiss for luck, Princess?"

An iron hand on Ptolemy's shoulder spun him around, and a fist connected with his chin, sending him sprawling. "Alexander!" Roxanne protested. "He meant nothing! He's drunk."

The king glared down at the unconscious figure and nudged him with a foot. "He'll think twice before he oversteps his bounds again, drunk or sober." A hush fell over the group as Alexander took Roxanne's arm roughly. "We were in the midst of a conversation, wife."

Kayan tensed, and Roxanne warned him with a glance not to try to interfere. Her cousin's shoulder wound was slow in healing in this Indian heat, and he was acting as captain of her guard until he recovered fully.

"Come to my pavilion, my lord," she said to Alexander. "There is no need to provide a show for your Companions."

"As you wish," he said, giving her a nudge. "But my own tent is closer. Let us go there." Kayan followed them as far as the pickets outside the High King's pavilion.

Alexander pushed her through the doorway. "Is it not enough you are disobedient. Now you must make a spectacle of yourself by flirting with my officers."

"Are you feverish again?"

"Ptolemy is not an ugly man."

"Neither are you," she soothed. "It was wrong to hit him. He's your friend."

"Is he? He urges me to turn back, you know. He thinks the Companions are ready to rebel." Alexander pulled her against him and kissed her roughly. "I will not stand by and see you in another man's arms. You are mine! Mine alone!"

"One Greek is enough, I assure you." She tried to free herself from his arms. A commotion at the entrance drew Alexander's attention.

"What is it?" he demanded with a foul curse. "What now?"

Roxanne followed him and listened to the exchange, not able to make out the message. Alexander returned and reached for his weapons. "The tiger. It has struck again."

"Not in daylight?"

"This one has. Come if you want to see a tiger hunt. King Porus is organizing his men now." Alexander's mood lifted as he put on his battered war helmet. "Arm yourself. We hunt from elephants."

"What was the tiger's prey?"

"An infant. He carried the child off into the jungle to devour it." He hesitated. "I should have taken the threat more seriously."

"You could not have expected the tiger to—"

218

"It is my business to know." He grimaced. "The child's death is on my head."

Beaters assembled in front of the elephants. Roxanne was assigned an elephant and mahout. She scrambled up into the howdah, and the beast rose to his feet. "Wait," King Ambhi called. The mahout signaled the elephant to kneel again, and the boy king climbed into the roofless howdah with her. "You have never hunted tiger before," he explained. "I am to be your guide and protector."

She laughed. "Thank you. I'm sure I will need both."

Ambhi was in his mid teens, she decided, still too young to have much of a beard. He was a pleasant companion, and she was glad to have him with her. He was armed with a bow and javelin and wore a fine new Macedonian helmet, a gift from Alexander.

"A tiger, especially a crazed man-eater such as this one, is never to be taken lightly," Ambhi said. His dark eyes were as large and intense as a girl's. "If he had not eaten, we would hunt differently. We might put out a freshly slain deer or goat as bait and trap him with a pitfall. But this one has taken its own meal. We will go east, and the beaters will circle and try to drive the tiger to us."

"But the beaters are not armed. What if the tiger doubles back through their ranks?"

"Sometimes they do." He shrugged. "But they are only beaters. They cannot expect to live forever. Usually, the tiger will be frightened by their noise and numbers and be driven toward the elephant line."

"I suppose it is better to be up here than down in the grass."

He grinned. "It is very exciting. I have seen my father slay two tigers in this manner."

Ambhi tried not to eye the well-shaped legs that brushed against him in the tight quarters of the hunting howdah. This woman was as exciting as the tiger hunt. His heart swelled with pride that the mighty Lord Alexander had entrusted him with the princess's safety. He flamed beneath his dark skin and tried to hide his arousal as he imagined what it would be like to possess her, to enter her secret garden.

219

Roxanne swallowed a giggle and stared hard at the elephant's head. Alexander was raving with jealousy and had locked her for an afternoon with a sex-crazed boy.

The great gray elephants lumbered through the jungle toward the spot designated as the catch area. There were twelve noble hunters in all: King Porus, Alexander, Hephaestion, Perdiccas, each on an elephant, Roxanne and Ambhi, and six Indian noblemen unknown to Roxanne. All were heavily armed.

A grown tiger was a fearsome opponent. A tiger would not hesitate to attack a horse or a man. The terrible claws could rend, the hind feet disembowel, and the fangs snap bone like straw. An angered tiger was the greatest of all game, and only brave men and women dared to hunt such prey with spear and arrow and often, in the end, with naked blade.

Once they had left the path behind, the entwined trees became thicker; the sky vanished in a mass of greenery. The jungle had its own smell, of ancient mold, of primordial life. Jungle sounds were all about them, hushing human voices until the only noise made by the hunting party was the grunting of the elephants, one to another, as they filed through the semi-twilight of the forest.

One hour passed and then two as they penetrated deeper and deeper into the living mass of vegetation. Then a silent signal passed from mahout to mahout and the elephants formed a line along a slight ridge at the edge of a twisted thicket of thorn. "Now we wait," Ambhi explained, "until the tiger comes. It is the job of the beaters to send the cat to us. We will surround and kill it."

"The elephants panicked on the battlefield. Will they face a wounded tiger?" Roxanne asked.

Ambhi had retreated to the farthest corner of the howdah. The temptation to fondle the lady was almost more than he could bear. "They will stand. These are trained tiger hunters. Each elephant is at least middle-aged. Elephants and tigers are enemies by nature. I have seen an elephant crush a tigress to death with a foot. You may have complete confidence in the beasts."

"What about the mahout? He's in a rather dangerous position."

"The elephant loves the handler more than anything in the world. And the mahout depends on his elephant to protect him." He looked away from Roxanne's full bosom. "We will have a wait. There is food in the basket, if you care to serve us."

"If I care to serve us?" She laughed. "Ambhi, you are a king by birth, are you not?" She took his ringed hand and turned it over to read the lines on his palm. "Ah, you have a lucky hand, a long life, wealth, and devoted children."

"Yes, of course. I am descended from the gods."

"Where have I heard that before?" she mumbled. "No, hear me out. Forget that I am a woman, Ambhi. You must try," she insisted. "In my own land I am born a prince as you are. In Sogdiana a woman may rule in her own right."

"I am constantly amazed at the outrageous customs of foreigners. It is very hard to believe."

"You have seen my fighting men and the Bactrians. Bactria is the twin kingdom I am also heir to. My land is very vast, Ambhi."

"Have you many elephants?"

"As many as the stars in the sky."

"Ayee!"

"So, you must understand I mean no disrespect to you as a brother king when I say—get your own food. When you are my guest, I will serve you and gladly. But I am no servant, not even to a king."

For a long moment, Ambhi deliberated on what she had said. "It is very difficult for me," he admitted. "You are very much a woman, and yet not a woman. Can it be that you are a goddess?"

"No." Roxanne unwrapped a loaf of bread and some rice and fruit and began to eat heartily. "No, Ambhi," she said between bites. "Only a princess far from home."

Reluctantly he reached for a piece of fruit. "I have never served myself," the boy confessed. "I did not mean to offend you." He drew himself up to his full height. "It is a rather novel experience."

"Many things happen on a hunt," Roxanne said seriously, "that would never be permitted otherwise."

He broke into a smile of relief. "You're right. It is a hunt." Magnanimously he offered her a flask. "Taste it. It's a spiced fruit juice, very refreshing."

Solemnly Roxanne took the flask and poured a small amount into the attached silver beaker. "To the hunt," she toasted. "A clean kill."

"A clean kill," he agreed, sipping from his own cup.

A wave of sound hit them, the clashing of metal on metal and shouts of men. Roxanne started. "It has begun."

"Yes." Ambhi put down the food and reached for his weapons. "Make ready," he advised. "Soon . . . soon now . . . the tiger comes."

Chapter Eighteen

Tension grew as the line of hunters waited. Louder and louder came the sounds of the beaters. Roxanne's pulse quickened. Brush snapped and small animals raced through the thicket, darting between the elephants to the thick jungle beyond. A startled doe leaped across the small clearing in front of Roxanne, passing so closely that she could see the terrified animal's white-rimmed eyes. And then a deep cough echoed through the foliage.

"Tiger!" Ambhi warned, clutching his javelin until the knuckles of his hand turned white. "Don't be afraid, Princess. I will protect you."

Roxanne glanced down the line to where Alexander waited on his elephant. He would be outwardly calm, smiling, and determined to have the kill at any cost. "Ormazd be with him," she muttered silently. Her husband's bravery went beyond daring, and she feared for his safety.

Although she was quite capable of hurling a javelin herself, Roxanne knew that she didn't have the strength to deliver a deathblow to a tiger. She readied her bow with its razor-sharp, iron-tipped arrows. She had no intention of shooting, but if she had to defend herself or the young prince, she wouldn't be empty-handed.

Alexander's famous luck held. As Roxanne expected, the huge black and orange tiger exploded out of the brush directly in front of him. Roxanne saw a snarling blur as the cat leaped upon Alexander's elephant and clawed ferociously. The cat's leap carried him into the mahout's lap. Alexander drove home his first javelin with lightning speed but little effect on the powerful tiger. Maddened with pain, his elephant lashed out with her trunk. The wounded mahout tumbled to the ground as the tiger clawed over him to reach Alexander.

The other hunters circled the battle; several javelins flew through the air, succeeding only in further wounding Alexander's elephant. The tiger's roaring was nearly drowned by the shouts of men and the trumpeting of the elephants. Alexander's sword flashed in the sunlight, and the tiger screamed.

Abruptly, out of the trees rushed a second tiger.

Ambhi swore and threw his javelin. It went wide, missing the tigress by two feet. So intense was the struggle around Alexander that it was several moments before any of the other hunters noticed the second cat. And when they did, they were too far away to intervene.

Roxanne drew her bowstring to her chin. If the tigress was willing to pass by, she was willing to let it. For the space of two heartbeats, Roxanne stared into the magnificent creature's golden eyes. And then the cat leaped onto a fallen tree and onto the back of Roxanne's elephant. Time froze as the tigress's hot breath scorched her face. Ambhi fell, knocked aside by a glancing blow from one powerful paw. Roxanne heard the mahout cry out as he tumbled to the earth. The tiger vaulted over the far side of the howdah into the foliage, and the enraged elephant charged after it. Nearly deafened by the trumpeting, Roxanne clung to the floor of the rocking howdah as overhanging branches lashed against the box.

Thick jungle closed in around them as Roxanne shouted useless orders to the elephant. "Stop!" she cried. The elephant tore up small trees and beat them against the ground, nearly knocking Roxanne senseless when a branch struck her head.

Only half conscious, Roxanne heard the cries of many men and what sounded like the clash of swords behind her. A spear with unfamiliar markings struck the rim of the howdah, and she caught a glimpse of armed soldiers in yellow turbans running through the jungle. Had Alexander's hunting party been attacked? And by whom?

Two bowmen appeared directly in front of the elephant. One shouted and waved his arms, but when the elephant bore down upon them, both bowmen leaped aside. The second man loosed an arrow. Roxanne couldn't tell if he hit the elephant or not, but the beast panicked and bolted once more, plowing through brush and crushing small trees. How far the elephant went, Roxanne couldn't tell, but nothing slowed the animal's mad rush until it began to rain.

Solid sheets of water soaked Roxanne to the skin. The downpour was so heavy that she couldn't see more than a few yards ahead. Then, without warning, the ground seemed to give way beneath her elephant. Roxanne peered over the edge of the shattered howdah to find the elephant sliding down a muddy bank into a river. All around there were floating logs. She caught her breath. The objects weren't logs; they were crocodiles. She threw herself face down in the box and held on.

When she felt the elephant wading ashore on the far side, Roxanne sat up and repeated the command to halt in as deep a voice as she could muster. The animal ignored her command, ripped off a branch, and tucked the leaves into her mouth. "Kneel!" Roxanne shouted. "Kneel!"

Abruptly the beast stopped and went down on her knees. Roxanne slid to the ground and backed away from the elephant. "Fool of a mountain on legs," she cried. "Stupid, lumbering . . ." She trailed off as the elephant chewed noisily and stared back at her.

Now that she was safely on the ground, she could admit to her fears for Alexander. She'd seen enough battles to recognize the sounds of fighting. Had the hunting party been ambushed or betrayed? Why hadn't the scouts reported enemy troops in the area? Had Alexander survived? And if he'd escaped the hostile troops, did he have any idea which direction the runaway elephant had carried her? If anything, the jungle here was thicker than on the other bank of the river. The trees and branches blocked out the sunlight and formed an almost impenetrable thicket.

Roxanne wiped a smear of blood from her cheek and examined herself for more serious injuries, finding none. Her sword was at her waist, her arrow case with three arrows over her shoulder. The bow was lost. Miraculously, one of Ambhi's javelins was dangling from the ruins of the howdah. She forced herself to approach the elephant and pull loose the javelin. It was intact.

"Well, what are you waiting for?" she demanded of the elephant. "Go! Do whatever it is you dimwitted creatures do when you've ruined your career!" The rain drowned her words and made her feel even more foolish. "Are you proud of yourself?"

The cow swung her trunk from side to side, moaning pitifully and grumbling pachyderm complaints before unleashing a stream of yellow urine. "You're stupid!" Roxanne said. "Stupid!" She shook a clenched fist at the elephant. "If you think I'm getting back up on you . . . think again!"

The elephant's trunk and ear were running with blood from the wounds of tiger claws. Roxanne's anger cooled as the noticed the injuries. "Poor thing," she soothed and cautiously came forward to touch the wounds. One was particularly deep, and the elephant shuddered as she ran her finger over it. Roxanne pressed hard and held. She knew the trunk was sensitive.

The beast gave low pitiful grunts. The wound was deep enough to be stitched, if there was any way to sew up an elephant. There was a great jagged tear in the right ear and deep cuts on the side and head. The rain would at least clean the open injuries. A tiger's claws would be filthy and leave infection if the wounds were not washed.

"I'm a fine one to accuse you of failing in duty," Roxanne said. "I never got off a shot." She released the pressure, and the wound oozed blood but remained closed. "That should stop it a bit, old girl." She patted the elephant's head. "You'll be all right."

The strain of not knowing what had happened to her husband and the others suddenly drained her of strength. Weary beyond belief, she looked about for some shelter from the rain. A huge tree with projecting roots seemed the driest; she crawled underneath, trying not to think about snakes, and huddled into a ball. She meant only to rest a few minutes, but instead fell into a deep sleep.

A withered hand on her face brought a silent scream. Roxanne's heart skipped a beat. The monkey shrieked and bounded away into the semidarkness. A monkey! Was she a child to be frightened by a harmless creature? She flushed in the darkness. How long had she slept? "Elephant? Are you still there?" A great shadowy form nearby answered the question. The rain had tapered off to a faint drizzle, muffling the night sounds of the jungle.

Thoughts of the tiger came spilling back. The jungle was no place to be alone in the dark for hours without a fire. It was the time of hunting. She walked toward the elephant, making soothing noises. "Pretty girl," she coaxed; "good girl." She gave the command to kneel, and when the elephant obeyed, Roxanne climbed back into the broken howdah. "Up!" Obediently, the elephant stood.

Now what? Without moon or familiar stars, how could she know direction or distance? The elephant's instincts would have to be good enough. Roxanne edged forward to grasp what was left of the mahout's harness. The javelin staff would have to do for a goad. Roxanne uttered all the Sanskrit words she remembered for "forward," and the elephant began to walk.

From somewhere off in the blackness, a leopard screamed, sending shivers down Roxanne's spine. Eyes were everywhere in the trees, glowing red and yellow. Twigs crunched under the elephant's feet. Roxanne tucked a foot around the harness and held on with one hand. The river, wherever it was, must be crossed to take them back in the direction of Alexander's camp. But she was hopelessly lost. "Take me somewhere," she begged the elephant. "Anywhere."

For hours, they wandered through the endless jungle, turning onto animal trails and crossing and recrossing seemingly identical rivers. The dawn was foggy with no real sunrise, just a gradual lightening of the steamy foliage above and around them. Once, they passed a herd of wild elephants. The bull trumpeted warningly and several cows collected calves and moved quickly away. Roxanne's elephant plunged ahead, seeming indifferent to her free cousins and their calls.

They crossed a small clearing and then another with fresh slash marks. The trail widened slightly, and Roxanne thought she saw the tracks of a man's bare foot. They were clearly nearing something, but what? She waited expectantly.

Suddenly the cow threw up her trunk and called. The signal was answered by another elephant. A man appeared on the path ahead of them, leading a hump-backed ox. He dropped the animal's lead and ran back the way he had come. Minutes later, a half-dozen mounted Indian archers rounded the bend and galloped toward Roxanne. "Halt," she ordered the big beast, and to her surprise, the elephant stopped and kneeled.

The soldiers surrounded the elephant menacingly, bows drawn. The leader shouted something incomprehensible to Roxanne. She straightened her back. "Greetings," she said in formal Sanskrit. "I bring you word from the great Lord Alexander, High King of Macedon, Greece, and Persia."

The officer said something to the man beside him, and then glared harder at Roxanne. Again he shouted. His accent was deplorable. It sounded like something about his Rajah and Porus.

"Alexander," Roxanne repeated. "Alexander and King Porus." A gleam of understanding showed in the man's eyes. A minute later, two soldiers seized her and threw her to the ground. She opened her mouth to yell, and the point of a javelin was pressed to her throat. The men stripped her of weapons, tied her wrists, and tossed her over the withers of the officer's horse.

They galloped back along the road, leaving the elephant

228

with two of the archers. "You're making a mistake," Roxanne protested. But she felt hers had been in mentioning Porus's name.

After a time, she lifted her head to see where they were going, earning a cuff on the cheek from her captor. They passed through thick stone walls into an enclosed town. Two-story buildings lined the paved streets as they galloped through the crowded thoroughfares, reining up at the foot of a wide set of steps.

Roxanne heard Porus's name distinctly as the archer conferred with guards at the bottom of the steps. Then she was shoved off the horse, barely catching herself. The officer dismounted, wound a hand in her hair, and pushed her up the steep stairs, followed by several of the guards. There was a set of doors at the top, also guarded. The conversation was repeated, and the group passed through into a vast inner courtyard.

A white-haired official in a long linen tunic approached slowly. Roxanne's captor bowed and began to repeat his story. "I am not a subject of King Porus," Roxanne interrupted. "I am the wife of the High King Alexander. Alexander!" Slowly the speech pattern her captors were using was filtering through to her. Ends of words were dropped and certain sounds lisped. "Alexander," she repeated.

The older man stared at her incredulously. He could not have been more surprised if an elephant had talked. Her captor twisted her hair cruelly, forcing her to her knees, and she cursed him roundly in Bactrian. Driving her head forward, using the full force of her legs, Roxanne butted him in the groin area as hard as she could. The man staggered backward, clutching his midsection, and began to be sick. A guard whipped out a sword and brought it to Roxanne's exposed neck.

"No!" The official waved his staff, and two burly men took her arms. He turned and marched toward the main buildings and they followed, dragging Roxanne between them. With great satisfaction, Roxanne heard the bowman retching and the laughter of onlookers.

Inside the building, they passed up two flights of stairs and down twisting corridors to an imposing reception room. The guards held Roxanne while the official went forward to speak with a blue-bearded man seated in an ornate chair.

Another wait, and then they went into a smaller chamber. An extremely thin young man entered. He was richly dressed and had an effeminate manner. He addressed Roxanne in a lisping but comprehensible manner. "I demand to know who you are and why you are here. Who sent you?"

"I have explained to these other gentlemen—" Roxanne's tone was crisp. "I am the wife of Lord Alexander, the great king and conqueror."

"These men say you come from King Porus. Why are you lying to me now?" The point of his beard was waxed, and he brought his face close to hers in an unpleasant way.

"King Porus was conquered by my husband, Lord Alexander. Is he an enemy of your Rajah?"

"A most ancient and cunning enemy."

"Do you know King Ambhi of Taxila?"

"He is equally despised by our great Rajah. Now you will ask no more questions. You will only answer them. What manner of spy are you?"

"I am no spy. I am the Princess Roxanne, wife to the High King Alexander."

"You are lying, woman. The consort of a king does not travel the jungle alone. Take her away. We will have her questioned in a more interesting manner." He clapped his hands, and two red-turbaned thugs appeared.

Roxanne's chin went up and she regarded him regally. "My husband and I were tiger hunting. My mahout was lost and the elephant panicked. I became separated from my hunting party. If you do not treat me with the respect due my station, you will be very sorry."

Roxanne stared at the gray blocks of stone. The room was small and bare, with not even a blanket to soften the floor, and the only light came from a slit in the wall high overhead. Her head hurt, and she hoped she wasn't getting sick. They had offered her no food or water and had taken away the dagger strapped to the inside of her leg. Poor hospitality, she thought wryly.

The cell stank of mold, and spider webs laced the corners and crept across the floor. The door was solid wood; she could not even see into the corridor. There was no sound in the room but that of her own breathing. Hours dragged by, and finally she slept, waking in total darkness and then sleeping again. On the second day, Roxanne was weak from hunger and beginning to imagine things. She forced herself to exercise and recite Chinese lessons from her childhood, pushing back the dread that she had been forgotten here.

"Come out, woman!" It was the lisping dandy. Roxanne got to her feet slowly. A peacock feather sprouted from his elaborate topknot. On a better day, she would have plucked it and placed the feather in a more appropriate position.

"Where are you taking me?" she demanded. Why was the room spinning so? She forced herself erect.

"You'll find out soon enough." One of the red-turbaned thugs took each arm. Good enough . . . walking unaided was difficult anyway. She found herself dragged down another flight of steps to a room lit with smoky torches.

Roxanne caught her breath as they slammed her against a wall and fastened her with a neck collar and wristlets of iron. "Wait a minute!" she protested. "Let's talk about this first!" The dandy pointed, and a guard ripped her tunic away. An oath worthy of a Sogdian camel driver escaped her swollen lips.

"Now, spy, perhaps you will answer my questions. Who is your master?" One of the guards came forward with a brazier and began to heat an iron in the red-hot coals. "It would be a shame to ruin such beauty," he taunted. "I will begin with the face." He touched her cheek lightly.

"I will speak, but only for the ears of the Rajah himself."

"You will speak for me, woman. You will say all you know." The guard lifted the branding iron and brought it to her eye level. Roxanne could feel the heat, and she forced herself to swallow the terror that threatened her reason. "Shall we start with the forehead? Or perhaps an eye?" He laughed. "When I am through, no man will look at you again."

"Alexander will nail your hide to the city wall, Indian. Only jungle will grow where your city stands if you touch a hair on my head."

"The kiss of iron will change your insolence." The brand touched Roxanne's bare skin, and an agony of torment swept through her. The smell of burning flesh filled the air, and she fell into a pit of blackness.

The tiger's claw ripped at her, and she struggled with the massive head. The amber eyes grew larger and larger, and Roxanne fell into the rending jaws, tumbling down and down. She hit bottom with a start, and her hand grasped the silken coverlet.

The pain was still with her. Her trembling hand traced the outlines of her face. It was smooth and unblemished. Tentatively she explored her arms and breasts. Was she weak or drugged? She wore strange clothing, soft to the touch. Silk?

A woman pushed aside the bed hangings, letting sunlight sweep across Roxanne's face. The first thing she saw was a pot of salve. The woman pointed at Roxanne's left thigh. "I fix," she said and held out the pot. "Fix burn." Her speech was slow and loud as one might speak to a dull child.

Roxanne threw aside the spread. An ugly burn on the top of her thigh throbbed. She took the salve from the servant and applied it herself; it numbed the ache somewhat. The burn would heal in time, but she would carry the outline of a leaping tiger to her grave. Silently she cursed the dandy and all his forebears. *I will have my vengeance,* she swore silently, *if I must trade my immortal soul for it!*

The woman stepped back, and Roxanne got out of bed. The chamber was large, with crimson and purple wall hangings and a wall of shuttered windows. Roxanne pushed one aside and stepped out on a wide stone balcony. Below her, the jungle spread out, a sea of green. "What is this place?" Roxanne asked. "Who is king here?"

"This is the palace of the Great Rajah, the breath of heaven," the woman replied. "His eldest son, Prince Nandin, has spared your life."

"Prince Nandin did this?" Roxanne pointed to the burn on her leg. "Did he put this mark on me?"

The woman snickered behind a well-manicured hand. "No, that was Purdy. He is a chamberlain of the third degree. Purdy is not even a man, if you take my meaning." She giggled again and made a gesture. "But he did brand you at the prince's command."

Roxanne looked at the woman more closely. "You are no ordinary servant. What is your place here?"

The woman frowned. "Once I was a favorite of the Rajah, but now I have seen too many years. I have my duties. You may call me Mistress."

"Not likely." Roxanne crossed to the latticework doorway. It was barred from the outside. "Guards?" she asked.

"Of course." She laid a hand on Roxanne's arm. "If you want to stay alive, you will follow my instructions. I will teach you how to please Prince Nandin."

"I am the wife of a great king, Alexander of Macedon! He has come with his army to conquer all of India. I serve no man but my lord." Where the hell was her great lord? It was his fault she was in this situation! He had better get her out of it, and quickly! Roxanne brushed off the woman's hand. "Do not touch me if you value your safety. I am a queen in my own land!"

"It matters not to me! I take orders from the prince. Here, you are a woman like any other. He requires many beautiful women for his service. You will comply, or you will be returned to Purdy. The chamberlain is permitted to profit from the prince's castoffs. There is a brisk market for even soiled goods among those who find pleasure in the pain of women." She pointed to a table. "There is food and drink. The prince has graciously instructed that you be given all you need to recover your strength before he calls for you." She went to the door, knocked, and was let out.

Roxanne circled the room, her eyes searching for some weapon or other exit. Finding none, she returned to the food and examined it carefully. The fruit still had skin on it; she would eat that. She would not partake of the rest, lest it be drugged.

For a week, Roxanne did not see the woman. Servants came to bathe and dress her hair and to bring perfumes and saris of brilliant colors. They did not answer her questions or give any sign that they understood her.

On the ninth day, the aging concubine returned. "Ah," she admitted. "You look more suitable to serve the prince. He has demanded that you come to him tonight."

Roxanne took a deep breath. "You do not understand me, woman. I am not a whore, and I will not act as one to your Prince Nandin."

The older woman walked around Roxanne critically. "Your skin is too pale. It resembles the belly of a snake, and your eyes are an unnatural color."

"Yours is a neck so skinny I could wring it like I would a pigeon."

Startled, the woman stepped back. "I have warned Prince Nandin that you may be deranged. He feels you will provide an interesting diversion. The prince's needs are somewhat different from those of lesser men. But any disobedience on your part will bring instant death." She took a shimmering length of silk from those spread on a couch for her consideration. "You will wear this. The prince is partial to gold. Prepare yourself—someone will come for you in an hour."

When she was alone, Roxanne went again to the balcony. The courtyard was far below, and enemy soldiers lingered there. She was trapped like a rabbit in a snare.

Slowly she put on the gilded costume. It would not do to alarm her captors yet. She'd no more play the whore for this prince than she would a Scythian. Alexander's fiends of Hades take them all. She had not yet used all her wit. From the dressing table she took jewelry and paints to do her face. If her beauty was a weapon, then it should be honed before battle.

Four men came to escort her to the apartments of Prince Nandin. They wore the red turbans that she assumed identified them as the palace guard. They were all big men, nearly six feet and broad, with thick black eyebrows and black curling mustaches. They did not lay hands on her, but walked closely before and behind her.

They escorted her up and down marble stairways and through open rooms and hallways until at last they reached a golden door guarded by four men in green uniforms and turbans. They stood with shields of gold before the door and would not give way until a steward came from inside with the order. The door opened again, and Roxanne was shoved inside. It closed behind her solidly, and she looked about the magnificently furnished chamber.

The walls, what she could see of them, were pink marble swirled with gray. Tapestries with hunting scenes hung everywhere, and the ceilings were draped with what seemed to be white linen clouds. A tiger skin lay under her feet, and a pair of green parrots swung from golden bars in an octagonal ivory cage. One bird squawked obscenities with an almost human voice, and Roxanne shivered despite the heat.

"Don't dawdle," a man called. "Come in so that I may see you, elephant woman." An archway led to an inner chamber. Roxanne passed ivory tables and benches and a vase of blue glass nearly as tall as a man. "Is your hair really the color of fire?" he questioned.

Roxanne stared into the black eyes of a young man, tall and muscular, wearing a robe of white linen covered with pearls. His sleek black hair was twisted into a knot in the fashion of the chamberlain and secured with a gold comb. The lower half of his face was covered with a veil, and one hand was twisted into a fist. "Come closer that I may see you clearly," he demanded. His voice was deep, not unlike the purring of some great cat. "I am the Prince Nandin. Have you a name, little bird?"

"I am the Princess Roxanne of Sogdiana and Bactria, wife to Alexander, Lord of Greece and Macedon, Lord of Asia and Conqueror of India," she answered defiantly. "And you would do well to remember it!"

Prince Nandin's amusement echoed through the vast apartments. "They said you were mad! Never mind, mad or not . . .

your body pleases me. I have never had an alabaster-skinned woman. Come here, I say."

Roxanne placed a chair between her and the prince. What did the veil hide? His eyes were ordinary enough, if a bit too close together. "Have you never heard of the High King Alexander?" she stalled.

"Si'kander? Yes, but he is far away. The rains have turned him back. The jungle and my father's army have defeated him."

"Alexander . . . Si'kander as you call him, will never turn back. He is more than a man! He is a god, and his vengeance will be terrible! He will level your city to rescue me. He will slaughter your people and sow salt in their fields. Not even your gods will be able to find a trace of where you once existed if you do not release me unharmed."

The prince came closer, and Roxanne moved away.

"There is nowhere to run, little bird. I tire of this game." Slowly he pulled the veil from his face, revealing scars so terrible as to be total disfigurement. "This is the mark of the tiger. I carry it also in my heart." His mouth was a bestial slash, revealing jagged teeth. "I have a tiger's lusts. If I must stalk you, you will know my anger." His normal hand closed on a lead-tipped whip. "You will feel only a little pain, and then I will you teach you joys sweeter than you ever dreamed of."

Chapter Nineteen

Roxanne dodged away. Nandin's whip cracked in empty space. She looked around frantically for a weapon. Her hand touched a marble bowl and she hurled it, striking the prince on the shoulder. He lashed out at her with the whip again, and she twisted to evade the blow. A flood of curses streamed from his mouth. His face contorted still more with anger.

Roxanne kept a healthy distance between them. She'd been trained in hand-to-hand combat, but she knew her strength could not compete with his. "What manner of man are you who must do battle against an unarmed woman?" she asked. "Give me the whip, and I will enjoy your game a little more."

He moved toward her, and she pitched a teakwood footstool at him. Nandin threw up an arm, and one leg struck his elbow, so that he gasped in pain. "I warn you," she said. "I'm not worth the effort." He kept coming, backing her into an inner chamber dominated by a great silk-curtained bed.

"Stop this idiocy. Kneel! Shall I have my guards strip and bind you? They will not be as gentle as I." Prince Nandin lowered the whip. "You cannot escape."

"Call your whole army if you like! But be prepared for the ridicule to follow. What manner of crown prince have they who cannot subdue a helpless woman?" From the corner of her eye, Roxanne saw a round copper shield and an ancient curved sword hanging on the wall beside the bed. She leaped onto a couch and yanked the weapon from its sheath.

Nandin rushed at her and grasped the bronze blade. Roxanne twisted the sword free. "Careful," she warned. "You have only one hand to lose."

The prince's eyes widened in astonishment as he stared down at his bloody palm. "You are no woman but a demon!"

"I am more woman than you are man!" Cold fury possessed her as she tightened her fingers on the hilt of the sword. Dull or not, the blade was still lethal. Eyes wild, Nandin stepped closer. Roxanne smiled. If he gave her the chance, she would slice this monster's head from his shoulders.

"You are mad," he said.

"Among my people, death in battle will carry me to paradise. Come, Nandin. I'll take you with me."

He crossed to the corner of the bed and yanked a heavy velvet cord. Instantly, guards ran into the room, swords drawn. "Take her," the prince ordered. "Alive!"

Roxanne backed against the wall. No swordsman on earth could stand off six. She raised the heavy weapon in mock salute and turned the point to her own throat, a fraction of a second too late. Rough hands wrenched the sword from her hands and threw her to the floor. She glared up into Nandin's grinning face.

"There!" he pointed. They carried her struggling to the bed and snapped a silver band around one ankle. A short chain ran to a brass ring in the floor. "Out!" the prince commanded. The guardsmen backed from the room bowing.

Roxanne wrenched at the chain. "I'll kill you."

"There is no need for such talk between us." The tip of his tongue flicked between broken teeth. "I will show you wonderful things. I promise . . . as long as you continue to please me . . . you will live. And you do please me, little savage." He stroked her arm. His fingers were cold and damp.

She shuddered. "A better man than you has called me savage."

Nandin went to a low table and poured amber liquid into a golden goblet. He sipped it slowly, as his gaze moved over her body. "I had not thought our meeting would be quite so physical," he purred. "You should be grateful to me. It was I who saved your life. My father's chamberlain believes you are a spy for King Porus. He went babbling to my father about my intervention."

"And you? Who do you think I am?" The image of the huge python that Alexander had killed in the jungle rose in her mind's eye, and it came to her that Nandin's eyes were like those of the snake. She struggled against the nausea that rose in her throat. If he came closer, she would spew all over him.

He shrugged. "It doesn't matter who you are. No woman ever leaves this room alive. If Si'kander comes, he won't know you were ever here. He will be told you died in the jungle. A pity—so young, so lovely. But the jungle is relentless." He began to remove his draped tunic.

Roxanne watched him intently. If he expected her to tremble like some half-grown virgin at the sight of his erect member, let him think again! Her hands were still free, and he would find it easier to bed a tiger.

Nandin dropped the linen undertunic, and she exhaled softly between clenched teeth. A knotted rope of flesh began at his left nipple and traversed his chest and belly to his groin. The tiger's claw had ruined his face, horribly scarred his body, and left devastation where his male parts had once hung.

"Look!" he commanded, his eyes glittering with dementia. "Does it sicken you to see a man who must pass water through a straw? Where are your cries of horror? Of disgust?" He picked up the leather whip. "You will scream in terror soon. I promise you."

Roxanne backed as far away as the chain would permit. Nandin seized her wrist, and she punched him in the face as hard as she could with her free hand. Cursing, he threw his full weight over her. She fought him with every ounce of her strength, but the prince forced her back, pinning her against the cushions. He spat blood and tried to bring his mouth down on hers. Roxanne wrenched a hand free and seized a fistful of his hair, yanking his head backwards.

Nandin struck her with his fist, momentarily stunning her, and then ripped away the tissue-fine fabric of her upper garment. Bare-breasted, Roxanne drove a knee into his groin and her head against the point of his chin. When he groaned and doubled up, she clawed her way out of his embrace.

"Spawn of a scorpion! I'll kill you!" He turned the weighted butt of the whip in his fist and raised it menacingly. Fists clenched, Roxanne glared at him, defying him to strike.

"Your Highness!" a male voice called. "Prince Nandin!" A servant threw himself facedown on the carpet, unable to conceal the horror in his eyes as he took in the extent of the crown prince's deformity.

"You dare to enter my private apartments without permission?" Nandin swung the whip's handle full into the man's face, following with two vicious blows to the back of his skull as he fell.

The prince kicked at the body with a bare foot and reached for his scattered clothing. "When I return, we'll finish what was begun," he promised Roxanne. He fastened the veil over his face. "We have a secret, you and I." He motioned toward his ruined manhood. "But the price of knowledge is high."

When he was gone, Roxanne sank to the bed, oblivious of her aches and bruises. The prince was a madman. She had only a short time, and she must escape before he returned. She gave the chain a few sharp yanks, but it was firmly secured to the floor. The silver shackles around her ankle unlocked with a key. But the key could be anywhere.

Roxanne rummaged through an ornate box on the low table beside the bed . . . no key here. An ivory toothpick rolled to the floor, and she seized it and began to work at the lock. Her fingers trembled, and she bit at her lower lip as tears of frustration rolled down her cheeks. It was useless.

She relaxed, closed her eyes, and breathed deeply, taking control of her emotions. Murmuring a prayer, she began to pick at the lock again. Minutes passed, and she had all but given up when the mechanism gave a dull click and the shackle fell open.

The delicate sandals she wore were worse than nothing; she kicked them off. A weapons chest by the wall produced an elegant dagger. Thus armed with the old sword and knife, Roxanne returned to the entranceway and knelt beside the figure on the floor. A touch told her that the man was dead. So would she be if she didn't act quickly.

She bolted the door. It would not hold the guards long, but it would slow them. She pushed a heavy table in front of the entrance, and then shoved furniture, bed hangings, and clothing against that.

She circled the apartments. There seemed to be only one entrance, the door she had blocked. She paused long enough to don an embroidered blue tunic and leg wrappings of linen. The tunic was too long, and she sliced it off just below the hip, and then slit the sides for mobility.

She glanced in a silver mirror. She was still too conspicuous; she must hide her hair. A turban would have to do. Galanus, the holy man, had taught her the art of winding the linen securely about her head. A charcoal brazier provided the black to mix with eye paint and cream. She spread the dark mixture over her exposed skin. It would have to do. Dawn was rising over the jungle. There was no time for further disguise.

The open balcony of the prince's apartment was too high for Roxanne to safely reach the ground. There was a garden below, but she suspected that this, too, would be well patrolled. Well, if she could not go down, she must go up. She tucked the prince's whip into her sash, and then emptied the charcoal brazier onto the pile of material at the entrance. The linen flamed up, and she jumped back. The parrots screamed, and she paused in her flight just long enough to open their cage.

The climb from the balcony to the roof above in the early morning light was terrifying. Roxanne pressed against the stones and clung to the crumbling masonry, inching her way upward. Once, she slipped, catching herself on the three-headed image of some foreign god. If anyone saw her on the wall, she would be lost.

A final last effort and one hand closed over the top edge. With a little cry, she scrambled up and over, lying prone on the flat roof while she caught her breath. She peered cautiously over the edge; black smoke was beginning to billow out of the royal apartments.

Roxanne raised her head in surprise. Smoke came also from the direction of the city. Roxanne scrambled higher over the rooftops of the palace, climbing toward a great bell-shaped dome. Sounds of fighting came faintly to her ears, and she suppressed a war whoop of pure joy. Alexander! In the distance two groups of struggling figures surged together. There were horses and elephants and the clash of swords above the screams of men.

Reports of battle came from a second direction and then a third. It was an all-out assault. There could be no doubt. Roxanne made out the colors of the Thracian Second. Alexander! How could he have known she was alive and prisoner here? She felt like jumping up and down and clapping her hands with joy.

Throughout the day, the battle raged. By noon, the Indians had retreated beyond the walls of the city to the palace itself. Would defenders be stationed on the rooftop? The palace was still burning, smoke coming from a hundred windows and balconies. The courtyards thronged with warriors. Roxanne wasn't sure how long the roof would be safe from the flames. Stone would not burn, of course, but sections were already crumbling, falling into the lower floors, and the surface of the roof was heating up.

Thick smoke hid the sun, and it was hard to breathe, let alone see. The reverberating sound of timbers striking the main gate came again and again. That would be the elephants. One after another, a file of elephants would swing the butts of logs against the ironbound wooden gates. Nothing could long bear the strain of such an assault. The sound stopped, and then a wave of human voices signaled the surge of an army through the crumbling gates.

Roxanne slid and scrambled down off the dome and ran across a flat roof, keeping low to avoid the blinding smoke. Breathing was difficult, and she wound part of the turban over her face. A third-floor balcony on the far side of the palace seemed her best hope. She hung from a ledge and then dropped catlike to the stone floor. When she parted the drapery, the room was empty with only a thin haze of smoke.

The halls were pandemonium. Soldiers and servants, reduced to the mentality of a mob, ransacked and plundered valuables and fled in all directions, often directly into the path of the fire. Roxanne passed among them unnoticed. Fights broke out and blades flashed; the floor was littered with bodies and scattered treasures. A thin boy dodged past two arguing soldiers, and Roxanne seized him by the arm, laying her dagger across his throat.

"Let me go!" he screamed, holding wide his empty hands. "I have nothing!"

"The way out!" she demanded. "Show me the way out of the palace."

"The foreign demons will murder us!"

"I'll take my chances with the demons. If you value your life, lead true."

Through a half-open door, Roxanne heard a woman's screams and caught a glimpse of two men throwing her to the floor. She steeled herself and gave the boy a shove. "Hurry!"

They passed through corridors and down stairs. Once, their path was blocked by flames, and they had to retreat and take another direction. As they turned the corner in a narrow servants' hallway, they came upon a man dragging a heavy iron-bound chest. The boy flattened himself against the stone wall in fear.

"Stand aside," the man lisped, raising a dagger menacingly.

"Purdy?" Roxanne's sword glittered in the firelight. The boy darted back the way they had come.

Purdy stared at Roxanne through the smoke.

The flash of her blade cut a ribbon across his cheek. He raised his knife clumsily. Curses tumbled from his lips as she backed him step by step down the hallway. He balked as the smoke became thicker and then dove at her with the dagger.

Roxanne sidestepped his charge, spun, and cut with a deft move. Purdy screamed, and his weapon clattered to the floor. He clutched his fingerless hand and howled like a wounded dog. "Mercy!" he cried.

"Not for all the jewels in India." Her blade slashed again, cutting away a portion of his left ear. The crackle of the flames became louder. "I will give you more than you gave me," Roxanne shouted. "I will give you a chance. Go! Run!"

Purdy looked over his shoulder at the burning hallway. "How? Where? I cannot!"

"But the exalted chamberlain cannot fear fire!" She raised her sword again, and with a shriek, Purdy dove into the smoke. Roxanne turned and ran, snatching up a velvet bag from the open chest and tucking the weight in the folds of her sash.

She stumbled into an open chamber. A score of Greek swordsmen were battling palace guards. The room was nearly clear of smoke. Realizing that she might easily be mistaken for an enemy, she backed up and dashed through another archway to a wide hall with a series of fountains down the center. A Macedonian battle helmet lay beside a slain youth. The fallen soldier's sword was better than the one she carried. Loosening belt and scabbard, she strapped them crossways over her shoulder, and donned the red-crested helmet. She'd not be so much a fool as to escape Nandin only to be murdered by her husband's troops, she thought as she wiped away some of the charcoal on her face.

Several highborn women fled wailing down the corridor, and Roxanne let them pass, moving cautiously in the direction they had come from. A red-turbaned guard appeared from a side passageway and attacked her. She kept him at bay until two Macedonians rounded the corner and the guardsman ran. Then she ducked into a huge, pillared hall.

The magnificent chamber was in shambles. Javelins and arrows flew through the air, and sword clashed on sword. The floor ran red with blood. Roxanne caught sight of Hephaestion, fending off two Indians. She put her back to a column and tried to think what to do. A mixture of sweat and charcoal ran into her eyes. A layer of smoke hung like a shroud over her head, sending her into a spasm of coughing.

Struggling for breath, she crouched closer to the floor. If Hephaestion was here in the thick of the fighting, she reasoned, her husband could not be far off. There! By the dais. That cap of blond curls could belong to no one but Alexander.

Glancing over her shoulder to see that she wasn't threatened from behind, she edged toward the throne, where Alexander battled a skillful opponent. The giant Indian soldier wielded his two-handed sword with deadly precision. He loomed a full head and shoulders over Alexander, yet the High King was on the attack. Roxanne's heart skipped a beat as Alexander dived beneath the oncoming blow to slash the turbaned man's midsection. The giant crumpled and Alexander was raising his sword to deliver the death stroke when suddenly Prince Nandin appeared from behind an ivory screen.

"Alexander! Behind you!" Roxanne screamed.

Her husband whirled to face the prince, blocking Nandin's blow with his sword. The bronze blade shattered, and Alexander hurled the pommel into Prince Nandin's veiled face.

"My lord!" Roxanne threw him the Greek sword.

He caught it and faced Nandin.

The prince closed in again, and Alexander attacked. Step by step, he drove the Indian back away from the throne. Nandin's blade nicked Alexander's forearm. Alexander feinted left, the prince blocked, and Alexander's sword cut through Nandin's defenses to pierce the prince's heart.

Roxanne rushed forward as Alexander withdrew the blade and wiped the blood on the dead man's tunic. Slowly she drew off her helmet and grinned up at the king. "Well done, my lord," she praised. "We will make a swordsman of you yet."

"Roxanne?" Stunned, Alexander stared at her. She threw herself into his arms and kissed the parted lips. "Roxanne, is it you?"

"Am I a ghost?"

She drew him aside into a sheltered alcove. "Didn't you come to rescue me?"

He held her, speechless.

"I cannot believe you are without words, Macedonian." She kissed him again.

"By the sword of Zeus, it is you." He covered her face and neck with kisses and wrapped his arms around her. "You are alive!"

"I kept waiting for you to come for me."

"I hoped you were a prisoner and not dead. The Rajah's soldiers hit us unaware just after I killed the tiger. If the tigress hadn't caused panic among the Rajah's men, we wouldn't have made it back to our camp. We were greatly outnumbered."

"The Rajah?"

"The king of this city. He murdered my peace emissaries and laid a trap for us in the jungle."

"I saw the soldiers. How did you escape with your lives?"

"Only some of us did." He shook his head. "We came back and searched for you, but found no trace. I thought the Rajah's men had captured you."

"In a manner, they did. The story, my lord, is a long and incredible one, better told between the sheets." She pulled away, her eyes moist, and pointed at the body. "This is the Crown Prince Nandin. The Rajah, I have never seen. But if you would save some of the booty, you must act quickly. The fire has consumed much of the palace . . . the fire I set for you."

"You? I should have guessed." He laughed. "The Rajah is dead, slain by his own men. They threw his head over the wall a few hours ago." He took her shoulders. "You were not harmed?"

"Beaten, tortured and starved, but not harmed . . . not in the way that would concern you, my lord." She crossed to the fallen prince and stripped away his lower garments. "Prince Nandin was my captor. He was not capable of taking that which you value most."

"No," Alexander said; "that is not what I value most." His eyes clouded with emotion. "I must see you to a place of safety, woman. You look more like a gutter thief than the wife of the High King. Hephaestion!"

"Roxanne? Congratulations, lady. You never cease to amaze me. You have more lives than a cat." Hephaestion saluted her mockingly.

"Take her somewhere safe," Alexander said. "I'll lick some order into these troops. And we'll strip the treasury before it falls about our ears." He kissed Roxanne again. "Guard her carefully, my friend. She slips through a man's fingers like mist."

Nearly forty Indian cities fell before Alexander's army as he swept to the Beas River. Through rain and flood, his troops marched and captured. Tales from beyond the Beas inflamed Alexander's imagination . . . wealthy cities . . . armies of elephants.

"India is far bigger than any realized," Alexander declared. "We will conquer it all, until we reach the ends of the earth." He stood before a gathering of his closest Companions, beaming, a brimming cup of wine in his hand. "Can't you see, Ptolemy? Hephaestion? The gods are with me! There is no limit to what I can do . . . only my own dreams."

"The men will go no farther," Hephaestion said wearily. "All your talking will do no good. They are tired, sick, and worn with fighting. They have so much treasure now that a man cannot carry it. We've left a trail behind us merchants would kill for. It's time to turn back."

"Aye," Perdiccas agreed. "Turn back. You've heard them. Not another step will they go, only home."

Alexander's good humor turned black, and his friends left the tent, leaving Roxanne cross-legged on a mat, polishing her dagger. "Well? Have you nothing to say?" he demanded.

"Nothing you would care to hear."

"Speak anyway. I value your advice, little Sogdian." He buried his head in his hands. "Why can't they understand?"

"My lord." She knelt by his feet and laid her head against his knee. "They are only men. You cannot expect of them what you expect of yourself. There are times when a leader

247

must go against his instincts. What good to be High King of the world if you have no followers? Give them what they desire, and you will have their loyalty again. You can turn this into a victory if you put your mind to it." She kissed his damp curls. "There are other lands, Alexander. You have said so yourself . . . Arabia . . . even the fabled land of Chin."

"Leave me . . . I would think on it."

"As you wish, my lord."

For two days, the high king remained in his tent alone and the army waited. On the third day, he came forth and assembled his troops to announce a great celebration. There would be feasting and games. Twelve magnificent altars would be erected in honor of the twelve gods of Greece. When the army had rested and recovered from wounds and illness, they would turn homeward toward Persia.

Ptolemy looked at Hephaestion meaningfully. "I didn't think he'd do it."

Hephaestion shrugged. "Something's brewing in that stubborn skull. He's as wily as an old midwife. But I for one will be glad to sleep in a real bed again and enjoy a little civilization. Cobras make for poor bed sport."

Ptolemy laughed. "Macedonia's a long way off, friend. I wouldn't count on seeing it anytime soon."

"Or ever." A shiver passed through Hephaestion, and he pushed through the joyous crowd to Alexander and slapped him on the back. "Maybe you're not totally mad after all."

Roxanne watched as men surged around the High King, cheering and lifting him on their shoulders. Home! Home was Sogdiana and the rolling steppes . . . home was the jagged mountains of Bactria. Oxyartes stepped from the tent nearby and went to his daughter, putting an arm around her shoulder. "So we are turning back," he said.

"Only as far as the Jhelum. We're going downriver from there to the sea. He didn't promise which route he was taking, only that he was returning to Persia."

"The rains are slacking, at least. This is an accursed country, fit only for Indians and serpents. I will rejoice to see the last of it."

Chapter Twenty

Almost as though the army's luck had changed when they turned back from the Beas River, the return journey to the Jhelum seemed charmed. The weather softened from rain to sunshine, and peace marked their steady progress. The soldiers and their women sang as they marched, and an air of laughter and good spirits filled the evening campsites.

It seemed to Roxanne that Alexander, too, had changed. His manner to her was gentler, more considerate, and gave evidence of a greater respect. "I thought I had lost you," he confided, "and the thought of waking every morning of my life alone was bitter." He began to bring Roxanne to council meetings and privately ask her opinion in matters of military judgment.

This morning they rode close, exchanging thoughts on the civil government of the satrapies Alexander had newly conquered. Roxanne glanced over her shoulder, careful to keep up her end of the discussion. Wolf had arrived at the camp the night before and brought with him a special gift for her lord. She meant to surprise Alexander, never an easy task.

Roxanne had embraced her silent guardian with tears of joy. Wolf had been a part of her life for so long that she hadn't realized what a hole his departure would leave. The dark eyes of the Bactrian were as impenetrable as ever, and his native costume seemed strangely out of place in this tropical jungle. Still, nothing would induce him to discard his rawhide tunic, trousers, and soft leather boots. He brought with him secret dispatches from rebel bands in the mountains of Bactria, reports from loyal friends, and the present she had requested he bring for her husband.

Alexander's warhorse had been slipping when they'd begun the journey into India, and Roxanne had guessed that Bucephalus's days were numbered. So she had instructed Wolf to seek out the finest stallion in the twin kingdoms for the High King. Wolf was a master equestrian and matchless in reading the inner heart of a horse.

A warhorse must be a special animal; speed, strength, and intelligence were vital but not enough. The mount that carried a man into battle must possess a certain something, difficult to put a name to. Roxanne called it heart. He must be utterly loyal to his master, willing to give up his life on the battlefield, yet canny enough to refuse a command that might take the life of his rider. This was the task she had given the Bactrian—find a worthy replacement for Bucephalus.

The black charger Wolf had brought from the mountains exceeded her dreams. Not only was he a magnificent animal with the coloring of Alexander's beloved friend, but he had been sired by Bucephalus himself, in Babylon. The price of the beast was staggering, but his training had been equal to his breeding. No saddle had touched his back until he was three years old. He had been broken gently, and then blooded in battle against the Scythians on the open steppes. This was indeed a horse fit to carry a conqueror.

"I should have taken more rubies from the chest in the Rajah's palace," Roxanne said wryly when Wolf signaled the sum he had promised for the warhorse. He stared at her blankly, and she shook her head. "Nothing, friend; I'm only worrying about finances."

Roxanne had stripped herself of jewels and coin when Wolf returned to Bactria. The Sogdian treasury had been emptied by Alexander. Slowly, Roxanne was replacing it. Her son, when he came to the throne, would need funds. Let her enemies complain of her extravagance. What they thought of her was meaningless. She would never lose sight of her duty as heir to the twin kingdoms.

Alexander's voice snapped her out of her thoughts. "I have decided that Ambhi can be trusted to govern his kingdom alone. He is young, but we have every confidence in his ability. His satrapy is three times as large as when we first crossed his borders; he can have no complaint."

"No, lord, you have treated him fairly and with honor. I feared for his life when the tigress attacked."

"He fought bravely against the Rajah's archers during our retreat from the hunt. He killed at least two men in hand-to-hand combat."

"And I'm certain he will remain loyal to you," Roxanne said.

Ambhi had greeted her like a lost sister when she returned to Alexander's camp. The young king's wounds had been slight, and healed without complication. Now he would have tiger scars to brag of to his ladies.

Roxanne smiled. "I have something for you, my lord." She signaled and Wolf galloped up, leading the black stallion. "A son of your Bucephalus, Alexander. May he carry you always to victory!"

Alexander's eyes sparkled as he slid off the bay he was riding and circled the young warhorse. The stallion arched his neck and pawed the ground, all the while watching Alexander with large, intelligent eyes. The horse's mane and tail flowed like rippling water, black as a starless night. His sleek hide was brushed until it gleamed, and his hooves were gilded.

"No one could replace Bucephalus, Alexander," Roxanne said. "But this is a noble animal. His name is Achilles."

Slowly Alexander approached the animal, lifting fingers to stroke the velvet nose and scratch the sensitive spot between his eyes. Achilles snorted, his ears twitched, and he sniffed the strange scent of the man before him. Deliberately Alexander blew his breath into the stallion's nostrils and whispered soothing endearments.

The horse nickered deep in his throat and rubbed his head against the man. "He is very like my Bucephalus," Alexander said hoarsely. "Was he truly sired by him?"

"Yes, my lord. The dam was one of the finest from King Darius's stables, a bay with white stockings. Achilles was foaled just outside of Babylon."

"Trained as a warhorse?"

Roxanne nodded. "If my lord would care to try him out? No man has ridden him since he was purchased in Bactria." That was the truth; no man had ridden him. She need not admit to the bruises on her own body. Achilles had spirit. He had tossed her twice last night before they'd come to an understanding. Dutifully she took the reins of Alexander's bay as he swung up on the black.

Man and horse became one, a harmony of pure movement, each the finest representation of his species. Alexander grinned boyishly and began to try out the black's paces, first a trot, then a slow canter. Alexander wheeled him in a tight pattern, and then dug his heels into the taut sides, and the stallion broke into an all-out gallop. "I've got to show him to Hephaestion," Alexander yelled.

Roxanne turned to the Bactrian. "Well done, friend. I think we can assume the king likes his present." She laughed, and then grew pensive. "Stay by me, Wolf. I have the taste of danger in my mouth. And I bid you, guard my lord as you would guard me. The future of our people lies in those strong hands." Wolf's feral eyes watched unblinkingly, and she could only guess what thoughts coursed within. "He is no longer our enemy, Wolf. Whether he is our friend, I do not know."

Alexander was back in moments. "This horse is a mount fit for Apollo!" he declared, stroking the noble arching neck. "What will you have as a reward for bringing us together?"

Roxanne frowned. "A Sogdian does not give gifts in hope of return. The honor is in your joy." Unconsciously, she stiffened. Did he think she was some petty Persian merchant to be offered a bribe? "I want nothing of you, my lord."

"Wait." He raised a hand. "I did not mean to offend you, Little Star. You are prickly as a jungle thorn. I am in your debt."

Alexander inclined his head, and then broke into the grin she could seldom resist. "Come, ride with me, I pray thee. I will be a faultless comrade."

Roxanne bit at her lower lip. "As my lord commands."

"You must come freely or not at all." His eyes were guileless as he offered a heavily muscled arm. She sighed and nodded, yielding, and he pulled her from the back of her own horse to ride before him.

They galloped past the troops, with Wolf keeping a safe distance behind. Alexander's left arm was locked around her waist, and she leaned against his firm body. "I love you, woman," he whispered into her hair. "And when our son is born, I will take you home to Macedonia and crown you queen of all my kingdoms. You are the daughter-in-law my mother deserves."

Roxanne's throat tightened; she had no wish to go to Macedonia or to wear Alexander's twin crown. She had her own. She would be a hated stranger in that far land. Could her son be less? Why was it that her flesh and Alexander's understood each other so well but never their souls?

"I swear, woman, you are armed to the teeth. Even my Silver Shields are less prepared! Do you think to hold off an army single-handed?"

Roxanne could not resist a gasp of amusement. "Why am I armed? You expect me to battle elephants, tigers, and all manner of hostile warriors without weapons?" Alexander guided the horse off the main trail into the jungle. "Where are you taking me?"

"Someplace we can be alone." His hand traveled up to caress her breast. Roxanne's nipples hardened as the familiar excitement coursed through her veins. "My lord, it is mid-morning," she protested weakly. She felt his passion growing.

"I like sharing a horse with you," he teased, exploring her body further with his gentle fingers.

"It is unfair." Roxanne drew a leg up and turned to face him, her arms around his neck. "This is better," she murmured, lifting her lips to be kissed and pressing against his broad, naked chest. *He smells sweet*, she thought and closed her eyes, blocking out all but Alexander's invading kiss.

A branch grazed his head. "Woman, you will kill me for love." He reined in the stallion and slid off, pulling her down with him. "Have you no shame?" His arms encircled her and clasped her tightly against him, while his hands moved down her back to cup her buttocks and fit her still closer to his form. "Enchantress." Breathing hard, he pushed her away and stamped the grass in a wide circle before spreading his scarlet cloak on the ground. "No snakes," he said. "Come lie with me."

Roxanne sank at his touch, allowing him to undress her. Lazily she raised her arms and stretched, pulling the ivory pins from her thick hair, so that her single braid fell forward over one bare shoulder.

"A man could drown in those eyes," Alexander murmured.

She trailed a finger from his brow down one cheek and brushed his sensuous lips. "You are too beautiful for a man, my lord. Perhaps you are the son of Apollo." She drew him down to taste those lips, her own parting eagerly to receive his hot, thrusting tongue.

The embers of her lust sparked, and, trembling, she caressed his sinewy shoulder and broad chest, stripping aside the thin cloth that covered his loins, and taking his throbbing erection in her hand. Alexander stretched beside her, and she moaned with joy as he cupped her breast and suckled. His free hand boldly searched out the secret places of her body, which opened, moist and warm, to his touch.

"Roxanne," he whispered hoarsely. "Roxanne . . ." He groaned, and his body trembled with passion as he entered her. She cried aloud at the moment of culmination, her teeth sinking into his flesh, drawing blood. "You are a tigress," he panted, his pupils large. He trailed a line of moist kisses across her damp throat. "I do love thee . . . and whatever you ask, though it be half my kingdom, I will grant it."

Tears filled Roxanne's eyes, and she buried her head in his shoulder, sobbing. He tipped up her chin and kissed her eyes and cheeks. "What is it? Why do you weep, heart of my heart?"

"Free my country, lord, and give me leave to return home."

His expression hardened. "You would leave me so easily?"

Roxanne pulled from his embrace. "I . . . I do not know. But . . . but if I may choose, I choose free will."

"Never! Never will I let you part from me, Roxanne! I will hold you even unto death. Nay—beyond death." He seized her roughly and drew her close. "You ask what I cannot give." His mouth closed on hers, a mouth no longer gentle. Roxanne yielded to his fierce assault and to the sexual act that followed. It was not an act of love, but the domination of a conqueror. Her body yielded, but her heart felt the icy chill of winter.

"You shall have the booty from the next city that falls," he promised later. "All that which is considered the High King's portion, I pledge to you. You may buy precious jewels or horses or mercenary troops. I care not."

She swallowed, choking back tears as he turned the full force of his charisma on her. "Do not be bitter, Little Star. I can't grant your request. If I free Sogdiana, why not Bactria? Why not all of Persia? You can see it is impossible!"

"If I cannot have Sogdiana, give me Bondoor to lead my new guards. Kayan returns to command your Flying Devils later this week. His injuries are finally improved."

"And Bondoor? He's recovered as well?"

Her captain had fought bravely beside her in the battle against King Porus until he took arrows in the chest and thigh. Bondoor's wounds had been so grave that he'd lain among the dead for a day and a night before he'd been found and taken to a field hospital. His recovery had been slow, complicated by an infection of the lungs, but Kayan felt that he was ready to take his post again.

"Yes," Roxanne replied. "Bondoor is fit, and we get on well."

"I fear the man isn't clever enough to deal with you, but who is? Besides me. Better he than that rascally cousin of yours." Alexander sat up and kissed the tip of her nose. "You have a perfect nose," he said. "In fact, you are quite perfectly arranged, although your chin is a bit too firm for a woman, and the mouth . . . the mouth . . ." He kissed her soundly. "A man cannot think straight for wanting to possess that mouth.

255

But your eyes are somewhat large, and they do have an unnatural slant."

Roxanne struck him a blow on the chest with her open palm. "You do not like my eyes or my chin or my mouth! Perhaps you would prefer to rearrange my features to suit your Greek expectations. You are a barbarian and know nothing of a woman's beauty."

"Gentle maiden," he soothed, his eyes dancing with mischief. He coughed and rubbed at his chest. "Have I not awarded you a perfect nose, even if it is freckled? But we must be fair, and one blow deserves another." An iron hand shot out and seized her, pulling her across his lap and delivering a stinging blow to her backside.

"Fiend," she protested. "I cannot reason with you. You are a madman."

Alexander took her hand and nibbled at the fingertips. "Am I demon or god? If you don't know, how can I? Surely no monster ever gave a wench such a pleasant ride." Roxanne pulled her hand away and lay back on the cape, laughing helplessly. He dropped beside her, chewing a blade of grass.

"We should stay here in the jungle, a man and a maid. It is the world that comes between us, Roxanne, for you are very like me."

"Me? Not likely, my lord. No one is like you." She relaxed and dreamily watched the multicolored birds above them. "The jungle is very beautiful at times, but it is not home."

"When we reach Susa, I will have a statue of you sculpted by the finest Greek artist, that all the world may remember your beauty."

"Better have one made of old Ox Head," she murmured sleepily. With luck, he would forget the statue. It was not the custom of her people to make a likeness of a person. Some said it captured the soul. Alexander had certainly had enough likenesses made of himself. His face stared out from coins and statues, paintings and palace walls. She would think on it. She burrowed closer to Alexander and took comfort in the feel of his arms around her. Who knew when or if such solitude and peace would come to them again?

That night Alexander hosted a banquet for his close friends and important allies. Roxanne was the only woman invited. The Persians, in particular, made no effort to conceal their dismay at her presence. They felt demeaned to share drink and talk with a mere woman. Still, Alexander would tolerate no insubordination and they attended, false smiles accompanying their bows to the Princess Roxanne.

Alexander was in a jovial mood, offering toasts to his Companions and to various officials. More and more, he was combining Greek and Asian troops, offering positions of trust to those who proved they were capable officers, regardless of race.

Roxanne sat at his right hand, Hephaestion at his left. She and Hephaestion had called a truce for the evening, trading small talk and laughter. Perdiccas sat on Hephaestion's left. Only Ptolemy was absent, kept to his tent by a recurring bout with malaria.

The Thracian reinforcements had arrived with pack trains of medicine and uniforms and newly forged weapons. The fresh troops were eager for their first taste of action, and their high spirits livened the entire army. The Thracian general eyed Roxanne coolly; he had heard tales of the foreign woman who held the High King's affections. Still, he was unprepared for her boldness in speaking out about military matters and the keenness of her observations.

"Offering no disrespect to your loyal Persians, my lord," Roxanne said. "But you can believe only half of what your Persian dispatches tell you of the situation in Susa and Persepolis. No Persian in his right mind would tell you of injustices or of diverted taxes."

A Mede stood, swaying righteously. "Your Majesty! These charges are unfounded! We have no reason to distrust . . ." He leaned forward on the table for support, spilling his wine goblet. A servant hurried to mop it and replace it with a full cup. "There has been a drought; naturally, crops are poor and revenue down."

"If my memory serves me, Lord Marzun, the area you speak of is well supplied with irrigation canals. The earth is fertile to

257

a depth of three meters. But surely you remember, the governor there is your cousin, is he not?" Marzun flamed and offered some slurred excuse.

Alexander laughed goodheartedly. "You must write this cousin, good Marzun, and inquire as to the crop and tax revenues. Perhaps some mistake has been made and can be easily rectified." He nudged Roxanne's knee beneath the table, and she saw the glow of admiration in her husband's eye. "Any relative of yours must be absolutely dependable. I trust in the honor of your family."

Oxyartes shook his head warningly. Why must his daughter delight in censuring these nobles publicly? A word to her lord in private would have served as well and gained her less animosity. Her lack of caution would be her downfall. As if reading his thoughts, the High King caught his eye and raised his cup in salute. Alexander loved Roxanne, of that Oxyartes was sure, and he would protect her. He prayed the Wise God it would be enough!

After midnight, the drinking grew heavier and the conversation coarser. Troops of dancing girls swirled in, black hair flowing as they bent and twisted to the wild strains of exotic music. Roxanne leaned close to Alexander and asked his leave to retire. "I am weary, my lord," she murmured.

"As you will," he answered fondly, kissing her and signaling Kayan to attend her. "A pleasant sleep. We will ride together again tomorrow."

Roxanne heard the laughter and shouts long after she left the royal pavilion. The rest of the camp was quiet, the pickets pacing their patrol vigilantly. Horses nickered softly, and from somewhere off an infant wailed. The heavy scent of cook fires lingered in the air, and a brilliant night sky arched overhead. "I miss my homeland," Roxanne said. "Remember the nights we climbed to the roof of the summer palace and watched the stars?"

Kayan nodded. "It seems another life."

"You used to point out pictures in the stars and tell me stories about them."

"Children's games."

"Kayan." She stopped in the shadows, wanting to touch him but not daring to put him in such danger. "You are too good a man to live alone. If the wife I chose for you makes you unhappy, divorce her and choose another."

"I want no other wife."

"Nonsense. It's your duty to your parents to provide legitimate grandchildren. Don't shut yourself off from life."

"As you are fond of saying, little cousin, perhaps this is our karma."

Two guards stood at attention outside Roxanne's tent. They were Bactrians and former members of the Flying Devils, appointed by Kayan to replace those men who had died with Parvona at the river camp. Roxanne waited beside them while Kayan took a torch and searched her quarters. She slept alone in her tent, with Soraya and her attending women in another pavilion close by. Many nights Alexander would come to her and share her bed until daybreak.

"It is safe, Princess," Kayan said as he came out. "Bondoor will be here in the morning. I ride at dawn to join my devils."

"So soon?"

"It is time," he answered.

She smiled to hide her distress. "May the Wise God watch over you and keep you safe."

"And you, noble lady." With a final salute, he walked away into the night.

She went inside, dropping the door cover behind her. Wolf had accompanied her to Alexander's banquet, and she'd insisted the Bactrian remain with her husband until his guests departed. It was true, she was tired, but her weariness was of the soul, not of the body. Parting with Kayan wasn't easy, but keeping him close might have meant disaster for them both.

She stabbed the point of her short sword into the earth beside her bed and slipped off her silk finery and heavy coronet. She had had a bit too much of the wine herself. Alexander was one for keeping cups full. She should know better. If she awoke with a splitting headache, she'd have no one to blame but herself.

She threw back the cover of her curtained bed and sat on

the edge of the platform to pull off her sandals. A movement caught her eye, and she flicked aside the sheet and froze.

In the dim torchlight, a cobra reared, spreading its hood and hissing menacingly. Roxanne fought back terror. She had seen a dozen men die of cobra bites, die horribly with blood oozing from every pore and the screams of their agony audible for half a mile.

Sweat trickled down her forehead as she stared at the snake. It was not large; perhaps two feet in length, but even a newly hatched cobra had venom enough to kill a grown man. The black and white speckled pattern of its body blurred before her eyes. If she wavered, even a hair's breadth, the cobra would strike. The hypnotic eyes and open mouth swayed before her. The snake's tongue flicked.

Roxanne caught the inside of her lip between her teeth and bit down until she tasted the warm saltiness of her own blood. She dared not cry out for help, but could only remain motionless on the chance the snake would tire of the game and slither harmlessly away.

The rustle of the entrance flap told her that someone had entered. She heard the soft tread of a man's boot. Still, she dared not stir or utter a sound. If an assassin was creeping close to drive a dagger into her back, she was helpless. She could not fight or even flee. Sweat beaded on her forehead. Her heart hammered against her ribs. And then, something hit the outside of the tent wall just beyond her bed.

The cobra veered to the left, drew back, and struck.

Chapter Twenty-one

A figure dove past her onto the bed, covering the snake with his body. Roxanne screamed and seized her sword, decapitating the cobra with one blow as it slithered onto the Persian carpet.

"Wolf!" She dropped the sword and grabbed his arm as her guards burst into the tent.

The snake's headless body thrashed harmlessly on the tent floor, and the Bactrian spat at it. Roxanne stared at him. "Wolf?" Slowly he bared his scarred chest, revealing the already blackening wounds where the cobra's fangs had torn at his flesh. Roxanne clutched Wolf's hand, her eyes overflowing with tears as the soldiers tore apart the bed in search of other snakes. They found one, smaller than the first, and quickly dispatched it.

As word spread through the camp of the assassination attempt against the princess, Oxyartes rushed to his daughter's side. Immediately after, Alexander and Perdiccas arrived. Roxanne paid them no heed. Her only thought was for Wolf as the bearded warrior slipped deeper and deeper into the grip of the cobra's lethal venom. That he was powerless to cry out in his agony made his dying seem all the worse to Roxanne.

Her father attempted to lead her away, but she shook off his hand. Wolf was her liege man, and it was her duty to see him on his final journey.

Wolf's last breath came almost as a relief, and for the first time, Roxanne became aware of Alexander's presence and the throng crowding into the pavilion.

"Are you hurt?" Her husband's fingers dug into her shoulders. "Roxanne? Answer me! Are you all right?"

She nodded and let Alexander pull her against him as her father gave orders for the care of Wolf's body. "He did it for me," she said, letting the tears flow. "The cobra's strike was for me."

"Wolf was your bodyguard," Alexander said. "It was his duty to protect you."

She closed her eyes and tried to rid her mind of the image of the striking snake. "I would not have asked it of him."

"It is not so hard a way to die for such as Wolf," Oxyartes said. "His path has ever been a sorrowful one. In paradise, he will regain his tongue."

"Perdiccas." Alexander released her and stepped back. "Take the princess to my quarters. Guard her with your life."

"No," she said. "Wolf must be—"

"Do as I say, woman. Your wild man is dead. Tonight, our concern must be for your safety."

"Let me take her with me," Oxyartes offered. "No one will—"

Alexander silenced him with a stare. "From this night, she sleeps with me. Perdiccas will keep her safe while I try to discover who wants her dead."

"We know who hates me enough to commit murder," Roxanne replied. "Your Companions. The Persians. The Indians. Half of your allies." She moved away from Perdiccas. "Am I such a fool that I'd go with him—who hates me as much as any of them?"

"What harm have I ever done you?" Perdiccas asked. He reached to grab her arm, and she drew her jeweled dagger. He stiffened, his hands doubling into fists. "By the gods, Alexander! Tame your own wife."

"I will not be shut away," Roxanne protested. "And I will not be subject to him."

"Or me, by your actions," Alexander said.

She didn't care if he turned his anger on her. From the gleam in his eyes and the manner in which he studied her guards, she feared that her own people would be the first to feel Alexander's rage. "It's not my subjects but your friends who did this."

He ignored her and Perdiccas. "Who has entered this pavilion tonight?" Alexander demanded.

"Only the princess's servants," the younger of the Bactrian guards said. "Two serving women. Arzu and . . ." The soldier shook his head. "I don't know the other one's name, lord, but she was Indian, young, dark-haired with a silver nose ring."

Roxanne nodded. "Durva. I've had no reason to distrust either of them. They came into my service after Parvona's death."

"Find them," Alexander said calmly. Roxanne shivered. When he spoke in such a tone, when his mouth grew thin and hard, someone would die.

Oxyartes shook his head. "Too late. They lie outside the women's tent with their throats cut. Soraya told me as I hurried here. They are certainly the guilty ones. But those who paid them have made certain that they will not talk."

Alexander glared at Perdiccas. "Are you still here? If you can't manage one woman, you're of no use to me tonight. Send Hephaestion."

Roxanne glanced at Oxyartes. "Father, please. Go to Soraya. Make certain she's safe." In the last months, she'd seen affection grow between the two of them, and she knew he was torn between wanting to be at her side and with Soraya.

"I'll not leave you," he answered. "Not when—"

Alexander bristled. "Think you I cannot care for my own wife?"

Oxyartes's chin went up. His features grew grimmer. "This is the third attempt on her life. The next may succeed."

"I would not have the two of you fight over me," she said. "I'll be fine, Father. I'll stay near my husband." She touched

Alexander's arm. "Don't send me away tonight, not when I need you most."

He motioned Oxyartes away, but the older man didn't budge. "I want your word, Highness, that this devilment is not by your order."

"If the High King wanted to be rid of me, he'd not need a cobra's venom to do his killing."

"Go, old man," Alexander said. "Get out of my sight while I remember you're my father-in-law." For seconds, Oxyartes glared back before placing his fist over his heart in salute, turning, and shouldering through the onlookers.

"My lord," Roxanne murmured. "I feel unwell. I . . ." She swayed against him. He caught her, gathered her in his arms, and laid her down on the bed.

"Out! All of you!" he bellowed.

She gripped his hand. "Don't leave me," she whispered. "I'm afraid."

"You should be," he answered when they were alone in the tent. "Do you take me for a fool to think I would believe such playacting?"

She sat up. "I'm sorry, but I was afraid you were about to do something you'd regret."

He scoffed, but laid his palm against her cheek. "You're wrong about my Companions. True, they hate you, but they love me more."

"You've been in the East so long, and yet you are still too trusting." She leaned against him. "You know how I hate snakes. And to have Wolf die so in front of me . . ."

"Speak no more of my friends." He leaned close and brushed his lips against her temple. "You're overwrought. To-morrow you will beg Perdiccas's forgiveness."

She averted her eyes meekly. "I'd sooner kiss his ass."

"All the more reason you will apologize. In public. Trust me, I'll find those responsible. I'll make them wish they'd never been born."

"Have you thought that the cobra might have been for both of us? If you'd come to my bed earlier—"

"If that's the plan, we'll make it easy for them. You will sleep

264

with me from now on, for otherwise I'd get no sleep worrying about you. You were right."

She looked at him with tear-swollen eyes. "When?"

"When you warned me not to bring you. You are nothing but trouble." He kissed her hair. "And I am a fool who has courted trouble all my life."

In the fall of 326 B.C., Alexander's army started downriver. Part of the force marched along each bank of the Jhelum. The remainder traveled by boat, his vessels nearing eight hundred in number. Dozens of enemy kingdoms lay between them and the sea, and Roxanne could see that Alexander was eager for new horizons, new adventures.

She wondered at the fleet her husband had built—flat-bottomed boats to ferry the horses, huge vessels for carrying grain and supplies, and magnificent galleys with three banks of oars. Soldiers had hired native workers to weave cloth for the sails and dye them a rich purple. It took thirty men to row the ship Roxanne stood upon. These sinewy oarsmen—all naked and sweating beneath the hot Indian sun—were experienced sailors from Egypt and Tyre and Greece under the capable guidance of Alexander's admiral and friend, Nearchus. For a woman of the mountains, it was a spectacular sight.

Alexander would need the fleet for exploring the coastline of the Indian Ocean and the Persian Gulf. The land ahead was known to be rugged, and the ships and land forces would aid one another in providing supplies.

The army fought its way from town to town until Roxanne tired of the constant warfare. Alexander had toughened, no longer seeking surrender before he attacked, almost as though he was turning his anger upon this new enemy for having been forced to retreat against the Indians. War was, after all, war, but Roxanne felt pity for the local tribesmen. This was no equal contest but slaughter.

"Would you have me leave these savages to fall upon our unprotected rear?" Alexander lashed out when Roxanne complained. "Shall I read you the day's list of our men and women slain from ambush?" She shook her head and retired to a shady spot on the trireme's deck. It was useless to argue with him when he was in such a mood. He was right, of course, but still wrong.

The Jhelum was treacherous with whirlpools and rapids, causing destruction among the ships and the threat of death from the huge crocodiles that infested its waters. Once, Alexander's ship collided with another trireme, and they were forced to swim for their lives. A crocodile snatched an archer barely an arm's length from Roxanne and devoured him alive.

They had passed by now into the country of the Mallians, a warlike and terrible race of ruthless fighters. Here, Alexander left the fleet and took command of a handpicked force of nearly eleven thousand of his finest cavalry. Seasoned and battle-wise, these veterans, many of whom were in their sixties, were nearly all Macedonians. Roxanne had pleaded with Alexander to add her own countrymen to this strike force, and he had surprisingly agreed. Her next request was not so easily granted.

"Take me with you, Alexander," Roxanne whispered as they lay close together beneath the sheets. "Let me dress as a man and take my place among my father's finest horsemen. You know that whenever you are gone from me, I get into trouble. And I have had a recurring dream. If you leave me here, you will never see me again." She was lying to him. She hadn't had any ominous dreams lately, but she did have an inner feeling of dread. To wait while he rode into danger would be torture. "Those who have tried to murder me will try again, and without you to protect me, my lord, they may well succeed."

"And what will men say of me—that I risk my own wife in battle?" He sat up, leaning on one elbow, and she felt the force of his stare in the darkness. "This will be a dangerous mission. The Mallians are not starving fishermen but warriors!"

"Since when have you cared what others thought, so long as you please yourself?" Roxanne coaxed. "Let it be known among Ptolemy's company that I am with the boats, and among Hephaestion's forces that you have put me in Ptolemy's care. When we are safely away, your men may recognize me, but who would dare to question you? I will be as secure with you and my own archers as I would be here. A crocodile nearly devoured me just last week." She trailed a finger across his bare chest. "You have seen me in battle, my lord. You know I am capable of defending myself, and I will wear armor if it pleases you."

"You looked ridiculous in that helmet." Alexander's voice was sharp, but she knew she had won her point. He was ever superstitious, and by not attacking her argument about the dream, he had already conceded the victory. "I will have no time to bother with you. We ride fast and hard. That cousin of yours and his Flying Devils shall have the honor of playing nursemaid to you, and if you receive even a scratch, I shall have his head."

"That's not fair!"

"As you say, woman, I care little for what others think." His mouth covered hers and he pressed her ardently back against the pallet. "And if you do not conceive soon, I will take that Persian princess to my bed. I must have a son, and a royal one, even if he be as timid as his mother."

"She speaks only her own tongue," Roxanne warned.

"Good! Perhaps I will get some peace from a woman's mouth."

The country was hot and dry, with great distances between wells. Alexander's force pressed hard, engaging small groups of hostile Mallians and destroying them to a man. A walled town was besieged and taken in two days, and the smoke of the ruined fortress blackened the sky for miles. Oxyartes ordered his Bactrians to drive the women and children to a hillside nearby and watch over them until the blood lust of the Macedonians had passed.

Alexander sent heralds to call for the surrender of the Mallian king. The army found the heralds' mutilated remains four days later. They had been blinded, nose and ears and male parts burned away. "Do you see what I am dealing with?" Alexander demanded as Roxanne gazed down at the pitiful bodies. "Look well, and think before you call my Macedonians savages!"

A sick taste rose in her throat, and she kept her eyes from his. There was a limit to Alexander's temper, and even she would not argue with him when that limit was reached. "This is the action of men without honor, my lord."

"A herald is unarmed, defenseless. No man fit to be a king would break the code!" he raged. "Such filth counts acts of mercy as weakness."

The army waited in the hot sun while the heralds were given proper burial rights, and the High King pledged a handsome pension to their families. Scouts rode in and Alexander conferred with them before announcing that the main Mallian army, under the direction of the king, had retreated to a great walled fortress city beside a river.

"My informants say this city cannot be taken!" Alexander cried to his Companions. "What say you?"

"Alexander! Alexander!" they roared. "It will fall before Alexander though it be the portals of hell!"

"And well it may be," Roxanne commented to her father as they shared dry bread at the next rest spot. "This is a godforsaken country my lord takes us into." She was hot in her heavy armor, and her mouth tasted like clay.

Kayan offered her a drink from his waterskin. "Not so loud," he warned. "Alexander's mood is not the best." His own features were streaked with dust, his beard as gray as an old man's. Kayan's eyes glowed through the mask of dirt as he watched Roxanne sip the warm liquid. Her fingers brushed his as she handed the waterskin back, and he flinched. "You are a great trouble to us all, Cousin," he said meaningfully. "I think you may be the greatest revenge our country has taken on the Greeks."

Roxanne shifted her heavy breastplate. "Armor in this heat is Alexander's subtle way of torturing me."

"It will keep an arrow from your chest," her father observed. "Still, I am easier with you here than back with the boats. I'll never be convinced that the Greeks didn't pay to have that cobra hidden in your bed."

"Nor I," Kayan agreed. The signal was given to move on, and they fell into a loose formation, urging the horses into a stiff mile-eating trot.

They rested the animals during the hottest part of the afternoon and rode on again through the night toward the Mallian fortress. It was a dry march, for the wells they passed were poisoned and only the experience of veteran campaigners kept them from dying horribly. Alexander's new mount, Achilles, proved his worth by demonstrating the endurance of his sire. With him, at least, Alexander was well pleased.

Dawn showed the enclosed city looming up on the horizon. The gates were closed and barred, and there was no smoke or sign of human activity. It might have been a fortress of the dead. Roxanne shivered as she scanned the ugly mud walls. "I don't like this place," she said to her father. "The city has an air of doom about it."

Fortunately, the river was too wide and deep to poison. The soldiers took their thirsty animals upriver to drink and then carried water back to the camp. The city's wastes would empty into the water in any case, and the invading army had no wish to drink their enemy's slops. Engineers set about constructing machines and ladders, and regular patrols were set up to prevent entrance or exit from the fortress.

"It is a large city," Alexander said to Perdiccas. "I have no doubt they have food and water enough for months. We will have to breach the walls. I've no time to waste on this worthless stretch of land."

With time on the side of the Mallians, Alexander's army had to keep up a constant attack on the city walls. By night, they launched fire missiles into the fortress, and by day, horsemen challenged the defenders. Having been severely warned by Alexander, Roxanne kept far enough away from the action to be bored. The days dragged out, one after another, as the siege continued, until she wished she had remained on the river. There, at least, the breeze was not ninety percent sand.

This was not a camp in which comfort was even a consideration. The officers' tents were only for sleeping, too low even to stand inside. The food was what they had brought, dry and monotonous with no fresh fruit and no meat. The Mallian king had blackened the countryside, destroying what could not be taken into the fortress, leaving nothing for Alexander's force to take. The hardships, Roxanne could endure without complaints. What she missed was her husband.

She was forced to admit to herself that she hated being separated from Alexander. His entire concentration was on the siege; he spoke not a dozen words to Roxanne in a day. He slept, when he slept, rolled in a blanket by Perdiccas's fire. Roxanne had to be content with the company of her father and Kayan. Even the nearness of her beloved cousin did not make up for the absence of her exasperating husband.

Roxanne busied herself in the mornings caring for the horses. Their legs and feet must be carefully inspected daily. A stone wedged in the frog of a hoof could lame an animal and cost the rider his life. She had brought medicines and bandages with her for man and horse. If she could not fight, she could care for those who would.

The two physicians Alexander had brought with him and their aides had seen enough of Roxanne's skill to welcome her assistance. In such a climate, any wound could fester and become fatal. A fractured bone usually meant amputation or a lingering death. Even insect bites could lead to serious complications. Medicine practiced under such conditions was crude at best, but the combined ability of the group was equal to any in the world.

Roxanne paused from stitching the forearm of a Macedonian to nod a greeting to Alexander. The boy hung, pinned between two sturdy Sogdian archers. "What happened?" Alexander demanded.

The youth flushed. "My horse bit me, Your Majesty."

Alexander motioned away an archer and took his place. "Here, let me." He glanced down at the lacerated flesh. "It's not too bad."

"I've cleaned it," Roxanne explained, "but it gapes, so we're sewing it shut. I'll coat the wound with honey and wrap it tightly." She held the ivory needle, strung with silk thread. "It bled freely, so I'm sure the evil humors have all escaped. I've offered to find him a more amiable mount, but he says he'll keep the one he has."

"One day you'll boast of this scar," Alexander told the injured boy.

"Ready?" Roxanne asked. The lad nodded and she quickly finished the job, and then bandaged it neatly. "Drink plenty of water and try to keep still for a day or so." She handed her supplies to an aide and followed Alexander as he walked away.

"How goes the siege, my lord?" she asked.

He answered with a foul curse, and she smiled at him.

"You'll take it," she said. "The man who captured the fortress at Tyre won't be stopped by a mud-walled city. Be patient." She held Achilles's bridle while Alexander swung up on his back. "Take no unnecessary risks. This place gives me an uneasy feeling."

"What did I tell you? Take a woman to war and she sees shadows behind every bush!" His eyes lit with amusement. "Patience is what I keep telling Perdiccas. It's something we both have little enough of." With a salute, he rode off toward the front line.

Roxanne did not speak with Alexander again before the morning meal of the following day. It was shared before dawn beside the embers of a watch fire. "Today we take the walls," he promised.

Roxanne watched silently as the first streaks of purple began to illuminate the starless sky. Even the sunrise here seemed foreign, as though this land possessed a different sun. The colors changed to red and gold, running together until the fiery ball rose above the dusty horizon. Uneasiness tugged at her heart, and she whispered a prayer for her lord's safety. Never before had nature's beauty failed to calm her restless mind. Was she indeed "seeing shadows behind every bush"?

The main attack was launched with fire and rock and a huge force of men flinging themselves at the fortress. Machines hurled missiles, and hundreds ran with ladders to scale the mud walls. Roxanne watched from horseback as Alexander rode back and forth shouting orders and lending support to the various assault teams. Even in the confusion, it was easy to spot the High King on his black charger. His gold battle helmet with its red crest gleamed in the sun and made a target for archers on the walls.

This was the type of warfare Roxanne liked least. Hand-to-hand fighting from horseback was simpler. In that case, you had the chance to see your opponent head on. Attacking a walled city was entirely different and involved noncombatants. She had no desire to ride within range of the archers or javelin throwers or have hot oil poured on her from above.

"Your husband takes too many chances," Kayan observed. "He would do better to wear plain armor, so he isn't so easily recognized. Alexander's luck will not last forever."

Roxanne turned fierce eyes on him. "And do you wish for that day, Kayan?"

He swore. "Are you never satisfied? Look at that!"

A new company ran forward carrying wooden ladders, leaned them against the walls, and began to climb, backed by lines of kneeling archers. The rugged Companions were veterans of this type of attack, and they swarmed up the narrow ladders, seemingly insensitive to the efforts of the defenders above.

Roxanne looked in the direction Kayan pointed. Alexander had dismounted and was climbing a ladder, sword in hand. "By the Wise God!" Roxanne cried. "He will be killed!" She put heels to her horse and galloped forward.

"Roxanne! No!" Kayan tried to head her off. "Stay back!" He lashed his raw-boned bay stallion up beside her and reached out.

Roxanne's leather whip cracked the air menacingly. "You're my bodyguard, Kayan! Not my master! Keep your hands off me!" She drew her gelding up so sharply that he reared, well behind the lines of Macedonian archers. "Did you think I planned to scramble up the ladder myself?" Her attention was riveted on the man in the red-crested helmet nearing the parapet.

A screaming Indian swordsman leaped naked over the wall,

and Alexander caught him on the point of his flashing weapon. Beside him, a ladder cracked under the weight of climbing men, and several tumbled more than twenty feet to the ground. Another instant and Alexander reached the top. His sword cut an arc of havoc around him, and two men followed him over the edge of the battlements. War cries of attackers and Mallians mingled with the screams of the dying, and Roxanne's horse shied at the scent of blood borne on the gritty wind.

Roxanne leaned forward anxiously. Was he truly protected by the gods? Other Macedonians were reaching the top, but the cost was terrible. Men fell, pierced with javelins and arrows. Some met death when their ladders were pushed off with long poles or were scalded by boiling water. Still the golden helmet moved freely.

Now there were only three Macedonians left on the parapet. The attack wavered as men slowed in the rush up the swaying ladders. Suddenly Alexander was silhouetted against the morning sky, sword upraised like some pagan god of war. He beckoned to his men, let out a cry, and leaped from the wall, not back to the ladders and freedom but into the fortress of his enemies. Without hesitation, his two Companions followed.

Roxanne heard a low groan and only numbly realized it was from her own throat.

"Alexander! Alexander!" the men cried.

"The High King! Alexander has fallen!"

"After him!" Roxanne shouted. "Follow your king! Are you men?" Her whip came down on her gelding's flanks, and archers scattered before the flying hooves. Roxanne drove among the Companions, her whip slashing. "Take the walls!" she ordered. "Capture the city or I will do it myself! Cowards! Will you leave Alexander to die alone?"

With mindless fury the Macedonians surged forward. Men formed human pyramids and climbed on each other's shoulders to reach the battlements. Soldiers propped new ladders against the walls. Others tore their way up the vertical surface by driving pegs into the dry mud and going up hand over hand with swords in their teeth.

Kayan reached Roxanne's side and grabbed her bridle. "Will you retreat, woman? Or must I knock you senseless and drag you!"

Roxanne wheeled her mount and galloped back toward the reserve troops. "Do you stand here like faint-hearted women while braver men take the fortress?"

From the left, Oxyartes's troops were massing on the main gate with fire, axe, and sword. Perdiccas waved, and his command followed him to the wall.

The Mallians could no more have stopped the assault than a man could turn a monsoon. The Macedonians swarmed over the walls in a dozen places at the same time the main gate cracked. Roxanne watched dry-eyed, caught in the grip of a fear she had never known before. It was not possible that Alexander had survived the leap into the Mallian den. Not possible, and yet it was not possible that he should die.

A rider galloped toward them. "He's dead! The High King is dead!"

Chapter Twenty-two

Roxanne's face hardened to a marble image. Numbness spread from her fingers and toes to encompass every inch of her body. Still, she did not move a muscle. *All is lost*, her mind cried. *He's gone*. Yet her heart could not accept that which was unthinkable.

"Not until I touch his cold flesh," Roxanne murmured only half aloud. "And place the coins on his dead eyes."

A second rider pounded across the dusty plain, and she waved him to stop. "Alexander?" she demanded.

"An arrow through the chest. He breathes, but barely." His dust-streaked face was wet with tears. "The physicians! They must come at once!"

Roxanne pointed toward the men he sought and then looked at Kayan. "Take me to him."

The king lay at the base of the wall, the sacred shield of Troy beside him. Heaps of dead and wounded Mallians were scattered about, mute testimony to the devastation of his sword. A sobbing Macedonian officer held Alexander's head in his lap.

Roxanne slid off her horse and approached her fallen husband. Silently the soldiers parted for her. Her throat tightened as she saw the long arrow protruding from Alexander's blood-covered chest. The wails of a dying city filled her ears, yet she heard nothing but the rasp of his breathing. Enraged, Alexander's army poured through the streets, dealing death and destruction to every living creature: man, child, or beast.

Roxanne pressed her fingertips to Alexander's throat . . . a faint pulse beat. The pink blood that oozed around the base of the arrow meant the shaft had pierced a lung. She knew that his condition was critical. Not one man in twenty survived such a wound. Not one in a hundred. Her husband's eyes were closed, his color like sour milk. "Oh, Alexander," she whispered. "My lord, what have you done?"

Perdiccas knelt beside her in the dust. "I'll have him carried back to camp."

Roxanne shook her head. "He cannot be moved so far."

"The arrow must come out—quick, if he's to have a chance." The general scowled at her. "This is no place for you."

Anger pierced her grief. "Order a room cleared," she said. "We need a table, water, and a fire." She glanced toward the open doorway of a dwelling across the street. "There. That will do."

"The physicians will be here soon," Perdiccas hedged. "They may—"

Roxanne stood and faced him with such venom in her eyes that Kayan stepped between them, hand on his sword. "Do as I say, Perdiccas," she said. "Lest I name you the king's murderer before your own army. What use to carry him to a field hospital on the bare plain when we can operate on him not thirty feet away?"

Perdiccas reddened. "I had not thought. You're right," he said. Hastily he gave the orders to have her demands carried out.

Roxanne knelt beside Alexander, placed her palm on his forehead, and closed her eyes in prayer. Kayan stood over her, fiercely protective.

The physicians arrived as men carried Alexander into the building. Roxanne dashed bowls and the remains of someone's supper onto the floor and spread clean linen on the table. The soldiers laid an unconscious Alexander on his back. A dozen of his friends crowded into the room, and Roxanne made no effort to send them away, asking only that they give the doctors room to work. The senior physician, Orestes, examined the arrow wound, and shook his head gravely.

"The arrowhead is lodged in the bone behind the lung," Roxanne said as she washed dirt and blood from Alexander's chest. Kayan handed her a jug of wine, and she poured that over the injury.

"I agree." Orestes turned away to wash his hands. "The arrow must be removed immediately." His voice trailed off hesitantly. "Under the best circumstances, this would be difficult. The High King has lost much blood, and there is danger of lockjaw. I would recommend purging at once."

The second doctor, a younger man by the name of Priam, joined them by the table. "The man with him remembers hearing the rush of air from the king's chest when the arrow struck. The lung is gravely wounded."

"I have removed arrows from a lung before," Orestes said, "but the men all died within hours, if not during the operation. I believe the High King will die no matter what we do. I will not operate on him and be accused of murder by his troops." He flushed. "It would be a useless gesture and only put him through more pain."

"Coward!" Roxanne said.

The man shrugged and turned away to confer with Perdiccas.

"He's right," Priam said to Roxanne. "Once, I had a patient with a lung wound who did live, but he was a cripple for life. He could walk no more than a few paces without losing his breath. If I cut out the arrow and Lord Alexander dies, they would crucify me."

"I'll do it myself," Roxanne answered. "Will you assist me?"

Priam fingered his dust-streaked beard with a ringed hand. "I will do so, Princess, if you command it. But I will not take the responsibility."

"Are you mad?" Perdiccas said. "If it is too risky for a physician, how can you allow a woman to cut him?"

Roxanne whirled on him. "Will you do it yourself, then? No? You have removed arrows on the battlefield! Alexander has too. One thing I know—he's dying. But death will not have him without a fight!"

Her eyes narrowed. "Have you nerve enough to hold him, Lord Perdiccas? And you?" She pointed to another friend of her husband. "I need four strong men. He is too weak for any drug. I must cut and pray the pain does not kill him."

A grizzled Macedonian in battered armor stepped forward, white-crested helmet dangling from a scarred hand. "I have been with him from the start, lady. If you're game, I am. I am no physician. But I know a dying man when I see one. Perdiccas?"

Cursing, Perdiccas stepped to Alexander's side and took hold of his left shoulder. "If you kill him, woman, I'll see you pay the price."

Ignoring him, Roxanne motioned to one of her guardsmen. He produced her velvet-lined medical case and opened it. Carefully she removed her instruments and carried them to the fire.

Flesh cut by fire-kissed steel was less prone to sicken. Whether it was the spiritual property of fire or some joining of metal and flame, she did not know. But her Indian teachers had insisted that infection was an enemy to healing and not an aid as the Greeks claimed.

Oxyartes pushed his way into the room.

He did not speak to her, but his presence lent her courage. Her father, at least, would not urge her to caution. She was not so foolish as to think her own life would be spared if Alexander died. Witch, they called her, and sorceress. She fervently wished it were so. She would need the powers of a sorceress. Her sharpest blade glowed red hot in the coals, and she carried it carefully to the table. Priam took his position across from her, and several of the doctors' assistants moved closer to await instructions.

Roxanne made no attempt to cut off the arrow shaft; that would only injure the lung further. She must cut deep and clean, freeing the iron arrowhead from the bone and removing the entire missile as quickly as possible. Then the wound would be cleaned with wine and closed. Alexander's body must do the rest. She hesitated and then leaned over her husband and kissed his cool, ivory lips. "Lend me your courage, Macedonian," she entreated silently, and began the fearsome task.

Alexander's eyes flickered as the knife cut into his chest, and he moaned, half conscious. Roxanne trembled inwardly, but her hand was steady. The point of the surgical knife grated on bone. She twisted the instrument and kept an even pressure on the arrow shaft. A second passed, then two, and suddenly the arrow was in her hand. Fresh blood bubbled up, and she dropped the arrow and pressed the wound together, raising her eyes to the Greek physician.

"He still breathes," the man assured her. "It was well done."

A murmur of approval came from the onlookers as Roxanne drenched the wound with more wine, padded it with fresh cotton gauze, and then wrapped it tightly with strips of linen. "He must have quiet now. If you could wait outside," Roxanne said. One by one, they filed out the low doorway.

She touched her lord's throat again. It seemed to her that his blood pulse was stronger now. "Attend the king," she ordered Priam. She turned to Oxyartes. "Father, I . . ."

Kayan's arm went around Roxanne, catching her as she fell. Oxyartes blocked the view from the outer door, and Kayan picked her up and carried her to the privacy of the adjoining room. Roxanne opened her eyes as Kayan applied a wet cloth to her face.

"What happened?" she murmured.

"You fainted. You grow soft, little cousin." His eyes lit with amusement. "You didn't faint when you cut that arrow from my knee . . . and it was your arrow."

"I couldn't have fainted," she protested. She sat up and sipped gratefully at the cup of water her father offered. "Did I?"

"We have successfully hidden your shame, Daughter," Oxyartes said gently. "Don't worry about it. I thought Perdiccas was going to puke when your knife grated on bone."

Roxanne sat up. "I'm all right now. I must go back to him." Oxyartes and Kayan exchanged glances. "I know what his chances are. But how many times have you seen him do the impossible? As you have so often told me, Father, Alexander is no ordinary man."

Through the long afternoon and evening, Roxanne sat beside him, moistening his lips and wiping the sweat from his pale face. Soldiers came and went, the physicians hovered in the background, and the sounds of the city died away.

"They are saying he is dead," Kayan told Roxanne. "Outside in the streets."

"See for yourself. His breath comes easier. He is asleep." She drew a linen coverlet over Alexander's chest. "It is a little cooler now, and he has a slight fever."

"You speak of me as though I were dead," Alexander said hoarsely. His lashes fluttered, and his gaze met hers.

"My lord! You are awake! Perdiccas!" Roxanne cried. She took Alexander's hand. "You took an arrow in the chest. We had to cut it out. How could you have done such a reckless thing?"

"The city?"

"Taken." Roxanne frowned. "They have slaughtered every man, woman, and child." The thought was repugnant; she pushed it to the far recesses of her mind. "They believed you dead."

"Do I look dead?" He tried to move and winced at the agony in his chest as he was shaken by spasms of coughing.

"Lie still, and be silent for once," she admonished. "You are badly wounded. If you die, they will murder me, and I have no wish to be ripped apart by a mob of angry barbarians!"

"I'm not—"

Roxanne covered his lips with her fingertips. "Shhh. Rest. I will drug you if I must."

He grimaced. "I'll be on a horse in a week."

"You may well be," Roxanne said. "But unless you want it

to be death's black horse and veiled rider, you'll follow orders instead of giving them!"

Within hours, the fever rose, and Alexander lapsed into semiconsciousness. He tossed and turned, every movement a detriment to healing. The physicians tried tying him, but so violent was the High King's reaction that they removed the restraints after only a few hours. Roxanne stayed by him day and night, touching him, whispering encouragement, and feeding him water as one might a baby, drop by drop.

Her voice calmed him as drugs and binding could not. So long as she sat by his side, held his hand, and continued talking to him, Alexander seemed content. And gradually, although he continued to suffer fever and chills, his breathing became easier and his pulse stronger.

It was impossible to remain long in the city among the unburied dead. The physicians ordered a litter to be stretched between horses, and Alexander was carried back across the desolate countryside toward the river and the rest of the army. Roxanne rode beside him, forcing frequent stops to change his linen and to give him water. She kept the sun from his fever-wracked body with a flimsy cloth shelter.

They met no resistance on the return trip. Word of the massacre of the Mallian city had spread, and the neighboring kings hastened to offer peace on any terms. Alexander held the country in the palm of his hand, and he was too weak even to lift that hand to his mouth to feed himself.

Roxanne's Bactrians hunted the sparse landscape for food, never returning empty-handed. The meat they brought back she boiled and mashed to liquid consistency, so that she could spoon the broth between her husband's lips. Gradually Alexander gained strength, each day waking for longer periods. At night, Roxanne slept beside him, listening for every noise and keeping him warm through the dark hours.

By the time the Jhelum River was sighted, Alexander was fully conscious and sitting up. "My lord!" a soldier called. "The river! I see purple sails!"

Alexander motioned to Roxanne. "Have them stop. And

bring me a horse. I will not have the army see me like this. They will believe I am a corpse."

"You will reopen the wound," she cautioned. "Leave well enough alone."

"A horse!" The familiar tone of command was back, even if the voice delivering it was weak and cracked.

Roxanne shrugged. "You heard the king." She signaled to an outrider. "Bring Achilles! My lord will ride." If Alexander's pride was up, he was not far from recovery. The black stallion was quickly led forward by eager hands and the king was helped onto the stallion's back.

White-lipped, Alexander took the reins. "Hephaestion would never let me hear the end of it if I was carried to his boat on a litter."

Roxanne knew the effort he made to hold his balance on the animal. She mounted and drew her own animal near him. "May we at least hold the horses to a walk?" she begged him. "Hephaestion would find even greater amusement if you tumbled into the dirt before his eyes." Alexander grinned, and the column started forward at a walk.

Riders and men afoot swarmed up the riverbank. Word had come of the High King's brush with death, and every man would see for himself if it was true. "Alexander! Alexander!" they cried. He saluted, and they went wild, screaming and whistling.

"Steady, my lord," Roxanne whispered. "Only a few hundred feet and we will have you on board the royal trireme. You can sleep for a week." She blinked back tears. Alexander had won the battle against death's veiled rider another time . . . but for how long? No matter . . . today was today, and Alexander rode at the head of his Companions.

Alexander paused long enough to recover and to build another city which he named Alexandria. Here, he divided the parts of India newly conquered between two satrapies, one to be ruled by a Macedonian and one by the tough old Sogdian, Oxyartes. His ships were refitted and restocked for the journey by sea. He had decided to send the elephants and many of his older Companions home by the old route to Susa. The ships would hug the coast under the command of Admiral Nearchas, and he would lead a force to explore a new road.

"It would be better if you went by water," Alexander urged Roxanne. "Or even with the elephants. The land ahead is barren."

Roxanne looked up from the manuscript she was copying. "I will only be parted from you by death, my lord. I cannot trust you alone. You are completely mad and must have a nursemaid."

Ptolemy roared with laughter. "If that is a declaration of love, it is the strangest I have ever heard."

"I suppose you think it is the act of a sane man to jump alone into the midst of hostile forces?" Roxanne was dressed in a tunic of sea green, embroidered with gold. An emerald the size of a man's thumb hung on a golden filigree wire in the center of her forehead. Her eyes and face had been made up in the Egyptian manner, and a subtle fragrance of frankincense and myrrh drifted from her elaborately coiled hair.

Ptolemy knew that Alexander had only last night returned to the lady's bed and nothing could shake his good humor. "You're right, Roxanne. He never showed much common sense as a boy either. Do you remember that raid on old Hector's—"

"Enough!" Alexander waved away the barber who was trimming his hair. The man was deaf and dumb and could carry no tales, but these two would destroy his face among the servants. "We will have no recitals of my boyhood pranks." He laid a hand on Roxanne's neck. "There is desert to be crossed in the new route we take. I only want you to know what I will be facing."

"Why? Why must you go by the desert? From what I hear, the land is impassable. The sand, the heat, the insects—"

"Impassable? Don't you know better than tell me that a thing cannot be done? The great Cyrus crossed that desert and survived. Am I less a king? Less a general? I tell you I will do it." He grinned. "Besides, we will need to dig wells along the coast for Nearchas's fleet to take on fresh water. He will provide us with fresh supplies before we enter the desert, and we will find the drinking water he needs. I have thought this out carefully. I can cross with my army. I will. And all those who scoff will be proved foolish old men."

"And foolish women. Yes, my lord." Roxanne smiled at him as she curled up on the low divan. "If you say you will, none shall attempt to stop you. But there is something else that concerns me. You have made my father the governor of this . . . this kingdom." She waved a hand. "Most of my people are remaining with him, as is only right. Father needs troops he can depend on while setting up the new regime."

"Where is this leading, lady?" Alexander asked. "Don't think that I'm leaving you here."

"I know better," she replied. "My father has no need of me now that he has taken a wife. Soraya will tend to his needs." The two had married only a week earlier, and although Roxanne would miss both Soraya and her father terribly, she could not wish to do anything to take away from what happiness they could find together.

"So what is it you want of me?" Alexander said.

"I would prefer that my ladies go by boat, but I am no sailor." She looked at him slyly. "Keep me by you, or I will run away to my mountains."

Alexander shook his head. "You heard her not two minutes ago promise faithfulness till death, and now she threatens to leave. A woman's mind is beyond comprehension. Come if you will." He chuckled. "I am only the High King here. What matters what I desire?"

"Thank you, my lord. I knew you could not bear to be parted from me."

Ptolemy drained his cup of wine. What was it about the Princess Roxanne that held Alexander so? She had great physical beauty, but that was true of many women, women with sweeter dispositions. Hers was the mind of a Persian general, as devious as any Ptolemy had ever known. In honesty, he had to admit he admired her spirit. Not that he would wish her in his bed, but he'd found a friendship with her such as he had never before experienced with a female. He set the cup down and turned his attention to what the lady was saying to Alexander.

"And you have promised, my lord," she continued, "that my father shall have only a temporary post here. He will not be happy away from the twin kingdoms too long."

"Oxyartes is tough enough to bring order here after we are gone. In a year or two, I will replace him and give him the governorship of your homeland." Alexander took the goblet his wife held out and offered a toast. "To Oxyartes, a man among men."

"May he live to see a hundred Sogdian summers." She cut her eyes to Ptolemy. "You are my witness. You heard my lord promise. Two years at most, and my father can return home."

"You are like some camel merchant, woman. Must I give you a written decree? When have I ever broken my word to you?" Alexander's eyes lit with merriment.

An official coughed at the doorway.

"It is time, my lord. You must review the veterans before they depart for Susa," Roxanne reminded him. She consulted a list. "You dine with Nearchas tonight and . . ."

Alexander threw up his hands. "I think I prefer the fighting." He took her hand formally. "Come, lady. I would have you with me. Tomorrow you will dress like some Scythian mercenary again. I must enjoy your beauty while I can."

Chapter Twenty-three

The desert route along the edge of the Arabian Sea was a difficult one. Rain was expected at this time of year to fill the sparse water holes that would enable a force of forty thousand to cross.

Mules and packhorses had replaced wagons, and only the strong were permitted to attempt the march. The land was desolate, barren rock, giving way to stretches of sand. The sun beat down by day, and nights were cool. The villages they passed were hardly recognizable as human habitations. The natives were almost naked with long hair and nails like savage beasts.

The army traveled by night and rested in the heat of the day. The wells were several days apart and too often dry. Wind howled over the sharp rocks and sand. Roxanne was glad she had sent her favorite horses with the elephants along the alternate route and was riding an Arabian camel. She had wound cotton cloth around her head and face in the nomad fashion to protect herself from the blowing sand, but nothing could keep the grit out of her eyes and mouth. Alexander rode horseback or walked at the head of the army when the sand was too deep to ride.

Night after night they marched, and the bitter land began to take a toll on the weaker members of the army. Pack animals foundered in the sand, breaking legs or simply collapsing with exhaustion. If it was impossible to get them on their feet, soldiers sliced their horses' throats to augment the short food supplies. The land became so fierce near the coast that when the fleet did not appear with promised supplies, it was necessary to cut inland and leave Nearchas to his own devices.

Roxanne had sent Bondoor with her women, but Kayan accompanied her. It was Kayan who had insisted that they be mounted on camels. The desert stretched for a thousand miles, and armies had perished there before. A camel could survive where a horse could not, carrying water within its great hump. The camels' broad, tough feet were well suited to the sand and crumbling rock, and the beasts did not seem to suffer from the heat as horses and mules did.

"Alexander was wrong to come this way," Kayan complained. "What if the rains do not come at all? We'll all die here." He scanned the forbidding desert that stretched as far as the eye could see. They'd passed no tree or patch of green in days. Hunters found no birds or game of any kind. Snakes there were aplenty. Kayan had lost two Flying Devils and three warhorses to their poisonous venom. "Even the sea with its unknown dangers would be better than this," he said.

Roxanne frowned. "It is not Alexander's fault if the rains are late." Her husband suffered as much as any man. Alexander's fair Macedonian complexion was darkened by the sun and his face lined with worry. The lung wound had weakened his constitution, and he slept only in snatched periods of time. It had taken all her feminine persuasion to get him to rest during the hottest part of the day.

"The children are dying." Kayan's hawk face was nearly hidden by folds of cloth. Were those tears that clouded his coal-black eyes?

The women that followed the army into the desert were mostly camp whores, common-law wives, and laundrywomen with their ragged children. The officers' wives had gone by ship or followed the elephants. Most of these women had no horses. They walked, staining the rocks with the blood of their feet. Some led donkeys or goats, and most were further burdened with children, cooking utensils, and household belongings.

The last well had been foul, and Alexander set armed soldiers to prevent any from drinking of it. What water they had was all but gone. Roxanne had given her own waterskin to a mother with a newborn. For the army to remain where they were would be a death sentence. The scouts had promised another water hole a day and a half ahead. The army must keep going, and those who could not march must be left behind.

"They were warned not to bring the children. They could have stayed behind or followed the main army," Roxanne reasoned. "Why were they so stubborn?" She had wept for the suffering of the little ones until her eyes were dry, but her main concern now was that Alexander keep his sanity. Without his leadership, there was no hope of crossing the hundreds of miles of desert still ahead.

Men who had carried treasure out of India found the booty too great a burden to bear and tossed it aside. There were greedy hands to seize it and carry it a few senseless miles more, but eventually the goblets, urns, and containers of precious spice were abandoned to the desert. Many of the soldiers were raw recruits, unused to discipline. It was no wonder that their courage was scoured away by the blistering winds and sinkholes of salt-encrusted mud. Roxanne lost count of those executed by their own officers for stealing water, or for draining the veins of horses to drink the blood.

The army was strung out for miles as the weaker fell farther and farther behind. Hephaestion had commanded the rear for days, before yielding his post to Perdiccas. Ptolemy had ridden three horses to ground on the right flank. Alexander's stallion had kept up the pace, although his ribs were beginning to show. All night, the High King had walked, resting the animal. Roxanne wondered if Alexander was truly flesh and blood.

Despite his protests, Roxanne had rubbed medicated cream

on his face and arms and had insisted he wear a cloak against the night chill. "Leave me, woman!" he said.

"You do what you must. Allow me the same privilege. Without you, my lord, there is no hope." She stood on tiptoe and kissed his forehead. "You will see us through to Susa, Alexander. The rains will come. Nearchas's fleet may land and send out scouts to find us."

"When? When the dead rise from their sea graves?" Cursing, he had taken his place at the head of the column, and Roxanne had mounted the waiting camel. His angry words slid off her back like grains of sand. Alexander must not lose faith in himself—not now.

Kayan drew his camel beside her and held out a waterskin. "Drink," he urged.

"Where did you get this?" Roxanne asked. "I thought we'd used the last."

"Drink."

There was no arguing when her cousin used that tone. She knew him capable of catching her and pouring it down her throat. A little vinegar had been added to the water to keep it fresh. It tasted heavenly, and she held the mouthful a long time before she swallowed.

"More," he commanded. Reluctantly she obeyed, then handed it back. Kayan tied the container closed without taking any for himself. "Will it do them any good for you to die of thirst? Even a water hole will only prolong their dying. We need the rains."

Kayan was party to information Alexander had not shared with his wife. The guides had deserted. Even the Companions believed the fleet lost. Crude maps and unfamiliar stars must guide them now. It was too late to turn back; they must go forward while their strength lasted.

Soldiers and camp followers began to drop that night. In the purple haze of dawn, Roxanne could see the trail the army had traveled by the vultures in the sky. Alexander had given the command that the dead were to be left where they lay. No energy could be wasted in giving them burial in the shifting sands. The army marched into mid-morning, putting as many miles behind them as they could before the sun reached its highest point.

Finally, when it became too hot to continue, Alexander gave the signal to make camp. Soldiers and camp followers erected flimsy sun shields and crawled beneath them. Some dug into the sand, seeking relief from the heat and biting flies.

Roxanne sought out her husband and found him with Hephaestion. "You must rest, Alexander," she said. She took a handful of dates from a leather pouch and offered them to the two men. They ate in silence, and Alexander shared his portion with Achilles.

Roxanne patted the stallion's neck and lifted each hoof to examine his feet. "He is more fit than you, my husband." She turned to Hephaestion. "Make him ride more. If he does not keep up his strength, his mind will begin to wander."

"Must you speak of me as though I weren't here?" Alexander's eyes were glassy, giving him the look of one half mad.

"I know you, my lord," she soothed. "No one questions your courage or your genius for command. But the desert heat saps us all. Human or god, your body is mortal and must have rest. You must drink." She motioned Kayan to bring a waterskin. "I have asked few favors of you, Alexander. But I ask this. Drink and sleep for a few hours. When you are rested, things will not be so bad."

Hephaestion nodded. "She's right."

Alexander swore a foul oath. "Do you think so little of me that I'd drink while my wife goes thirsty? While my men die?" He shook his head. "Better I pour it on the sand."

"You would, too," Hephaestion said. "No need to be that noble." He glanced at Kayan. "Take the water away before he makes fools of the lot of us."

"If you won't drink, at least lie down for a while," Roxanne pleaded.

Still swearing, Alexander crawled into the nearest shelter. "I will not sleep!" he warned her. But she sat beside him, applied damp cloths to his face, and fanned him until he drifted off. He did not stir until the first shadows of evening.

Roxanne smiled down at him. "Better?" she asked softly.

Alexander caught her hand and brought it down to his dry lips. "You were right, as usual." He turned her palm over and kissed her cracked knuckles. "I'll do what I should have done yesterday," he said. "The army will rest here through the night. I'll take a handful of men and find that damned water hole myself. If it's dry, at least we won't go out of our way for nothing."

"Take Hephaestion with you," she urged.

"Ptolemy. Hephaestion remains here to command my army."

"Take my camel," she said. "He is the strongest. Ptolemy can ride Kayan's beast. Your chances will double if you all use camels. And you can carry more water back."

Alexander nodded agreement. "I'll leave you Achilles," he said. "Hephaestion has the maps. We have only to hold out a little longer. The rains are overdue. This desert has been crossed before. We can cross it." He looked at her with haunted eyes. "The cost has been high. The children—"

Roxanne became brisk. "If you are going to hunt out that water hole, do so. You waste the hours of coolness lying here."

"When your tongue is sharp, I worry less about you, woman." Alexander laughed. He sent a scout to fetch Ptolemy.

"You know the right time to call me." Ptolemy held out a partially cooked piece of meat. "Your dinner."

"What is it?" Alexander bit into the gristly chunk.

"Mule." They both laughed, and Alexander finished the meat while he explained his plan.

Roxanne hurried to find Kayan and the camels before Alexander changed his mind. "Fasten that waterskin to Ptolemy's camel. Ptolemy, at least, will be sensible. If they die, so do all of us."

After they had ridden off, Roxanne slept fitfully in the shelter. Alexander's luck would hold, she told herself. If he said he would find water, he would. It was the first real rest she had had in days, and it was already morning when Achilles's soft, grumbling woke her. She sat up and rubbed gritty eyes. Her mouth felt as dry as old papyrus. Painfully she got up and stretched, braided her matted hair, and tucked it under the cotton cloth head-covering.

"Kayan?" Her cousin's face appeared at the opening. "See if you can find something for Achilles to eat. I want to ride back along the column and see if I can help with the women and children."

He shook his head. "I have my orders from the king. The army is desperate. They could turn their anger on you. You're to remain here until Alexander returns."

The hours passed slowly, and despite the biting flies, Roxanne drifted off to sleep again before being awakened by joyous shouts. "Alexander! Alexander!" She rushed outside to see five camels outlined on the horizon. Kayan led the black stallion forward, and she leaped on his back and galloped to meet her husband and his followers.

Alexander's beaming face answered her questions before she could ask. "My lord, you are safe?"

"There is water to the east, enough for all. We march in that direction as soon as the sun is lower. It's not far. We had to dig for it or we would have returned sooner."

The news raced through the army like wildfire. "Water! Water! Alexander has found us water!"

Men laughed and women wept with joy. What fools they had been to lose heart! Had Alexander ever failed them before? They were under the protection of the gods. Hardships were forgotten as the army turned toward the new wells with fresh hope.

The water holes marked the halfway point of the desert crossing, and soon after the army refreshed itself there, the skies began to cloud and the winds to smell of rain. Showers fell, filling outcrops of rock with small pools of water. The land did not become gentler, only harsher. There were ravines and valleys of deep sand, rocky outcrops, and wallows of waist-deep dust to struggle through. The army trudged on, gladdened by the thought that most of the desert lay behind and not ahead.

They camped that night on rough ground, making small

fires from dry brush to cook horseflesh. The thunderstorms made it difficult to keep the flames going, and most ate their meat nearly raw. Roxanne had refused the first portion Alexander offered. "You eat it. It would turn my stomach. This bread is like stone, but at least it won't whinny on the way down."

"Women!" He laughed. "Meat is meat, and I have eaten far worse." By the firelight, Roxanne noticed threads of silver in Alexander's golden curls. He remained in the full strength of his manhood, yet hardship had taken a toll on him.

"No doubt you have eaten worse, my lord," she replied. "But you are only a Greek barbarian." Hephaestion laughed as he gnawed at a bone. "Scythians will eat anything, too," Roxanne continued. "Dog is considered a delicacy."

"I can't say we've ever eaten dog," Ptolemy said. "But we did eat lion. Do you remember—" An ear-splitting crash of thunder deafened them. Lightning flashed, and rain began to beat on the threadbare tent, soaking them all.

"He promised me palaces," Roxanne grumbled, "and treasures of India. This is what I get." Alexander put his arm around her and pulled her close, kissing her soundly with greasy lips. "Ughh!" She grimaced and wiped her mouth. "Horse lips!"

The others roared with laughter, and Roxanne felt a sense of companionship and acceptance she had seldom realized among her husband's friends. Only Perdiccas remained cool, avoiding eye contact as though she were an embarrassment.

There was barely room to sit in the small enclosure which Alexander had ordered assembled on a rise in the middle of the camp. Jammed in together, they shared a skin of sour wine in the semidarkness. "You wanted to come campaigning, woman," Alexander teased.

"I did not. I begged to remain in Sogdiana."

"Begged? You have never begged for anything. Well"—Alexander laughed lecherously—"maybe for some things." His Companions howled, and Roxanne tried to crawl out of the shelter. Iron fingers closed on her wrist. "Stay, lady," he teased. "The conversation is just getting interesting."

She muttered a Bactrian curse under her breath.

"A toast," Ptolemy said. "To Roxanne's silence!" The toast was cheered and shared by all but Alexander, who had his hands full and was unable to reach his cup.

The storm was directly overhead now, unleashing torrents of rain. Suddenly a roar greater than thunder filled their brains; the earth seemed to shake beneath them. "Flood!" Alexander shouted. He dragged Roxanne outside in time to see a wall of water engulf the camp. There was no time to run. They stood helplessly as men and horses were swept away by the fury of the flash flood rushing down the canyon.

Kayan appeared at Roxanne's side, and Alexander thrust her into his arms. "Take care of her!" he ordered.

Kayan led her through waist-high water to a rocky hill. "Get down," he said. Lightning struck nearby, and thunder continued to boom overhead. They watched speechless as animals ran, soldiers screamed, and figures struggled to keep their heads above water. Beating rain mingled with the tears on Roxanne's cheeks.

Dawn showed the extent of the disaster. The river had dried up as quickly as it had come. Now there were only damp sand and scattered bodies. The numbers of dead were beyond belief. Nearly all the women and children had drowned. Counting the soldiers, more than five thousand lives had been lost. The numbers of pack animals and horses were decimated. Achilles and the royal party's riding camels survived; they had been hobbled beside Alexander's shelter. But Roxanne's heart bled for both the humans and magnificent horses that now were only rotting meat on the merciless sand.

There was nothing to do but to move on. The rest of the journey blurred in Roxanne's mind. Numbly she heard Alexander instructing Kayan to tie her to the camel saddle. The days and nights slid together. Gradually, the landscape began to change; the brown began to show spots of pale green. The terrible desert had been conquered by Alexander's army; but of the forty thousand that went in, no more than twenty-five thousand reached the far side.

At last, they reached the first outposts of habitation. The shattered army found food to restore their bodies and wine to numb their tortured minds. Rough tracks led to the broad road which led to Persepolis. Word came that the fleet under Admiral Nearchas—which all had believed lost—was safe; and Alexander's troops met and joined the main army force with the veteran Companions and the elephants.

The great procession entered Persepolis. Alexander was again draped in the trappings of an Oriental monarch. At her lord's insistence, Roxanne rode on Tuma's back, the roof of the magnificent howdah removed so all could view the flashing gems and beauty of the High King's wife. Crowds lined the streets, throwing flowers and screaming their approval. Alexander smiled back and waved, his eyes murderous behind the royal façade.

Roxanne knew the depths of her husband's fury. Long before they entered Persepolis, Alexander had received word of the treasonous actions of those he had left in power. Macedonians and Persians alike had betrayed his trust, embezzling funds, severely taxing the people, and ignoring laws which should have protected the citizens of the land in his absence. Worse, Harpalus, a man Alexander had known and trusted since childhood, had robbed the royal treasury and fled the High King's wrath.

Looters had violated the sacred tomb of Cyrus the Great, ravaging the sarcophagus and spilling the skeleton of the mighty king across the stone floor. Heads had already rolled for that crime. Alexander's honor had been challenged when the final resting place of such a monarch was disturbed, and the High King's revenge was terrible.

Everywhere the kingdom was uneasy. In Bactria, the Greeks had revolted. Philip, the Macedonian Alexander had left as satrap in India, had been murdered. Ambhi had put down the insurrection and awaited further orders. The Hindu Kush was in flames, and Oxyartes had marched on the rebels. For once, Alexander could not drop everything and lead troops to punish the offenders himself.

With a stroke of the pen, he gave Philip's satrapy into Ambhi's keeping; the boy king had earned his reward. Oxyartes's satrapy was quiet. He would leave it under the rule of his father-in-law's second-in-command while Oxyartes took back the Hindu Kush. The mountain passes must be kept open, and Oxyartes was the man to do it. The Hindu Kush was not Sogdiana, but it would be more to the tough old warrior's liking. Alexander dispatched fresh troops and supplies to aid in the struggle.

The High King sent another army under the leadership of a loyal Macedonian general to Bactria. The penalty for treason was death, and there would be no mercy for the rebels. Roxanne's heart chilled at the thought of more blood spilled in her beloved mountains; at least this time the graves would be only Greek.

Alexander would deal with those in Persepolis personally. He launched a vendetta against the government officials, trying, sentencing, and executing within hours. One corrupt governor rode out to meet the High King with excuses, and Alexander's answer was a royal spear through the throat.

Roxanne retreated to her own quarters of the palace. She did not care for this ruthless side of Alexander. She had ordered men's deaths before, but never with unfeeling cruelty. It seemed to her as though the desert sun had burned away every ounce of her husband's humanity and tenderness.

Chapter Twenty-four

Alexander got up from the bed and walked to an open balcony. Roxanne rose on one elbow and covered her naked body with a silk sheet. They had lain abed late this morning, and the sun was already high. In the palace gardens, birds sang and the blue sky was cloudless. "Will you dine here, my lord?" Roxanne asked. "Shall I call a servant to bring food?" None would dare to disturb the High King in the private apartments of the princess, no matter how late the hour.

Alexander stretched and ran a hand through his tousled curls. A light sheen of moisture covered his nude body. His face was smooth and unlined after a night of heated lovemaking. He grinned at her with the old boyish sparkle in his eyes. "Today I will do no work. Hephaestion and I are going to hunt lions. Would you like to come?" He crossed to a low bench and dressed in a single linen garment.

"You will enjoy yourself more alone. Bring me a cub if you find one. I miss my leopard." She propped herself against a bolster, unashamedly letting the sheet drop to her waist. After weeks of turmoil, the political tensions had eased. It would do Alexander good to relax and leave the cares of kingship behind for a few hours.

"Cover yourself, woman, or I will come back to bed and ravish you. Hephaestion has waited long enough this morning." He rummaged about and found an unopened bottle of wine and a goblet. "Is this safe?"

"It should be. Bondoor bought it in the market." Here, in the splendid Persian city of Susa, Roxanne was not so foolish as to take strange food or drink without caution. Poison would be too handy a weapon for her enemies, and in many ways, greater perils lurked here than in the trackless desert.

"I had to set things right, you know. They didn't believe I'd return alive from India. Any show of weakness, and they'd be at our throats like a pack of wolves." He drank deeply from the silver goblet, and his eyes clouded to the color of winter frost, always a dangerous sign. "I am well aware of your disapproval."

His gaze seemed to charge the air between them, and tiny hairs prickled on the nape of her neck. Forcing a smile, she draped a gown around her body, and softened her tone. He was up to something, and arguing with him about what she could not change would gain her little advantage. "This is not my country, my lord. I would not presume to advise you on matters of state."

He scoffed. "Not presume? Admit it, little Sogdian, you are squeamish about beheadings." He offered her the goblet.

She sipped and handed it back. "I don't like senseless killings," she admitted, careful not to make him suspicious by overplaying the role of obedient wife. "I am but a weak woman, as you have so often reminded me. Your methods are harsh, but they work. Your kingdom is peaceful. I can find no fault with that." She began to massage the hard muscles in his neck and shoulders. "It may be that you must rule Persians by fear. I've never had to deal with foreign subjects."

"They aren't foreign subjects. All peoples will be one under my hand: Persian, Indian, Greek, Bactrian—all one. I will unite them. My army of young men is nearly ready. You remember the thirty thousand I recruited before we left Sogdiana?"

"Do I forget anything you do, son of Apollo?"

"Careful—one day you will mock me once too often," he admonished lightly before continuing. "My youngsters speak Greek, and they are trained in the use of Greek weapons. They owe their loyalty to Macedonian and Greek officers. Around such a force I will build my armies of the future. Many of the Companions are ready to retire. I'll send them home, replace the veterans with Macedonian and Asian youths. In a generation or two, we will have one language, one nation stretching to the ends of the earth." Alexander's voice took on a strained tone as he gripped her hand. "You understand me, Roxanne?"

"I'm not your enemy, my lord." She brushed his cool lips with hers and pulled free. "I understand what you're trying to create. But it isn't easy to change old loyalties and customs." She took an ivory and boar's hair brush and began to run it through her waist-length hair.

"Leave it," he said, when she began to twist the heavy length into a knot. "I like to see your hair flowing around your shoulders. You are a vision of loveliness."

Obediently she let her hair fall, splashed water from a basin of beaten gold on her face, and dried it with a length of linen. Her thin silk robe molded itself to the curves of her body as she returned and knelt by his feet. "I have a gift for you," she murmured.

"What now? Another horse? A new bow? You spoil me." His eyes danced with curiosity. "I promise not to offend you this time with offers of repayment."

She laughed. "For this gift, all your wealth could not buy me a present of equal value."

"Am I to be kept in suspense? Where is it?" He pulled her to her feet and draped an arm around her. "Where is this wondrous gift? Is it something I have never seen before?"

"Yes!" She caught his hand and pressed it to her belly. "Here. I carry your child, here, under my heart. By summer you will have a son." Tears glistened on her lashes. "I have waited to tell you until I passed the most dangerous months. Yesterday I felt him kick."

"You're certain? There's no doubt?"

She nodded. "I will hunt no lions until he is old enough to ride."

"A son . . . a son to inherit the throne. Alexander IV." He hugged her and buried his face in her hair. "It is a gift beyond price."

A chilling frisson of doubt pierced her triumph. Something was wrong. Alexander had said the right words, but . . . She backed away. "What is it?"

He averted his gaze, but not before she saw a flash of color in his cheeks. "Nothing," he said. "What could be wrong? It comes as a shock. After all this time, I thought . . ."

"You thought I was barren? I'm not, am I? Do you doubt that this child is yours?"

"You know better than that." He caught the hand she raised against him. "Calm yourself, Roxanne. The news you give me is more welcome than any other I could receive. You are my beloved wife. Barren or not, I would have loved you so long as you drew breath, with or without an heir from your body. But . . ."

"But? Speak, my lord. What have you done to us?"

"I have promised to wed the Princess Barsine."

"What?" Rage made her reckless, and she struck him in the chest. "You promised to marry the Persian? Do you put me aside for her? Make our son a bastard before he is born?"

"Don't be a fool." Anger washed away shame. "This marriage will bring a union of East and West. It has nothing to do with you. It is politics, nothing more. There's no reason for you to go into a jealous tantrum." He released her and scowled.

She rushed at him. "You bastard! You cold, calculating Macedonian bastard," she cried. Without thinking, she slapped him hard across the face.

"How dare you?" he bellowed.

"You made love to me last night, knowing you were going to have Barsine?" The imprint of her fingers raised welts on his cheek.

Alexander drew back a clenched fist. "I should—"

"Do it, damn you! Or better yet, cut off my head. I struck

300

the High King. But you're not just a king, are you? You aim higher! What punishment for a woman who'd dare raise her hand to a god?"

"Roxanne—"

"Go! What do I care? But I'm not staying here while you wallow with your whores. I'm going home. Divorce me or have me killed. It matters not to me! I'm going home to Sogdiana."

He stopped and faced her, his face white with rage. "You will go nowhere I do not send you. You are my wife and my property. There will be no divorce. You will conduct yourself properly, or I will have you placed under house arrest. The decision is yours, Roxanne. I will marry Barsine and both her sisters if I feel like it." His gray eyes flashed with warning. "I will excuse your hysterics this time, because of your condition. Do not expect the same forebearance a second time." With that he strode from the room.

Roxanne's fury knew no bounds. She ripped the bed hangings away and threw them on the floor, clearing the dressing table with a single swipe of her sword, and kicking a golden bowl across the room. Sharin, one of her ladies-in-waiting, peered cautiously into the room, and Roxanne hurled a shoe in that direction. "Leave me alone," she screamed. "Alone." Her gaze fell on the jewelry box by the bed. She seized it and pitched it against a wall, scattering necklaces, earrings, and golden chains in all directions.

"Shame me, will he? I'll show him a thing or two about shame. I'll sleep with half his army." The absurdity of her statement pierced the hysteria, and she began to laugh, sinking to the floor and drawing her knees up as she had done as a child. The laughter turned to healing tears and she wept, letting out the hurt and anger and leaving nothing but cold reason.

Once again in control of her emotions, Roxanne dressed and left the ruins of her inner chamber and passed through the outer ones. Beyond the double doors, she saw that her personal guards were augmented with Macedonians. "Am I confined to my rooms?"

"No, Princess," the captain stammered. "But . . ."

"I am or I am not? Which is it?" Involuntarily the soldier took a step backward. Roxanne brushed past him, and the guards fell in step behind as she made her way down the corridor.

Twenty minutes later, Roxanne was mounted on Achilles and galloping through the streets of Susa with two score men in attendance. Pedestrians scattered before them, speculating on the identity of the beautiful red-haired noblewoman astride the magnificent black stallion.

Outside the city, she let loose the reins and urged Achilles into a run across the open green fields. With the wind in her hair and the movement of the horse beneath her, she could try to deal with the awful emptiness that filled her soul. *Alexander*, she cried silently. *Alexander!* She lashed the stallion faster as though to outrun her pain.

At dusk she returned to the palace, dirt-streaked and weary. She would bathe and dress and attend Alexander's formal dinner. And no man, she vowed, would guess the workings of her heart, least of all the king.

Alexander was in no way deceived by the courteous and gentle lady who sat beside him at the banquet. He had not wanted to hurt her, least of all now when she carried his child. Why was a woman's mind so illogical? That she was jealous pleased him. Roxanne had never said she loved him, and he had professed his love for her many times. Was it her heart or her pride that was injured? No matter; she would yield. He would have them both.

The woman Barsine did not matter. He wasn't marrying her for her looks, but for her bloodline. As Darius's daughter, she commanded the loyalty he must have of the Persian nobility. That she was only a second wife was inconsequential. If she produced children for him, so much the better. Roxanne's child, if it was a boy, would be his heir. If it was female, they would make others.

"Have you heard I am to be a bridegroom also?" Hephaestion leaned toward Roxanne, the kindness in his eyes contradicting the sarcasm in his voice. "The king has graciously informed me that I am to wed Barsine's sister."

"I can think of no one more suited to be kin to Alexander." Roxanne sipped her wine. "Your children will be cousins."

He laughed. "I suppose they will."

"And does the lady please you?"

Kayan motioned to Roxanne, willing her to mind her tongue. Word of her temper had spread quickly through the palace. To insult Alexander publicly would be disastrous. Here in Susa, the administrative center of the Persian Empire, Kayan remained both her guardian and commander of the Flying Devils, who now acted as her private escort and personal troops.

"I have not met the princess who is my intended," Hephaestion confided. "Persian women are not so open. I was informed we shall meet at the ceremony. I won't be alone. Eighty of the officers are to marry noble Persian ladies."

"And ten thousand of my Greeks will marry the women they have taken as concubines," Alexander said. "Their children will be legitimate, an example of the blending of our peoples."

"To your wedding, my lord," Roxanne raised a cup. "May you find the happiness you deserve."

Kayan's hand touched her back, a forbidden act. "Caution," he murmured. When Roxanne mouthed sweet words, it was time for him to duck for cover. Kayan felt her stiffen, and he pinched her hard through the thin material of her gown.

Roxanne stifled a gasp. The temptation was great, but her cousin was right. She had pushed her Macedonian husband beyond the breaking point. To make a scene before the Persian nobility and Alexander's friends would do her cause no good. It might even place her child in jeopardy. She stood. "Lord Alexander; gentleman." She inclined her head slightly. "If you will pardon me, I am somewhat weary," she said. "I bid you all a good evening." Regally she rose and swept from the room, a dozen armed men, including Kayan and Bondoor, in attendance.

Halfway down the hall, Roxanne wrenched off her coronet and tossed it aside. Kayan caught it without breaking stride. He took her arm and pulled her into the shadows. "You are pregnant again?" He took her silence for affirmation. "Then don't behave like a stupid girl. You won't block Alexander's marriage to the Persian woman." He shook her. "You walk a knife's edge, Roxanne. If Alexander casts you out, it will mean your death."

"And yours?" She gasped, ashamed of what she had just said. "No, I'm sorry, Kayan. I know better. You're right, of course. It's just . . . he makes me so furious. He goes his merry way when it pleases him. Why must he yield to pressure on this?"

"This is not the time or place to discuss the king's failings, Cousin. My men are loyal, but this is Susa. Doubtless the walls are lined with listening holes."

"Alexander is a royal bastard," she snapped. "There! If there are spies, give them something worthy to report." She caught up the train of her elaborate lavender robes and continued on to her apartments, with ladies, guards, and officers trailing behind.

Sharin met her in the doorway, plainly distraught. "My lady, did the High King . . ."

Roxanne shook her head and murmured a few words of apology to Kayan in the hall, then closed the doors and stood before them, arms crossed. "Well, Sharin, what now? Not bad news of my father?" Her eyes lit with alarm.

"No, nothing like that, Your Highness. It is the Persian Princess Barsine. She is coming here. We received a courier a few minutes ago. She wishes to speak with you."

"Barsine? Here?" Roxanne let slip a barracks-yard oath. "By the Wise God, she is a fool or a saint to place herself in my hands this night. I'll skin her rosy hide for a wall hanging."

"My lady," Sharin sputtered. "You must remember your position." She smoothed Roxanne's tousled hair and set the coronet carefully in place. "Come to the reception rooms. You must meet her with all ceremony or you will lose face."

Protesting, Roxanne allowed herself to be ushered to the marble-columned chamber and took a seat on the raised dais. Roxanne's apartments had been last used by the Persian queen mother, grandmother of the Princess Barsine. The throne was low and delicate as befitted a woman, cunningly wrought with flowers and grazing ibex in silver and beaten gold. Two of Roxanne's younger handmaidens wore bows and quivers and carried swords. They took positions directly behind her. No man was permitted inside the apartments but the High King; even the guards here must be female.

A procession wound through the corridors and halted before the entrance. Several Persian noblemen and two lines of guards protected the closed litter. A haughty eunuch announced the arrival of Princess Barsine to Bondoor, who looked to Kayan for orders.

"I am the commanding officer here. State your business," Kayan said harshly, glaring at the painted creature before him.

"I am the First Chamberlain to the—"

Kayan's hand went to his sword hilt. "Save your pretty words for one who will appreciate them. What do you want?"

"The Princess . . . the Princess Barsine, daughter of the High King Darius, wishes to see the first wife of the High King Alexander."

Kayan nodded, and two fierce Bactrians barred the eunuch's way with crossed spears. He turned to Bondoor and repeated the message, and Bondoor rapped at the door. A serving girl answered, and the message was relayed to Roxanne in the throne room.

"Horse feathers," she shouted. "If the goose is here, show her in. Am I to be afraid of a Persian blossom?"

The reply was sanitized and reported to the First Chamberlain, who demanded to know if the Princess Roxanne's chambers were free of any uncastrated males. Kayan smiled. "Send in your princess, sweetie. She's safe enough from any man. More than that I cannot promise."

After much consultation, the slaves lowered the litter to the tile floor, the draperies were pulled back, and a veiled figure emerged. Surrounded by other veiled women and several armed eunuchs, the Princess Barsine entered the throne room.

Roxanne watched as the tall, slender, swathed form made her way toward the dais, and then offered the slightest of formal bows. "Princess Roxanne." The feminine voice was high-pitched and clipped.

Brown eyes, large, intelligent, and heavily made up with black liner, showed above the fuchsia veil. Roxanne struggled to fathom the message they revealed. A little of her anger drained away, and she spoke, not unkindly. "Princess Barsine." Roxanne inclined her head courteously, but less than the lady had done. "Please remove your veil. There are no whole men here, and I dislike speaking to a mask. I would prefer seeing your face."

Trembling, the lady removed her veil. Her hands were long and thin with beautiful nails; her thumbs heavy with rings. Her oval face was in proportion to the rest of her body, not homely, but plain, with King Darius's strong nose and a smooth olive complexion. Against the canvas of her features, her large eyes looked sad. Barsine's hair was thick and black, arranged severely without adornment.

"They told me you were very beautiful, lady," she said, looking closely at Roxanne, her dark liquid eyes squinting. Barsine's father had suffered from poor vision. This daughter must have inherited the fault, Roxanne decided.

"You are too kind. But beauty in a woman is not always an asset, Princess Barsine." Roxanne glanced about at the curious onlookers. "May we not speak in private?"

"Oh, yes—could we?" Barsine agreed.

The First Chamberlain frowned and started to protest, but Roxanne silenced him with a steely glare. "The Princess Barsine is the intended bride of Alexander. She is as safe in these apartments as she would be at the foot of Zeus's throne." Since Zeus was Alexander's god and none of hers, Roxanne felt the blasphemy would go unpunished.

Roxanne led the way to a small curtained alcove lit by a single oil lamp. The cubicle was pleasantly scented with a pungent spice, and a priceless Chin carpet of sky blue covered the floor. Roxanne waved the lady to a low divan and sat beside her. "Let us talk, then, without the ears of those partridges. Why have you come here, Barsine? I admire your courage. You must know I oppose this marriage."

Barsine flushed. "I do. And I was very frightened to come. They say you . . ." Her voice dropped to a whisper. "They call you an Amazon. But I can see with my own eyes they lie. You are a most gracious noblewoman."

"You did not come to compliment me, Barsine." Roxanne looked at the soft, delicate hands of the Persian princess. Would her lord cherish such dainty hands that had never drawn a bow or dug for water in desert sand? Barsine was a woman such as Roxanne had never had for a friend and had often scoffed at. *This is truly a lady,* she thought; and then a little regretfully, *a lady such as I will never be.*

"I do not wish the marriage either!" Barsine cried. "I am afraid. Please, you must help me. My uncles . . . the nobles . . . all insist I must wed Lord Alexander. Even my grandmother, who has always been like a mother." Tears welled in the charcoal-smudged orbs and spilled down cheeks that had never felt the rays of unfiltered sun. "I do not wish to marry, ever. And especially not to the High King. I am so afraid." She buried her face in her thin, soft fingers and wept.

Roxanne sighed and laid a hand on the girl's shoulder. No . . . she was not a girl. She was a full woman and long past the time of marriage. Her age was close to Alexander's. Roxanne's anger was gone, and in its place was something akin to pity.

"I can do nothing, Barsine. I would if I could. Not for you, but for the child I carry. Alexander has said he will wed you, and if he breathes, he will do so, and quickly. We are but pawns on the gameboard of politics. You are the pawn of the Persian hierarchy, and I . . . I . . ." She laughed. "I am not even sure what hand directs my moves. Reconcile yourself. You must marry the High King. It is no use wasting tears over what cannot be changed."

"I can't," Barsine sobbed. "I can't. I have never . . . Lady . . . I have never thought of a man in that way. I spend my days in prayer and with my music. The High King . . ." Her eyes grew larger, and flickers of fanaticism lit the irises. "He is a foreigner. I cannot even speak his language. How can I let such a man touch me? I would as soon couple with a . . . with a beast of the steppes!"

Roxanne smiled. "Not quite, Barsine. The High King is somewhat more human than a Scythian. He is gentle with women who do not displease him. Obey him in all things and he will not harm you."

"But . . ." Her voice dropped even lower. "My maids whisper of strange practices . . . of a phallus so large that . . . I will die before I permit my body to be so desecrated."

"Lies," Roxanne soothed. "Old wives' tales. Alexander is quite an ordinary lover," she lied smoothly. "Although somewhat . . . how to put this gently . . . more generously endowed than most men. But I assure you that the royal member is both vigorous and normal . . . for one so large."

Barsine paled and bit her lower lip.

"Lord Alexander expects a virgin. You are virgin, aren't you?"

"Of course!" The Persian princess flushed. "I have never—"

"Naturally, naturally," Roxanne soothed. "I meant no dishonor on your family. As I said, the High King expects a virgin bride. You need do nothing but obey him. He cannot abide a woman with a sharp tongue or willful disposition."

Barsine nodded. "I understand. He is much like my uncles."

"Exactly," Roxanne continued. "You are a woman. Sex with a husband is a natural part of life. You may even come to enjoy it."

Barsine let out a tiny gasp.

"Well, maybe not enjoy, but it will only be painful the first few times . . . if you are careful to use oils and lie perfectly still."

The Persian lifted her tear-stained face and tried to compose herself. "If what you say is true, perhaps it will not be so bad. I have been trained in obedience all my life. I would never dare to oppose Lord Alexander, but—"

"But nothing. Be gentle, be silent, and be obedient. Hide your inner emotions. Say as little as possible. Alexander speaks your tongue, if roughly. He will be kind; and perhaps he will only remain with you a few nights, to please the nobility."

"Do you truly think so?" Hope showed in her liquid eyes. "I could stand it if I thought it would not be forever."

"Nothing is forever." Roxanne stood. "Come, let us return to the others before we are accused of plotting against the state." She smiled with her eyes. "You have nothing to fear from me, Barsine. I can see we are not enemies."

"Never. I have no wish for power. I ask only to be left alone. I have an ibex. Did I tell you? I raised her from a baby. She eats from my hand. The king will not make me send her away, will he?"

"You may have as many ibexes as you wish, Barsine. Alexander likes wild things. And silent women." Roxanne took the cool, ringed hand. "Come. We both have duties. Do not trouble your heart any longer on these things."

The Princess Barsine dipped into a graceful bow. "Thank you, Your Highness. I will never forget your kindness."

"Do not forget," Roxanne reminded, her eyes twinkling with mischief. "Obedience in all things. So will you please my lord. We will be sisters now. Do not hesitate to come to me at any time for advice. What else are sisters for?"

Chapter Twenty-five

For the wedding of Greece and Persia, Alexander would spare no expense. Skilled workers erected awe-inspiring pavilions with multicolored roofs and gilded columns more than thirty feet high. Private apartments with a hundred richly furnished bedrooms for the bridal couples were arranged; and for the High King, craftsmen created the most magnificent chamber of all, with a golden couch for the wedded pair to recline upon. Authorities imported companies of musicians and casts of Athenian actors for the occasion. The soldiers, main characters, and supporting players alike were all garbed in new uniforms. Weapons were polished to a gem finish.

Cooks and bakers pressed every oven into service to provide food for the great day. A tent city of tailors, leather makers, sutlers, wine merchants, and entertainers sprang up overnight. Sweetmeat sellers, jewelers, cloth dealers, and carpenters pushed and shoved to find the best spot to ply their trade. Herds of cattle, sheep, and geese were driven through the dusty streets, and the air was thick with the smell of animal dung, roasting meat, and newly baked bread.

Priests, magi, and holy men of every description assembled to provide the spiritual guidance the ceremony demanded.

Detachments of soldiers marched in the open squares, refining military precision and spit and polish. It was a pickpocket's dream. Rascals of Persian, Scythian, and Greek origin slinked and stole in the hustle and bustle.

In her apartments, the Princess Roxanne bathed and listened to Persian poets and laughed at the tricks of a troupe of performing dogs. A constant stream of jewelers had passed through the gardens of her suite. Here the well-guarded, unveiled Sogdian princess purchased a dozen king's ransoms in uncut gems, gold chains, coronets, pearl necklaces, hundreds of yards of Chin silk, silver and gold chalices, and dinnerware. She chose three new crowns, one of diamonds, one of pearls, and the last of emeralds, as well as bracelets and earrings to match each coronet.

Roxanne ordered huge jars of rare spices and dozens of Persian carpets, as well as two hundred of the finest Scythian horn bows with engraved bow cases of sterling and boxes of steel-tipped arrows for the princess's ladies.

Seamstresses cut and sewed lengths of silk into garments for Roxanne and her household. Uniforms for Kayan and his guard were stitched of sapphire and aureate cloth, each trimmed in pearls; and all must be mounted on matching white chargers with jeweled saddle cloths. For herself, she demanded a new chariot and a team of horses.

On the afternoon of the day following her purchase of the animals, Kayan cornered Roxanne in a chamber off her private bath. "Are you mad?" he demanded. "What use have my Flying Devils of gem-encrusted swords and silver arrows? Alexander will kill you."

"Hush." She placed two fingers on his lips. "I'm neither addled nor suicidal. My husband has not forbidden me to spend what I would on the celebration of his wedding."

"To make fools of my troops? To make me a laughingstock?"

"Peace, Cousin. Half of what I've purchased is already on its way to Sogdiana. Every camel and mule train that departs Susa carries gold, weapons, rubies, pearls, diamonds, and emeralds to the twin kingdoms. Someday that wealth will be of use to our cause."

"He is no fool. If he guesses—"

"I carry his heir. Hephaestion may boast the title of Vizier, but until this child is delivered, I stand second only to the High King in power. What you see is only a fraction of what I've done since the day I wed Alexander. Until his death, Wolf carried my messages. Now it must be you, Kayan. I can trust no other. Even my father doesn't know the extent of what I've bled from the Greek treasury and acquired elsewhere."

"How?"

She chuckled and spread her hands, palms up. "This is Persia, no different from India. Men believe that I influence my husband. What is a mere woman to do if they offer me small tokens of their esteem?"

"And do you plead their cases once you've taken their bribes?"

She frowned. "You wound me. I promise nothing. Have you known me to lie—"

"Yes. When it suited you."

She shrugged. "This is war. A woman must use what weapons the Wise God gives her. Besides, most who offer me expensive gifts are greedy men who seek only to oppress the common people."

"Once Alexander weds the Persian princess, you may no longer hold his favor. If she gives him a son, who is to say that her child—"

"Do you think I care who sits on the Macedonian's throne? My child will rule the twin kingdoms."

"Had you been born a man, Alexander would have met his match at the borders of Bactria."

She smiled. "Perhaps, perhaps not. I'm only mortal, and as he so often tells us, he is a god."

"And you believe that?"

"As much as I believe that Barsine will give him a healthy son."

Kayan looked puzzled. "That makes no sense. Why? You're not planning . . ." He stepped back into the passageway and looked up and down to make certain their conversation was unheard. "You wouldn't plot her death, would you?"

"I have no quarrel with the lady, so long as she does not take what is mine or threaten my child. But I will do what I must."

The palace treasurer trembled with apprehension as the bills began to filter into his office. The first royal wife was charging enormous sums. To ignore such amounts would mean his position—his head. But who would dare to complain to the High King of Roxanne's expenditures? When the invoice for two hundred iron short swords and helmets arrived, the bureaucrat was compelled to action.

Hephaestion opened the official missive, stamped with the seal of the royal treasury, and convulsed with howls of glee. Alexander, who'd been suffering the ministrations of a nervous tailor, jumped, stabbed himself with a pin, and cursed foully. "Enough!" Alexander roared. The tailor fled, and Alexander crossed to his friend. "Well, what's so funny?"

Chuckling, Hephaestion handed the letter over for inspection. "Roxanne is taking her revenge in a woman's favorite occupation, spending your ill-gotten gains as recklessly as a Cretian sailor." Both he and Alexander had been drinking heavily, and the jest seemed the best Hephaestion had enjoyed in weeks. "Are you certain you can afford two wives?" he asked.

The courier stood frozen, hardly daring to breathe while the High King read the message twice. "Well, what are you waiting for?" Alexander demanded. The boy squirmed, and his face turned a dark shade of plum. "Tell your master to pay the bills, fool! And tell him I appreciate the information. I will consult with the lady in question—personally."

The boy prostrated himself and edged out of the chamber, then leaped up and fled. His sandals clicked and slid down the marble corridor.

"Can I watch?" Hephaestion asked. "Give me an hour's time. I can win back half your loss by arranging wagers on the contest between you and Roxanne. What did you call me in Persepolis? A money-grubbing merchant, when I balked at the price of those greaves?" Tears of amusement rolled down the tall Macedonian's face.

Alexander joined him in laughter. "She's a bitch, but a royal one. Nearly my match. One way or another, this will be the most expensive lay in Persian history. Helen of Troy would be jealous." He threw up his hands and grinned. "What am I to do with her?"

"Send her packing. Give her Bactria, Sogdiana, and Chin to boot. It would be cheaper."

"It might be at that."

Not long after, a page arrived at Princess Roxanne's apartments, begging to be admitted to the lady's presence. Since he was unarmed and under the age of twelve, Kayan permitted him to pass, and the boy was duly ushered into Roxanne's bedchamber. "I bring a gift from the High King," he squeaked. A servant took the silver box and passed it to Roxanne.

"What has my lord sent? A viper?" She lifted the lid to find another, smaller red lacquer box, and inside that, one of finest amber. That box was wrapped in parchment, and written in Alexander's strong hand was the message: "Take pity on me, I'm destitute."

Smiling, Roxanne opened the amber box, and the maid gasped in wonder. A brilliant diamond pendant sparkled against a black silk lining.

Roxanne yawned and dangled the precious gem in the rays of sunlight streaming through an open window. "It is a pretty bauble. Thank the High King . . . and"—she smiled sweetly— "deliver this to the Princess Barsine. She may want it for some minor feast day."

The boy blanched. His mouth opened and closed, and he dragged a hand through his close-cropped brown hair.

"Do as I say," Roxanne commanded. "Take it to the Persian lady's apartments at once." She waved a hand imperiously. "Tell Alexander that an Amazon has no need of such trinkets. Tell him also that I desire nothing but his company."

The wedding ceremony was set for dusk, so that the guests might not suffer from the excessive heat of Susa. The celebration and feasting would go on for days with free food and drink for all, noble and commoner alike. The citizens were jubilant. It was an event which would not be duplicated in a thousand years. The streets thronged with dancing men, and the wine shops gave free refreshment at the High King's expense.

Representatives from all parts of the empire gathered to do homage to Alexander and his new bride. The Princess Barsine, heavily veiled and hidden from prying eyes, was transported to a special pavilion and there concealed until the actual vows were to be exchanged. Outside the royal pavilion, rows of stately war elephants and mahouts were flanked by ten thousand Asian bowmen in splendid uniforms of red and blue. Row upon row of Persian elite fighting corps called Immortals and staunch Macedonian Companions marched with Indian, Scythian, and Thracian troops.

Alexander was garbed in kingly purple robes so encrusted with gold and precious gems, he could hardly walk. Persian costume blended with his native Macedonian so that all men could admire his glory. On his head he wore a simple wreath of laurel, the Greek symbol of a hero.

Hephaestion, sighting him, swore lustily. "He could have made his fortune as an actor." As second-in-command, Hephaestion's finery was nearly as magnificent.

Near the palace steps, another procession formed. Kayan and his Bactrians on their white horses waited impatiently for the Princess Roxanne. Not willing to hide during the High King's wedding to the Persian princess, Roxanne had declared her intention to graciously bear witness to her husband's folly.

A golden chariot waited by the wide marble staircase. Persian grooms struggled to hold the matched pair of ebony Arabian stallions that tossed their heads and pranced in golden harness. Kayan dismounted and stood by the chariot, watching as Roxanne emerged and made her leisurely way down the steps.

"Artemis," he murmured. "Virgin goddess of the moon."

"If I'd wanted to portray the Grecian goddess, I would have worn silver," Roxanne replied.

A golden bow was slung over one of her shoulders beside a Scythian bow case engraved with golden figures and set with flashing emeralds. Her flowing gown was Grecian style, of azure blue silk, and upon her alabaster brow she wore the plain gold crown of Sogdiana. The mass of red gold curls hung freely, falling nearly to her waist.

Kayan dropped to one knee and inclined his head to hide the love and admiration all must read there. Rising, he took her hand to help her into the chariot and whispered, "If we die for this, it matters not." Her touch shot shafts of fire to his loins, and he longed to throw her across his horse and gallop headlong for the snow-capped mountains of home.

A trace of a smile tugged at the corner of Roxanne's lips, and she winked before taking the gilded leather reins firmly between her hands. "Shall we go? It would not do to keep the bridegroom waiting."

Through the main thoroughfare of the city they thundered with a hundred of Alexander's mounted cavalry behind the splendid Bactrians. Heads turned to watch the golden chariot spin past, roll beneath the great arch, and approach the wedding grounds.

Kayan's features were expressionless, harsh as the crags of his native Sogdiana, as he led his men past the elephant corps and Macedonian troops to the entrance of the royal pavilion. Shock waves ran through the assembled guests.

Inside, the High King frowned at Hephaestion, who turned to Ptolemy and shrugged. "Ares, save us," Hephaestion said. "What now? Go and tend to it. You are the only one not encumbered by a simpering bride."

Alexander grunted at his terrified wife-to-be and motioned to the priests to begin the ceremony. "What are you waiting for?"

The Princess Barsine swayed. She was hot under the silk robes and triple veils; she felt faint. She'd eaten nothing since yesterday morning, and she was afraid she'd be sick. Worse, the Greek savage beside her was a full head shorter than she. The thought of how they must look together blurred her already poor vision and she felt her knees give.

Hephaestion shoved a stool under the lady, and Alexander grunted in relief. He didn't feel half so ridiculous with the wench seated. His hand steadied her, and she flinched as though he had slapped her. Conscious or unconscious, he'd have her wedded and bedded before the dawn. At least on a bridal couch, he wouldn't have to worry about her towering over him like a mahout in a howdah.

The purple robes did nothing for her olive skin. The only things visible on the lady were her long, thin fingers weighed down by too many rings, and her frightened eyes. By Zeus's phallus! No one appreciated what a monarch went through for his people.

The priest repeated his question a third time before clearing his throat. Alexander sighed and made the correct response. Did this have to drag on forever? Once the Greeks were done, there would be a Persian ceremony. Alexander's head pounded, and he felt the need to piss. This would be a very long night.

Outside, Ptolemy pushed his way through the crowd. "Princess Roxanne. I might have guessed." He leaped into the chariot and jerked the reins from her fingers. "Are you mad to let her come here like this?" he demanded of Kayan. Kayan didn't answer. Ptolemy turned the team and cracked the whip over the blacks' heads. "This is no place for you, lady," he said. "Alexander's in a foul mood as it is."

Roxanne clung to the side and struggled to hold her balance in the swaying chariot. "What happens between us is none of your affair!" The vehicle lurched as it struck a rut and she fell against him, and then recovered. "Give me the reins!"

"Smile at the people, Roxanne. They'll talk about you for months. You've done what you came for. You've stolen the stage from the bride. Now sheath your sword and retreat gracefully." Ptolemy smiled and waved grandly at the bystanders.

"You son of a bitch! No one forbade me to go to the wedding!"

"For once, woman, heed your tongue." Ptolemy cracked the whip again, and the horses raced on with Kayan and the Bac-

317

trians riding behind. The Macedonian said nothing more until they reached the palace steps. There, he reined in the team and passed the leathers to a waiting groom. "Kayan!" Ptolemy ordered. "See Her Royal Highness to her quarters and hold her there—for a week."

Roxanne turned on him, enraged. "How did you escape a noble bride, Ptolemy? Are you out of favor?"

"Just luck, I guess. And don't let this wedding make you crazy. A thirty-one-year-old virgin is no prize."

"I'll not stand for it," Roxanne flung back. "I'll not be shamed like this. First Europa and now Barsine. I tell you—"

"Europa?" Ptolemy scoffed. "She's Hephaestion's."

"But my husband slept with her," Roxanne insisted. "I know he did."

Ptolemy grasped her hand and lifted it to his lips. "How can you know him so well, and yet not at all? You hold his heart, lady. Only you. He has not lain with another woman since he took you to wife."

"Liar!" she protested. "I found that whore in his bed."

"Hephaestion's idea of a joke. Alexander was drunk enough that night to swive a goat, but he didn't. You prevented that."

"If you're telling the truth, why did Alexander let me believe he was unfaithful? Why didn't he tell me—"

"And let you think you could control him?" Ptolemy shook his head. "He has to be in control. I promise you, if you use your wits and don't do anything else stupid, he'll be back in your bed in a week."

Roxanne's reply was so original, Ptolemy chuckled all the way back to the wedding pavilion. He had borrowed a horse from Kayan and arrived in time to see the blessing of the troops and their ten thousand Persian brides. He hoped everyone had the good sense to omit telling the High King about Roxanne's appearance until after the bridal night. It was at times like this that Ptolemy wished he'd stayed in Macedonia and taken up farming as his mother had wanted.

A second gift arrived for Roxanne from her husband the following morning, an Egyptian collar of flashing green emeralds and diamonds. That, she passed to Kayan. "Sell it in Egypt," she commanded. "It should buy enough weapons and armor to outfit and mount a regiment of soldiers for Sogdiana. Someday my son will have need of a mighty army to defend his homeland."

She wept no more tears over Alexander's wedding; her grief was too bitter for tears. Instead, she busied herself with the translation of an ancient Chin medical treatise.

The week of festivities was marred by one tragedy. Calanus, the Indian holy man who had followed Alexander so far, was dying. He was well liked and respected, and the High King left his new bride to go to the old man's side along with many of his officers and men. Roxanne, too, went to pay tribute to Calanus and his wisdom.

Calanus lay on a mat under a sun shield as friends passed by to bid him farewell. His skin was the color of old parchment, and the flame seemed to have gone from his eyes. He could barely speak as Roxanne knelt beside him. "Must you leave us, Calanus? I treasure your advice, even though I know I've been a poor pupil."

He forced a feeble smile. "Clouds will come, Daughter, but you must hold fast. The sun will break forth in all its glory, and you shall triumph over all."

A murmur of voices signaled the arrival of the High King. Roxanne kissed the old man's hand and stepped away. Alexander wept as he took Calanus in his arms. "Not yet," he protested. "I have need of you, my friend."

"For us, Alexander, this is not goodbye. I will see you again in Babylon."

Roxanne grew chilled at Calanus's words, and she murmured a prayer of protection for her husband. Such words could be thought to be prophesy, and no good could come of them.

When the holy man closed his eyes for the last time, he was given funeral rites in his own religion. A great pyre was built and his earthly body was committed to the flames. It cast a pall over the high spirits of the city, and men began to take up their daily duties and worries again.

Roxanne's informants were meticulous in bringing exact information to her on the state of affairs between Alexander and his new wife. The general consensus was, as Ptolemy had predicted, that the High King was thoroughly bored with Barsine. A page assured Roxanne that Alexander had spent only two nights with the princess before retiring to his own quarters.

Not that the king made public complaint against his second wife. That was not his way. She was his wife and must have all due respect from his subjects. But the two seemed to have little personal affinity for each other; indeed, no one had heard them exchanging conversation.

"Serves him right, the bastard!" Roxanne sent another arrow into the target from a distance of thirty yards. The garden had been transformed into a training ground for the day, and her ladies practiced at swordplay and archery. Roxanne loved the palace gardens of Susa. They were a spot of greenery in an otherwise brown landscape. The climate was hot and dry, and any land not irrigated quickly turned to dust.

Here in the royal gardens grew lush trees and shrubs and flowers from many lands. Fountains bubbled, and pools illuminated the corners of the parkland. All was enclosed in a high wall with spear points set in the top and heavily armed guards on the far side. The women's quarters of the palace were defended as vigorously as any state treasury, and any trespassers were rewarded with instant death.

Roxanne's pregnancy, thus far, had been an easy one. She bloomed with rosy cheeks and sparkling eyes above the sadness of her heart. She wanted the father of her child with her, but she wanted him on her terms. Soraya had warned her of coming to trust him too much. She must turn her attention to the child she carried. He would never betray her as Lord Alexander had.

A week to the day after the wedding, Ptolemy appeared at the gates of the first wife's apartment and asked formally for an audience with the Princess Roxanne. Kayan, on duty that morning, carried his message, and Roxanne appeared almost immediately, clad in riding clothes.

"What is it, Ptolemy?" she asked. "You just caught me. I'm going riding. If I stay shut up in this prison much longer, I'll go mad. You did order Kayan to hold me captive for a week. The week is up."

"Save your honeyed words for Alexander, lady. I would speak with you in private." They walked together to a main reception hall beyond the women's quarters. Bondoor and three Bactrians followed at a respectful distance.

"I have another gift for you from Alexander," Ptolemy said. "I think you'll like this one." He raised a hand to ward off a possible blow. "I am not the gentleman Alexander is. If you hit me, I'll hit back,"

"I'm not a child to strike out senselessly." Her anger with Ptolemy had cooled somewhat. It had been both foolish and dangerous to go to Alexander's wedding in such a manner, but the king had deserved it.

Ptolemy waved her to a bench and sat beside her. "I can't abide this place," he said. She looked at him expectantly. "You and the king did not part on the best of terms. He won't return to your quarters to be driven out again."

"Why come at all? He has a new lady. I'm already pregnant. He has no need to waste his royal seed on me." She raised her chin, and her back stiffened. "If he would grant me the divorce I asked for, I would gladly return home or even go to my father in Hindu Kush." The forest green of her Sogdian costume suited her coloring, and she seemed even more attractive to Ptolemy when she was angry.

"We cannot keep going over and over his marriage to Barsine. Listen to me! You have a mind, use it. His wedding of the Persian princess was inevitable from the day he took Darius's throne. You have no idea how many plans were shattered when he took you to wife first. Your attitude will ruin your marriage to Alexander if you allow it. You know how he feels about you. Accept his gift, smile, and tell him you're sorry."

321

"I'm sorry?" Roxanne jumped to her feet. "Me?" Her cheeks flamed.

"It won't be the first time you've lied to him." Ptolemy refused to allow his temper to get the best of him. "Stop thinking like a woman, Roxanne. Your child will be his heir. Alexander needs you. As devious as you are, you're loyal to him and you're a good influence on him. Without you, he begins to believe he's immortal. You bring him back to reality."

She realized the wisdom of his advice, even as she protested. "Everyone worries about the king losing face. What about me?"

"Since when has an Asian queen lost face because her husband took another wife, or a dozen? Darius had, what? . . . three hundred concubines?"

"Three hundred and sixty-four," she corrected. "Officially."

"Did that bother his chief wife?"

"It is the custom of Sogdiana to have one wife, as in your culture."

"Fine, but do the Sogdian nobles have concubines? Did your own father?"

She nodded, reluctantly. "A concubine is not a wife, but any children of the union are considered legitimate and have all the rights of those born to the marriage."

He shook his head, thoughtfully rubbing his long nose. "Must make for interesting politics. And intrigue."

"We are not Greeks," she answered. "In living memory, no member of our ruling house has murdered a brother or a sister to claim the throne."

"Who decides which son will inherit the title?"

"The throne goes to the one who is most fit. Daughters are equal to sons."

Ptolemy laughed. "You expect me to believe that a king would bypass a male heir and give power to a female?"

She sighed. "Unlikely, men thinking as they do. Fortunately, in my case, it was not a problem. I am Prince Oxyartes's only living child. My brothers are all dead."

"That aside, Princess, we have established that you believe in a man having one wife, as does Alexander. The first wife—

you—are his true companion. This match with the Princess Barsine is a political necessity, a move to please his advisers."

"It would please my advisers if I divorced Alexander and took another man to my bed."

"That might be so, for a few hours. But once Alexander found out . . ." He shrugged. "Use logic, Roxanne. I've always felt you have a general's mind. Will you throw away all you've won out of jealousy?"

"Very well," she agreed. "I will accept my lord's presents. What else would you have me do? Run naked through the hallways and cast myself at his feet?" She moistened her lips thoughtfully. "Perhaps—"

"No." He raised both hands in mock horror. "Not another scene. Consider. You are going riding. It would be easy to accidentally cross paths with the king's hunting party, and natural for you to take that opportunity to apologize. If you and Alexander return together, the unpleasant incident is over. You are mother of his heir-to-be; no one would expect the king to be harsh with you."

"He has gravely wronged and insulted me. And you wish me to throw myself on his mercy and beg forgiveness?"

Ptolemy laughed. "Somehow, I think Alexander will find it more painful than you." The tall Macedonian turned to an aide and nodded, and the man hurried down the hall, returning quickly with a squawling bundle of fur and claws.

"Ohhh!" Roxanne exclaimed and went down on her knees to take the lion cub. Needle-sharp milk teeth nipped her, and she cuddled the cub against her breast. "He's beautiful."

"*She*, lady. The cub is female."

"She's beautiful." Roxanne stroked the tawny-gold fur; it was as soft as duck down. "What's this?" Parting the thick fur, she found a magnificent ruby and diamond collar. Laughing, she said, "He is a tactician, I'll give him that. You may tell my lord that I will ride today. Mention also that his Flying Devils are mounted so poorly that they are the laughingstock of the other companies."

Ptolemy struggled to keep his composure. "And do you have suggestions for improvement?"

"Me?" She glanced up with a feigned expression of amazement. "A woman? Advise the High King on military matters?"

Ptolemy folded his arms across his chest. "What else do you want?"

"Camels. Bactrian camels. I hear that there is a large consignment for sale in the market. Racing camels, the finest stock. Surely they would be invaluable to—"

"May I tell the king that you will give public apology today?" She smiled up at Ptolemy. "Who knows what may happen?"

"Make sure that babe you carry has balls, lady. He'll need them with you for a mother."

Roxanne, fully veiled and swathed in azure silk garments, rode out of Susa into the countryside with Kayan, Bondoor, and an escort of twenty Bactrian guards. As mount, the princess chose an Arabian mare the color of bright copper. The animal's flowing mane and tail were braided with strings of pearls and silk azure ribbons to match Roxanne's exquisite costume. The horse's hooves were gilded, and her saddlecloth and bridle were adorned with pearls and sapphires.

Roxanne's company crossed paths with the High King's hunting party seven miles from the city. Alexander, equally royally garbed in a golden tunic and sandals and wearing his favorite lionskin cap, reined in his black charger and waited as Roxanne and Kayan approached.

"Good day to you, my lady." The king's features remained stern.

Kayan saluted before dismounting and lifting the princess down from the mare's back. Taking hold of the bridle, he stood rigidly at attention. Roxanne approached Alexander and knelt in the dust, eyes cast down in submission. "My lord," she murmured, then raised her gaze to his and winked at him.

Alexander laughed. Vaulting off Achilles, he pulled her to her feet, enveloped her in his arms, and kissed her for all to see. "Little sorceress," he whispered, and then spoke louder so that his comrades could hear. "Will you hunt with us today, Princess? I promise we will go gently." He pulled her close so that wisps of her hair that peeked out from under her head-dress brushed his cheek. "By all that's holy, I've missed you," he murmured in her ear.

"Whatever my husband desires, so will I do," she answered and then smiled up at him. "I love the lion cub."

Kayan watched, his hawk eyes hooded. Did Alexander believe the fortress so easily taken? No, he decided. The king was no fool. He knew Roxanne better than that. It was a truce between them, and the best that either side could hope for on this terrain.

"Come then, wife. I've promised Hephaestion fresh meat for dinner. You will dine with us." Alexander turned the full force of his charm on her. "Won't you?"

"As you wish, my lord." She allowed him to help her mount and gathered the reins. "You will shoot, and I will watch. I brought no bow with me today. I am weaponless. All honors shall be yours."

It was the most natural thing in the world that the Princess Roxanne should retire with the High King to his bedchamber after the evening meal. The servants exchanged knowing looks and whispers. Once the king had left the room, Hephaestion tossed a bag of golden darics to Ptolemy. "I didn't doubt the outcome," he said, "only the time element."

Ptolemy laughed and raised his goblet. "To the Sogdian princess. May she bear twins."

"And all our troubles be doubled."

Roxanne posed naked on the edge of Alexander's private bathing pool and then dove in and swam to the center to emerge like a nymph from the water, her hair a mantle around her shoulders. Alexander came up under her, seizing her legs and lifting her, threatening to dunk her. She locked her arms around his neck and gazed into his beautiful eyes. "I am furious with you," she said.

He let her slide down until her wet breasts pressed against the hard muscles of his scarred and muscular chest. "Don't be. You know I love only you." His mouth met hers, and their kiss deepened. Her pulse quickened as he trailed strong fingers down her spine to caress her bare buttocks. "You're a fire in my blood, Roxanne."

"And if I came to you after leaving another man's bed? What then?" Her sensuous nature quickened to his touch, but the hurt remained, weighing on her like a great stone.

"I am a man, Roxanne. It is not the same."

He kissed her again, and then lowered his head so that his face rested against her bare breasts while he tenderly caressed her swollen belly.

"It is exactly the same," she said.

He slipped an arm behind her knees, cradled her against him, and carried her to the tiled edge of the pool. Lifting her up, he laid her on a bed of cushions. "Let me love you, darling."

"Alexander," she murmured. "You are the High King. Have I any choice?"

He stretched out beside her, wet and beautiful and magnificent in his male glory. Closing his hand on hers, he guided her fingers to the proof of his arousal. "Say the word," he murmured hoarsely. "Tell me to go, and I will abandon the siege, heart of my heart."

Tears clouded her eyes as she brushed his hard, throbbing erection. "You know I cannot," she whispered.

He groaned, brushing her breast with his lips. "You know there is no other woman but you."

She stiffened. "How can you say that to me? Barsine—"

He nuzzled her throat and breasts, then pushed himself up on one arm and looked into her eyes. "Two nights I spent in the lady's bed," he said. "But you weep for nothing. Barsine is as untouched as when I took her to wife."

"You expect me to believe that you slept with her and didn't—"

"Why would I?" He chuckled. "She is as thin and dry as a spear shaft. All she did was weep and wail. And pray. She does a great deal of praying."

Hope surged in Roxanne chest. "Swear to me," she said. "Swear you are telling the truth."

"On Hephaestion's life."

"Then I care not," she cried, pulling him close to cover his face with kisses. "Take a hundred wives, so long as you save this for me."

Chapter Twenty-six

To Roxanne's delight, Alexander moved on from Susa, leaving the Persian Princess Barsine behind. As so often after his periods of brief inactivity, Alexander was his old self, bursting with plans for exploration and conquest. His first command was that a new fleet be constructed under the command of Admiral Nearchas. While they were waiting for the armada's completion, Alexander and his royal party took ship to investigate the marshes and waterways, sailing up the Tigris River and founding another new city.

Oxyartes had subdued the rebellion in the Hindu Kush and had taken over the position of governor in Alexander's name. But the struggle had been costly, and he wrote to Roxanne asking that additional loyal Bactrians be dispatched to ride under his banner. Regretfully she approached Kayan and asked him to go to Oxyartes.

"You're mad!" he swore. "You need me at your side more than ever before." He indicated her obvious pregnancy. "Prince Oxyartes can have most of the Flying Devils, if Alexander will send them, but I stay with you. Bondoor can lead the Bactrians. He's earned the command."

"Don't you believe Alexander capable of defending his own

wife?" She shrugged. "I'm in his favor now. He'd lay down his life for me."

Kayan scowled. "Mutiny is brewing again, and you know it. With the arrival of his thirty thousand boy soldiers from Bactria and the melding of Asian and Greek units, there will be trouble. Alexander has many enemies, and most would give their right hand to see you dead! Especially since you carry his heir—a child that the Greeks openly call a half-breed. Are you so wrapped up in your coming motherhood that your wits have ceased to function?"

She placed a hand on her cousin's shoulder. "Send Bondoor, then, and as many of the Bactrian cavalry as you can spare. I'll have the usual goods for them to transport when they leave." Selfishly, she was glad she didn't have to part with Kayan, even for her father. All was well with her and her husband and with her pregnancy, but she was haunted by uneasiness, a sense of impending danger.

The journey up the Tigris River had been leisurely, and there were peaceful periods when she and Alexander could be alone. They often shared the wide couch in the luxurious, curtained pavilion he'd ordered constructed on the deck of their boat. There, screened from the curious eyes of fellow passengers, she could watch the banks of the river glide by, engage in love play with the High King, or play the boardgame of strategy involving kings, foot soldiers, and elephants that they'd learned in India. Today, they had only talked and laughed together while Alexander massaged her body with scented oils and made plans for their coming child.

"I'm directly descended from Achilles," he boasted as he slowly dangled a rope of pearls back and forth across her swelling belly.

"Achilles?" Roxanne replied sleepily. "You'd not told me that." She snatched the pearls from his fingers and tucked them under her pillow. "That tickles."

"Through my mother's family. My son is descended from heroes and gods. He'll have much to live up to."

"Leave him the fabled lands of Chin, my lord. You have all of Arabia and Africa to conquer, and there are always the

Misty Isles to the north." She took his hand and kissed the battered knuckles, one by one. "The world is wide, and any son of yours will have great dreams." She smiled at him affectionately. "It could be a girl, you know."

"Then she shall be Alexandra. I'll give her India as her portion, and marry her off to Hephaestion's first son." He laid his head on her belly, and she ran her fingers idly through his golden hair. "We'll have no talk of girls," he said. "This is a boy."

She closed her eyes, reveling in the slight breeze off the river, enjoying the Sogdian musicians playing on the far side of the curtains. "Since when does Hephaestion have a son?" she teased.

"He has none yet, but I've ordered him to waste no time. His boy will be a companion to ours." Alexander kissed the mound of her belly, which seemed to her to grow more ungainly every day.

"Soon I'll be so fat you'll not want to share my bed. And I am scarred and ugly." She touched the brand of the leaping tiger on her thigh.

"Never. If anything, the tiger makes you more desirable, more mysterious. You even smell good." He caressed her bare hip, trailed a hand down her thigh and calf, and began to rub her ankle and the arch of her foot. "I like my women round and soft."

"Mmm." She sighed. "That feels good." It never ceased to surprise her how thoughtful Alexander could be when it suited him. "Do you find me soft?"

"Only your body. Your heart is as fierce as a lion." He sat up, poured more oil in his palm, and began to massage her other foot. "That first night I took you to bed, I knew you were worthy to be the mother of my son."

"I thought you a savage," she admitted. "I still do."

He chuckled. "You bring out the beast in me." He squeezed and rubbed her calf in slow, sensual circles before continuing up her knee and thigh.

"Oh, you've got the best hands." She groaned in pleasure. "You'd make a wonderful bath attendant."

"I knew I had to have you that morning on Sogdiana Rock, when I saw your hair."

"I would have shaved it if I'd guessed."

"It's not been that bad, has it, my Little Star? But you were a handful, even for me. It would have been easier taking your leopard to wife." He wiped his hands on a towel and stretched out beside her again.

She turned to him and brushed his lips with the tip of her fingers. "Had I known you admired Akheera so, I would have kept her better hidden," she teased.

"Who knows?" Capturing her right hand, he spread her fingers, pressing her flesh, palm to palm against his own. "There are probably some who accuse me of swiving that accursed leopard. My enemies spread such tales of my moral vices and sexual perversions that fools will believe anything."

He kissed her fingertips, then turned them over, produced a small kidskin bag, and poured a sparkling stream of glittering diamonds into her cupped hand. "For your collection."

"Thank you, my lord. You are too generous."

"Send those to your mountain homeland with the rest of my treasury."

"I wondered when we'd get around to that," she replied, before leaning close to moisten his lower lip with the tip of her tongue. "But you cannot escape the list of your faults so easily. You drink too much unwatered wine, but I've yet to see these perversions." She smiled mischievously. "Other than a hero's capacity for prolonging that which delights a wife most."

"So you say." His eyes lit with desire.

Laughing, she lay back against the cushions and opened her arms. "Who would know better?"

"We must take care for our son."

"Ah, but there are ways and ways, my Macedonian barbarian. And I've yet to teach you all Neerja's secrets."

He put a hand on either side of her head and lowered himself over her, his blue-gray eyes heavy-lidded with desire. "You think you can distract me so easily from your crimes of extortion?"

331

"Perhaps." She stroked his chest, skimming the powerful muscles to linger sensually on his nipple.

He inhaled sharply. "Play your power games, little wife," he said. "Steal what you will from my riches. So long as you remember who is your master and to whom you owe your loyalty, we will have no quarrel."

She laughed and arched her hips to his. "Then we remain the best of friends."

"And lovers," he answered huskily. "Always lovers."

Roxanne was content. She had begged Alexander to take her to Sogdiana for the birth of the child, and they had compromised on the magnificent summer palaces of the Persian Empire in Hamadon. It was wooded, mountainous country and much like home. The hunting in Hamadon was superb, and Alexander would be well occupied while she waited here for her delivery.

At Opie, Alexander's party joined with Hephaestion and the main army. Many of the Macedonian troops were in their sixties and seventies, of age to be retired and sent home, richly rewarded for their service. Still, they were not happy to be replaced with younger Asians. The Macedonians protested and complained bitterly, even when Alexander wiped out their debts from his own personal coffers. As days passed, drink made the veterans ugly, and grumbling flared to open rebellion.

A Macedonian king ruled by sheer force of his personality, and the army who followed Alexander faithfully across half the world would have killed him had he lost control. By the strength of his own will, he turned their mutiny to hero worship once again and shouted down their opposition. He brought Asian and Greek troops together in a great feast of peace and brotherhood, quelling the mutiny and causing the old soldiers to shout the High King's name in abandoned hysteria.

Tearfully, Roxanne bid Bondoor and the Flying Devils farewell, embracing each fierce mountaineer and giving personal messages to carry home to her people. "You must marry," she said to Bondoor. "In your heart, you will always remember Parvona, but she would not want you to be alone in your old age. You should have children and grandchildren to bring laughter to your house."

She had rewarded her captain with a huge grant of land and a stronghold on the border of Sogdiana and Bactria. "You have been faithful. Serve my father well and Lord Alexander has promised you title to the territory when your term of service is expired."

Bondoor mounted and saluted, too full of emotion to answer in words. The lady had been difficult to serve, but his heart swelled with pride that he had known her. She had extracted his blood oath to support her child should he come to the twin thrones in the future. His saddlebags were heavy with precious jewels, an addition to the treasury of Sogdiana. That the Princess Roxanne had such faith in him was a greater gift than either the fortress or lands.

Mounted on an even-gaited mare, Roxanne rode beside the High King as the army made its way into the high country of Media. The Nicaean Fields were the traditional breeding grounds of warhorses of the Persian Empire. Thousands of mares and colts and magnificent stallions grazed the green pastures.

"They are riches beyond number," Roxanne cried hoarsely. "Oh, my lord, look!" Have you ever seen such a sight!" She leaned forward eagerly and swept a hand to encompass the vast herds. "The treasury at Susa is dross compared to this!"

Alexander frowned. "The numbers are a third of what they should be. The count is near fifty thousand; the rest have been stolen or lost through carelessness while we were in India. I have replaced the governor and his staff here. In a few years, we should see an increase."

Roxanne bit her lower lip pensively. She knew where a few thousand of the missing horses had been driven. Before his death, Wolf had informed her of Bactrian raids on the High King's breeding grounds. She watched Alexander warily from the corner of her eye. Did he know? "Fifty thousand or a hundred thousand, they are more than any other king has commanded. You might try introducing some Arabian mares in the herd. They are lighter, but have more heart than any animal I have ever seen."

"Such a horse might carry a woman or a boy." He smiled. "We will hunt out a likely colt for my son while we are here. When he is ready to begin his training, the colt will be old enough to ride."

"A Sogdian pony, my lord, surefooted as a goat and steady," she suggested. "Not a charger for a small princeling."

"I would seek out Pegasus if I could. No matter, we will teach him to ride like a Scythian." Alexander put heels to Achilles and led them down toward the horse pastures at a gallop, his army strung out behind for miles.

Roxanne settled into the turreted palace at Hamadon to wait out the last few months before the birth of her child. The hunting was excellent and Alexander, Hephaestion, and Ptolemy rode out nearly every day. Alexander gave up nights of drinking and carousing with his friends to spend time with her. After the heat of Susa, the cool heights were doubly welcome, and Roxanne enjoyed the sights of the ancient city. Magi had been brought from Sogdiana to assist at the birth of the prince, and her husband made certain that she was cosseted, pampered, and given every desire.

Here again, grumbling broke out between the Greeks and Persians; and Alexander decided to distract the men with a celebration of athletic games and competitions. Eager as children for a holiday, the soldiers threw themselves enthusiastically into the foot races, wrestling, and boxing contests.

"Will you compete, my lord?" Roxanne demanded.

"Certainly, with a king of equal rank," Alexander said wryly. "Inform me if any appear."

Workmen built a sheltered balcony for Roxanne's use, so that she might view the games without being seen in her advanced condition. Alexander, Ptolemy, and Perdiccas joined her there, sharing wine and specially prepared delicacies. Only Hephaestion was absent, laid low by a recurring bout of swamp fever. "He said he felt a little better this morning," Alexander said. "I left the physician with him."

"A shame when a man's bowels interfere with his enjoyment," Perdiccas commented. "He wanted to compete."

Ptolemy laughed. "I, for one, am content to leave the games to younger men. Every year my sword seems to get a little heavier."

Roxanne sipped at an iced fruit drink and wished the days would take wings. Her body was awkward, and it was harder and harder to sleep at night. So far, her lord had slept at her side every night, but sooner or later some pretty face might catch his eye. The quicker the child was in her arms, the better.

A white-faced courier burst into the royal box and threw himself face down on the floor. "Your Majesty . . ." His voice cracked.

Alexander sprang to his feet and moved in front of Roxanne, hand on his sword. "What is it?" Ptolemy and Perdiccas tensed.

"Lord Alexander, it is General Hephaestion. He is stricken. He begs you to come."

"Ptolemy, stay with Roxanne!" Alexander ran from the balcony, Perdiccas at his heels. They arrived at Hephaestion's quarters too late. He had already drawn his last breath.

Alexander's grief knew no bounds. For three days and nights, he stayed by Hephaestion's body, refusing food or drink. A page whispered to Roxanne that the High King had cut his own hair short with Hephaestion's knife. The physician who had been tending Hephaestion fled, but not far enough. With or without the High King's order, the unlucky soul was captured and hanged.

Alexander declared a general mourning throughout the empire. Public prayers were said for the soul of the departed hero, and the manes and tails of all horses were cropped. All commerce came to a halt, and the country waited with bated breath while rumors of Alexander's near-crazed condition multiplied and spread.

On the fourth day, at Ptolemy's insistence, Roxanne went

to her husband. Attendants had prepared Hephaestion's body for funeral rites and sealed the corpse in an elaborate coffin. Alexander turned as she entered the room and came to take her hands. "This is no place for you, little Sogdian." His face was pale and lined, but no trace of madness showed in his red-rimmed eyes.

"We were worried about you." She embraced him.

"I've lost the best friend in all the world."

"I know, my lord. We have all lost a friend."

"You two did not always agree."

"No, usually not. But as long as I was faithful to you, Hephaestion would have defended me and my child." She motioned to a servant. "I have brought you wine and a little bread. You must eat, my lord. A kingdom does not run smoothly without a leader."

Hephaestion's death was a terrible blow to Roxanne. Although he'd never pretended to approve of their marriage, Hephaestion was second-in-command and loyal to Alexander beyond heaven and hell. Who would step into that spot now? It would not be Ptolemy, her best and perhaps only friend among the Macedonians. Alexander loved him like a brother, but Ptolemy was more statesman than general. Her husband was too shrewd a king to pick him as vizier.

Alexander took the wine goblet from the servant and drank. "What will I do without him? I'd trade my eyes to have him back. I'd give my kingdom."

"He was a lion of a man. You must build him a fitting memorial," she said softly, "so that men in ages to come will know of Hephaestion's deeds and his greatness."

"Yes." For a moment, life came back to Alexander's stony face. "I'll build him a monument such as has never been." His voice cracked. "He would have stood as godfather to our son."

"Come, my lord. Your generals are waiting. You must see them," she urged. "Later, when you've rested, you can draw plans for Hephaestion's monument. He deserves all the honor we can show."

* * *

Within weeks, Alexander decided he could not abide the city of Hephaestion's death. After commissioning an enormous stone lion to be carved in his friend's honor, Alexander announced his decision to move on to Babylon. Roxanne's protests were useless. "You can remain here at Hamadon until the child comes if you like," he said. "I ride tomorrow."

"Let us return to Susa. Anywhere but Babylon," she replied. "I fear the towers of Babylon."

"A breeding woman's fancies."

"No, my lord. It is an evil place where much wickedness has been played out. And it isn't just me. The omens are not good. Your diviners sacrificed a bull and claim that the liver was abnormal and missing parts."

"Superstitious nonsense. In Babylon, I will build my true memorial to Hephaestion. Come with me or stay, as you choose," he said stubbornly.

Since Hephaestion's death, Alexander no longer came to her bed. Instead, he spent his nights with his comrades, drinking, and mourning his dearest friend. Alexander had become moody and taciturn, and no longer confided his thoughts to her.

"Where you go, I go," she said. "Shall our son be born without his father to receive him?"

Reluctantly Roxanne gave orders for her women to pack. The journey to Babylon would be difficult in her condition, but she would not be left behind, despite her growing dread of the city. Without Alexander to protect her, anything could happen to her child. Her circle of enemies grew larger every day, and even a trusted midwife might be bribed to deliver a dead infant rather than a live one.

In Babylon, Alexander had commanded that a new harbor be created to hold his huge fleet of ships. Once Roxanne was safely delivered and his heir proclaimed to the empire, he would lead the fleet in new explorations of conquest against Arabia. He drew up plans for sailing around Africa and taking all the land encompassed for his kingdom. Ambassadors from many nations flocked to his court to pay homage to the great god-king, Lord Alexander. Their offerings filled his coffers and paid for the building of ships and the equipping of new armies.

The Princess Roxanne remained within the palace during the games and festivities held in honor of Hephaestion. A second funeral service was held here, and the priests declared that the dead hero Hephaestion must be honored as a god. Alexander commanded that sections of Babylon's walls be pulled down so that the bricks could be used to construct Hephaestion's monument. Once completed, he declared, the tomb would be one of the wonders of the civilized world.

Roxanne welcomed the excuse of her coming confinement to avoid the pageantry of the funeral games. She found Babylon oppressive. Not even the beauty of the famed hanging gardens could raise her spirits, and she prayed daily before the sacred fires of Zoroaster for her lord's safety and his reason.

Here in Babylon, the luxurious women's quarters were even more isolated than those at Susa. Nightly, Alexander came to inquire of her health and sometimes to share the evening meal, but he slept in his own palace, surrounded by courtiers and servants. Here in the city she hated, she slept alone and afraid, plagued by evil dreams.

"I cannot bear to touch you and know that I can't express my love," Alexander had explained. "I will take no chance of injuring you or the baby because of my lust. There will be many nights for us, Little Star. Now it is better you sleep alone."

"But I want you beside me," she said. The sheer white linen robe she wore gave only the illusion of covering.

He laughed merrily. "I think you are beautiful." He held her against him, with her back to his chest, and rubbed her swollen belly. "He is impatient to be born, our little son. You must call me when your labor begins, no matter what the hour. I will be with you then, I promise. You can grip my hands when the pain is the worst. We will do this great thing together, and I will be the first to look on my son's face."

"The physicians and midwives will not let you. It would be improper." Roxanne pushed the heavy hair off her neck. Babylon was hot, and she hated it. It was past time for the child to be born, and still he had not come. How long must she wait?

"I will come. Just don't make it tonight. Medius of Thessaly has invited me to a feast. I doubt if I'll be up to delivering a baby after that. You know his parties never break up until dawn." Alexander kissed her and strode from the room.

"Take care, my lord," she called after him. Who was this Medius? She knew nothing of his politics. Hephaestion had left a void impossible to fill. She had worried less about her husband when the two of them were together. No matter how drunk Alexander was, Hephaestion would never let him come to harm.

Roxanne woke up with a start, fear acrid in her mouth. Somewhere a dog howled, and she shivered, the dream still dominant in her clouded mind. The smell of incense was heavy in the air, and a single ray of moonlight spilled through a window panel to shine on the tiled floor. The ancient mud-brick palace crushed down on Roxanne like a mountain of earth. She closed her eyes and saw again the awful images of her dream . . . the towers of Babylon beginning to crumble, burying the wailing inhabitants.

She shook herself awake and reached for a jar of tepid water. A small whimper caught her ear, and she padded silently to the lion cub's box and carried her back to bed. "You can't sleep either?" she whispered, and cuddled the baby lion against her. "This is no place for wild things, is it? No place for either of us."

The following morning, Roxanne woke cranky and out of sorts from her restless night. The day was much like the one before, long and tedious. She busied herself with inspecting the infant's cradle and tiny clothing. A volume of Homer's *Iliad* that Alexander had forgotten lay on a small table beside the empty cradle. In Hamadon, he'd left it by their bed, and it had been mistakenly packed with her things. Knowing how important his books were to him, Roxanne decided to take the epic saga to her husband's apartments.

The protocol necessary for the princess to cross to the High

King's palace was maddening. Here in Babylon, she must call for an enclosed litter, lest she shock the throngs of Persians with her exposed face. When she finally arrived at Alexander's gate, suitably guarded by Kayan and two dozen Bactrians, she found the way barred by four burly Macedonians.

"No one is to be admitted," the nearest guard said gruffly. "The High King is ill."

"Tell him the Princess Roxanne is here," Kayan growled back. "He will see her."

"My orders are plain. No one!"

Roxanne drew aside the curtain. Kayan took her hand to assist her out. "I am here to see my husband," she declared. "Stand aside if you value your skin." A curved dagger glittered in her hand. "Touch me on your life, Macedonian." Red-faced, the soldier backed away. Roxanne nodded, and Kayan shoved open the door.

It was all she could do not to show her dismay when she caught sight of Alexander. His hair was wet with sweat, his complexion a pasty tallow. A stout, heavily bearded physician in Babylonian dress turned away from the couch and motioned her to silence. "The High King is sleeping, Your Majesty. It is nothing to alarm yourself over. Only a touch of summer fever."

Roxanne chilled. Fever? Hephaestion had died of fever. She ignored the physician and went to Alexander, placing a hand on his damp brow. "Why was I not informed he was sick?"

The older man cleared his throat importantly and lowered his voice. "Lord Alexander drank heavily last night at the feast. What he needs is rest and a good purging. You should not be here."

"He is my husband. Where else should I be?" Roxanne took up a wet cloth, wrung it out, and placed it on his temple.

Alexander opened his eyes. "Roxanne? What are you doing here?"

"Hush, my lord. I've come to care for you." She kissed him tenderly. "How do you feel?"

"Like an elephant stepped on me." He forced a laugh. "You shouldn't be here. It might harm the baby."

340

"This child must be as tough as his father, my lord, if he is to survive. Sleep; I will stay with you." Roxanne turned to Kayan. "Have someone fetch my medical kit and order fresh water and fruit juices."

"I can assure you, Princess," the doctor said, "I have what is needed to care for the High King."

"Send for Ptolemy, Kayan. These leeches will trouble me with petty annoyances." She glared at the physician. "I am not without skill in medicine myself, Babylonian."

In the late evening, Alexander opened his eyes and exchanged a few words with Ptolemy and Roxanne. She slept beside him that night, fully dressed, waking instantly whenever he stirred, giving water or medicine as the occasion demanded. Still, the fever rose again, and the physician returned to the king's chambers with Greek priests and more physicians.

Ptolemy took Roxanne aside and spoke in a low, concerned voice. "This is more than the aftereffects of a night of drinking, lady."

"I don't need you to tell me that." Her face was pale. "I fear he has been poisoned."

Ptolemy shook his head. "Speak that word no more," he warned. "Rumors are already about that you have poisoned him." Roxanne's eyes widened. "Calm yourself; he is strong. He has recovered from nine wounds that would have killed an ordinary man. But I think it best if you return to your own palace. This can do your coming child no good, and if worse comes to worst, Alexander's heir is what will matter most."

"I won't leave him," she protested.

Perdiccas arrived with a group of Companions, and Alexander raised himself painfully to speak with them. "Princess," Perdiccas called. "The High King Alexander would have a word with you."

Her husband struggled to sit up, and she knelt by his side and took his hand, raising it to her lips. "Lie still, my lord," she pleaded. "You must rest."

His eyes glittered with fever. "Nothing to worry yourself

about," he whispered between cracked lips. "You must think of my son. Return to your palace. I'll come as soon as I shake this. You look worse than I do."

Roxanne could not stop trembling. "My lord, I would stay by you."

"Perdiccas." Alexander gripped her hand. "I commend my lady and her son to your care. If I die, he is to inherit my throne." A fire flickered in the gray eyes. "And she . . . she is the dearest thing I have ever conquered."

Perdiccas took hold of Roxanne. "Come, lady. You must go back to your apartments. The king will be fine."

Roxanne broke away and kissed her husband's lips. "I love you," she whispered, and then allowed them to hurry her away.

For six days, Alexander drifted between consciousness and coma, growing steadily weaker. In the women's palace, Roxanne waited, dry-eyed, the agony of her fears growing greater by the hour. On the seventh day, Kayan brought word that the High King had roused enough to greet his Companions; soldiers filed by his bed, one by one, to see that he still lived.

On the thirteenth of June, Alexander, age thirty-two, King of Macedonia, King of Greece, High King of Persia, Lord of Bactria, Lord of Sogdiana, and India, took a final gasp of breath and gave up his soul. The muffled drums carried the message to his wife faster than any human messenger could run, and Roxanne wept for all that had not been done or said between them.

Chapter Twenty-seven

Roxanne knelt beside the bed, Alexander's cold and lifeless hand in hers. He looked so youthful lying there, so beautiful. His body showed none of the results of days of sickness and fever and still smelled fresh to her despite the sultry Babylonian heat and the burning torches that lit the bier. Was he only sleeping? Was he an immortal caught in a spell and destined to sleep for a thousand years?

Roxanne was dry-eyed, her tears all shed. A Greek priest glared at her and muttered to another beside him. A day ago he would not have dared, she thought. The vultures were closing in.

As if reading her thoughts, the voices of the gathered Macedonian elite grew louder. Ptolemy moved to her side. "It might be better, lady, if you did not linger. Your condition . . ."

"Who is to be his successor?" she asked.

Ptolemy helped her to her feet. "You must retire to your quarters. Your concern now must be for his heir and your own well-being."

"Who?" she demanded.

Ptolemy hesitated for a fraction of a second too long. "Perdiccas stood closest to him at the end." He glanced at the

343

scowling vizier. "He claims the High King's last words were that his crown should pass 'to the strongest.'"

Heartsick, Roxanne nodded and leaned down to brush Alexander's cool lips with hers one final time. When she turned to face the hostile faces of Perdiccas, Leonnatus, and the others, her demeanor was regal and as expressionless as that of her dead husband.

Had Alexander crowned her queen, then perhaps Ptolemy would have rallied to her cause with men and arms. Now, she realized, she was on her own.

"Allow me to escort you to—" Ptolemy began.

Roxanne shook her head. "No," she said quietly. "Save yourself."

"He loved you, you know. His last thoughts were for you and your child."

"And he loved you," she answered. "Go, my friend, while you can." Ptolemy could not hide the relief in his eyes. She knew that he and Perdiccas had always hated one another. Now that Perdiccas grabbed for power, Ptolemy would not linger long at Alexander's wake. Too wise to pit his troops against the other generals, Ptolemy would turn his gaze toward Egypt while the others scrabbled like dogs over the spoils.

"May his luck protect both of you," Ptolemy said.

Perdiccas stepped forward. "This is no place for you, Princess."

"So I have been told."

The vizier's unshaven face was hard, his eyes puffy and bloodshot. Grief or guilt had aged him years in the last few days. "You need not fear for your safety," Perdiccas said. "You remain under my protection."

She nodded and swept from the room, trying not to listen to the angry rumbles that rose behind. Let her enemies tell what lies they pleased . . . whisper their tales of poison. She had not yet played her last game piece. While they hesitated, she would act.

The child moved within her, and she winced. Her contractions had begun in the night. Alexander's son clamored to be born, and the world that would receive him was fraught with danger. Outside the chamber, she allowed the servants to help her into a carrying chair and sighed with relief as the curtain dropped, shielding her from view.

She had seen Alexander's ring of command on Perdiccas's finger. Did he seek to be High King? If Alexander had been poisoned, was Perdiccas to blame? Alexander's swift death so close on that of Hephaestion's had all the marks of treachery—if not Perdiccas, who?

Roxanne laid her head back as the porters traversed the halls to her quarters. She would be safe there for a while. The attendants and guards in her palace were yet loyal. If only her father were in Babylon. The Hindu Kush was far away, and by the time he received the message of Alexander's death, it would be too late. If she was to save her infant's life, she must do it alone.

Sharin sent away the chair attendants and followed Roxanne into the dim coolness of her bedchamber. With a wave, the high-born waiting woman dismissed the maids, slaves, and musicians, and then removed Roxanne's silken robe herself. "You must get into bed," she urged. "I will fetch the physician. Your pains have begun, haven't they?"

"Not yet." She gripped Sharin's hand. "The child is in great danger. We both know it."

"Lady, you are overwrought. No one will harm you or the baby. Be it boy or girl, it is Alexander's only heir. Even the Greeks, barbarians that they are, must respect the law." She wiped Roxanne's damp forehead with a perfumed cloth. "The shock of his death is too much for you, but you have the child to consider."

"By the sacred fires! I think of nothing else! How did Alexander reach his own throne? Through his father Philip's death! For generations—centuries—the Greeks have murdered son and father, brother and kin to the fourth degree! The Mediterranean must run red with the blood of murdered royalty! Are you so foolish as to think that a half-Sogdian infant will live to claim the throne of Alexander? Cut clothes of mourning for his name day. My son's birth will be but the first day of his funeral feast!" She brushed away Sharin's hand. "The Wise God give me strength! I must find a way."

Sharin drew the embroidered draperies around the wide bed. "You have eaten nothing, lady. You must take something." She offered a goblet of goat's milk. "It is safe. I milked the animal myself. You must keep up your strength."

Moistening her lips with the liquid, Roxanne forced herself to breathe deeply. Another cramp began in her back. Her eyelids flickered. "Can I trust you, Sharin?"

"Yes, lady. To the death."

"All right. Send away all the women. Tell them my head aches, and I weary of their idle chatter. There must be none but you and me in my inner chambers. And fetch me Kayan. I need him now." She reached for a jewelry box and dumped pearl and ruby earrings, diamond bracelets, and golden chains onto a silken pillow. "Take all of it," she said. "I want you to have it. But hide it well, lest it be stolen."

Sharin began to weep. "You don't have to bribe me, Princess. I will remain faithful. I swear it."

"Who knows what tomorrow may bring? Take the jewels, and bring Kayan."

"It is forbidden for any man to enter your inner court, even the captain of your guard. They will accuse you of whoring on your husband's bier. Let me carry a message to him. You must do nothing to increase the danger."

"Bring me Kayan!" Roxanne's dark eyes flashed. "Here, or I will seek him out myself. The game nears its end. We must risk all on a final throw."

Shaking her head in despair, Sharin slipped from the room by a little-used doorway that led to the enclosed gardens.

Roxanne rose from the bed and went to her dressing table. An ivory brush lay on top. She picked it up, thinking of the many times Alexander had brushed her hair with it. Swallowing the lump in her throat, she ran the brush through her hair, and then swiftly braided the tresses into a single plait in the style she favored for riding.

She found herself staring into the mirror, a treasure brought from far Chin and worth its weight in gold. Her face reflected back, eyes dark with torment. "Do not fear," she whispered to the babe within her womb. "I will not let harm come to you, I swear by my father's soul. You will live, son of Alexander. You will survive to reign in Sogdiana."

A firm step sounded on the marble tiles, and she turned to face Kayan. "We have to flee Babylon while there is still time," he said with urgency.

She took his strong hands in hers and looked up into his face. The crow-black of Kayan's hair was streaked with premature white, adding to his noble appearance. Oh, what might have been, were it not for Alexander, she thought. "You and your Bactrian guard? What are there left—twenty?"

"Two score," he answered, and a faint flush colored his olive tan cheeks. "They are the best."

"So, with two score mountain fighters and a Sogdian hero we will fight our way across half of Persia. As my father said, Kayan, you are a general, but no prince. Heart of my heart, it would be hopeless, we both know it." She raised his hand to her lips and kissed it. "I love you, Kayan, as I have always loved you."

"But not more than the Macedonian." He spoke gruffly, clearly shaken. "Now, above all, we must be honest with each other."

"On my soul . . . I do not know." She gripped his hand so fiercely that her nails dug into his flesh. The contraction had caught her unawares, robbing her of breath and sapping her strength.

"The child comes?" Kayan swept her into his arms, protesting, and carried her to the bed. "You need your women."

"Not yet, Kayan. Listen to me. Listen well and heed me, if you ever have. My son you must take home to our mountains. You who are dearest to me in all the world, you must take him and make of him a prince."

Kayan frowned.

"Do you think I'm a fool?" Roxanne asked. "I know they would not let the child escape alive . . . if they knew he lived. Go and seek out another infant, one with a Persian mother

347

and Greek father, fair of skin as my babe shall be. I'll switch them and claim the foundling as my own."

"Impossible."

"Not impossible," she insisted. "Even your loyal guards could not protect me, but a lone man on a Bactrian racing camel? Who would notice a single rider carrying so small a bundle? No creature on earth runs as swiftly as a Bactrian racer. The distance is far; the Greeks will never hold the twin kingdoms without Alexander. They will scramble for Persia and Greece like beggars for crusts in a gutter! When he is old enough, you can safely crown him Prince of Sogdiana and Bactria. None will have the power to challenge him."

"It will never work," Kayan said. "And it would mean leaving you in the hands of the Greeks. I have sworn to stay by your side as long as I draw breath. Don't ask this of me."

"It will work, and it will only work if I play my part. It may be that I can ally myself with Ptolemy or Perdiccas. Even Olympias may champion her only grandchild. If I know my son is safe, I will be free to plot with the best of them."

"A journey so far . . . with a baby. How could I—"

"You must," she said. "Make certain the camel you choose is a female that has recently given birth. Alexander's son will thrive on camel's milk."

"What if it be a girl?"

"No, this is a man child. Alexander knew it. I know it." Her gaze held his. "On your oath, I demand it." Her breath was coming in short gasps. "We have no more time. You must do as I command! If you love me . . ."

He nodded, his eyes bright with tears. "I will be father to your babe. Would that it were mine and not Alexander's. I swear, if he lives, he will be Lord of Sogdiana."

"Go at once and find a healthy newborn. I've heard that many women abandon their Greek bastards in a ravine outside the city walls."

"How will we carry out such a deception?"

"I'll go into the outer courts and be seen loudly mourning. When I think it is near time, I will retire to my bath. None must be there but my woman Sharin. She is faithful. The exchange

348

must be made at the minute of birth, and I do not think we have much time left. We will smear the slave's child with blood, and I will scream so loudly the whole palace will come running."

"If it is a girl, we need not go through with it," he said. "A girl would not be such a threat to the Greeks. She would be valuable as a prospective bride."

"Could I value a daughter less than a son?"

"And what payment will you give me?" The tears spilled down his weather-lined face.

"Payment?" Her heart lurched. "What can I give you but my hopes and my trust?"

"One last kiss," he said. "I would not trade an hour of your life for all the kingdoms on earth—but I can deny you nothing. I ask only for that which I have longed so many nights . . . your lips on mine."

Trembling, she tilted her head to receive his kiss. Kayan's lips were warm, but strangely, his intimate touch stirred nothing but brotherly love in her heart. No thrill of forbidden passion so long denied.

What have I done? she thought. Too late . . . too late. Why hadn't she realized until now that Alexander had truly captured her heart? That he had commanded her love, leaving nothing but friendship to give another man . . . not even to her faithful Kayan.

She hugged him tightly. "Go, and the Wise God go with you."

He released her and stepped back to salute her, and in the flicker of lamplight, she read the sorrow in his eyes and realized that he knew.

Servants had extinguished all fires in the palace. The only light shed was that from smoky oil lamps and torches. A drumbeat, slow and solemn, echoed through the shadowy halls, accompanied by the sound of wailing. Roxanne had streaked her face with charcoal and covered herself with veils. The concubines of the old king kept up a steady weeping, and she added her cries to theirs. The eunuchs put their heads together

349

and talked in hushed voices. Who knew what behavior to expect from this barbarian princess?

Sharin clapped her hands. "My lady will have her bath now." She waved at the eunuchs. "She must have privacy in her grief. I will call you when you are needed." Together, she and Roxanne went into the sunken bath. The heavy bronze door swung shut, and Roxanne sank onto the marble floor. Sharin saw that Roxanne's lower lip was bleeding where she had bitten it.

"Bid the musicians to play loudly," Roxanne whispered. "Is Kayan here yet?"

Sharin pointed to an alcove. "He arrived nearly an hour ago. He has the child in a laundry basket. It is fair and healthy, born early this evening. His cord is still attached."

"Send him to me. I will lower myself into the bath; perhaps it will ease the pains."

"Drink this." Sharin offered a dark liquid. "It will not slow the birth." Kayan joined them by the edge of the pool, and together they helped her out, then walked her back and forth. The contractions were close together.

"My son is eager to be born," Roxanne moaned. "Impatient as my lord always was."

They laid her on the silken cushioned divan and Kayan took both her hands in his and slipped a leather glove between her teeth. "A little longer," he coaxed. "Be brave a little longer."

Another sharp contraction doubled her body and she bit into the leather. "Another push, lady," Sharin ordered. "Again!" The child's head slid between her fingers, and she drew it from Roxanne's body, laying it on her stomach with the cord still pulsing.

"It is a son?" Roxanne stroked the wet head. The child's blue-gray eyes were open wide, yet he did not cry.

Sharin nodded. "A boy, lady."

"Alexander, Alexander IV . . . my little love." Roxanne nestled him against her breast and kissed him as they cut the cord. The rosebud mouth opened strongly for the nipple. For a few seconds, she gave him suck, and then turned her face away.

"Kayan, take him. Bring me the other, quickly. The Wise God speed you." She did not look again as they took the slave child from his nest and dipped him in the heated waters of the pool. She did not open her eyes until she heard the door close at the far end of the room. "Now?" she whispered.

"Aye," Sharin said. She laid the wailing boy infant between Roxanne's legs. Roxanne drew a deep breath and let out an ungodly scream.

Sharin ran from the room. "Physicians! Physicians!" she cried. "My lady! My lady's time has come!"

A week after her son's birth, robed and bejeweled, Roxanne received Perdiccas, Leonnatus, Callisthenes the historian, the two priests she had seen at Alexander's bier, and several of Perdiccas's closest comrades in the stateroom off her apartments. Her face was carefully made up, her eyes painted in the Egyptian fashion, and a thin gold coronet framed her forehead.

Haughtily she studied the assembly as they approached her throne. "Greetings, friends of Alexander. You honor me by your presence."

Perdiccas cleared his throat. "We have come to see the child."

Roxanne glanced at a servant and gestured. A nurse glided in, bearing the child, wrapped in a single purple blanket.

Perdiccas flipped back the cloth to reveal the infant's sex. "This is the son of the late High King Alexander III?"

"Of course. Whose did you think it was? Or have you come here to insult me?"

Perdiccas laid his scarred hand on the baby's head. "We have come to view the boy. He appears healthy enough. And we meant no disrespect. It shall be my personal duty to protect and guide you both. It will be many years until he will come to his throne."

Leonnatus smiled down at the child. "You need have no fear, Princess Roxanne. Perdiccas is a man of honor."

"I'll take you both to Macedon where you will be safe," Perdiccas said. "This is a time of turmoil. The boy's grandmother, Queen Olympias, will wish to have him near her. She'll be a comfort to you."

Roxanne shook her head. "I don't wish to leave Persia." Her eyes sought those of Perdiccas. "I will not be welcome in Macedonia . . . the foreign wife. You know that as well as I."

Perdiccas fingered the golden ram's-head torque that encircled the infant's neck. "Politics, Lady Roxanne, is not the realm of women. You have been placed in my care and I will do with you as I see fit. It is common knowledge even your guard has deserted. I have taken the liberty of providing you with another." A dozen Greeks in full battle armor filed into the room. "They are enjoined with your safety, on pain of death."

"See that you do your duty, then," she replied, "on peril of your immortal soul. This is Alexander's legitimate son and heir, and his is the only true claim to the throne." She took the infant from the nurse and cradled him in her arms. "I am not queen and have never sought to be. Now that my lord is dead, my son is my only concern. Treat him fairly and we will have no quarrel, noble Perdiccas."

With a cool nod, she rose and walked proudly from the room, followed closely by the guards. The trap has closed, she thought, but the hawk flies free!

There had been a final meeting with Perdiccas before Roxanne and the child were taken to Macedonia. The guard had ushered her to the great chamber of state, where Lord Perdiccas sat on Alexander's throne and issued decrees, like a king. He had not risen when she entered the room, and no hint of compassion flickered in his eyes.

"Well, Perdiccas, you value yourself highly these days," Roxanne said boldly.

"Quiet, bitch! Your days of power are over. I give the orders now." He glared. "It has taken me long enough to rid myself of you!"

Roxanne's eyes narrowed. "Then it was you who tried to have me murdered . . . the poison . . . the assassins . . . the cobra. You, noble Perdiccas! And did you also murder Alexander?"

He leaped to his feet, covered the distance between them, and backhanded her across the face. "Silence, or you and the brat will not live to see Macedonia! If I ever hear that you have breathed a word of accusation against me, I will have your son boiled alive!"

Fury warred with caution, and Roxanne forced herself to maintain control. "Not my son," she begged. "Do not harm my baby!" The bile rose in her throat and threatened to choke her. She longed to seize the sword of the nearest guard and plunge it into Perdiccas's heart.

"Take her away!" Perdiccas thundered, and then delivered a passing threat. "Do not breathe easily, Sogdian sorceress. For I shall decide the hour of your death."

Roxanne sprinkled the papyrus with sand and blew it away. It was finished. Even within the bowels of the mountain prison, she could feel the sunset. The last day was gone.

So much to regret. So much yet undone. Her sorrows were heavy . . . and yet, life had been good to her. And she had always tried to meet misfortune boldly with a strong heart. She had remained strong when Perdiccas's men carried her to Macedonia, more hostage than regent for Alexander's heir. And she had shed no tears when her cruel mother-in-law, Olympias, had abandoned all pretenses and ordered her and Alexander IV imprisoned in this cave for so many years.

Roxanne sighed. Olympias was as bloodthirsty, vengeful, and power-seeking as Alexander had always claimed, but the harpy had reaped the full harvest of her own wickedness amid the madness of betrayal and slaughter in the years following Alexander's death. In the end, Cassander's army had trapped Olympias in a walled city, forcing her to devour not only her starving elephants but the bodies of her own maids before she died.

Now Cassander could safely dispose of Alexander's widow. . . .

Rolling the papyrus carefully, Roxanne put it into the oiled leather pouch and eased aside the wide stone beside her bed. It had taken months to hollow out the precious space, months in which she had painstakingly disposed of the earth, a spoonful at a time. The time would come when it was safe for her secret to be revealed. Roxanne placed the manuscript inside and set the rock securely in its place.

She dressed carefully in her finest robes and jewels, pausing to offer a prayer for the soul of the dear little boy she'd raised as her own, the laughing child with the weak heart who'd died peacefully in her arms nearly a year ago. She had grown to love that Alexander over the years, not flesh of her flesh and bone of her bone, but the child of her heart. As Alexander IV, he would have his place in history. None would take it from him. How he had listened to her tales of flowers and grass and birds. Surely those wonders surrounded him in paradise.

And last, she prayed for young Alexander, the son she had only seen at the moment of his birth. "Know that I sent you away so that you might live," she whispered, "and don't judge me too harshly."

Thoughts of the other Alexander—the one who had captured her mountain fortress and her heart—surged in her, and she smiled through her tears. "I have beaten them, my lord," she murmured. "My son rules in Sogdiana. Our son! Ptolemy has slain the treacherous Perdiccas. Your Macedonians did not outflank me. The royal house of Sogdiana will continue. I have won."

For a moment, she saw him standing before her as she had seen him for the first time in all his glory, Alexander of Macedon.

The image wavered and then shone clear and bright. "Indeed you have won, my lady," he seemed to say. The smile spread to his blue-gray eyes. "As I always said, the prize goes to the strongest."

Alexander tilted his head and laughed. "It is very like you, Roxanne, to claim all the credit. Think you I would let them destroy my son? He is the best of both worlds, East and West, as I told you he would be." He held out his hand to her. "Come, my darling, it is time."

Heavy footsteps sounded in the passageway, then the rattle of iron keys. From her girdle, Roxanne slipped a gold ring with a silver ram's head. With a twist, she turned the carving aside and tipped the black powder onto her tongue. It burned like fire, shooting flames of crimson through her head. She barely heard the soldiers' tread on the rock floor. The burning crept toward her heart, and the room was bathed in silver mist.

Across a Sogdian meadow a black stallion pranced, and on his back was a golden rider. "Alexander," she cried. "Alexander, my lord!"

And then she was in his arms and riding swiftly away into eternity.

Connie Mason

The Laird of Stonehaven

He appears nightly in her dreams—magnificently, blatantly naked. A man whose body is sheer perfection, whose face is hardened by desire, whose voice makes it plain he will have her and no other.

Blair MacArthur is a Faery Woman, and healing is her life. But legend foretells she will lose her powers if she gives her heart to the wrong man. So the last thing she wants is an arranged marriage. Especially to the Highland laird who already haunts her midnight hours with images too tempting for any woman to resist.

Lionheart
Connie Mason

Lionheart has been ordered to take Cragdon Castle, but the slim young warrior on the pure white steed leads the defending forces with a skill and daring that challenges his own prowess. No man can defeat the renowned Lionheart; he will soon have the White Knight beneath his sword and at his mercy.

But storming through the portcullis, Lionheart finds no trace of his mysterious foe. Instead a beautiful maiden awaits him, and a different battle is joined. She will bathe him, she will bed him; he will take his fill of her. But his heart is taken hostage by an opponent with more power than any mere man can possess—the power of love.

TO BURN
CLAUDIA DAIN

He has sworn to battle the empire wherever he finds it, and an isolated Roman villa in Britannia seems the perfect target for his revenge. He and his fierce Saxon warriors will sweep through it like an inferno, destroying all in their path. From the moment he sees her, he knows she embodies all that Rome stands for: pride, arrogance, civilization . . . beauty. She is a woman like no other, fighting with undaunted spirit even as he makes her his slave. She calls him barbarian, calls him oaf, calls him her enemy. Yet when he takes her in his hard-muscled arms, her body trembles with excitement. But will the fire flaring between them conquer him or her? Is the passion that burns in their souls born of hatred, or of love?

CLAUDIA DAIN

THE MARRIAGE BED

It starts with a kiss, an explosion of longing that cannot be contained. He is a young knight bent on winning his spurs; she is a maiden promised to another man; theirs is a love that can never be. But a year's passing and a strange destiny brings them together again. Now his is a monk desperately fleeing temptation, and she is the lady of Dornei, a woman grown, yearning to fulfill the forbidden fantasies of girlhood. They are a couple with nothing in common but a wedding night neither will ever forget. Eager virgin and unwilling bridegroom, yielding softness and driving strength, somehow they must become one soul, one purpose, one body within the marriage bed.

___4933-3 $5.99 US/$6.99 CAN

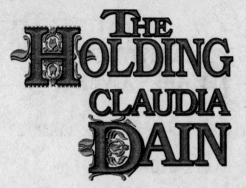

THE HOLDING
CLAUDIA DAIN

It is done. She is his wife. Wife of a knight so silent and stealthy, they call him "The Fog." Everything Lady Cathryn of Greneforde owns—castle, lands and people—is now safe in his hands. But there is one barrier yet to be breached. . . . There is a secret at Greneforde Castle, a secret embodied in its seemingly obedient mistress and silent servants. Betrayal, William fears, awaits him on his wedding night. But he has vowed to take possession of the holding his king has granted him. To do so he must know his wife completely, take her in the most elemental and intimate holding of all.

__4858-2 $5.50 US/$6.50 CAN